Mr. Murdstone slowly and gravely walked me up to my room.

When we got there, he suddenly twisted my head under his arm.

"Mr. Murdstone! Sir!" I cried. "Please don't beat me. I've tried to learn, but I can't learn while you and Miss Murdstone are there. I can't."

"Can't you, David?" Mr. Murdstone said. "We'll see." He held my head as in a vise, but I pressed up against him and stopped him for a moment, begging him not to beat me. He struck me heavily with the cane. In the same instant I bit the hand by which he held me. He beat me then as if he'd beat me to death. Above all the noise we made I heard my mother and Peggotty running up the stairs and crying out.

A Background Note about
David Copperfield

In the England of Charles Dickens' time, society offered children little protection from severe exploitation and other abuse. British law did not require that all children receive an education. Young children commonly were put to work in factories and warehouses. Parents and other adults routinely battered children without fear of penalty. Physical "punishment" of children was standard in lower-class schools. Teachers and principals legally could twist their ears, strike them with a ruler, beat them with a cane, and otherwise assault them. They also could publicly humiliate children in ways that society doesn't tolerate today—for example, by making them wear a placard or conical paper hat as a sign of disgrace. In *David Copperfield*, children who lack the protection of a loving parent or other relative have a hard time of it.

David Copperfield

CHARLES DICKENS

Edited, and with an Afterword,
by Joan Dunayer

 THE TOWNSEND LIBRARY

DAVID COPPERFIELD

TP THE TOWNSEND LIBRARY

For more titles in the Townsend Library,
visit our website: www.townsendpress.com

All new material in this edition is
copyright © 2009 by Townsend Press.
Printed in the United States of America

0 9 8 7 6 5 4 3 2 1

Illustrations copyright © 2009 by Hal Taylor

Townsend Press, Inc.
439 Kelley Drive
West Berlin, NJ 08091
cs@townsendpress.com

ISBN-13: 978-1-59194-091-3
ISBN-10: 1-59194-091-5

Library of Congress Control Number:
2007928924

Contents

Chapter	1	1
Chapter	2	5
Chapter	3	11
Chapter	4	20
Chapter	5	25
Chapter	6	32
Chapter	7	43
Chapter	8	50
Chapter	9	57
Chapter	10	71
Chapter	11	83
Chapter	12	92
Chapter	13	103
Chapter	14	115
Chapter	15	127
Chapter	16	134
Chapter	17	142
Chapter	18	149
Chapter	19	153
Chapter	20	161
Chapter	21	168
Chapter	22	173
Chapter	23	180
Chapter	24	185
Chapter	25	191

Chapter 26 204
Chapter 27 211
Chapter 28 216
Chapter 29 219
Chapter 30 223
Chapter 31 227
Chapter 32 235
Chapter 33 241
Chapter 34 253
Chapter 35 257
Chapter 36 265
Chapter 37 275
Chapter 38 279
Chapter 39 286
Chapter 40 293
Chapter 41 300
Chapter 42 303
Chapter 43 316
Chapter 44 327
Chapter 45 336
Chapter 46 340
Chapter 47 345
Chapter 48 363
Chapter 49 368
Chapter 50 382
Chapter 51 390
Chapter 52 398
Chapter 53 406

Afterword

About the Author 410
About the Book 415

Chapter 1

In reading my story, you'll decide whether I'm the hero of my own life or someone else is. I was born at Blunderstone in Suffolk. My father, David, had died six months before, at the age of thirty-nine. His aunt, Betsey Trotwood, was the head of the family. Aunt Betsey had been married to a younger man who had been very handsome and was said to have abused her. They had separated. Aunt Betsey had taken back her birth name, bought a seaside house in Dover, established herself there as a single woman with one servant, and lived in near-seclusion. It was believed that her husband had gone to India and died there ten years later. My father had been a favorite of Aunt Betsey until his marriage, which had deeply offended her. She never had met my mother, Clara. However, because my mother had been only nineteen when she married my father, then thirty-eight, Aunt Betsey had taken offense and referred to my mother as a "wax doll." My father and Aunt Betsey had never seen each other again.

The day before I was born was a bright, windy March day. My mother was in poor health and in low spirits. Dressed in mourning because of my father's recent death, she sat in the parlor by the fire shortly before sunset. When she lifted her sad eyes to the window opposite her, she saw an unfamiliar lady coming up the walk. The lady was Aunt Betsey. Her posture was rigidly upright and her face composed. Instead of ringing the doorbell, she looked in at the window, pressing her nose against the glass. Startled, my timid mother got up and stood behind her chair. Aunt Betsey scanned the room until her eyes reached my mother. Then she frowned and gestured to my mother to open the door. My mother did.

"Clara Copperfield?" Aunt Betsey said.

"Yes," my mother replied faintly.

"Betsey Trotwood. You've heard of me?"

"Yes," my mother answered. "Please come in."

They went into the parlor. When they both were seated, my mother, after vainly trying to restrain herself, started to cry.

"Oh, tut, tut!" Aunt Betsey said. "Don't do that."

But my mother cried until she was cried out.

"Take off your cap, child, and let me see you," Aunt Betsey said.

My mother did so, and her luxuriant hair fell around her face.

"Why, bless my heart!" Aunt Betsey exclaimed. "You're just a baby."

Sobbing, my mother said, "I'm afraid I'm a childish widow and will be a childish mother."

"What's the name of your servant girl?"

"Peggotty," my mother answered.

"Peggotty!" Aunt Betsey repeated with some indignation. "What kind of name is that?"

"It's her last name," my mother said softly. "David called her Peggotty because her first name is Clara, the same as mine."

Opening the parlor door, Aunt Betsey called, "Peggotty! Come here! Bring tea. Your mistress is a little unwell. Don't dawdle." Having thus spoken to the amazed Peggotty, who was coming along the passage with a candle at the sound of a strange voice, Aunt Betsey shut the door again. She sat down with her feet on the fender of the fireplace, the skirt of her dress tucked up, and her hands folded on one knee. "I have no doubt that your baby will be a girl," she said to my mother with satisfaction.

"It might be a boy," my mother responded.

"I'm sure it will be a girl," Aunt Betsey insisted. "Don't contradict me. From the moment of her birth I intend to be her friend. I intend to be her godmother. She must be well brought up and taught not to trust people who shouldn't be trusted. Please name her Betsey Trotwood Copperfield."

My mother didn't say anything.

"Was David good to you, child? Were you happy together?" Aunt Betsey asked.

"We were very happy. David was very good to me," my mother answered.

"He spoiled you, I suppose. You were an orphan, weren't you?" Aunt Betsey asked.

"Yes."

"And a governess?"

"I was a governess to young children in a family where David came to visit. He was very kind to me and paid me lots of attention. Then he proposed to me," my mother said.

Aunt Betsey frowned. "Do you know anything about keeping house?"

"Not much, I'm afraid," my mother answered.

"Did David leave you well provided for?"

"I have a hundred and five pounds a year."

When Peggotty came in with the tea things and candles, she glanced at my mother and saw that she was ill. Peggotty brought my mother upstairs to her bedroom and immediately sent her nephew, Ham Peggotty, to fetch a doctor. Ham had been staying in the house for the past few days for just this purpose.

While Aunt Betsey remained in the parlor, Dr. Henry Chillip attended my mother. At 12:30 a.m. he came downstairs and said to Aunt Betsey, "I'm happy to congratulate you. It's all over now, ma'am, and well over."

"How is she?" Aunt Betsey asked.

"I hope that she'll soon be as comfortable as we can expect a young mother to be under these sad circumstances of widowhood," Dr. Chillip answered.

"And *she*. How is *she*?" Aunt Betsey said sharply.

Not understanding, Dr. Chillip tilted his head a little to one side.

"The baby!" Aunt Betsey said with annoyance. "How is she?"

"Ma'am, the baby is a boy," Dr. Chillip responded.

Outraged, Aunt Betsey put on her bonnet and, without a word, walked out.

Chapter 2

One night when I was seven years old, Peggotty and I were sitting alone by the parlor fire. I had been reading to her about crocodiles. I was dead sleepy. I'd been granted permission, as a treat, to stay up until my mother came home from an evening at a neighbor's. I looked at Peggotty as she sat sewing with a brass thimble on her finger.

"Peggotty, were you ever married?" I asked.

She stopped sewing and looked at me, with her needle drawn out to its thread's length. "Lord, Master Davy. What put marriage into your head?"

"Were you ever married, Peggotty?" I repeated.

"No, and I don't expect to be."

"You're a very handsome woman, aren't you?" Although Peggotty's skin was rough and somewhat red and she was so plump that her form was rather shapeless, I thought that she was lovely, especially her eyes, which were a very dark brown.

"Me handsome, Davy? Lord, no, my dear! But what put marriage into your head?" she asked again.

"I don't know." After a pause, I asked, "If you marry someone and the person dies, can you marry again?"

"Yes," Peggotty answered, looking at me curiously. She laid aside the sock she was sewing and hugged my curly head. "Let me hear some more about the crorkindills." She couldn't get the word *crocodile* right.

So I read on about crocodiles and then moved to alligators.

The garden bell rang, and Peggotty and I went to the door. There was my mother, looking unusually pretty, I thought. With her was a gentleman with beautiful black hair and whiskers. He had walked home with us from church on Sunday. I later would learn that he was Edward Murdstone.

As my mother stooped at the threshold to take me into her arms and kiss me, Mr. Murdstone said that I was a more privileged little fellow than a monarch, or something to that effect.

"What does that mean?" I asked him over my mother's shoulder.

Mr. Murdstone patted me on the head, but I didn't like him or his deep voice. I also didn't like that his hand touched my mother's as he patted me on the head, so I moved her hand.

"Davy!" my mother scolded.

"Dear boy," Mr. Murdstone said. "I don't blame him for being devoted to you," he said to my mother.

My mother blushed and scolded me for being rude. She turned to thank Mr. Murdstone for bringing her home. As she spoke she put out her hand to him. She glanced at me as he met her hand with his own.

"Let's say good night, my fine boy," Mr. Murdstone said to me.

"Good night," I responded.

"Let's be the best friends in the world," Mr. Murdstone said, laughing. "Shake hands."

My right hand was in my mother's left, so I gave him my left hand.

"That's the wrong hand, Davy," Mr. Murdstone laughed.

My mother drew my right hand forward, but I still gave Mr. Murdstone my left hand. He shook it heartily. "You're a brave fellow," he said. He walked away but turned around in the garden and gave us a last look with his black eyes. My mother and I went inside.

Peggotty, who hadn't moved or said a word, instantly bolted the door. We all went into the parlor. Contrary to her usual habit of coming to the armchair by the fire, my mother stayed at the other end of the room, where she sat singing.

"I hope you had a pleasant evening, ma'am," Peggotty said, standing stiffly in the center of the room with a candlestick in her hand.

"Thank you, Peggotty," my mother replied cheerfully. "I had a *very* pleasant evening."

I briefly dozed off. When I awoke, I found Peggotty and my mother talking and both in tears. "Not a man like this one," Peggotty was saying. "Mr. Copperfield wouldn't have liked him. I'm sure of it."

"How can you say such awful things, Peggotty?" my mother exclaimed.

"It won't do!" Peggotty said with conviction. "No."

We all went to bed greatly dejected.

The next Sunday Mr. Murdstone was in church, and afterwards he walked home with my mother, Peggotty, and me. He came into the house, supposedly to look at a geranium we had in the parlor window, but he didn't take much notice of the plant. Before he left, he asked my mother to give him a blossom. She plucked it for him and put it into his hand. He said, "I'll never, ever part with it." I thought that he must be a fool not to know that it would fall apart in a day or two.

Peggotty started spending less time with my mother and me in the evenings. My mother still deferred to her, and the three of us still were great friends, but we all were less comfortable. Gradually I got used to seeing Mr. Murdstone, but I continued to dislike him.

One autumn morning I was with my mother in the front garden when Mr. Murdstone came by on horseback. He reined up his horse to salute my mother and said that he was going to Lowestoft to see some friends who were there with a private boat. He merrily proposed to have me ride in front of him on his saddle if I'd like to. The air was clear and pleasant, and Mr. Murdstone's horse seemed to like the idea of the ride because he stood snorting and pawing at the garden gate, so I decided to go. My mother sent me upstairs to Peggotty to be made spruce. Meanwhile Mr. Murdstone dismounted. With his horse's bridle over his arm, he walked slowly up and down on the outer side of the sweetbriar fence while my mother walked slowly up and down, in parallel, on the inner side. Peggotty and I peeped out at them from my little window. Then Peggotty turned cross and brushed my hair the wrong way, too hard.

Mr. Murdstone and I soon were off, trotting on the green turf by the side of the road. I sat in front of him. He held me easily with one arm. Every now and then I turned my head and looked up into his face. I marveled at the blackness of his eyes, hair, and whiskers; the squareness of his jaw; and the dotted indication of what would have been a thick black beard if he hadn't shaved close every day. Although I disliked him, I thought he was very handsome.

We went to a hotel by the sea and entered a room where two men were by themselves, smoking cigars. Each of them was lying on at least four chairs and wore a large, rough jacket. Two overcoats were in a heap in a corner. When we entered, the two men rolled onto their feet in an untidy way. Mr. Murdstone greeted them as Quinion and Passnidge.

Mr. Passnidge said, "Hello, Murdstone. We thought you were dead."

"Not yet," Mr. Murdstone said.

"Who's the boy?" Mr. Quinion asked.

"David Copperfield," Mr. Murdstone answered.

"The encumbrance of the bewitching Mrs. Copperfield, the pretty little widow?" Mr. Quinion asked.

"Watch what you say, Quinion," Mr. Murdstone warned.

Mr. Quinion rang the bell for some sherry. When it came, he made me have a little with a biscuit.

After that we went to a private boat. The three men descended into its cabin, where they busied themselves with some papers. I saw them hard at work when I looked down through the open skylight. They had left me with a man with thick red hair. He wore a small shiny hat and a shirt with horizontal stripes and the word *Skylark*. When I called him Mr. Skylark, he told me that Skylark was the boat's name, not his.

Mr. Murdstone seemed grave and was mostly silent, whereas Mr. Quinion and Mr. Passnidge seemed merry. Mr. Quinion and Mr. Passnidge joked with each other but not with Mr. Murdstone, who seemed smarter but also colder than they were.

Mr. Murdstone and I had dinner at the hotel with Mr. Quinion and Mr. Passnidge and went home early in the evening. It was a very fine evening. My mother and Mr. Murdstone had another stroll by the sweetbriar while I was sent in to have my tea. When Mr. Murdstone left, my mother asked me all about the day I'd had and what Mr. Murdstone had said and done. I mentioned what Mr. Quinion had said about her, and she laughed. She said that he was an impudent fellow who talked nonsense, but I saw that she was pleased.

When I went to bed, my mother came to bid me good night. She kneeled down by the side of my bed, laid her chin on her hands, and laughed. "What was it they said, Davy? Tell me again."

"'Bewitching Mrs. Copperfield' and 'Pretty little widow.'"

"What foolishness!" my mother cried, delighted.

We kissed each other over and over, and I soon fell asleep.

Chapter 3

One evening soon after, while my mother was visiting a neighbor, Mrs. Grayper, Peggotty said to me, "Master Davy, how would you like to go to Yarmouth with me and spend two weeks at my brother's? Wouldn't that be a treat?"

"Is your brother nice?" I asked.

"Very," Peggotty said. "And there's the sea, and boats, and the beach, and my nephew Ham to play with."

"It would be a treat, but what will Mother say?"

"I'll ask her as soon as she comes home," Peggotty said.

"What will she do while we're away?" I asked, putting my small elbows on the table. "She can't stay by herself."

"She's going to stay with Mrs. Grayper for two weeks. Mrs. Grayper is going to have lots of company."

The day soon came for the trip to Yarmouth. Shortly after breakfast John Barkis, a local carter, was at the gate with his cart, to drive Peggotty and me. My mother kissed me, and we both cried. I never had left home before. When Mr. Barkis started to drive away, my mother ran out at the gate and called to him to stop so that she could kiss me again. As we left her standing in the road, Mr. Murdstone came up to her and seemed to scold her for being so emotional. I was looking back around the cart's awning and wondered what business it was of his. Peggotty looked back on the other side and seemed displeased.

Mr. Barkis's horse shuffled along with his head down and periodically coughed. Mr. Barkis, too, kept his head down. He drooped sleepily forward as he drove, with one arm on each knee. At times he whistled.

Peggotty had a basket of refreshments on her knee. We ate and slept a lot. Peggotty slept with her chin on the basket's handle and snored. She never lost hold of the basket.

I was very glad when we reached Yarmouth, although it looked very soppy and flat, scarcely separate from the sea. When we got into the street and smelled the fish, pitch, oakum, and tar and saw the sailors walking around and the carts jingling up and down over the cobblestones, I felt better about the place.

"There's Ham! He's grown beyond all recognition," Peggotty said.

Wearing a canvas jacket and stiff trousers, Ham was waiting for us at the inn. He had grown into a strong, broad fellow six feet tall with curly blond hair, round shoulders, and a friendly smile on his boyish face. He asked me, "How are you doing?" as if we were old friends. He took me onto his back and carried me to the house while carrying a small trunk of mine under his arm. Peggotty carried another small trunk. We turned down lanes strewn with bits of wood and sand and went past gasworks, forges, and shipyards until we emerged on the wasteland I had seen from a distance.

"That's our house, Master Davy," Ham said.

I looked in all directions over the flatland, sea, and river, but I didn't see any house. There was only an old barge on the ground not far off, with an iron funnel sticking out of it for a chimney and smoking very cozily.

"That's it?" I exclaimed. "That barge?"

"That's it, Master Davy," Ham answered.

I was charmed with the romantic idea of living in a barge on land. The barge was roofed in. There was a delightful door cut in one side of the barge, which had little windows. The barge was beautifully clean and tidy inside. The furnishings included a chest of drawers and a table with a clock. On the chest of drawers was a tray with a Bible surrounded by cups, saucers, and a teapot. Framed pictures of biblical scenes hung on the walls, and some large, empty hooks were lodged in the ceiling. Because there were only a few chairs, some trunks and footlockers served as seats. Peggotty opened a little door and showed me my bedroom in the barge's stern. The room had a little window where the rudder used to go through. A little mirror framed with oyster shells was nailed to the wall at just the right height for me. There was a little bed and just enough room for me to get into it. A small bunch of seaweed filled a blue mug on the table. The walls were whitewashed, and the patchwork bedspread was bright. A fish-like smell permeated the barge. When I mentioned this to Peggotty, she told me that her brother dealt in lobsters, crabs, and crayfishes. At any given time many of these crustaceans were confined, in a heap, in a small wooden shed where pots and kettles were kept.

Wearing a white apron, a woman I assumed to be Mrs. Peggotty welcomed us. I had seen her curtseying at the door when I was on Ham's back about a quarter of a mile off. I offered to kiss Emily, a beautiful little blue-eyed girl with a necklace of blue beads, but she wouldn't let me. She ran away and hid. We dined on boiled flatfishes and potatoes with melted butter.

By and by, Peggotty's brother Daniel came home. A hairy man with a good-natured face, he gave Peggotty a hearty kiss on her cheek and called her "lass." He said to me, "Glad to see you, sir. You'll find us rough but ready."

"Thank you, Mr. Peggotty," I said. "I'm sure I'll be happy in this delightful place."

"How's your ma, sir?" Mr. Peggotty asked me. "Did you leave her pretty jolly?"

"Oh, yes," I said. I added (untruthfully), "She sends you her compliments."

"I'm much obliged to her," Mr. Peggotty said. "Well, sir, if you can get along here for two weeks, we'll be proud of your company." Remarking that "cold water never would get the muck off," Mr. Peggotty went out to wash himself in a kettleful of hot water. He soon returned, greatly improved in appearance but looking quite red.

After tea the door was shut, and all was made snug, the nights being cold and misty. It enchanted me to hear the wind rising out at sea, to know that the fog was creeping over the desolate flatlands outside, and to look at the fire and think that there was no house near this one and this one was a barge. Having overcome her shyness, Emily sat by my side on a footlocker that fit into the chimney corner and was just big enough for the two of us. The woman I thought was Mrs. Peggotty, knitted on the opposite side of the fire. Peggotty did her needlework. Ham, who had given me my first lesson in walking on all fours, was trying to remember how to tell fortunes with cards and was putting a grimy thumbprint on every card that he turned. Mr. Peggotty smoked his pipe.

"Mr. Peggotty," I said, "did you name your son Ham because one of Noah's sons was named Ham and you live in a sort of ark?"

"No, sir. I didn't name him," Mr. Peggotty replied.

"Who did, then?" I asked.

"His father," Mr. Peggotty answered.

"I thought *you* were his father."

"No, my brother Joe was his father," Mr. Peggotty said.

"He died?" I asked.

"Drowned," Mr. Peggotty answered.

Glancing at Emily, I asked, "Emily is your daughter, isn't she, Mr. Peggotty?"

"No, sir. My brother-in-law Tom was her father."

"He died?" I asked.

"Drowned," Mr. Peggotty said.

"Don't you have *any* children, Mr. Peggotty?"

"No, Master," he answered with a short laugh. "I'm a bachelor."

"A bachelor!" I cried. "Why, who's that, then?" I pointed to the woman I had thought was his wife.

"That's Mrs. Gummidge," Mr. Peggotty answered.

Peggotty motioned to me not to ask any more questions. I was silent until it was time for me to go to bed. Then in the privacy of my own little cabin, Peggotty informed me that Mr. Peggotty had adopted Ham and Emily, who had been destitute orphans. Mrs. Gummidge was the widow of Mr. Peggotty's fishing partner, who had died very poor. Mr. Peggotty was poor himself, Peggotty said, but "as good as gold and as true as steel."

I heard Peggotty go to bed in a little room like mine at the opposite end of the barge. Mr. Peggotty and Ham hung up two hammocks for themselves on the hooks in the ceiling. The wind howled out at sea and came across the flatland so fiercely that I had a slight fear that the great deep would rise in the night. But I remembered that I was in a barge and that a sailor such as Mr. Peggotty was a good person to have on board if anything happened. With those thoughts I fell asleep.

Almost as soon as morning shone on the oyster-shell frame of my mirror, I was out of bed and out on the beach with Emily. "You're quite a sailor, I guess," I said to her.

"No," she replied, shaking her head. "I'm afraid of the sea."

"Afraid!" I cried with a becoming air of boldness. Looking at the mighty ocean, I said, "*I'm* not."

"I've seen the sea tear a boat as big as our house to pieces," Emily said.

"I hope it wasn't the boat that . . . "

"That my father drowned in? No. I never saw that boat."

"Did you ever see your father?" I asked.

Emily shook her head. "Not to remember."

"I've never seen *my* father. My mother and I always have lived happily by ourselves."

"I never knew my *mother* either," Emily said. She started looking around for shells. "Your father was a gentleman, and your mother is a lady. My father was a fisherman, my mother was a fisherman's daughter, and Uncle Daniel is a fisherman."

"He's very good, isn't he?" I said.

"He's more than good," Emily said. "If I ever became a lady, I'd give him fine cotton trousers, a red velvet vest, a sky-blue coat with diamond buttons, a cocked hat, a large gold watch, a silver pipe, and a box of money."

"I'm sure he deserves those treasures," I said. We went on picking up shells. "You'd like to be a lady?"

Emily nodded. "I'd like it very much. We'd all be gentlefolks together: me, Uncle Daniel, Ham, and Mrs. Gummidge. We wouldn't mind when stormy weather comes—not for our own sakes, at least. We'd mind only for the sake of the poor fishermen, and we'd help them with money if they came to any harm." Walking near the edge of a wharf, she said, "I wake up when the wind blows over the sea and tremble to think about Uncle Daniel and Ham. I think I hear them crying out for help. That's why I'd like to be a lady."

We strolled a long way, loading ourselves with shells. We carefully put some stranded starfishes back into the water. Then we made our way home. Before entering the barge, we exchanged a kiss. We ate breakfast glowing with health and pleasure.

Hour after hour Emily and I walked together on Yarmouth's dim flatlands. "I adore you, Emily," I announced earnestly. "Unless you say that you adore me, too, I'll have to kill myself with a sword."

"I adore you, too," she assured me.

Mr. Peggotty and Mrs. Gummidge admired Emily and me. In the evenings when Emily and I sat lovingly side by side on our little footlocker, they'd whisper, "Lord, aren't they beautiful?" Mr. Peggotty would smile at us from behind his pipe, and Ham would grin all evening.

At dinner I always was served first, as a visitor of distinction. In the evenings, Mrs. Gummidge would knit in her corner, Peggotty would sew, Mr. Peggotty would smoke his pipe, and Ham would busy himself with something, such as patching a large pair of water boots. Sometimes, with Emily by my side, I'd read to everyone.

The two weeks slipped away. Only the tide changed and, with it, the times that Mr. Peggotty and Ham went out and returned. When Ham wasn't busy, he sometimes walked with Emily and me to show us the boats and ships. Twice he took us for a row.

I especially remember one Sunday morning on the beach. The bells rang for church. Emily leaned against my shoulder. Ham lazily tossed stones into the water. The sun, away at sea, just broke through the heavy mist, showing us the ships.

At last the day came for going home. I bore up against separating from Mr. Peggotty, Mrs. Gummidge, and Ham, but I felt agony at leaving Emily. She and I went arm in arm to the inn where the stagecoach stopped, and I promised to write to her. We grieved at parting.

But the closer I came to my own home, the more excited I became at the thought of seeing my mother and running into her arms.

Chapter 4

Peggotty and I arrived home on a cold afternoon with a gray sky that threatened rain. In my pleasant agitation I was half laughing and half crying. The door opened, and I looked for my mother. Instead I saw an unfamiliar servant.

"Why, Peggotty, hasn't Mother come home?" I asked with dismay.

"Yes, Master Davy," Peggotty said. She looked agitated. "She's home. Wait a bit, and I'll . . . I'll tell you something." She took me by the hand, led me into the kitchen, and shut the door.

"I feel afraid, Peggotty," I said. "What's wrong?"

"Nothing's wrong, Master Davy dear," she answered, trying to seem merry.

"Something's wrong. I can feel it. Where's Mama? Why didn't she come out to the gate? Why are we here in the kitchen?" I started to cry.

"Bless the precious boy!" Peggotty cried, hugging me.

"She isn't . . . dead, Peggotty?"

"No!" Peggotty exclaimed. She sat and said, "I should have told you before now." Untying her bonnet with shaking hands and speaking in a breathless way, she said, "You have a new father."

I trembled and turned white. "A new father?"

Peggotty gasped as if she were trying to swallow something. She put out her hand. "Come see him."

"I don't want to see him!" I said.

"And your mama," Peggotty added.

I ceased to draw back, and we went straight to the parlor, where Peggotty left me. My mother sat on one side of the fire. Mr. Murdstone sat on the other. My mother dropped her work and rose hurriedly but timidly.

"Now, Clara, my dear," Mr. Murdstone said with a tone of warning. "Remember. Control yourself. Always control yourself. Davy, my boy, how are you?"

I gave him my hand. Then I went and kissed my mother. She kissed me, patted me on the shoulder, and sat down again to her work. I couldn't look at her or Mr. Murdstone. I knew he was watching my mother and me. I turned to the window and looked out at some shrubs that were drooping their heads in the cold.

As soon as I could steal away, I crept upstairs. My old, dear bedroom was changed. I was to sleep in another room. I went back downstairs to find anything that was like itself. Everything seemed altered. I roamed into the yard. I soon started back because there was a large black dog in a kennel, with a deep bark. He growled and sprang at me. I went up to my new bedroom, hearing the dog in the yard bark after me as I climbed the stairs. I sat down and looked around the room. I noticed cracks in the ceiling and flaws—ripples and dimples—in the window glass. I noticed that the three-legged washstand was rickety. Feeling cold and desolate, I wept. I missed Emily and felt unwanted in my own home. I rolled myself up in a corner of the bedspread and cried myself to sleep.

I was awakened by Peggotty saying, "Here he is," and uncovering my head. She and my mother had come to look for me.

"Davy, what's the matter?" my mother asked.

"Nothing." I turned over onto my face to hide my trembling lips.

"Davy, my child," she said.

I hid my tears in the bedclothes. When my mother tried to lift me up, I pressed her from me with my hand.

"This is your doing, Peggotty, you cruel thing!" my mother said. "You've turned my own boy against me."

"God forgive you for saying such a thing, Mrs. Copperfield!" Peggotty responded.

"You shouldn't envy me a little peace of mind and happiness, especially when I'm a new bride," my mother said to Peggotty. "Davy, you naughty boy!"

I felt the touch of a hand that I knew was neither my mother's nor Peggotty's and slipped to my feet at the bedside. The hand was Mr. Murdstone's. He kept it on my arm as he said, "What's this? Clara, my love, have you forgotten? Firmness, my dear."

"I'm very sorry, Edward. I meant to be very

good, but I'm so uncomfortable," my mother said.

"Indeed! That's bad, Clara," Mr. Murdstone said. He drew my mother to him, whispered in her ear, and kissed her. My mother's head leaned against his shoulder as if she had no will or strength of her own. Her arm touched his neck. "Go downstairs, my love," he said to her with a nod and smile. "David and I will come down together." After watching my mother leave the room, Mr. Murdstone turned to Peggotty with a dark face. "My friend, do you know your mistress's name?"

"She's been my mistress a long time, sir," Peggotty answered. "I ought to know it."

"As I came upstairs I heard you address her by a name that no longer is hers. She now is Mrs. Murdstone. Please remember that."

With an uneasy glance at me, Peggotty curtseyed and left the room.

Mr. Murdstone shut the door. He sat on a chair and had me stand in front of him. Holding me by my arms, he looked steadily into my eyes. My heart beat quickly. "David," he said, making his lips thin by pressing them together, "if I have an obstinate horse or dog to deal with, what do you think I do?"

"I don't know," I answered in a breathless whisper.

"I beat him."

I was silent.

"I make him wince and smart," Mr. Murdstone continued. "I say to myself, 'I'll conquer that fellow,' and I'd do it even if it cost him all of his blood." He paused. "What's that on your face?"

"Dirt," I lied. I knew that he was referring to traces of tears and that he knew what they were.

"Wash your face, and come down with me." He pointed to the washstand and motioned with his head that I should obey him.

I did as ordered, feeling that he would strike me if I didn't.

When Mr. Murdstone walked me into the parlor with his hand on my arm, he said, "Clara, my dear, you won't be made uncomfortable anymore. We'll soon improve this boy."

My mother seemed sorry to see me standing there scared. When I stole to a chair, she sorrowfully followed me with her eyes, but she didn't say anything to comfort me.

The three of us dined. Mr. Murdstone and my mother seemed very fond of each other. I gathered from what they said that Mr. Murdstone's older sister, Jane, was coming to stay and would arrive that evening. I learned that Mr. Murdstone and his sister had some share in a London wine company.

After dinner when we were sitting by the fire and I was longing to escape to Peggotty, a coach drove up to the garden gate. Mr. Murdstone and my mother started out to greet his sister. I timidly followed. At the parlor door my mother turned around, hugged me, and gently whispered, "Love and obey your new father." Secretly extending her hand behind her, she held mine until we came near to where Mr. Murdstone was standing in the garden. Then she let go of my hand and drew hers through his arm.

Chapter 5

Jane Murdstone was a dark, gloomy-looking woman. She greatly resembled her brother in face, voice, and manner. She had heavy eyebrows that nearly met over her large nose. She had two black trunks with her initials on the lids in brass nails. When she paid the coachman, she took her money out of a steel purse. She kept the purse in a bag that hung on her arm by a heavy chain and snapped shut like a bite. I never had seen such a metallic person.

Miss Murdstone was brought into the parlor with many tokens of welcome. She looked at me and said, "Is that your boy, sister-in-law?"

"Yes," my mother answered.

"Generally speaking, I don't like boys," Miss Murdstone said. "How do you do, boy?"

"Very well, thank you. I hope that you're well, too," I said with no enthusiasm.

Miss Murdstone announced, "He lacks manners," and asked to be shown to her room.

From then on I regarded that room with dread. Sometimes I would peek into it while Miss Murdstone was out. I never saw her two black trunks unlocked. Whenever she dressed up, Miss

25

Murdstone adorned herself with numerous little steel fetters and rivets; these usually hung on her mirror.

The day after her arrival Miss Murdstone was up at dawn and ringing her bell. When my mother came down to breakfast and was going to make tea, Miss Murdstone gave her a peck on the cheek, which was her nearest approach to a kiss, and said, "Now, Clara my dear, you know that I've come here to relieve you of all the trouble that I can. You're much too pretty and thoughtless to have any duties that I can undertake. If you'll give me your keys, I'll attend to everything from now on." From then on, Miss Murdstone kept the keys all day and put them under her pillow at night.

One night when Miss Murdstone had been sharing certain household plans with her brother, of which he approved, my mother objected, "I might at least have been consulted."

"Clara, I wonder at you," Mr. Murdstone said sternly.

"It's fine for you to say that you wonder, Edward, and fine for you to talk about firmness, but you wouldn't like it yourself," my mother replied. "It's very hard that in my own house . . . "

"'*My* own house'?" Mr. Murdstone questioned.

"*Our* own house," my mother said. "You know what I mean, Edward. It's very hard that in our own house I have no say in domestic matters. I managed very well before we were married. I did very well when I wasn't interfered with." She started to cry.

"Edward," Miss Murdstone said, "let there be an end to this. I'll leave tomorrow."

"Be silent, Jane," her brother ordered.

"I don't want anyone to go," my mother said, still crying. "I'm not asking for much. I'm not unreasonable. I'm very much obliged to anyone who assists me. I only want to be consulted sometimes. You once were pleased with my being a little inexperienced and girlish, Edward. Now you seem to hate me for it. You're severe."

"You astound me, Clara," he responded. "Yes, I derived some satisfaction from the thought of marrying an inexperienced and artless person, and forming her character, and infusing some needed firmness into it. But when my sister is kind enough to come to my assistance in this endeavor and to assume, for my sake, a condition something like a housekeeper's, and when she meets with ingratitude . . ."

"Oh, please, Edward. Don't accuse me of being ungrateful. I'm sure I'm not. I have many faults but not that," my mother said.

"When my sister meets with ingratitude," he repeated, "my feeling toward you is chilled and altered."

"Don't say that, my love!" my mother cried. "I couldn't live with coldness or unkindness. Jane, I don't object to anything. I'd be brokenhearted if you left."

"This isn't a fit scene for the boy. David, go to bed," Mr. Murdstone ordered.

Having tears in my eyes because my mother

was so distressed, I left the room. I didn't have the heart to say good night to Peggotty or get a candle from her, so I groped my way up to my room in the dark. When Peggotty came up about an hour later, she woke me and said that my mother had gone to bed feeling unwell.

Going down next morning somewhat earlier than usual, I paused outside the parlor door on hearing my mother's voice. She was begging Miss Murdstone's forgiveness, which Miss Murdstone granted.

From then on, I never knew my mother to give an opinion on any matter without first consulting Miss Murdstone. Whenever Miss Murdstone moved her hand toward her bag as if she were going to take out the keys and offer to resign them to my mother, my mother looked frightened.

The religion of Edward and Jane Murdstone was as severe as they were. Every Sunday I filed into the pew first, like a guarded captive. Wearing a black velvet dress suitable for a funeral, Miss Murdstone followed close behind me, then my mother, then Mr. Murdstone. Peggotty no longer accompanied us to church. Miss Murdstone would mumble responses, emphasizing all the dread words and phrases, such as "miserable sinners." Sandwiched between Mr. and Miss Murdstone, my mother would timidly move her lips, with Mr. and Miss Murdstone muttering near her ears like low thunder. If I moved a finger or relaxed a muscle of my face, Miss Murdstone would poke me in the side with her prayer book.

As we walked home, I'd notice neighbors looking at us and whispering. My mother, Mr. Murdstone, and Miss Murdstone went arm in arm, and I followed. I wondered if any of the neighbors were recalling, as I was, how my mother and I had previously walked home together.

I was taught at home, ostensibly by my mother but always in the presence of Mr. and Miss Murdstone, who would continually tell my mother that she wasn't firm enough with me. I had been an apt and willing pupil when my mother and I had lived alone. The gentleness of her voice and manner always had cheered me on. But these solemn lessons were drudgery and misery. They were long, numerous, and hard. I think that they bewildered my mother as much as they bewildered me.

One morning after breakfast I came into the parlor, as usual, with my books, an exercise book, and a slate. My mother was ready for me at her desk. Mr. Murdstone pretended to be reading a book in his armchair by the window. Sitting near my mother, Miss Murdstone was stringing steel beads. The sight of Mr. and Miss Murdstone made it hard for me to remember the words I had tried to memorize. I handed the first book to my mother and started off aloud at a racing pace while I had the words fresh in my mind. I tripped over a word. Mr. Murdstone looked up. I tripped over another. Miss Murdstone looked up. I reddened, tumbled over half a dozen words, and stopped. My mother looked as if she'd show me the book if she dared, but she didn't dare. "Oh, Davy," she said softly.

"Now, Clara," Mr. Murdstone said. "Be firm with the boy. Don't say, 'Oh, Davy.' That's childish. Either he knows his lesson, or he doesn't."

"He *doesn't* know it," Miss Murdstone declared.

"I'm afraid he doesn't," my mother said.

"Then, Clara, you simply should give him back the book and make him learn it," Miss Murdstone said.

"Yes," my mother said. "I intend to do that, my dear Jane. Now, Davy, try once more, and don't be stupid."

I tried again but stumbled even before I got to the previous place. I couldn't think about the lesson. I thought about the amount of lace in Miss Murdstone's cap and the price of Mr. Murdstone's bathrobe. Mr. and Miss Murdstone made impatient movements. My mother glanced at them submissively, shut the book, and laid it aside. She and I exchanged a despairing look.

During a lesson my mother sometimes tried to give me a clue by moving her lips when she thought neither Mr. nor Miss Murdstone was looking. Miss Murdstone then would warn in a deep voice, "Clara." My mother would start, color, and smile faintly. Mr. Murdstone would rise from his chair, take the book, hit me with it (often on the side of my head), and turn me out of the room by the shoulders.

At the end of each lesson Mr. Murdstone would give me a math problem. For example, he might say, "If I go into a cheese shop and buy five thousand cheeses at fourpence-halfpenny each, how much do I pay?" I would pore over the problem until dinner, when, having covered myself with chalk dust, I would be unable to deliver the answer. I would be considered in disgrace for the rest of the evening.

When I got through a lesson reasonably well, I didn't gain much because Miss Murdstone never could bear to see me without a task. If I foolishly made any show of being unemployed, she would call her brother's attention to me by saying, "Clara, my dear, there's nothing like work. Give your boy an exercise." And I'd be given some new task to master.

I rarely was allowed to play with other children because Mr. and Miss Murdstone considered children little vipers who contaminated one another.

Chapter 6

After six months of this treatment, I had become sullen, dull, and dogged. Each day I felt more alienated from my mother. I found some comfort in reading. My father had left a small collection of books in a little room upstairs that adjoined mine. In that blessed little room, which didn't interest anyone else in the house, I found many novels that kept me company. They kept alive my imagination and my hope of something beyond that place and time. Sometimes I would look out of the window and see other children at play. Then I'd return to my book.

One morning when I went into the parlor with my books, I found my mother looking anxious, Miss Murdstone looking firm, and Mr. Murdstone binding something around the bottom of a limber cane. He stopped binding when I came in and poised and switched the cane in the air. "I tell you, Clara," he said, "I've often been flogged myself."

"To be sure," Miss Murdstone said.

"Certainly, my dear Jane," my mother meekly faltered. "But . . . do you think it did Edward good?"

"Do you think it did me harm, Clara?" Mr. Murdstone asked gravely.

"That's the point," Miss Murdstone said.

"Certainly, my dear Jane," my mother said.

Mr. Murdstone looked at me. "Now, David, you must be far more careful today than usual." He gave the cane another poise and switch, laid it beside him with an impressive look, and took up his book. The words of my lessons slipped away by the page. I began badly and continued worse. Book after book was set aside as a failure. When I finally came to the five thousand cheeses—except Mr. Murdstone had substituted canes for cheeses that day—my mother burst out crying.

"Clara," Miss Murdstone said in her warning voice.

"I'm not quite well, my dear Jane," my mother said.

Mr. Murdstone winked at his sister as he rose. Taking up the cane, he said, "Jane, we hardly can expect Clara to bear with perfect firmness the worry and torment that David has caused her today. That would be stoic. Clara is greatly strengthened and improved, but we can hardly expect so much from her. David, you and I will go upstairs, boy."

As Mr. Murdstone took me out the door, my mother ran toward us. Miss Murdstone said, "Clara, are you a perfect fool?" and kept her from leaving the room.

Mr. Murdstone slowly and gravely walked me up to my room. When we got there, he suddenly twisted my head under his arm.

"Mr. Murdstone! Sir!" I cried. "Please don't beat me. I've tried to learn, but I can't learn while you and Miss Murdstone are there. I can't."

"Can't you, David?" Mr. Murdstone said. "We'll see." He held my head as in a vise, but I pressed up against him and stopped him for a moment, begging him not to beat me. He struck me heavily with the cane. In the same instant I bit the hand by which he held me. He beat me then as if he'd beat me to death. Above all the noise we made I heard my mother and Peggotty running up the stairs and crying out.

Then Mr. Murdstone was gone, the door was locked from the outside, and I was lying on the floor—torn, sore, and, in my puny way, raging. When I quieted, an unnatural stillness filled the house. I crawled up from the floor and saw my face in the mirror, so swollen, red, and ugly that it frightened me. My stripes were sore and stiff and made me cry when I moved, but they were nothing compared to the guilt that I felt. I felt like an atrocious criminal.

For a long time I lay alternately crying and dozing. At twilight the key was turned, and Miss Murdstone entered with some bread, meat, and milk. Without a word she put these on the table, glared at me, and left, locking the door again. Long after dark I sat there, wondering if anyone else would come. I undressed and went to bed. I began to wonder fearfully what would be done to me. Had I committed a criminal act? Would I be taken into custody and sent to prison? Would I be hanged?

When I awoke the next morning, I was weighed

down by the oppression of remembrance. Miss Murdstone appeared before I was out of bed, told me that I was free to walk in the garden for half an hour and no longer, and left, leaving the door open. I walked in the garden and did so every morning of my imprisonment, which lasted five days. If I had been able to see my mother alone, I would have gone down on my knees to her and begged for her forgiveness, but I saw no one other than Miss Murdstone except at evening prayers in the parlor. She would escort me there after everyone else was in place. I would be stationed alone near the door, like an outcast. My mother would be as far from me as she could be and would keep her face turned away. Mr. Murdstone's bitten hand was bound in linen. Before anyone rose from their devotional posture, Miss Murdstone would lead me back to my room.

Those five days felt like years. I listened to all the incidents of the house that I could hear: the ringing of bells, the opening and shutting of doors, the murmur of voices, the footsteps on the stairs. In my solitude and disgrace, any laughing, whistling, or singing outside seemed like mockery. Each day boys played in the churchyard. I watched them from my room but at some distance from my window. I was ashamed to show myself at the window because I didn't want them to know that I was a prisoner. The monotony of fear, gloom, and remorse was broken only when I was brought something to eat and drink. When I went to sleep, I had nightmares.

On the last night of my imprisonment, I was awakened by Peggotty's whispering my name. I started up in bed, put my arms out in the dark, and said, "Is that you, Peggotty?"

Peggotty whispered again through the keyhole. I groped my way to the door and, putting my lips to the keyhole, whispered, "Is that you, Peggotty dear?"

"Yes, my precious Davy," she replied. "Be as soft as a mouse, or the cat will hear us."

I understood "the cat" to mean Miss Murdstone. "How's Mama, dear Peggotty? Is she very angry with me?"

Peggotty cried softly. Then she answered, "Not very."

"What are they going to do to me, Peggotty? Do you know?"

"They're going to send you to school near London," Peggotty answered.

"When, Peggotty?"

"Tomorrow."

"Will I see Mama?"

"Yes. In the morning," Peggotty answered. After a pause she whispered, "Davy, dear, if I haven't been as intimate with you lately as I used to be, it isn't because I don't love you. I love you more than ever. It's because I thought it better for you and your mother. Can you hear me, Davy?"

"Yes, Peggotty," I sobbed.

"My poor darling! What I want to say is that you mustn't ever forget me. I'll never forget *you*. I'll take as much care of your mama, Davy, as I ever took of you. I won't leave her. The day may come when she'll be glad to lay her poor head on my arm again. I'll write to you, my dear."

"Thank you, dear Peggotty," I said. "Will you promise me one thing, Peggotty? Will you write and tell Mr. Peggotty and Emily, and Mrs. Gummidge and Ham, that I send them all my love, especially to Emily? Will you do that, Peggotty?"

Peggotty promised. We both kissed the keyhole because we couldn't kiss each other. I also patted it with my hand as if it had been her honest face. And we parted.

In the morning Miss Murdstone appeared as usual and told me that I was going to school. She informed me that when I was dressed, I should come down to the parlor and have my breakfast. There I found my mother, very pale and with red eyes. I ran into her arms and begged her pardon.

"Oh, Davy," she said. "That you could hurt anyone I love! Try to be better. Pray to be better. I forgive you, but I'm so grieved, Davy, that you should have such bad passions in your heart."

Mr. and Miss Murdstone had persuaded my mother that I was wicked. She was sorrier about that than about my going away. I tried to eat breakfast, but my tears dropped onto my buttered bread and trickled into my tea. My mother looked at me sometimes and then glanced at the watchful Miss Murdstone and looked down or away.

When we heard wheels at the gate, Miss Murdstone ordered a servant, "Bring down Master Copperfield's trunk." I looked for Peggotty, but neither she nor Mr. Murdstone appeared. The driver, Mr. Barkis, came to the door. My trunk was taken out to his cart and lifted in.

"Clara," Miss Murdstone said in her warning voice.

"Ready, my dear Jane," my mother said. "Goodbye, Davy. You're going for your own good. Goodbye, my child. You'll come home at the holidays. Be a better boy."

"Clara," Miss Murdstone warned again.

"Certainly, my dear Jane," my mother said. She was holding me. "I forgive you, my dear boy. God bless you."

"Clara," Miss Murdstone repeated. She took me out to the cart, saying, "I hope you'll repent before you come to a bad end." I got into the cart, and Mr. Barkis and I drove off.

By the time the cart had gone half a mile, my pocket handkerchief was soaked from tears. Suddenly Mr. Barkis stopped short. Looking out to see why, I was amazed to see Peggotty burst from a hedge and climb into the cart. Without saying a word, she took me into her arms and squeezed me to her. Then with one arm she reached down into her pocket and brought out some paper bags of cupcakes that she crammed into my pockets and a purse that she put into my hand. After another tight hug, she got down from the cart and ran away.

"Go," Mr. Barkis said to his horse, who went.

I examined the purse, which was of stiff leather and had a snap. In it were three bright shillings. Two half-crowns were folded in a sheet of paper on which my mother had written, "For Davy. With my love." I cried again. When my crying subsided, I asked Mr. Barkis if he were going all the way.

"All the way where?" he asked.

"To the school near London," I answered.

"Why, my horse would be deader than pork before we got halfway there."

"Are you going only to Yarmouth, then?" I asked.

"Yes. I'll put you on the stagecoach there. It will take you the rest of the way." I offered Mr. Barkis a cupcake, which disappeared into his big face as he ate it in one gulp. "Did Miss Peggotty make it?" he asked, slouching forward on the cart's footboard with an arm on each knee.

"Yes. She makes all of our pastry and does all of our cooking."

"Does she?" Mr. Barkis pursed his lips. After a while he asked, "Does she have any sweethearts?"

Thinking that he wanted something else to eat, I said, "Did you say sweet tarts, Mr. Barkis?"

"No. Sweet*hearts*," he answered. "Does she go walking with any man?"

"Does Peggotty go walking with anyone?"

"Yes."

"No. She's never had a sweetheart," I said.

Mr. Barkis pursed his lips again. "So she makes all the apple pastries and does all the cooking?"

"Yes."

"Will you be writing to her?" Mr. Barkis asked.

"Definitely."

Slowly turning his eyes toward me, he said, "When you write to her, would you say, 'John Barkis is willing'?"

"'John Barkis is willing,'" I repeated innocently. "Is that the whole message?"

He considered. Then he said, "Yes. 'John Barkis is willing.'"

"But you'll be back in Blunderstone tomorrow, Mr. Barkis," I said. "You'll be able to see Peggotty any time you want to. Don't you want to give her the message yourself?"

He shook his head no.

Worn out by everything that had happened, I lay down on a sack in the cart and fell asleep. I slept soundly until we reached Yarmouth in the afternoon. We drove into the inn yard and I wished that I could see Mr. Peggotty and Emily. The stagecoach was in the yard but without horses. Mr. Barkis put my trunk down on the yard pavement. A lady looked out of a bay window where some dead chickens and geese and some joints of meat were hanging and asked Mr. Barkis, "Is that the little gentleman from Blunderstone?"

I answered, "Yes, ma'am."

"What's your name?" she asked.

"David Copperfield, ma'am," I answered.

"No, you aren't the boy, then," she said.

"Have you been told 'Murdstone,' ma'am?" I asked.

"If you're Master Murdstone, why did you give another name?" she asked.

I explained.

The lady rang a bell and called out, "William! Show this boy to the coffee room." A waiter came running out of a kitchen on the opposite side of the yard.

The coffee room was a large, long room. I sat down, with my cap in my hand, on the chair nearest the door. When the waiter laid a tablecloth for me, I blushed with modesty. He brought me some chops, potatoes, and vegetables and took the covers off the serving dishes in a bouncing manner. He placed a chair at the table for me and said, "Now, Six-foot, come on."

I thanked him and took my seat but found it difficult to handle my knife and fork with any dexterity or avoid splashing myself with gravy while he was standing opposite me staring, making me blush every time I caught his eye. When I had finished, he brought me pudding.

As soon as I was done, I asked him for a pen, inkstand, and paper. He brought them immediately and watched me as I wrote to Peggotty:

> My dear Peggotty,
>
> I've arrived in Yarmouth. John Barkis is willing. My love to Mama.
>
> Yours affectionately.
>
> P.S. Mr. Barkis says that he particularly wants you to know **John Barkis is willing**.

The stagecoach horn blew in the yard. I rose and hesitantly asked if I had to pay anything. "You need to pay for the letter paper," the waiter answered. "Did you ever buy letter paper before?"

"No."

"It's expensive," he said. "Threepence. The only other thing to pay for is me."

"How much is it right to pay a waiter?" I asked with embarrassment.

"I have to support my family, my sister, and an aged parent," he claimed, "and some of them are sick."

Believing him and feeling sorry about his misfortunes, I felt that any payment less than ninepence would be hardhearted. I gave him one of my three bright shillings, which he received with much professed humility.

The coach set out from Yarmouth at 3:00 p.m. Whenever we passed through a village, I pictured to myself what the insides of the houses were like and what the inhabitants were doing. Whenever boys came running after the coach and jumped up to grab hold of it and swing there for a little way, I wondered if their fathers were alive and if they were happy at home. I tried to remember what *my* home had been like before my mother had married Mr. Murdstone.

The coach stopped for supper and then traveled through the night. Although it was midsummer, the night got chilly. Having been placed between two men, I was nearly smothered by their falling asleep and pressing against me. Sometimes they squeezed me so hard that I couldn't help crying out, "Oh! Please." Also, they snored. Opposite me was an elderly lady wrapped in a large fur cloak. She had a basket with her that she placed under my short legs. It cramped and hurt me, but if I moved at all, the movement made a glass in the basket rattle against something else. Then the lady would wake up, poke me with her foot, and say something like, "Don't fidget. *Your* bones are young enough, I'm sure." All together, I didn't get much sleep.

Chapter 7

At last the sun rose, and I saw London in the distance. Finally we arrived at an inn in the Whitechapel district. The coachman took me to the booking office and said, "Is there anyone here for a youngster named Murdstone, from Blunderstone, Suffolk? He's to wait here until called for."

No one answered.

"Try 'Copperfield,' if you please, sir," I said.

"Is there anyone here for a youngster named Copperfield? Come! *Is* there anyone?"

There was no one. I looked around anxiously. The horses were taken to the stable, the luggage removed, and the coach wheeled off by some hostlers. Still no one came to claim me.

The clerk on duty invited me to wait behind the counter of the booking office, where I sat on the scale used to weigh luggage. I sat looking at the parcels and inhaling the smell of stables. All sorts of frightening thoughts passed through my mind. What if no one fetched me? How long would my money last? Would I have to sleep in a luggage bin and wash myself at the pump in the yard in the morning? Would I be turned out every night and

43

have to come back every morning until someone called for me? What if Mr. Murdstone had planned it so that I simply would be left here? If I immediately left and tried to walk home, how would I find my way or walk so far? Even if I managed to get home, how could I trust anyone but Peggotty? Being only eight years old, I couldn't join the army or navy.

A gaunt, sallow young man entered. He told the clerk, "I'm Charles Mell from Salem House. Is a boy named David Copperfield here? He's a new pupil."

The clerk indicated me.

"I'm one of the teachers at Salem House," Mr. Mell said to me.

I bowed and felt awed.

"Where's your luggage?" Mr. Mell asked me.

I indicated my trunk. "Someone from Salem House will call for the trunk around noon," Mr. Mell told the clerk, who nodded.

I left the office hand in hand with Mr. Mell. Clean-shaven, he had hollow cheeks. His dark brown hair looked dried out. He was dressed in a worn black suit that was too short in the sleeves and legs. He wore a dirty white neck scarf.

"Is it far to Salem House?" I asked.

"It's about six miles from here, down by Blackheath. We'll go by coach."

"I'm rather hungry," I said, "I'd be obliged if you'd let me buy something to eat."

He stopped, looked at me, and said, "My mother lives near here. I'd like to call on her. You can buy some bread, or something else if you'd prefer, and have breakfast at her house."

So we stopped at a bakery, and I bought a loaf of brown bread for threepence. Then I bought an egg and a slice of bacon at a grocery store.

We went through the tumult of London's crowded streets, which confused my weary head, and over London Bridge until we came to a community of almshouses. An inscription on a stone alongside the gate said that the community consisted of twenty-five houses that had been built for poor women. All of the houses were alike, small two-story buildings with little black doors and two small diamond-shaped windows. Mr. Mell lifted the latch of one of the doors. We entered the ground floor's only room. It had an open corner cupboard, square-backed chairs, and a narrow staircase leading to the upper floor. The only decoration I remember was three peacock's feathers displayed over the mantel. Mrs. Mell was kneeling in front of the fire, using a bellows to increase the flames to make the contents of a little saucepan boil. On seeing her son, she stopped, got up, and said, "My Charlie!"

"Hello, Mother." Mr. Mell kissed her on the cheek, and they briefly embraced. "This young gentleman is a new boy at Salem House."

Mrs. Mell rubbed her hands and made a half curtsey.

"Would you cook his breakfast for him?" Mr. Mell asked.

"Certainly," his mother said.

Mrs. Mell cooked my food, and I sat down to a delicious meal of bread, egg, bacon, and milk, with Mrs. Mell having contributed the milk. While I ate,

Mr. Mell and his mother softly talked to each other.

When I finished, Mr. Mell took me away. We found the coach nearby and got up on the roof. I was so sleepy that when the coach stopped on the road to take up another passenger, Mr. Mell and the coachman put me inside by myself so that I could sleep. I slept deeply until I was aware of the coach's slowly mounting a steep hill. Then it stopped. It had reached its destination.

Salem House was surrounded by a high brick wall and looked very dreary. A board with "Salem House" on it hung over a door in the wall. We rang the bell, and a surly face surveyed us through a grating in the door. The door was opened by a stout man with a bull neck and a wooden leg. His hair was cropped very short all around his head. I later learned that he was Mr. Tungay.

"The new boy," Mr. Mell said to Mr. Tungay.

Mr. Tungay eyed me all over, locked the gate behind us, and kept the key. Mr. Mell and I started toward the house, which was among dark, heavy trees. "Mr. Mell!" Mr. Tungay called. We looked back. Mr. Tungay was standing at the door of a little lodge, where he lived. He had a pair of boots in his hand. "The cobbler was here while you were out," he said to Mr. Mell. "He said he can't mend your boots anymore. He said there ain't a bit of the original boots left and he wonders that you expected him to be able to fix them." Mr. Tungay tossed the boots toward Mr. Mell, who went back a few paces to pick them up. He looked at them disconsolately, and we went on. I observed then for the first time that the boots he had on were much the worse for wear. One of them had a hole through which one of his toes slightly protruded in its sock.

Salem House was a square, bare-looking brick building with wings. It was so quiet all around that I said to Mr. Mell, "I suppose the boys are out."

"It's vacation. You didn't know that?" he said in a kindly way, seeming surprised. "All the boys are at their homes. You were sent here during vacation as punishment for your misdeeds. Mr. Creakle, the principal, is at the seaside with his wife and daughter."

Mr. Mell took me into a schoolroom. I gazed at it, the most desolate place I'd ever seen. It was a long room with three long rows of desks. The room bristled all around with pegs for hats and slates. Scraps of old workbooks and exercises littered the dirty floor. Two miserable little white mice, left behind by their owner, ran back and forth inside a moldy castle made of cardboard and wire, looking in all the corners with their red eyes for anything to eat. A bird in a cage scarcely bigger than himself alternately hopped onto his perch, two inches high, and hopped back down. He neither sang nor chirped. Every so often he made a mournful rattle. The room had a strange, unwholesome smell like that of rotting apples. There were ink stains all over the place.

Mr. Mell left me while he took his irreparable boots upstairs. At the upper end of the room, I came across a cardboard placard lying on a desk. It read, "Beware of him. He bites." Startled, I looked around for a ferocious dog. When Mr. Mell returned, I asked, "Is there a dog, sir?"

"Where?" he responded.

"Here. The sign says, 'Beware of him. He bites.'"

"No, Copperfield," Mr. Mell answered gravely. "That doesn't refer to a dog. It refers to a boy. You, Copperfield. I've been instructed to put this placard on your back. I'm sorry to make such a beginning with you, but I must do it." With that he tied the placard to my shoulders like a backpack.

You can imagine what I suffered from that placard. Even when I was alone, I always imagined that someone was reading it. Whenever Mr. Tungay saw me leaning against a tree or wall, he roared out from the door of his lodge, "You! Copperfield! Show that badge, or I'll report you." The playground was a bare gravel yard open to the whole back of the house and the offices. Whenever I was ordered to walk in the yard, I knew that the servants read the placard and that everyone, such as the butcher and baker, who came to or from the house read it. I dreaded the return of the other students, fearing that they would mock and bully me. Mr. Mell told me that there were forty-five of them. Night after night I dreamed that people stared at me and screamed because I had nothing on but my nightshirt and the placard.

Every day I had long lessons with Mr. Mell. I got through them without disgrace. Mr. Mell never said much to me, but he never was harsh. Before and after my lessons, I walked around, watched by Mr. Tungay. I vividly recall the dampness around the house, the cracked flagstones in the courtyard, an old leaky water cask, and the discolored trunks of some of the grim trees. Each day at 1:00 Mr. Mell and I ate lunch at the upper end of a long, bare dining room that smelled of fat and was filled with tables made of pine boards. Then we did more lessons until tea. Mr. Mell drank his tea out of a blue teacup, and I drank mine out of a tin pot. All day long, until 7:00 or 8:00 at night, Mr. Mell worked hard at his schoolroom desk with pen, ink, ruler, books, and writing paper, making out the bills for the last semester. When I went to bed after further study, I sat on my bed—the only occupied bed among many empty ones—and wept. I longed for a comforting word from Peggotty. In the morning I came downstairs and looked through a long, narrow staircase window. Through it I saw the school bell hanging on the top of an outbuilding with a weathercock above it. I dreaded the time when the bell would ring.

Chapter 8

After about a month, Mr. Tungay began to stump around with a bucket of water and a mop. I inferred that preparations were underway to receive Mr. Creakle and the students. Before long Mr. Tungay brought his mop into the schoolroom and turned out Mr. Mell and me. For days Mr. Mell and I kept moving from place to place for our lessons and meals. It seemed we always ended up in the way of two or three cleaning ladies. We were so continually in the midst of dust that I sneezed a lot.

One day Mr. Mell informed me that Mr. Creakle would be home that evening. In the evening after tea, I heard that Mr. Creakle had come. Before bedtime Mr. Tungay brought me to Mr. Creakle.

Mr. Creakle's part of the house was much more comfortable than the part the students occupied. He had a snug little garden that looked pleasant after the bare, dusty playground. I went, trembling, into his presence. When I was ushered into the parlor, I hardly noticed the presence of his wife and daughter. I was focused on Mr. Creakle, a stout gentleman with a thick watch chain. He sat in an armchair, with a bottle and drinking glass beside him.

"So," Mr. Creakle said, "this is the young gentleman whose teeth should be filed. Turn him around." He had an odd voice that was almost a whisper.

Mr. Tungay turned me around to exhibit the placard. Then he turned me back with my face to Mr. Creakle and went to stand beside him. Mr. Creakle's face was fiery. His eyes were small and deep in his head. He had thick veins in his forehead, a little nose, and a large chin. He was bald on the top of his head and had some thin, wet-looking hair that was just turning gray brushed across each temple so that the two sides interlaced on his forehead. "Now," he whispered, although he appeared to be trying to speak with normal loudness. "What's the report on this boy?"

"Nothing against him yet," Mr. Tungay answered. "There really hasn't been any opportunity."

Mr. Creakle looked disappointed. I now glanced at his wife and daughter for the first time. Both were thin and quiet.

"Come here, sir," Mr. Creakle said, beckoning to me.

"Come here," Mr. Tungay said to me, repeating the gesture.

"I have the pleasure of knowing your stepfather," Mr. Creakle whispered, taking me by the ear. "He's a worthy man of strong character." He pinched my ear hard.

I flinched with pain.

"When I say that something should be done, I

mean it," Mr. Creakle whispered. He twisted my ear and then released it. "You may go." He turned to Mr. Tungay. "Take him away."

"If you please, sir," I timidly began.

"Huh? What's this?" Mr. Creakle whispered, his eyes burning into me.

"If you please, sir," I faltered. "May I take this placard off before the boys come back? I'm very sorry for what I did."

Mr. Creakle burst out of his chair with such violence that I ran out and all the way to my bedroom. Finding that I wasn't pursued, I went to bed. I didn't fall asleep for a few hours; I felt too scared.

The next morning Mr. Sharp returned. He was the head teacher, Mr. Mell's superior. Mr. Mell took his meals with the boys, but Mr. Sharp ate at Mr. Creakle's table. He was a limp, delicate-looking gentleman with a large nose and a habit of carrying his head to one side as if it were a little too heavy for him. His hair was very smooth and wavy. But the first boy who returned—Tommy Traddles—told me that it was a secondhand wig and that Mr. Sharp went out every Saturday afternoon to get it curled.

Tommy introduced himself and then asked me for a full account of myself and my family. He enjoyed my placard so much that he saved me from the embarrassment of trying to hide it from other students or explain it to them. As soon as any boy returned, Tommy presented me to him with these words: "Look here. Here's a game." Happily for me, most of the boys came back so low-spirited that they weren't nearly as boisterous at my expense as I had expected. Most of them couldn't resist pretending that I was a dog. They patted and soothed me so that I wouldn't bite, calling me "Fido" and mock-commanding, "Lie down." This treatment cost me some tears, but on the whole it wasn't nearly as bad as I had anticipated.

I wasn't considered formally received into the school until James Steerforth accepted me. I was brought to him as if to a magistrate. At least six years older than me, he was very handsome and was reputed to be a great scholar. He had a melodious voice, fine face, and dark, curly hair. In front of a shed on the playground, he publicly asked me about the circumstances leading to my punishment. When he expressed the opinion that my having to wear the placard was "a damned shame," I felt enormously grateful. Now that James had passed favorable judgment, the gathering broke up.

"What money do you have, David?" James asked, taking me aside.

"Seven shillings," I answered.

"You'd better give it to me for safe keeping," he said. "That is, if you want to. You don't have to."

Hastening to comply, I opened Peggotty's purse and turned it upside down so that the contents spilled into James's hand.

"Do you want to spend any of it now?" he asked.

"No, thank you, sir," I replied.

"You can if you like, you know," he said. "Just say the word."

"No, thank you," I repeated.

"Maybe you'd like to spend a couple of shillings on a bottle of wine that we can enjoy up in the bedroom," James said. "You're in the same bedroom as I am, I find."

"Yes. I'd like that," I said.

"Good. Would you like to spend another shilling or so on almond cakes?"

"Yes. I'd like that, too," I answered.

"And another shilling on biscuits and another on fruit?"

I smiled because he smiled, but I was a little troubled.

"Well," James said, "we must stretch your money as far as we can. I'll do my best for you. I can go out whenever I like. I'll smuggle the items in." He put the money into his pocket and said, "Don't you worry. I'll take care of it."

I feared that the planned purchases were a waste of my money, but I went along with James's plan.

That evening after we went upstairs to bed, James laid the seven-shillings' worth of refreshments out on my bed in the moonlight. "There you are, young David," he said. "A royal spread."

I asked him to do me the honor of presiding over the feast, and the other boys in the room seconded my request. James sat on my pillow, I sat to his left, and the other boys sat grouped around us on the nearest beds and on the floor. James handed out the food in equal amounts to everyone present. He dispensed the wine in a little glass that was his own property.

A small amount of moonlight entered through the window, painting a pale window on the floor. Otherwise we were in darkness. I think we all delighted in the secrecy of our forbidden feast. At one point Tommy pretended to see a ghost in one corner. We all laughed, pretending not to be frightened. Whenever James wanted to look for something, he briefly lit a match. Speaking in whispers, the boys talked to one another and told me all sorts of things about the school and its staff. They said that Mr. Creakle was the most severe of principals and that he charged in among them, every day, slashing away mercilessly with his cane. According to James, Mr. Creakle knew less than the most ignorant boy in the school. The boys said that many years ago Mr. Creakle had been a small hops dealer. He had used up all of his wife's money and gone bankrupt. Then he'd gone into the business of schooling. The boys said that Mr. Tungay had assisted in Mr. Creakle's hops business, had broken his leg in Mr. Creakle's service, had done dishonest work for him, and considered everyone in the school his enemy except for Mr. Creakle. I heard that Mr. Creakle had a son who disliked Mr. Tungay and who objected to his father's cruel treatment of the students and of Mrs. Creakle. As a result, Mr. Creakle had turned his son out of doors. Mrs. and Miss Creakle had been sad ever since. But there was one boy in the school whom Mr. Creakle never dared to abuse: James. "If he ever started to lay a hand on me," James said, "I'd knock him down." This statement made the rest of us breathless. I heard that Mr. Sharp and

Mr. Mell both were wretchedly underpaid and that whenever there was hot and cold meat for dinner at Mr. Creakle's table, Mr. Sharp was expected to say that he preferred the cold meat. I heard that Mr. Sharp's wig fit him so poorly that his own red hair was visible underneath it. I heard that one boy, a coal merchant's son, had been taken as a pupil in payment of coal bills. I heard that everyone at the school regarded Miss Creakle as being in love with James. I heard that Mr. Mell wasn't a bad fellow and that he didn't have as much as sixpence.

When the eating and drinking ended, most of the guests went to bed. The rest of us remained whispering until we finally went to bed.

"Good night, young David," James said. "I'll take care of you."

"You're very kind," I gratefully returned. "I'm much obliged to you."

"Do you have a sister?" James asked.

"No," I answered.

"That's a pity. If you did, I think she'd be a pretty, timid, bright-eyed little girl. I would have liked to know her. Good night, David."

"Good night, sir," I replied.

After I went to bed, I raised myself to look at James where he lay in the moonlight, with his handsome face turned up and his head resting on his arm. In my eyes he was a person of great power.

Chapter 9

School began the next day. After breakfast the roar of voices in the schoolroom suddenly changed to a death-like hush when Mr. Creakle entered and stood in the doorway, looking at us like a storybook giant surveying his captives. Mr. Tungay stood at Mr. Creakle's elbow. Even though all of the students already were silent and motionless, he roared, "Silence!"

Mr. Creakle whispered, and Mr. Tungay then repeated so that everyone could hear, "Now, boys, this is a new semester. Take care what you're about. I advise you to put fresh energy into your lessons because I'll be putting fresh energy into the punishments. I won't flinch. You won't be able to rub off the marks that I'll give you. Now get to work, all of you!"

Mr. Tungay stumped out, and Mr. Creakle came to where I sat. "If you're famous for biting," he said to me, "so am I." Showing me his cane, he said, "What do you think of *that* for a tooth?" He gave me a fleshy cut with it that made me writhe and begin to cry. "Is it a sharp tooth?" he said. Another cut. "Does it bite?" Another cut. "Does it bite hard?" Another.

Such abuse was by no means limited to me. Most of the boys, especially the smaller ones, received similar treatment as Mr. Creakle made his way around the schoolroom. He delighted in slashing at the boys, especially the chubby ones. Often he would hit a boy on the hands with a ruler. All of us would watch Mr. Creakle, in constant dread. Some unfortunate boy, having failed to learned the assigned lesson, would approach at Mr. Creakle's command. The boy would falter excuses and say that he was determined to do better tomorrow. Mr. Creakle would make a joke before beating him. Servile and afraid, we all would laugh at the joke, our faces white, our hearts sinking into our boots. How abject we were to the tyrant! We didn't dare to meet his eyes.

Once I sat at my desk on a drowsy summer afternoon. My head was heavy. I sat with my eyes on Mr. Creakle. Then sleep overpowered me for a minute. He came up behind me and woke me with a red ridge across my back.

While we boys were on the playground, Mr. Creakle would watch us through a little window. One day Tommy accidentally sent a ball crashing through the window. Poor Tommy! Wearing a sky-blue suit that was too tight for his chubby arms and legs, he was the merriest and most miserable of all the boys. He always was being caned. I think that Mr. Creakle caned him every day that semester, except one day when Mr. Creakle only struck him on both hands with the ruler. Tommy always was going to write to his uncle about the abuse, but he never did. After laying his head on the desk for a little while, he somehow would cheer up, begin to laugh again, and draw stick figures all over his slate before his eyes were dry. Tommy was very honorable. He considered it a solemn duty in the boys to stand up for one another. He suffered for this belief on several occasions, especially once when James laughed in church and the beadle thought it was Tommy and took him out for a beating. Tommy never said that James was the actual offender. He was caned so that he still smarted the next day and was imprisoned many hours. In response to Tommy's self-sacrifice, James told the rest of us, "There's nothing of the sneak in Traddles." We all considered that the highest praise, and I thought it worth the price of being beaten and imprisoned.

To see James walk to church in front of us, arm in arm with Miss Creakle, was one of the joys of my life. I didn't think that Miss Creakle was as beautiful as Emily and I didn't love her, but I thought that she was a young lady of extraordinary attractiveness and unsurpassed gentility. When James, in white trousers, carried her parasol for her, I felt proud to know him. I thought that Miss Creakle had no choice but to adore him. In my eyes Mr. Sharp and Mr. Mell both were notable personages, but James was to them what the sun is to two stars.

James continued to protect me. None of the boys dared to annoy me because I had his favor. However, he didn't defend me from Mr. Creakle, who was very severe with me. Whenever Mr.

Creakle beat me worse than usual, James would say to me, "You should have more pluck, as I do. I'd never submit to such abuse." I took his words as encouragement and considered them very kind. There was one advantage to Mr. Creakle's severity. Because he found that my placard was in the way when he wanted to cut me on my back, it soon was permanently removed.

One day while James was doing me the honor of talking to me on the playground, I happened to mention some of the stories I'd read.

"And do you remember them?" he asked.

"Oh, yes," I replied.

"Then, I'll tell you what, young David," James said. "You'll tell them to me. I have trouble falling asleep at night and get up very early. Tell me a different story every night and every morning."

I felt extremely flattered. That same night I told James the first story. From then on I narrated a tale every night. I did this even when I felt very tired and would have liked to go to sleep, because I wasn't willing to disappoint or displease James. I also told him a story every morning, even when I felt weary and would have preferred to sleep for another hour. James would wake me before the wake-up bell and force me into a long story. In return for my storytelling, he helped me with arithmetic and other subjects that I sometimes found difficult. But I would have told him the stories even if he'd given nothing in return, because I worshipped him. Some of the other boys, especially Tommy, often listened to my narrations. Tommy showed great delight at the comic parts and pretended to be frightened by the alarming parts.

Peggotty's promised letter arrived a few weeks into the semester and with it a cake, oranges, and two bottles of wine. I felt duty-bound to lay these treats at James's feet and ask him to dispense them. James said, "I'll tell you what, young David. You keep the wine to wet your throat when you're telling me stories. I've noticed that sometimes you get a little hoarse." So the wine was locked up in his trunk, and he dispensed it to me when he thought my voice needing restoring.

Mr. Mell assisted me in my studies. He had a liking for me for which I remain grateful. It always pained me to observe that James treated Mr. Mell with systematic disparagement and seldom lost a chance to wound his feelings or incite others to do so. Soon after meeting James I had told him about my having met Mrs. Mell and about her living in an almshouse.

One Saturday afternoon when (to the joy of every student) Mr. Creakle had stayed at home because he wasn't feeling well, Mr. Mell was in charge of the class. The boys had been given some light tasks, but they were in an uproar. Mr. Mell was seated at his desk, trying to help me with some reading, and I was standing beside him. He bent his aching head, supported on his bony hand, over the book and wretchedly tried to continue teaching me. Boys darted in and out of their places, playing tag. Boys laughed, sang, talked, danced, howled, and shuffled their feet. They whirled around Mr. Mell, grinning, making faces, and mimicking him behind his back and before his eyes. They mocked his poverty, his boots, his coat, his mother, everything associated with him.

Suddenly getting up, Mr. Mell cried, "Silence!" and struck his desk with a book. "This is impossible to bear. It's maddening. How can you do it to me, boys?"

I continued to stand beside him, following his eyes as they glanced around the room. I saw the boys all stop, some suddenly surprised, some half afraid, and some sorry perhaps. James's place was at the back of the long room. He was standing with his back against the wall and his hands in his pockets. When Mr. Mell looked at him, he whistled.

"Silence, Mr. Steerforth!" Mr. Mell said.

"Silence yourself," James responded. "Whom do you think you're talking to?"

"Sit down," Mr. Mell said.

"Sit down yourself, and mind your own business," James replied.

There were titters and some applause. But Mr. Mell was so white that silence immediately followed. One boy, who had darted behind Mr. Mell to imitate his mother again, changed his mind and pretended to want a pen mended.

Mr. Mell said, "I'm well acquainted, Steerforth, with the power that you exercise over the other boys. You urge your juniors on to every sort of outrage against me."

"I don't give myself the trouble of thinking about you at all," James said coolly.

Mr. Mell's lips trembled. "You use your position of favoritism here to insult a gentleman."

"A what? Where is there a gentleman? I don't see one," James retorted.

"For shame, Steerforth!" Tommy bravely cried out. "This is unworthy."

"Hold your tongue, Traddles," Mr. Mell said. Then he said to James, "It's mean and base to insult someone who is less fortunate than you, sir, and who never has given you the least offense. You're old enough and smart enough to know better. Copperfield, go on." Mr. Mell sat back down at his desk.

"Wait, David," James said, coming to the front of the room. "Mr. Mell, when you take the liberty of calling me mean, base, or anything of that sort, you're an impudent beggar. You *always* are a beggar, but when you do that, you're an *impudent* beggar."

Mr. Mell stood again, and James approached him. For an extremely tense moment I thought that they might come to blows. Suddenly Mr. Creakle was in the midst of us with Mr. Tungay at his side. Mrs. and Miss Creakle were looking in at the door with expressions of alarm. Mr. Mell and all of the boys were silent and still.

"Mr. Mell," Mr. Creakle said, "you haven't forgotten yourself, I hope?"

"No, sir," Mr. Mell answered, shaking his head.

Mr. Creakle turned to James. "Now, sir, what is this about?"

At first, James was silent. He looked at Mr. Mell

with scorn and anger. Even then I thought how noble James was in appearance and how homely Mr. Mell was by comparison.

Then James said to Mr. Creakle, "He accused the school of favoritism."

"Favoritism?" The veins in his forehead swelling, Mr. Creakle turned back to Mr. Mell and angrily demanded, "What did you mean by that, sir?"

Mr. Mell answered in a low voice, "I said, Mr. Creakle, that no pupil has a right to use his position of favoritism to insult me."

"Insult *you*?" Mr. Creakle responded. "Allow me to ask you, Mr. What's-Your-Name, whether, when you talk about favoritism, you show proper respect to *me*, the principal of this establishment and your employer."

"It wasn't judicious of me to say what I did, sir," Mr. Mell said. "I admit that. I wouldn't have said it if I hadn't been angry."

"He also said that I'm mean and base," James struck in. "Then I called him a beggar. Maybe I wouldn't have called him a beggar if *I* hadn't been angry. But I did, and I'm ready to take the consequences."

There was a low stir of admiration among the boys. Even though James never faced any consequences for his words and actions, we thought his words very brave. I glowed with pride at what I considered to be his gallantry.

Mr. Creakle said, "Your candor does you credit, Steerforth, but I'm surprised that you would attach such an epithet to anyone employed at Salem House."

James gave a short, scornful laugh.

"That's no answer to my remark, sir. I expect more than that from you, Steerforth," Mr. Creakle said.

"Let him deny it," James said, referring to Mr. Mell.

"Deny that he's a beggar, Steerforth?" Mr. Creakle cried. "Why, where does he beg?"

"He may not be a beggar himself, but his mother is," James replied, glancing at me.

Mr. Mell gently patted my shoulder. I looked up with a flush on my face and remorse in my heart, but Mr. Mell's eyes were fixed on James.

"Since you expect me to justify myself, Mr. Creakle," James continued, "I'll say that his mother lives on charity in an almshouse."

Still patting me kindly, Mr. Mell softly said to himself, "I thought so."

Frowning, Mr. Creakle turned to Mr. Mell. "Mr. Mell, please set this gentleman straight."

"What he says is true," Mr. Mell responded.

At first Mr. Creakle was shocked into silence. Then he said, "In that case, be so good as to declare publicly that I was unaware of this."

"I believe you were unaware of this," Mr. Mell stated.

"Why, you *know* I was, don't you, man?" Mr. Creakle demanded.

"Surely you've known that I have little money," Mr. Mell responded. "You know what my position is, and always has been, here."

"I now know that you've been in the wrong position, Mr. Mell. You've mistaken this school for a charitable institution. We'll part, if you please. The sooner the better."

"There's no time like the present," Mr. Mell answered.

"'Sir' to you!" Mr. Creakle declared.

"I take my leave of you, Mr. Creakle, and all of you," Mr. Mell said, glancing around the room. "James Steerforth, the best wish with which I can leave you is that you may come to be ashamed of what you've done today. At present I wouldn't want you as a friend, and I'd prefer that anyone I care about not associate with you." Once more he laid his hand on my shoulder. Then, taking a few books from his desk and leaving the key in it for his successor, he left the school.

Mr. Creakle then made a speech, through Mr. Tungay, in which he thanked James for asserting (although perhaps too warmly) Salem House's independence and respectability. He wound up by shaking hands with James while all of us boys gave three cheers. All of us except for Tommy, that is. He wept over Mr. Mell's departure. Although I, too, felt miserable, I joined in the cheering because it was for James. When Mr. Creakle noticed that Tommy was weeping instead of cheering, he caned him. Tommy then sat with his head down on his desk, and Mr. Creakle returned to his quarters.

Left to ourselves, we boys all looked blankly at one another. I suffered from self-reproach and wanted to weep, but James kept looking at me, so I held back my tears, fearing that he would consider tears undutiful toward him.

James was very angry with Tommy and said to him, "I'm glad you were caned."

Tommy responded, "I don't care about that. Mr. Mell has been abused."

"Who abused him, you girl?" James said.

"You did," Tommy replied.

"What did *I* do?" James questioned.

"You hurt his feelings and cost him his job," Tommy answered.

"His feelings?" James said scornfully. "His feelings aren't like yours, Miss Traddles. As for his job—it hardly was a good one, was it? Also, I'm going to write home and see that he gets some money."

We thought this intention very noble of James. It was said that his mother, a wealthy widow, would do almost anything that he asked. We all thought that James had answered Tommy admirably.

"Besides," James added, looking around at his entire audience, "I did what I did for all of *you.* You go to this school and shouldn't associate with beggars."

James initially taught some of Mr. Mell's classes. He didn't use any books but seemed to know the lessons by heart. Then a new teacher was hired. He came from a grammar school. Before he started, he was introduced to James at dinner. James told us boys that he highly approved of the new teacher. But the new teacher never would take the pains with me that Mr. Mell had.

One afternoon when Mr. Creakle was even more brutal than usual, Mr. Tungay came in and bellowed, "Visitors for Copperfield!" Mr. Tungay exchanged a few words with Mr. Creakle. I was told to go by the back stairs and put on a clean suit and then go to the dining room. I hurriedly obeyed.

Hoping that the visitors included my mother but fearing that they might, instead, be Mr. and Miss Murdstone, I collected myself enough to enter the parlor. There, to my amazement, were Mr. Peggotty and Ham. They hugged me, and I laughed with joy. Then I started to weep.

Mr. Peggotty looked very concerned.

"Cheer up, Master Davy," Ham said. "How you've grown!"

"Have I?" I said, drying my eyes with my handkerchief.

"Yes," Mr. Peggotty said.

I asked, "Do you know how my mother is, Mr. Peggotty, and my dear, dear Peggotty?"

"They're fine," Mr. Peggotty answered.

"And Emily and Mrs. Gummidge?"

"Fine," Mr. Peggotty said.

There was a silence. Mr. Peggotty took the bodies of an enormous crab and two large lobsters out of a sack and handed them to Ham to hold. "And here's shrimps," he said, picking up a large canvas bag. "Mrs. Gummidge boiled them."

"Thank you!" I said.

"The wind and tide were favorable, so we sailed to Gravesend," Mr. Peggotty said. "My sister wrote me the name of this place and said that if I ever happened to be in Gravesend I should come and ask for you, give you her good wishes, and tell you that your family is fine. When I get home, Emily will write to my sister that I saw you and found you were fine."

"Thank you." Blushing, I said, "Tell me about Emily."

"She's getting to be a woman," Mr. Peggotty said. "Ask *him*." He indicated Ham, who beamed. "Her pretty face!" he said, with his own shining.

"Her learning!" Ham exclaimed.

"Her writing!" Mr. Peggotty added. "It's as black as jet and nice and large." His bluff, hairy face radiated joyful love. His broad chest heaved with pride. His strong, loose hands clenched in earnestness.

Suddenly James entered, singing. Seeing me in a corner speaking with two strangers, he stopped singing and said, "I didn't know you were here, David." He started to leave the room.

Wanting him to know how I came to have friends such as Mr. Peggotty and Ham, I called out, "Don't go, James, if you please. These are two Yarmouth boatmen—very kind, good people— who are relatives of my nurse. They've come from Gravesend to see me."

"Oh?" James said, returning. "I'm glad to see them. How are you both?" His manner was breezy but not swaggering.

I thought how handsome and charming James was. Mr. Peggotty and Ham seemed to open their hearts to him in a moment.

"Mr. Peggotty, when you send that letter to Peggotty, please let her know that Mr. Steerforth is very kind to me and that I don't know what I'd do here without him," I said.

"Nonsense!" James said, laughing. "You mustn't

write anything of the sort, Mr. Peggotty."

"And if Mr. Steerforth ever comes to Suffolk while I'm there, Mr. Peggotty, I'll bring him to Yarmouth to see your house if he'll let me. You never saw such a good house, James. It's made out of a barge."

"Made out of a barge?" James said. "I guess that's the right sort of house for a boatman."

"So it is, sir," Ham said, grinning.

"Thank you, sir, for your welcoming manner," Mr. Peggotty said. "My house ain't much, but it's at your service if you ever come along with Master Davy to see it."

Ham echoed this sentiment, and James and I parted from Mr. Peggotty and Ham in the heartiest manner. Unobserved, we took the crab, lobsters, and shrimps up to our room. That evening we had a feast.

Chapter 10

As the weather turned cold, so did the students of Salem House. It was cold when we got up and cold when we went to bed. In the evening the schoolroom was dimly lit and inadequately warmed. In the morning we all shivered in it. The beatings with canes and rulers continued.

When the holidays approached, I feared that I wouldn't get to go home. But when the time came, I was inside the Yarmouth stagecoach and going home. That night the coach stopped at an inn, and I was shown up to a nice little bedroom. I was very cold despite the hot tea that a waiter had given me in front of a large fire downstairs. I was very glad to get into the bed, pull the blankets around me, and sleep.

Mr. Barkis, the driver, was to call for me at 9:00 a.m. I got up at 8:00, a little giddy from the shortness of my night's rest, and was ready for him before the appointed time. He received me as if no more than five minutes had passed since we had last seen each other. As soon as I and my trunk were in the cart and Mr. Barkis was seated, the horse walked away with us at his usual slow pace.

"You look very well, Mr. Barkis," I said.

He rubbed his cheek with his cuff but didn't acknowledge the compliment.

"I gave Peggotty your message, Mr. Barkis," I said. "I wrote to her."

"Ah," Mr. Barkis said, seeming dissatisfied.

"Didn't I give the right message, Mr. Barkis?"

"I suppose the message was fine, but it ended there."

Not understanding, I asked, "What ended there, Mr. Barkis?"

"When a man says he's willing," Mr. Barkis explained, "he's proposing marriage. She never answered."

"Oh!" My eyes widened at this realization. "Maybe she didn't understand. Why don't you talk to her?"

"No," Mr. Barkis said.

"Would you like me to tell her, Mr. Barkis?"

Mr. Barkis looked at me. "What's her first name?"

"Clara," I answered.

"If you would, you might tell her, 'Barkis has been waiting for an answer.'" After nudging me in the side with his elbow, he took a piece of chalk from his pocket and wrote, "Clara Peggotty" on his cart. Then he slouched over his horse in his usual way. Nothing more was said on the matter.

Although anxious to be home with my mother and Peggotty, I also felt dread and sorrow, knowing that Mr. and Miss Murdstone were sure to be there. When I arrived at the house, the bare elm trees were wringing their many hands in the bleak, wintry air. Mr. Barkis put my trunk down at the garden gate and left. I walked along the path to the house, glancing at the windows and fearing to see Mr. or Miss Murdstone glowering out of one of them. No face appeared, however. I opened the front door and entered with a quiet, timid step. From the hall I heard my mother's voice in the parlor. She was singing softly, as she had sung to me when I was a baby. My heart overflowed. Sensing that she was alone, I softly entered the room. She was sitting by the fire, breast-feeding an infant who was a few weeks old and whose tiny hand she held against her neck. She was looking down at his face as she sat singing to him.

"Mother," I said softly.

My mother started and cried, "Davy dear!" She came halfway across the room to meet me, kneeled on the floor, and kissed me. She laid my head on her bosom near the baby who was nestling there and put his hand to my lips. "He's your brother Stevie," she said, fondling me. "Davy, my pretty boy, my poor child." My mother kissed me again and again and clasped me around the neck. She was doing this when Peggotty came running in. Peggotty bounced down onto the floor beside us and was in raptures over me for a quarter of an hour.

I hadn't been expected so soon. Mr. Barkis had arrived much before his usual time. Mr. and Miss Murdstone had gone to visit a neighbor and wouldn't return before nightfall. Peggotty, my mother, and I dined by the fire. I used my old plate with a brown man-of-war in full sail painted on it. Peggotty had kept the plate safely hidden somewhere the whole time I'd been away. I used my old mug with "David" on it and my own little knife and fork. While we were at the table, I told Peggotty about Mr. Barkis. Before I had finished, she started to laugh and threw her apron over her face.

"What's this about, Peggotty?" my mother asked.

"Drat the man!" Peggotty cried. "He wants to marry me."

"It would be a good match for you, wouldn't it?" my mother said.

"I don't know," Peggotty answered. "I wouldn't have him if he had heaps of gold. I wouldn't have *anybody*."

"Then, why don't you tell him so, you ridiculous thing?" my mother said.

"He's never said a word to me about it." She laughed again and went on with her dinner.

I noticed that my mother was changed. Her pretty face was careworn. Her hands were so thin and white that they seemed almost transparent. Her manner was anxious and fluttered. Looking grave, she affectionately laid her hand on Peggotty's and said, "Peggotty, dear, you're not going to marry?"

"Lord bless you, no!" Peggotty exclaimed.

Taking her hand, my mother said, "Don't leave me, Peggotty. It won't be for long, perhaps. What would I ever do without you?"

"Leave you, my precious? Not for the world," Peggotty said. "I know two people who'd be mighty pleased if I did, but they won't have that satisfaction. No, I'll stay with you until I'm old, deaf, lame, and blind, and of no more use. Then I'll go to my Davy and ask him to take me in."

"And I'll make you as welcome as a queen, Peggotty," I said.

"Bless your dear heart," Peggotty said. "I know you will." She kissed me. Peggotty took Stevie out of his little cradle and held him. Then she cleared the dinner table. After that she came in with her sewing box.

We sat around the fire and talked delightfully. I told Peggotty and my mother what a harsh principal Mr. Creakle was, and they pitied me very much. I told them what a fine fellow James was and what a patron of mine. Peggotty said that she would walk many miles to see him. I took Stevie in my arms when he was awake and fondled him. When he was asleep again, I crept close to my mother's side and sat with my arms around her waist and my little red cheek on her shoulder and once more felt her beautiful hair drooping over me. I was very happy.

Peggotty darned a sock as long as she could see and then sat with it drawn on her left hand like a glove and her needle in her right, ready to take another stitch whenever the fire flared up. "I wonder," she said, "what's become of Davy's great-aunt."

"Whatever made you think of her?" my mother asked.

"I don't know," Peggotty replied.

"Would you like her to visit?"

"God forbid!" Peggotty cried.

"No doubt, Aunt Betsey is shut up in her house by the sea and will remain there," my mother said. "At any rate, she isn't likely to trouble us again."

"No," Peggotty mused. "That certainly isn't likely. I wonder, if she was to die, if she'd leave Davy anything."

"Don't be silly, Peggotty," my mother said. "You know that she took offense at the poor dear boy's being born."

"Maybe she's forgiven him," Peggotty said.

"Why would she?" my mother replied rather sharply.

"He has a brother now," Peggotty said.

"Are you saying that Davy will inherit nothing now that he has a brother? How dare you suggest such a thing! Maybe you'd better go and marry Mr. Barkis."

"That certainly would make Miss Murdstone happy," Peggotty responded.

"What a bad disposition you have, Peggotty," my mother said. "You're jealous of Miss Murdstone. I suppose you'd like to keep the keys. You know that she does that out of kindness and the best intentions."

"Best intentions, indeed!" Peggotty muttered.

"Haven't you heard her say, over and over, that she wishes to spare me a lot of trouble to which she doesn't think I'm suited and to which *I* doubt I'm suited. And isn't she up early and late, going to and fro? And doesn't she do all sorts of things, and grope into all sorts of places, such as coal holes and pantries, that can't be very pleasant? You also slight Mr. Murdstone's good intentions. If he seems to have been somewhat stern with Davy, it's only because he thinks it's for Davy's own good. He loves Davy for my sake. He's a better judge of these things than I am. I know that I'm a weak, silly, girlish creature, whereas he's a firm, serious man. He takes great pains with me, and I should feel very grateful."

Peggotty sat with her chin on the foot of the sock, looking silently at the fire.

"Let's not argue, Peggotty," my mother said, changing her tone. "You're my true friend. I know that. You've been good and true to me ever since Mr. Copperfield first brought me home here and you came out to the gate to meet me."

Peggotty gave my mother a hug.

When we finished our tea, and the ashes were thrown up and the candles snuffed, I read Peggotty a chapter of the crocodile book in remembrance of old times. Then we talked about Salem House, which brought me back to James, who was my favorite subject. It was almost 10:00 before we heard wheels. We all got up. My mother hurriedly said that Mr. and Miss Murdstone approved of early hours for young people, so I'd better go to bed. I kissed her and went upstairs with my candle before Mr. and Miss Murdstone came in.

The next morning I was reluctant to appear at breakfast and face Mr. and Miss Murdstone, but I forced myself to go down. I presented myself in the parlor. Mr. Murdstone was standing in front of the fire with his back to it while his sister made tea. He looked at me steadily as I entered but made no sign of recognition. After a moment of confusion, I went up to him and said, "I beg your pardon, sir. I'm very sorry for what I did. I hope you'll forgive me."

"I'm glad to hear that you're sorry, David," he replied. He gave me the hand that I had bitten. My eye rested for a moment on a red spot on it. I reddened when I met his sinister glance.

"How are you, ma'am?" I said to Miss Murdstone.

She gave me the tea scoop instead of her fingers and asked, "How long is your holiday?"

"A month, ma'am."

"That long?" She looked very displeased.

Later in the day I came into the room where Miss Murdstone and my mother were sitting. Stevie was on my mother's lap. I carefully took him into my arms. Suddenly Miss Murdstone gave such a scream that I nearly dropped him.

"My dear Jane!" my mother cried.

"Good heavens, Clara! Do you see?" Miss Murdstone exclaimed.

"See what, my dear Jane?"

"He has the baby!" Miss Murdstone cried. She was limp with horror. Then she stiffened, darted at me, and took Stevie out of my arms. She solemnly forbade me from touching my brother again.

I could see that my mother wished otherwise, but she said, "No doubt you are right, my dear Jane."

On another occasion my mother was looking at Stevie's eyes as he lay on her lap. "Come here, Davy," she said, and she looked at my eyes.

Miss Murdstone laid down her beading work.

"I declare," my mother said. "They're exactly alike. I guess they're both the same color as mine. They're wonderfully alike . . . "

"What are you talking about, Clara?" Miss Murdstone said harshly.

"My dear Jane," my mother said, a little abashed, "I find that Stevie's and Davy's eyes are exactly alike."

"Clara!" Miss Murdstone said, rising angrily. "Sometimes you're an absolute fool."

"My dear Jane," my mother remonstrated.

"An absolute fool," Miss Murdstone repeated. "Who else would compare my brother's baby with *your* boy? They aren't at all alike. They're utterly dissimilar in all respects, and I hope they'll remain so. I won't sit here and hear such comparisons be made." She marched out and slammed the door behind her.

I was completely miserable in the presence of Mr. or Miss Murdstone. If I entered a room in which my mother and Miss Murdstone were talking and my mother seemed cheerful, an anxious cloud would steal over her face the moment I entered. If Mr. Murdstone was in his best humor, I reduced his cheer. If Miss Murdstone was in her worst mood, I intensified it. In their presence my mother was afraid to speak to me or be kind to me. I resolved to stay out of Mr. and Miss Murdstone's way as much as I could. I spent many hours sitting in my cheerless bedroom, wrapped in my little overcoat, poring over a book.

In the evening I sometimes went and sat with Peggotty in the kitchen. I was comfortable there and not afraid to be myself. But Mr. and Miss Murdstone soon decided that this shouldn't be permitted.

"David," Mr. Murdstone said one day after dinner when I was going to leave the room as usual. "I'm sorry to observe that you have a sullen disposition."

"Extremely sulky," Miss Murdstone added.

I stood still and hung my head.

"A sullen, stubborn disposition is the worst kind," Mr. Murdstone continued.

"And the boy's is the most sullen and stubborn I've ever known," Miss Murdstone said. "I think, my dear Clara, even *you* must have noticed this."

"I beg your pardon, my dear Jane," my mother said, "but I'm not quite certain that you understand Davy."

"I'd be ashamed of myself, Clara, if I couldn't understand the boy or any other boy," Miss Murdstone said.

"No doubt, my dear Jane, your understanding is very vigorous. I profit by it in many ways," my mother responded.

Arranging the small fetters on her wrists, Miss Murdstone said, "Yet you say that I don't understand your boy. Apparently he's too deep for me. Given that I share my brother's opinion, you must also think that *he* fails to understand the boy."

"I think that you aren't the best judge of the matter, Clara," Mr. Murdstone said in a low, grave voice.

"Edward," my mother said timidly, "you're a far better judge of all questions than I pretend to be. Both you and Jane are. I only said . . . "

"You only said something weak and

inconsiderate," he replied. "Try not to do it again, my dear Clara. Watch yourself."

"Yes, my dear Edward," my mother murmured.

Turning his head and eyes stiffly toward me, Mr. Murdstone said, "I was saying, David, that you have a sullen disposition. That is not a disposition that I can allow to develop without an effort at improvement. You must try, sir, to change it. We must try to change it for you."

"I beg your pardon, sir," I faltered. "I haven't meant to be sullen."

"Don't lie, sir!" he returned so fiercely that my mother involuntarily put out her trembling hand as if to interpose between us. "In your sullenness you've continually withdrawn to your own room. You've stayed there when you should have been here. Know now that I require you to be here. Further, I require you to bring obedience here. I will have it done. Your bearing toward me, Miss Murdstone, and your mother will be receptive and respectful. Now sit down."

I obeyed.

"There's one more thing," he said. "I observe that you have an attachment to low and common company. You aren't to associate with servants. The kitchen won't improve you in the many respects in which you need improvement. I won't say anything about the woman who abets you"—he turned toward my mother—"since *you*, Clara, have a weakness with regard to her that you haven't yet overcome."

"It's a most unaccountable attachment!" Miss Murdstone cried.

Mr. Murdstone resumed, addressing me. "I disapprove of your preferring such company as Miss Peggotty. You're to abandon that attachment. Now, David, you understand me, and you know what the consequences will be if you fail to obey me."

I no longer retreated to my room or took refuge with Peggotty. Instead day after day I sat wearily in the parlor, looking forward to bedtime. I sat hour after hour, afraid to move an arm or leg lest Miss Murdstone should complain of my restlessness. I sat listening to the ticking of the clock, watching her shiny steel beads as she strung them, and wondering if she ever would marry and, if so, to what sort of unhappy man.

I took solitary walks down muddy lanes in the bad winter weather. I ate my meals in silence and with little appetite, always feeling unwelcome. In the evenings I didn't read an entertaining book. Instead I had to pore over some arithmetic textbook. It always was a relief when the clock struck nine and Miss Murdstone ordered me to bed.

At last the holiday was over, and Mr. Barkis was at the gate. As before, Miss Murdstone said in her warning voice, "Clara" when my mother bent over me to bid me farewell.

I kissed my mother and Stevie and felt very sad, not to be leaving but to be separated from her even when she and I were in the same room. She embraced me. I was in Mr. Barkis's cart when I heard her calling to me. I looked out. She stood at the garden gate, holding Stevie up in her arms for me to see.

Chapter 11

My birthday, two months later, was a damp, frosty day. Here and there in the schoolroom, a sputtering candle lit up the foggy morning. I could see the breath of the boys in the raw, cold air as they blew on their fingers and tapped their feet on the floor in an effort to get warm. It was after breakfast. We had been summoned in from the playground.

Mr. Sharp entered and said, "David Copperfield is to go to the parlor."

I brightened at the order, expecting a birthday hamper, filled with goodies, from Peggotty. As I hurried out of my seat, some of the boys around me asked me not to forget them when it came to distributing the anticipated goodies.

"Don't hurry, David," Mr. Sharp said in a tone of sympathy that I didn't register until afterwards. "There's time enough, my boy."

I hurried away to the parlor. There I found Mr. Creakle sitting at his breakfast with his cane and a newspaper in front him. His wife had an opened letter in her hand. "David," she said, leading me to a sofa and sitting down beside me, "I have something to tell you, my child."

I looked at Mr. Creakle. Without looking at me, he shook his head, briefly sighed, and ate a very large piece of buttered toast.

"You're too young to know how the world changes every day and how the people in it pass away," Mrs. Creakle said. "But we all have to learn it at some point, David."

I looked at her earnestly.

After a pause she asked, "Was your mother well when you left home at the end of the vacation?"

I trembled and didn't speak.

"I grieve to tell you that your mama has been ill."

Tears started to stream down my face.

"She is dead."

I gave a desolate cry.

Mrs. Creakle was very kind to me. She kept me there all day and left me alone sometimes. I cried until I wore myself out, slept, awoke, and cried again. When I couldn't cry any more, I felt anguish. Mrs. Creakle said that Stevie, too, had been ill. He wasn't expected to live.

The boys treated me with kindness and sympathy. They paid so much attention to me that I felt quite important. That feeling comforted me a bit. Tommy insisted on lending me his pillow that night. I don't know what good he thought it would do me; I had one of my own. I suppose that Tommy lent me the pillow because he just wanted to give me something and show support.

The next day in the afternoon I left to go home for the funeral. The stagecoach traveled very slowly and didn't reach Yarmouth before 9:00 the next morning. I looked for Mr. Barkis, but he wasn't there. Instead a fat, little old man, short of breath, came puffing up to the coach window. Although he wore black, including black stockings, he was merry-looking, with a broad-rimmed hat and little bunches of ribbons at the knees of his breeches. "Master Copperfield?" he panted.

"Yes, sir."

"I'm Mr. Omer. Will you come with me, young sir, if you please?" He opened the coach door. "I'll have the pleasure of taking you home."

Wondering who he was, I put my hand in his, and we walked to a shop in a narrow street. The sign in front of the shop said, "Omer's Funeral Clothing and Supplies." It was a stifling little shop full of fabric and clothing. We went into a little back workroom, where three young women were at work on an abundance of black materials that were heaped on the table. Scraps from the materials littered the floor. There was a good fire in the room. The three young women, who appeared to be very industrious and comfortable, raised their heads to look at me and then went on with their sewing. A steady hammering came from a small workshop, visible through the window, at the other end of the backyard.

"How's it coming, Minnie?" Mr. Omer asked one of the women.

"Don't worry, Father. We'll be ready," she replied gaily without looking up.

Mr. Omer took off his hat, sat down, and panted. He was so fat that he panted for some time before he could say, "Good." Then he turned to me, "Would you walk into the shop, Master Copperfield, so that we can measure you for clothes?"

I preceded Mr. Omer, who showed me a roll of cloth that he said was too fine a fabric for mourning anyone other than a close family member. He took my measurements and wrote them down. Then, panting, he took me back to the workroom. He called down some stairs behind a door, "Bring up that tea and bread and butter!" After some time a tray appeared, which turned out to be for me.

"I've been acquainted with you a long time, my young friend," Mr. Omer said while I tried to eat a little.

"Have you, sir?"

"I knew your father. He was five-foot-nine-and-a-half, and he lies in twenty-five feet of ground."

"Do you know how my little brother is, sir?" I asked.

"He's in his mother's arms."

"Oh! Is he dead?" I cried.

"Yes. The baby's dead."

I grieved anew. I left my scarcely tasted breakfast and went and rested my head on another table, in a corner of the little room. Minnie hastily cleared that table so that I wouldn't stain any fabric with my tears. She was pretty and good-natured. She put my hair away from my eyes with a soft, kind touch and was very cheerful about having nearly finished her work.

Presently the hammering stopped, and a good-looking young fellow came across the yard into the room. He had a hammer in his hand, and his mouth was full of little nails, which he now removed.

"Well, Bob, how's it coming?" Mr. Omer asked.

"It's done, sir."

Minnie blushed, and the two other young women smiled at each other.

"What? You worked on it by candlelight last night?" Mr. Omer said.

"Yes," Bob answered. "You said that if I finished the coffin in time, we could make a little trip of it and go over to the house together: Minnie and me . . . and you."

"I thought you were going to leave me out," Mr. Omer said, laughing until he coughed.

The two young women who had still been sewing now finished. They brushed bits of cloth and thread from their dresses and went into the shop. Minnie stayed in the workroom to fold up what they had made and pack it into two baskets. She did this on her knees, humming a lively tune. Mr. Omer went for the carriage, and Bob stole a kiss from Minnie. Then Bob went out again. Minnie put her thimble and scissors into her pocket and neatly stuck a needle threaded with black thread into the bosom of her dress. At a little mirror behind the door, she put on her smart-looking overcoat. I saw the reflection of her pleased face.

I observed all of this while sitting at the table in the corner with my head leaning on my hand. The carriage soon came to the front of the shop. It was black and pulled by a black horse. The baskets were put in. Then I got in, followed by Mr. Omer, Minnie, and Bob.

The others enjoyed the ride. I didn't feel angry with them for their cheerfulness. Instead, I felt entirely different from them. Mr. Omer sat in front to drive, and Minnie, Bob, and I sat behind him. Whenever Mr. Omer spoke to them, Minnie and Bob leaned forward, one on each side of his chubby face, and made much of him. I silently grieved. When we stopped so that the horse could be fed, I couldn't eat. The others ate, drank, and enjoyed themselves.

When we reached my home, I dropped from the carriage as quickly as I could. Before I got to the door of the house, I was in Peggotty's arms. Her grief burst out. Then she controlled it and took me into the house. She spoke in whispers and walked softly. She hadn't slept for a long time. She had been sitting up each night, keeping watch over my mother's body.

Mr. Murdstone was in the parlor. He took no heed of me when I entered the room. He sat in his armchair by the fireside, weeping silently and pondering. Miss Murdstone was busy at her writing desk, which was covered with letters and papers. She gave me her cold fingernails and coldly asked, "Have you been measured for your mourning clothes?"

"Yes," I answered.

"Have you brought your shirts home?" she asked.

"Yes, ma'am. I've brought all of my clothes home."

She said nothing more to me. The whole rest of the day she sat at her desk, scratching composedly with a hard pen, never relaxing a muscle of her face or softening the tone of her voice.

Mr. Murdstone sometimes opened a book and looked at it as if he were reading, but he remained for an hour without turning the page and then put it down and paced. Hour after hour I sat, with folded hands, watching him. He seldom spoke to his sister, and he never spoke to me. Except for the ticking clocks, he seemed to be the only moving thing in the house.

In the days before the funeral I saw little of Peggotty. When I went up or down the stairs, I always found her close to the room in which my mother and Stevie lay. She came to me every night and sat by the head of my bed while I went to sleep. A day or two before the funeral she took me into my mother's room. She was about to turn back the clean white cover over the body when I cried, "No!"

The day of the funeral there was a bright fire in the parlor. Wine shone in decanters. There was a faint smell of cake and of Miss Murdstone's dress. We all wore black.

Dr. Chillip came up to me. "How are you, Master David?" he said kindly. I gave him my hand, which he held. Smiling meekly, with tears in his eyes, he said to Miss Murdstone, "Dear me! Our little friends grow up around us, don't they, ma'am?" She didn't answer, only frowned. Discomfited, Dr. Chillip took me into a corner and said nothing more.

A bell sounded, and Mr. Omer and someone else came to ready us for the funeral procession. Mr. Murdstone, our neighbor Mr. Grayper, Dr. Chillip, and I went out the door. The pallbearers were in the garden with the coffin. They moved before us down the path, past the elms, through the gate, and into the churchyard, where I had so often heard birds sing on summer mornings.

We stood around the grave. The day seemed different from every other day. Light was weaker; colors were duller. There was a solemn hush. We stood bareheaded. His voice sounding remote in the open air, the clergyman said, "'I am the Resurrection and the Life,' saith the Lord." Peggotty sobbed. Among the small gathering I recognized some faces that I'd seen in church. The funeral service ended. The grave was filled in with earth, and we turned to leave. Dr. Chillip talked to me. When we got home, he had me drink some water. I asked him if I could go up to my room, and he dismissed me with great gentleness.

Peggotty came to my room and sat down beside me on my little bed. She held my hand and sometimes stroked or kissed it. "She wasn't well for a long time," Peggotty told me. "She was uncertain in her mind and unhappy. When Stevie was born, I thought at first that she'd get better, but she was more delicate after the birth and sank a little every day. Before Stevie came, she often sat alone and cried. But after he was born, she sang to him. She became more and more timid and frightened. Any harsh word was like a blow to her. My poor, sweet girl!" Peggotty stopped and patted my hand a little while. "The last time that I saw her like her old self was the night you came home, my dear. The day you went away, she said to me, 'I'll never see my darling boy again. I'm sure of it.'" She tried to hold up after that. Mr. and Miss Murdstone often told her that she was foolish. She didn't tell Mr. Murdstone about her illness until about a week before her death. Then she said to him, 'My dear, I think I'm dying.' When I saw her to bed that night, she said, 'It's off my mind now, Peggotty. Edward will believe it more and more over the next few days, and then it will be over. I feel very tired. Sit by me while I sleep. Don't leave me. God bless both my children! God protect and keep my fatherless boy!' From then on, I never left her. Right to the end she loved those two downstairs. She couldn't bear not to love anyone around her. But she never fell asleep until they left her bedside. On the last night she kissed me and said, 'If Stevie also dies, please have them lay him in my arms. Please see that we're buried together. Tell Davy I blessed him a thousand times.' Stevie lived only one day beyond your mother." Peggotty again patted my hand. "Pretty late into the night, she asked me for something to drink. When she'd taken it, she smiled at me. As the sun rose, she told me how kind and considerate Mr. Copperfield always had been toward her. Whenever she had doubted herself, he had told her that a loving heart was better and stronger than wisdom and that he was a happy man in having her love. 'Peggotty, my dear,' she said, 'lay your good arm under my neck, and turn me toward you. Your face seems far away, and I want it to be near.' I did as she asked and—oh, Davy!—she died, died like a child who had gone to sleep."

Chapter 12

The day after the funeral, Mr. Murdstone gave Peggotty a month's notice. Much as Peggotty disliked the Murdstones, I believe she would have stayed on for my sake if they hadn't fired her. She told me what had happened, and we condoled with each other. I'm sure the Murdstones would have been happy if they could have dismissed *me* with a month's notice as well.

I mustered the courage to ask Miss Murdstone when I would be going back to school. She dryly answered, "I don't think you'll be going back." I was told nothing more. I was very anxious to know what was going to be done with me. So was Peggotty.

There was one positive change in my situation. I no longer was forced to sit with Mr. Murdstone or his sister. In fact, several times when I took a seat in the parlor, Miss Murdstone frowned to me to go away. The Murdstones never sought me out or asked my whereabouts. I could spend time with Peggotty.

One evening while I was warming my hands at the kitchen fire, Peggotty said to me, "Davy, my dear,

I've tried to get a suitable job here in Blunderstone, so that I could still be near you, but I haven't been able to."

"What will you do, Peggotty?" I asked.

"I suppose I'll go to Yarmouth and live there."

"I can visit you there," I said, brightening a little.

"As long as you're here in Blunderstone," Peggotty said, "I'll come see you once a week."

That promise greatly reassured me.

"I'll stay with my brother for a while and look for work. Maybe the Murdstones will let you go with me."

I felt joy at the thought but then feared that the Murdstones wouldn't permit my escape. Miss Murdstone happened to enter the kitchen soon after. With a boldness that amazed me, Peggotty asked if I could accompany her to Yarmouth.

"The boy will be idle there," Miss Murdstone said, looking into a pickle jar, "and idleness is the root of all evil. On the other hand, he would be idle here or anywhere else in my opinion."

I saw that Peggotty had an angry answer ready, but she swallowed it for my sake and remained silent.

Still eyeing the pickles, Miss Murdstone said, "It's of paramount importance that my brother not be disturbed or discomfited. I suppose I'd better say yes."

I thanked her without showing any joy. (Any sign of joy might have caused her to withdraw her consent.)

A month later, Peggotty and I were ready to leave. Mr. Barkis came into the house for Peggotty's boxes. I'd never seen him pass the garden gate before, but on this occasion he came into the house.

He gave me a meaningful look as he shouldered the largest box and went out.

Peggotty was naturally in low spirits at leaving what had been her home so many years. She had walked in the churchyard very early, as if to say a final goodbye to my mother, my father, and Stevie. She got into Mr. Barkis's cart and sat in it with her handkerchief at her eyes.

Mr. Barkis sat in his usual place and remained silent and motionless as long as Peggotty was crying. But when she began to look around and speak to me, he nodded and grinned several times.

"It's a beautiful day, Mr. Barkis," I said as an act of politeness.

"It ain't bad," he responded.

"Peggotty is quite comfortable now, Mr. Barkis," I remarked for his satisfaction.

He eyed her and said, "*Are* you comfortable?"

Peggotty laughed and said yes.

Mr. Barkis slid nearer to her on the seat and nudged her with his elbow. "Are you really and truly comfortable?"

"Yes," Peggotty repeated.

Mr. Barkis stopped at an inn and treated us to broiled mutton and beer.

When we reached Yarmouth, Mr. Peggotty and Ham were waiting for us. They received Peggotty and me with much affection and shook hands with Mr. Barkis. They each took one of Peggotty's trunks.

We were going away when Mr. Barkis signaled to me with his forefinger to come under an archway. "It's all right, then," he said. Not knowing what he meant, I nodded. He shook my hand. Peggotty called me away.

As she and I were going along, she asked me what Mr. Barkis had said.

"He said, 'It's all right, then,'" I answered.

"Impudence! But I don't mind." After a pause Peggotty asked, "Davy dear, how would you feel if I thought of getting married?"

"Why, I suppose you'd still like me as much as you do now," I answered.

Peggotty stopped and embraced me. When we walked on, she asked, "What would you say, my darling, if . . . ?"

"If you married Mr. Barkis, Peggotty?"

"Yes."

"I think it would be a very good thing because then you'd always have a cart and horse to bring you over to see me, and you could come for free."

"Just my thoughts, my dear!" Peggotty cried. "And I'd be more independent. I could work in my own house instead of somebody else's. I don't know that I'd like to be a servant to a stranger. And if I married Mr. Barkis, I'd always be near your mother's resting place and be able to see it whenever I like."

Neither of us said anything for a while.

"But Davy, I wouldn't give marrying another thought if you were in any way against it," Peggotty resumed.

"Look at me, Peggotty, and you'll see how glad it would make me."

Peggotty hugged me. "Well, I'll think about it, then. I'll talk to my brother about it. In the meantime, Davy, let's keep it to ourselves, just between you and me. Mr. Barkis is a good, plain man. I think I'd be comfortable with him."

Mr. Peggotty's house looked just the same except somewhat smaller to my maturing eyes. As before, Mrs. Gummidge was waiting at the door. Everything inside was the same, down to the seaweed in the blue mug in my bedroom. But I didn't see Emily, so I asked Mr. Peggotty where she was.

"She's at school, sir," he replied, wiping sweat from his forehead after carrying Peggotty's trunk. He looked at the table clock. "She'll be home in about half an hour. We all miss her during the day."

Knowing the way that Emily would come, I strolled down the path to meet her. Before long she appeared in the distance. When she neared, I saw that her eyes were bluer and her dimpled face brighter than ever. She still was very petite. When she recognized me, she laughed and ran ahead of me. I ran after her and didn't catch up with her until we almost were back at the house. I was going to kiss her, but she covered her cherry lips with her hands and said, "I'm not a baby anymore." And she ran, laughing, into the house. She seemed to delight in teasing me, which was a change that I wondered at.

The tea table was ready, and our little foot locker was put in its old place. But instead of coming to sit by me, Emily sat next to Mrs. Gummidge. Everyone in the household adored Emily and spoiled her. But she was so affectionate and sweet-natured and had such a pleasant way of being sly and shy at the same time that she captivated me more than ever. She was tenderhearted, too. When we sat around the fire after tea and Mr. Peggotty alluded to my mother's death, tears came into Emily's eyes and she looked at me with great kindness.

"Here's another orphan, sir," Mr. Peggotty said, running his hand through Emily's curls. "And here's another, although he doesn't look like one," he said, giving Ham a backhanded knock in the chest.

"If I had you for my guardian, Mr. Peggotty, I don't think I'd feel like an orphan either," I said.

"Well said, Master Davy," Ham said. "To be sure, you wouldn't." He returned Mr. Peggotty's backhander.

Emily got up and kissed Mr. Peggotty.

"How's your friend, sir?" Mr. Peggotty asked me.

"James Steerforth?"

"That's the name! Steerforth!" Mr. Peggotty cried, turning to Ham. "I knew it was something like that."

"You thought it was Rudderford," Ham said, laughing.

"Well, you steer with a rudder, don't you?" Mr. Peggotty retorted. "How is he, sir?" he asked me.

"He was very well when I left, Mr. Peggotty."

"He's a handsome fellow," Mr. Peggotty said, smoking his pipe.

"Yes. He *is* very handsome," I said, pleased with the compliment.

"Bold, too," Mr. Peggotty said. "He doesn't seem afraid of anything."

"Yes. He's as brave as a lion. He says just what he thinks."

"I bet he's good at book learning, too," Mr. Peggotty said.

"Yes," I said. "He knows everything. He's very clever. He seems to do everything easily. He's the best cricket player I ever saw, and he beats everyone at checkers. He's such a persuasive speaker that he can win anyone over to his point of view. And I don't know what you'd say if you heard him sing."

Mr. Peggotty shook his head in amazement.

"He's also a fine, generous, noble fellow. No praise does him justice. I'm very grateful to him. He has generously protected me." Suddenly I noticed that Emily was bending forward, listening with the deepest attention. Her blue eyes sparkled, and her cheeks were flushed. She looked so earnest and pretty that I stopped in a sort of wonder. Everyone else looked at her.

"Emily would like to see him," Mr. Peggotty said.

Embarrassed, Emily looked down and blushed more deeply. When she glanced up through some stray curls and saw that we still were looking at her, she ran away to her room and stayed away until nearly bedtime.

I lay down in the little old bed in the barge's stern. The wind moaned across the flats as it had before. But this time it seemed to moan for my mother. Before I fell asleep, I said a prayer in which I expressed the hope that I might grow up to marry Emily.

The days passed pretty much as they had before, except that Emily and I rarely wandered on the beach. She had school lessons to learn and needlework to do. She was absent most of each day. But I felt that we wouldn't have wandered as we had even if Emily weren't so busy. She was more womanly now, more distant. She still liked me, but she laughed at me and tormented me. When I went to meet her, she stole home by another route and was laughing at the door when I came back disappointed. The best times were when she sat quietly at work in front of the house and I sat on the wooden step at her feet, reading to her. At those times I felt I'd never seen such bright April afternoons or such sparkling sky, water, and sailing ships.

On the first evening after our arrival, Mr. Barkis appeared with a bundle of oranges tied up in a handkerchief. After his visit he left the oranges for Peggotty. He then appeared every evening at the same hour, always with a little bundle that he left for Peggotty. These offerings of affection were of an odd variety. I remember pigs' feet, a huge pin cushion, half a bushel of apples, a pair of jet earrings, some onions, a box of dominoes, a canary in a cage, and a leg of pickled pork. Mr. Barkis's wooing of Peggotty was peculiar. He rarely said anything. Instead he sat by the fire in much the same way that he sat in his cart and stared at Peggotty, who sat opposite. He seemed content. Even when he took Peggotty out for a walk on the flats, he hardly said a word. Now and then he would ask her if she was comfortable. Sometimes after he left, Peggotty would laugh for half an hour.

When my stay was almost over, Peggotty asked Emily and me to accompany Mr. Barkis and her on a day trip. I slept poorly that night because I was so excited about spending a whole day with Emily. In the morning we all were up early. While we were eating breakfast, Mr. Barkis appeared in the distance, driving a carriage. Peggotty was dressed as usual, in her neat and quiet mourning, but Mr. Barkis bloomed in a new blue coat that was too large for him, so that the cuffs hung down over his hands. The collar was so high that it pushed his hair up on end. His bright buttons, too, were exceptionally large. He wore drab pantaloons and a yellow vest. I thought him the image of respectability.

Soon we all bustled outside. Peggotty kissed everyone goodbye, and she, Emily, and I climbed into the carriage. Emily and I sat side by side. Away we went. The first thing we did was stop at a church, where Mr. Barkis tied his horse to some rails and went in with Peggotty. I took that occasion to put my arm around Emily's waist. I said that since I was going away very soon, we should be very affectionate to each other all day. Agreeing, Emily allowed me to kiss her. I declared that I never could love anyone else and that I was prepared to shed the blood of anyone who aspired to her affections. Laughing, Emily called me a "silly boy."

Mr. Barkis and Peggotty were in the church quite a while. When they finally came out, we drove away into the countryside. As we were going along, Mr. Barkis turned to me and said, with a wink, "What name was it that I wrote on the cart?"

"Clara Peggotty," I answered.

"What name should I write there now?" he asked.

"Clara Peggotty again?" I suggested.

"Clara Peggotty *Barkis*!" he cried, laughing so hard that the carriage shook.

He and Peggotty had married. Peggotty had wanted the wedding to be as quiet as possible. She hugged me, and we drove on. At a small inn where we were expected, we had a very comfortable dinner. Mr. Barkis ate a lot of pork and greens. Peggotty was as much at ease as she would have been if she'd been married for ten years. She, Emily, and I went for a stroll while Mr. Barkis stayed at the inn, I suppose smoking his pipe and contemplating his happiness. When we returned for tea, Mr. Barkis ate a large quantity of boiled bacon. Soon after dark we drove back, looking up at the stars and talking about them. Emily and I made a cloak out of an old wrapper and sat under it for the rest of the journey. How I loved her! I blissfully imagined marrying her, never growing older, living with her among trees and fields, and always rambling hand in hand through sunshine and flowery meadows.

When we arrived at Mr. Peggotty's house, the Barkises bade us goodbye and drove away to their own home. I felt then for the first time that I had lost Peggotty. Sensing my sadness, Mr. Peggotty and Ham were ready with some supper and their hospitable faces. For the only time during my visit, Emily came and sat beside me on the footlocker. It was the perfect end to a wonderful day.

In the morning, Peggotty called to me under my window. After breakfast she took me to her new home, a beautiful little place. The kitchen had a tile floor and the parlor a wonderful bureau of dark wood with a top that opened and came down to form a desk.

That day I look leave of everyone at Mr. Peggotty's house and spent the night at Peggotty's in a little room just under the roof. On a shelf by the head of the bed was the crocodile book from which I used to read. With her arms around my neck, Peggotty said that it always would be there for me. "Davy dear, as long as I'm alive and have this house over my head, you'll find that bedroom as if I expected you here any minute. I'll keep it as I used to keep your old little room, my darling."

"Thank you, Peggotty," I said with much love and gratitude.

The next morning I went home in the cart with Peggotty and Mr. Barkis. They left me at the gate of my house, not easily or lightly, and I felt desolate as the cart drove away, taking Peggotty.

Chapter 13

I immediately fell into a solitary condition. I had no companions. I would have welcomed being sent to the harshest school. The Murdstones largely ignored me—sullenly, sternly, steadily. I wasn't beaten or starved but utterly neglected. When the Murdstones were at home, I ate with them; otherwise I ate and drank alone. I lounged around the house and neighborhood.

Dr. Chillip, who was a widower, often asked me to come visit him, but I seldom was permitted to go. When I did, I delighted in reading some book that was new to me or pounding some concoction into medicine under his mild direction. Similarly, I seldom was allowed to visit Peggotty. Faithful to her promise, she came to see me, or met me somewhere nearby, once every week. One of the rare times that I was permitted to go to Peggotty's house, I learned that Mr. Barkis was something of a miser. He kept a heap of money in a box under his bed, but it was only with difficulty that Peggotty could get him to give her even small amounts for expenses.

One day while I was out loitering in my usual listless manner, I came across Mr. Murdstone walking with Mr. Quinion.

"Mr. Quinion, you remember David," Mr. Murdstone said.

"How are you getting on?" Mr. Quinion asked me. "Where are you being educated?" He had put his hand on my shoulder.

I glanced at Mr. Murdstone.

"He's at home at present," Mr. Murdstone said. "He isn't being educated anywhere. I don't know what to do with him. He's a difficult subject." His eyes darkened, and he turned his frowning face away.

"Hmph," Mr. Quinion said, looking at us both. "I suppose you're a pretty sharp fellow," he said to me.

"Yes, he's sharp enough," Mr. Murdstone said impatiently. "Let him go. He won't thank you for troubling him."

Mr. Quinion released me, and I made my way home. Looking back as I turned into the front garden, I saw Mr. Murdstone leaning against the churchyard's fence while Mr. Quinion talked to him. They were both looking at me. I felt that they were talking about me.

Mr. Quinion stayed at our house that night. After breakfast the next morning, I was leaving the room when Mr. Murdstone called me back. He went to another table while his sister sat down at her desk. Mr. Quinion, with his hands in his pockets, stood looking out of the window. I stood looking at all of them.

"David," Mr. Murdstone said, "young people should take action. They shouldn't mope around."

"As you do," Miss Murdstone said to me.

"Jane Murdstone, leave this to me, if you please," Mr. Murdstone said. "As I was saying, David, young people should take action. Your disposition requires a great deal of correcting. You must learn the ways of the working world."

"Stubbornness won't do," Miss Murdstone said. "It must be crushed, and it *will* be."

Mr. Murdstone gave her a look, half of remonstrance, half of approval, and went on. "I'm not rich. You've already received considerable education. Education is costly. Even if I could afford it, I wouldn't think it advantageous to you to be kept in school. What is before you is a fight with the world. The sooner you begin it, the better. Have you heard of the wine warehouse?"

"The wine warehouse, sir?"

"Of Murdstone & Grinby," he replied.

"I think I have heard the business mentioned, sir," I said.

"Mr. Quinion manages that business."

I glanced at Mr. Quinion as he stood looking out of the window.

"He has suggested that I employ you in the business," Mr. Murdstone continued.

Half turning around, Mr. Quinion said in a low voice, "He having no other prospects, Murdstone."

With an impatient, somewhat angry gesture, Mr. Murdstone resumed talking to me. "You will earn enough to buy food and drink and have pocket money. I've arranged for your lodging. I'll pay for your lodging, clothes, and washing. So you're now going to London with Mr. Quinion to begin life on your own."

"In short, you're provided for," Miss Murdstone said, "and will please do your duty."

I knew that the purpose was to get rid of me. I would leave the next day with Mr. Quinion.

The next morning Miss Murdstone had me dress in stiff corduroy trousers, a black jacket, and an old white hat with a black band of mourning. My meager possessions were packed into a small trunk. I sat with Mr. Quinion in a carriage that would take us to the London stagecoach at Yarmouth. I lost sight of my house, the church, and finally its spire.

At age ten I became a laborer at Murdstone & Grinby. The company's warehouse was at the waterside, down in Blackfriars. It was the last building at the bottom of a narrow street that curved downhill to the river. The street had some stairs at the end, where people took boat. The warehouse was an old building with a wharf that abutted on the water when the tide was in and on the mud when the tide was out. Its paneled rooms were discolored with the dirt and smoke of a hundred years. The floors and staircase were decaying. Rats squeaked and scuffled in the cellars. I entered the building with my hand trembling in Mr. Quinion's.

Much of Murdstone & Grinby's business was supplying wine to packet ships. I became one of three boys employed to examine empty wine bottles against the light and reject them if they were flawed, wash empty bottles, put labels on full bottles, fit corks into bottles, put seals on corks, and pack finished bottles into casks. My workplace was a corner of the warehouse where Mr. Quinion could see me when he chose to stand up on the bottom rail of his stool in the counting house and look at me through a window above his desk. On the first morning Mick Walker, the oldest of the boys, was summoned to show me what I should do. He wore a ragged apron and a paper cap. He told me that his father was a bargeman. He also told me that our principal coworker would be another boy whom he introduced as Mealy Potatoes, a name bestowed because of his pale, mealy complexion. Mealy's father was both a waterman and a fireman.

I felt despair at having to associate with my new companions, especially when I compared them to James Steerforth, Tommy Traddles, and other boys at Salem House. My hopes of growing up to be a learned, distinguished man were crushed. I felt misery. When Mick walked away that first afternoon, my tears mingled with the water with which I was washing bottles.

When the counting-house clock indicated 12:30, there were preparations for lunch. Mr. Quinion tapped at the counting-house window and beckoned me to enter. I went in and found there a stout, middle-aged man in a shabby brown overcoat, black tights and shoes, and prominent shirt collar. A monocle hung on the outside of his coat. He carried a jaunty stick with a large tassel at the end. His large head was completely bald and shiny. He turned his broad face fully toward me.

"This is the boy, Mr. Micawber," Mr. Quinion

said to him with reference to me.

"Master Copperfield," Mr. Micawber said in an exaggeratedly genteel way. "I hope you are well, sir?"

"Very well, sir. I hope you are, too," I politely responded.

"I am, thank heaven, quite well," Mr. Micawber said, smiling. "I have received a letter from Mr. Murdstone in which he asks me to rent you a room in the rear of my house. It's currently unoccupied."

"Mr. Murdstone knows Mr. Micawber," Mr. Quinion said. "Mr. Micawber takes orders for us on commission when he can get any. You're going to lodge with him."

"My address is Windsor Terrace, City Road," Mr. Micawber said with his genteel air.

I bowed.

"Because you don't know your way around London and could get lost trying to find the house, I'll be happy to return this evening and show you the way," Mr. Micawber said.

"Thank you, sir," I said with sincere gratitude.

"What time should I . . . ?" Mr. Micawber began.

"At eight," Mr. Quinion interrupted.

"At eight, then," Mr. Micawber said. "Good day, Mr. Quinion." He put on his hat and went out, with his cane under his arm, very upright and humming a tune once he was clear of the counting house.

Mr. Quinion then formally hired me at a salary of six shillings a week. He paid me a week in advance, and I gave Mealy sixpence to have my trunk carried to Windsor Terrace that night. I paid sixpence more for my lunch, which was a meat pie, and passed the lunch hour walking around the streets.

At 8:00 Mr. Micawber returned. I washed my face and hands, and we walked to his house. As we went along, Mr. Micawber told me the names of the streets. When we arrived at the house, I saw that it was shabby but decent. The entire first floor was unfurnished. The blinds were kept down so that the neighbors wouldn't see this. Mr. Micawber introduced me to his wife Emma, a thin, faded lady who was sitting in the parlor with a baby at her breast. The baby was one of twins. There were two other children: a four-year-old boy and a three-year-old girl.

With the baby still in her arms, Mrs. Micawber led me upstairs. My room was at the top of the house at the back. It was a small, scantily furnished room. The wallpaper was patterned with what looked like blue muffins. Mrs. Micawber sat down to take a breath. "Before I was married, when I lived with my parents, I never thought I'd ever find it necessary to take a lodger," she said. "But we're in financial difficulties, so considerations of privacy must give way."

"Yes, ma'am," I said.

"At present our difficulties almost are overwhelming. I'm not sure that we'll make it through. Mr. Micawber's creditors want to be paid."

Creditors did, indeed, come at all hours, and some of them were quite ferocious. One dirty-faced man—a boot maker—would edge himself into the passage as early as 7:00 a.m. and yell up at the second-floor windows to Mr. Micawber, "You ain't out of it yet, Wilkins Micawber! Pay us! Don't hide. You just pay us, do you hear?" Receiving no answer, he would yell, "Swindler! Robber!" But that, too, would have no effect. Within a half hour Mr. Micawber would polish his shoes and go out, humming a tune. Mrs. Micawber was equally resilient. She could be thrown into a fit of crying by a creditor at 3:00 and eat lamb chops and drink ale (paid for with two pawned teaspoons) at 4:00.

I always bought my own breakfast: a penny's worth of bread and another penny's worth of milk. I kept a small loaf of bread and some cheese on a particular cupboard shelf and always had bread and cheese for supper. Often, as I went to work in the morning, I couldn't resist buying some stale pastry displayed at half price in a bakery. Then I had to go without lunch or could afford only a roll, or some pudding with raisins. For my main meal I usually had sausage and a penny-loaf of bread, or a fourpence plate of beef, or bread and cheese and a glass of beer. We had half an hour for tea. When I had enough money, I would get half a pint of coffee and a slice of bread and butter.

Underfed and shabby, I worked from morning until night. I never told anyone how I had come to be at Murdstone & Grinby or how much I suffered there. I soon was as skillful as Mick and Mealy. They and the men usually called me "the little gent." A man named Mr. Gregory, the foreman of the packers, and a man named Mr. Tipp, in charge of carting, sometimes called me David. To spare Peggotty sorrow, when I wrote to her I never told her how miserable I was.

I became attached to the Micawbers and worried about their debts. One evening Mrs. Micawber said to me, "Master Copperfield, our difficulties have reached a crisis."

I sympathetically looked at her eyes, which were red from weeping.

"With the exception of some cottage cheese, we have nothing left to eat," she said.

"Dear me!" I said in great concern. I hastily produced the three shillings in my possession and begged Mrs. Micawber to accept them as a loan.

She kissed me and made me put the shillings back in my pocket. "No, my dear Master Copperfield," she said. "But there *is* something you can do for me."

"Please name it," I said.

"We still own a few things that we can part with. Mr. Micawber's feelings never would allow him to dispose of them. Would you see what you can get for them?"

That very evening I began to dispose of the smaller possessions. Mr. Micawber had a few books. I carried them to a bookstall and sold them for whatever they would bring. Over some days, I also pawned other things. Each time I returned with the money, Mrs. Micawber made a supper.

At last Mr. Micawber was arrested early one morning and taken to the King's Bench Prison. On the first Sunday after he was taken there, I went to see him. I went up to his room on the next to the top floor, and we both cried. As a warning to me, he said, "If a man has an annual income of twenty pounds and spends nineteen pounds, nineteen shillings, and sixpence, he'll be happy. But if he spends a single

shilling over twenty pounds, he'll be miserable."
Then he borrowed a shilling from me for beer, gave
me an IOU for the amount, put his handkerchief
away, and cheered up. We sat in front of a little fire
until another debtor, who shared the room with Mr.
Micawber, came in with a loin of mutton. There was
something agreeable in the dinner, like camping out.
When I returned home, I gave Mrs. Micawber an
account of my visit.

Except for the beds, a few chairs, and the kitchen
table, what was left of the household furniture was
sold and taken away in a van. Mrs. Micawber, the
children, and I lived in nearly bare rooms. Finally
Mrs. Micawber decided to move into the prison,
where Mr. Micawber had obtained a private room.
I took the key to the Micawbers' house to the
landlord, who was very glad to get it. All of the beds
but mine were sent over to the prison. A little room
was rented for me near the prison. I was glad to
stay near the Micawbers. My room was a quiet back
garret with a sloping roof and a pleasant view of a
lumberyard.

Some relatives of the Micawbers came to their
aid and saw that they lived comfortably in the prison.
I visited the Micawbers every evening. Mr. Micawber
applied for release under the Insolvent Debtors Act,
which he expected would set him free in about six
weeks. "And then," he said, "I'll begin again and live
in a different way—that is, if something turns up."

To my joy Mr. Micawber was discharged under
the Act. Mrs. Micawber told me that they had decided
to move to Plymouth, where relatives of hers had

some influence, with the hope that Mr. Micawber would work in the customhouse there. Suddenly she started to cry. "I never will desert Mr. Micawber!" she said. "He has his faults. I don't deny that he's careless about money. He may have concealed his financial difficulties from me when we first married, but his optimistic nature probably led him to believe that he would overcome them. The pearl necklace and bracelet that I inherited from my mother have been sold for less than half their value, but I'll never desert him."

That night I had trouble sleeping, knowing that I would be friendless without the Micawbers. I never heard from Mr. Murdstone. On two occasions Miss Murdstone had sent me a parcel of mended clothes with a note saying, "Jane Murdstone trusts that David Copperfield is applying himself to business and devoting himself wholly to his duties."

The Micawbers rented rooms, for a week, in the house where I lived. Mr. Micawber came down to the counting house to tell Mr. Quinion that he was moving to Plymouth and to praise my character. Mr. Quinion called in Mr. Tipp, who was a married man and had a room to rent, and they agreed that I would lodge with Mr. Tipp.

I spent every evening of the Micawbers' last week in London with them. On the last Sunday, they invited me to dinner. We had pork loin, applesauce, and pudding. As parting gifts, I gave the little boy a spotted wooden horse and the little girl a doll. We had a very pleasant day, although we all grieved at our coming separation.

"Master Copperfield, we'll always remember you with fondness and gratitude," Mrs. Micawber said. "Your conduct toward us always has been delicate and obliging. You haven't been a lodger but a friend."

"My dear Copperfield has a heart that feels for others and a head that plans," Mr. Micawber said.

"Thank you," I said. "I'll be very sorry to part from all of you."

"My dear young friend, I have nothing to give you but advice," Mr. Micawber said. "Never do tomorrow what you can do today. Procrastination is the thief of time. My other advice is, as you know, never spend beyond your income."

The next morning I met the whole family at the coach office and, with a desolate heart, saw them take their places on the outside of the coach.

"Master Copperfield, God bless you," Mrs. Micawber said.

"Copperfield, farewell," Mr. Micawber said. "I wish you every happiness and prosperity. If I'm ever in a position to improve your prospects, I'll be extremely happy to do so."

Mrs. Micawber sat at the back of the coach with the children while I stood in the road looking at them wistfully. Suddenly she gestured to me to climb up. She put her arm around my neck and gave me a motherly kiss. I barely had time to get down before the coach started. The family waved goodbye as they drove off. I went to begin my weary day at Murdstone & Grinby.

Chapter 14

I decided to run away. Somehow I would go to my only living relative, my great-aunt Betsey Trotwood, and tell her my story. Although my mother had thought Aunt Betsey harsh and intimidating, I remembered her saying that Aunt Betsey had gently touched her hair. That gesture gave me hope that my great-aunt might take pity on me. Not knowing where she lived, I wrote a long letter to Peggotty and asked her, incidentally, if she knew. I also asked if she could lend me half a guinea, for which I'd be very grateful and which I'd repay. I told Peggotty that I'd explain at some later time why I needed the money.

Peggotty's answer soon arrived and was, as usual, full of affectionate devotion. A half guinea was enclosed. Peggotty told me that Aunt Betsey lived in or near Dover, but she didn't know exactly where. I resolved to set out at the end of the week. Because I had been paid a week in advance when I started at Murdstone & Grinby, I wouldn't take my final pay. When Saturday night came and we were all waiting in the warehouse to be paid, I asked Mick to tell Mr. Quinion, when it was my turn to be paid, that I had gone to move my trunk to Mr. Tipp's.

Then I started toward my former lodging. My trunk still was there. While at work I had written a card that I planned to attach to the trunk: "Property of Master David Copperfield. To be left, until sent for, at the office of the Dover stagecoach." As I walked, I looked around for someone who would take my trunk and me to the stagecoach office. I spotted a long-legged young man with an empty donkey cart and asked him if he'd like a job.

"What job?" he asked brusquely, chewing straw as he spoke.

"To help me get my trunk downstairs and then take it and me to the office of the Dover stagecoach," I answered. "Will you do that for sixpence? The trunk is in my lodging, which is down that street there."

"Get in," he said. As soon I was in, the young man quickly drove us to my lodging. I took him upstairs to my room, and we brought the trunk down and put it onto his cart. I now prepared to attach the identification card to the trunk. As I removed the card from my pocket, my half guinea fell out. The young man saw it and snatched it up.

"Give me my money," I said.

He pushed me down, jumped into the cart, and drove off with my trunk and half guinea. I ran after him as fast as I could, but I had no breath to call out with. A number of times I narrowly escaped being run over. I would see him, then lose him, then see him again. When I got close, he would swipe at me with his whip. I fell into the mud and got back up. Finally, exhausted and overheated, I gave up. Panting and crying, I sat and rested. Fortunately, it was summer and fine weather. When I had recovered my breath, I got up and started walking toward Dover. Although I had nothing but three halfpence, I didn't even consider going back. As I trudged on, I imagined being found dead in a day or two and my death's being reported in a newspaper.

After some time I passed a little shop with a sign hanging over the door that said "Dolloby's Secondhand Clothes." A man I assumed to be Mr. Dolloby was sitting at the door in his shirtsleeves, smoking. Two feeble candles burned inside, revealing many coats and trousers dangling from the low ceiling. I went up the next side street, took off my vest, rolled it neatly under my arm, and came back to the shop door.

"If you please, sir," I said, "I'd like to sell this vest for a fair price."

Mr. Dolloby took the vest, stood his pipe on its head against the door post, and went into the shop, followed by me. He spread the vest on the counter and looked at it. Then he held it up to the light and looked at it some more. Finally he said, "What do you call a fair price for this little vest?"

"You know best, sir," I replied.

"I can't be both buyer and seller," Mr. Dolloby said. "Put a price on the vest."

"How about eighteen pence?" I suggested.

Mr. Dolloby rolled up the vest and gave it back to me. "I'd rob my family if I offered more than ninepence for it."

Because my circumstances were so pressing, I said I'd take ninepence for it. Grumbling, Mr.

Dolloby gave me ninepence. I wished him good night and left.

I decided to sleep behind the wall at the back of Salem House, in a corner where there used to be a haystack. With some difficulty I found my way to Salem House and the haystack and lay down by it. I fell asleep and dreamed of lying in my old school bed, talking to the boys in my room.

The ringing of the wake-up bell at Salem House woke me. If James Steerforth had been there, I would have lurked until he came out alone, but I knew he must have left the school by now. Tommy Traddles might still be a student there, but I couldn't trust that he would be discreet, and I didn't want to burden him with my situation. So I crept away from the wall as the boys were getting up and struck into the long, dusty track that I had known to be the Dover Road when I was a student.

In due time I heard church bells. I plodded on. I met people who were going to church and passed a church where the congregation was inside. The sound of singing came out into the sunshine. I felt ashamed in my dirt and dust, with my tangled hair.

That day I walked twenty-three miles on the straight road. As evening closed in, I crossed the bridge at Rochester, footsore and exhausted. I bought bread and ate it for supper. One or two little houses with signs saying "Lodgings for Travelers" had tempted me, but I was afraid to spend the few pence that I had. So I toiled on into Chatham. I crept onto a grassy artillery area that overlooked a lane, lay down near a cannon, and, comforted by the presence of a nearby sentry who remained unaware of me, slept soundly until morning.

I awoke very stiff and footsore. I felt that I could go only a very little way that day. At a dealer in secondhand clothes, I sold my jacket for much less than it was worth. Trudging on, I managed to travel only seven miles. My bed at night was under another haystack. I rested comfortably after washing my blistered feet in a stream.

The next morning I took to the road again. It lay through a succession of hop fields and orchards. In a few places hop pickers already were at work. That night I lay down to sleep among the hops.

On the sixth day of my flight I set foot in Dover. I stood, dusty, sunburned, and only half-clothed, in ragged shoes. I inquired about my aunt among boatmen, fly drivers, and shopkeepers. No one knew her. I felt desperate. My money was all gone. I was hungry, thirsty, and exhausted. I had worn the morning away in useless inquiries. I was sitting on the step of an empty shop at a street corner near the marketplace when a fly driver came by with his carriage and dropped a horsecloth. As I handed it up, something good-natured in his face encouraged me to ask him if he could tell me where Miss Betsey Trotwood lived.

"Trotwood," he said. "Let me see. I know the name. Old lady?"

"Yes," I said.

"Pretty stiff in the back?" he said, making himself upright.

"Yes. I think so," I said.

"Carries a big bag? Is gruff and sharp?"

My heart sank as I acknowledged this description's accuracy.

"Why then, I'll tell you what. If you go up there," he said, pointing with his whip toward the heights, "and keep on until you come to some houses facing the sea, I think you'll hear of her. It's my opinion that she won't give you anything, so here's a penny for you."

I accepted the gift thankfully and bought a loaf of bread with it. As I ate, I went in the indicated direction. I walked on a good distance without coming to the houses that the fly driver had mentioned. Finally I saw some ahead. Approaching them, I went into a little general store and asked the man behind the counter if he could tell me where Miss Betsey Trotwood lived. He was weighing some rice for a neat, pretty woman about twenty years old. The woman turned around quickly and said, "My mistress? What do you want with her, boy?"

"I want to speak to her, please."

"To beg of her, you mean," my aunt's maid retorted.

"No, indeed," I replied, blushing.

My aunt's maid put her rice into a little basket and walked out of the shop, saying, "You can follow me if you want to know where Miss Trotwood lives."

I followed on shaky legs. We soon came to a neat little house with cheerful bay windows. In front of the house was a small, square flower garden, carefully tended and emitting wonderful fragrances.

"This is Miss Trotwood's house," the maid

said. "Now you know, and that's all I have to say." She hurried into the house, leaving me standing at the garden gate. I looked disconsolately over the top of the gate toward the parlor window and saw a curtain that was open in the middle and a large, round green fan fastened to the windowsill.

My shoes were in woeful condition. The soles had disintegrated, and the leather uppers had cracked open. My hat was crushed and bent. My shirt and trousers were torn and also stained with sweat, dew, grass, and soil. My hair hadn't been combed since I'd left London. My face, neck, and hands were sunburned. From head to foot I was powdered with chalk and dust.

Looking up at the house's upper story, I saw a gray-headed, pleasant-looking gentleman looking out of a window. He winked, nodded to me several times, laughed, and left the window. A lady now came out of the house. Her handkerchief was tied over her cap. She wore a pair of gardening gloves and carried a large knife. I immediately knew her to be Aunt Betsey because she came marching out of the house exactly as my poor mother had often described her marching up our garden path at Blunderstone.

"Go away!" she said, shaking her head and making a distant chop in the air with her knife. "Go along! No boys here!" She marched to a corner of her garden and stooped to dig up some small root.

I quietly entered the garden and stood beside her. Touching her with my finger, I said, "If you please, ma'am."

She started and looked up.

"If you please, Aunt."

"What?" she exclaimed in a tone of amazement.

"If you please, Aunt. I'm your nephew."

"Oh, Lord!" She plopped down in the garden path.

"I'm David Copperfield of Blunderstone, Suffolk, where you came on the night when I was born and saw my dear mama. I've been very unhappy since she died. I've been neglected, denied an education, put to work, and left to fend for myself. I ran away to you. I was robbed when I first set out, so I've walked the whole way. I haven't slept in a bed since I began the journey." I burst into tears.

My aunt, who had been staring at me up to that point, started up from the gravel, collared me, and took me into the parlor. She unlocked a tall cupboard, took out several bottles, and poured some of the contents of each into my mouth. They tasted like aniseed water, anchovy sauce, and salad dressing. As I continued to sob, my aunt put me on the sofa with a shawl under my head and the handkerchief from her head under my feet so that I wouldn't soil the slipcover. Then, sitting down behind the green fan attached to the windowsill so that I couldn't see her face, she periodically cried out, "Mercy on us!" After a while she rang the bell.

"Janet," my aunt said when her maid entered, "go upstairs and tell Mr. Dick I want to speak to him."

Janet looked surprised to see me lying stiffly on the sofa, but she did as instructed. With her hands behind her, my aunt walked up and down the room until the man who had winked at me from the upper window came in laughing. He had a reddish complexion. His eyes were large and, like his hair, gray. He wore a loose gray jacket, a gray vest, and white trousers.

"Mr. Dick," my aunt said, "don't be a fool. No one is more sensible than you when you choose to be. So don't be a fool."

Mr. Dick immediately turned serious. He looked at me, I thought, as if he were asking me to say nothing about his having winked at me.

"Mr. Dick," my aunt said, "you've heard me mention David Copperfield."

"Oh, yes," Mr. Dick replied.

"This is his son."

"Indeed!"

"Yes," my aunt continued. "He's the image of his father except that he also looks like his mother. He's run away. What should I do with him?"

"What should you do with him?" Mr. Dick scratched his head.

"Yes," my aunt said gravely. "I want sound advice."

"Why, if I were you," Mr. Dick said, considering and looking at me, "I'd . . . " Suddenly he seemed inspired. "I'd wash him."

"Janet," my aunt said, turning around with a triumphant air, "as usual, Mr. Dick knows the right thing to do. Heat the bath."

My aunt was a tall, hard-featured woman but by no means homely. There was a rigidity in her face, voice, gait, and bearing, but her features were rather handsome. She had quick, bright eyes. Her gray hair was parted down the middle and mostly covered with a cap that fastened under her chin. Her dress was lavender, simple, and neat. At her side she wore a man's gold watch and chain. Her shirt collar and cuffs also resembled those worn by men.

The room in which I was lying was as neat as Janet or my aunt. A sea breeze entered, mixed with the perfume of flowers. The old-fashioned furniture was brightly polished. There was a table by the round green fan in the bay window. The room also contained a wool carpet, a kettle holder, some old china, a punchbowl filled with dried rose leaves, and a tall cupboard with all sorts of bottles and pots. A cat lay curled up on the carpet, and two canaries were perched in a cage.

Janet had gone downstairs to get the bath ready when my aunt, to my great alarm, suddenly became rigid with indignation and cried out, "Janet! Donkeys!" Janet came running up the stairs, darted out onto the green in front of the house, and warned off two ladies on donkeys. My aunt rushed out of the house, seized the bridle of a third donkey ridden by a child, turned the donkey, led him off the green, and boxed the child's ears. To this day I don't know if the green was public property or my aunt's, but she was determined that no donkey would travel over it. She kept sticks behind the door and jugs of water ready as weapons against any boy who showed up on the green riding a donkey.

My aunt came back inside and gave me broth out of a tablespoon. The bath was a great comfort. My limbs ached, and I was so tired that I hardly could stay awake. When I had bathed, Janet and my aunt put me into a shirt and pants belonging to Mr. Dick and tied me up in two large shawls. I felt very hot. Feeling faint, I lay back down on the sofa and fell asleep.

I awoke with the impression that my aunt had come and bent over me while I slept, brushed my hair away from my face, laid my head more comfortably, and then stood looking at me. I felt that she had said "Pretty fellow" or "Poor fellow." She now sat in the bay window gazing at the sea from behind the green fan, which was mounted on a swivel and could be turned in any direction.

We soon dined on roast goose and pudding. I was anxious to know what my aunt was going to do with me. But she ate in silence except when she occasionally looked at me sitting opposite and said, "Mercy on us!"

Some sherry was put on the table, and I had a glass. My aunt sent up for Mr. Dick again. He joined us. When my aunt asked him to listen to my story, he seemed to try to look as wise as he could. Then, by a series of questions, my aunt gradually drew my story from me.

"Whatever possessed your poor mother to remarry?" she asked when I had finished.

"Perhaps she fell in love with her second husband," Mr. Dick answered.

"Fell in love!" my aunt scoffed. "What did she

want with a man? She'd already had one husband. Why would she want another, certain to mistreat her? She already had a child. What more did she want? But she went and married a man with a name similar to Murderer. And then that woman, Peggotty, also got married! Hadn't she already seen the evil that comes of marrying?"

"Please don't speak ill of Peggotty!" I cried. "She's the most faithful, devoted, and self-denying friend and servant in the world. She loved my mother dearly and always has loved *me* dearly. She held my mother's dying head on her arm, and my mother's last kiss was for her. I would have gone to her for shelter, but because of her humble station I feared that I'd bring some trouble upon her." Then I broke down and hid my face in my hands.

"Well, well," my aunt said. "The child is right to stand up for those who have stood by *him*."

When dusk came, my aunt again asked Mr. Dick what she should do with me.

"I would put him to bed," Mr. Dick said simply.

"Janet!" my aunt cried with the same satisfaction she had shown when Mr. Dick had said that I should be washed. "If the bed is ready, take the boy up to it."

I was led upstairs, my aunt going in front of me and Janet behind. When I was left in the room, I heard them lock my door from the outside. The room was a pleasant one at the top of the house. It overlooked the sea, on which the moon was shining brilliantly. I said my prayers and sat looking at the moonlight on the water. I felt grateful for my soft, white-curtained bed. I nestled into the snow-white sheets and fell into a deep sleep.

Chapter 15

When I went downstairs in the morning, I found my aunt musing at the small, round breakfast table. During breakfast I repeatedly glanced at her and saw her looking at me in a thoughtful manner. When she had finished her breakfast, she leaned back in her chair, knitted her brows, folded her arms, and stared at me. I was so embarrassed that my knife tumbled over my fork, tossing bits of bacon into the air, and I almost choked on some tea that went down the wrong way.

Suddenly my aunt said, "I've written to your stepfather. I've sent him a letter that he'd better attend to."

"Does he know where I am, Aunt?" I asked, alarmed.

"I told him," my aunt said with a nod.

"Will I have to go back to him?" I faltered.

"I don't know," my aunt said. "We'll see."

"Oh!" I exclaimed. "I don't know what I'll do if I have to go back to Mr. Murdstone!"

Not appearing to take much heed of me, my aunt put on a coarse apron with a bib, which she took out of the cupboard, and washed the teacups. Next she put on gloves and swept up the crumbs with a little broom until there didn't seem to be a speck left on the carpet. Then she dusted and arranged the room, which already had been thoroughly dusted and neatly arranged. When she had done all of this to her satisfaction, she took off the gloves and apron, folded them, put them back into a corner of the cupboard, took out her sewing box, brought it to her table near the open window, and sat down to work. As she threaded her needle, she said, "Why don't you go upstairs and ask Mr. Dick to show you his kite?"

I immediately rose.

Eyeing me as narrowly as she had eyed her needle while threading it, she said, "I suppose you think that Mr. Dick is a short name, eh?'"

"Yes, Aunt."

"His real name is Richard Babley, but don't call him that. He hates the name Babley. He's been abused by some who bear that name. So call him Mr. Dick."

"Yes, Aunt."

I went upstairs and asked, "Mr. Dick, would you be good enough to show me your kite?"

Pointing to a large kite in one corner of the room, Mr. Dick said, "What do you think of that for a kite?"

"It's beautiful," I answered. The kite must have been seven feet tall.

"I made it. You and I will fly it. There's plenty of string, and it flies high." His expression was so enthusiastic that I laughed. He laughed, too.

When I went back downstairs, my aunt asked me, "What do you think of Mr. Dick?"

"I think he's a very nice gentleman," I answered.

"He's been called insane," she said, laying down her work. "I'm delighted to say that, because if he hadn't been declared insane, I wouldn't have had the pleasure of his company and the benefit of his advice these past ten years. Mr. Dick is a distant relative of mine. If it hadn't been for me, his own brother would have shut him away for life, and only because Mr. Dick is a little eccentric. Mr. Dick's brother didn't like to have him be seen around the house, so he sent Mr. Dick to a private asylum, even though their father had left Mr. Dick to his brother's care in his will. So I stepped in. I said to Mr. Dick's brother, 'Your brother's far saner than *you*. Let him have his little income and come live with me. I'm not afraid of him. I'm ready to take care of him. And I won't mistreat him as some people (besides the asylum folks) have.' After a lot of squabbling, I got him. He's been here ever since. He's the friendliest person alive, and he always gives excellent advice." My aunt smoothed her dress and shook her head. "He had a favorite sister, a good woman who was very kind to him. But she did what they all do: took a husband. And *he* did what they all do: made her wretched. It had such an effect on Mr. Dick that, combined with his fear of his brother, he fell ill. That was before he came to me, but the memory of his sister's unhappiness and his brother's unkindness upsets him even now. He likes to fly a kite sometimes. Well, what of it? Benjamin Franklin flew a kite."

My aunt's generosity toward Mr. Dick made me hope that she'd protect me as well and made me warm towards her. I started to have faith in her. As I awaited Mr. Murdstone's reply to her letter, I felt extreme anxiety. When the letter came, my aunt informed me, to my terror, that Mr. Murdstone was coming to speak to her the next day.

The next day late in the afternoon, I saw Miss Murdstone ride a donkey, sidesaddle, up to the house. Because the incline to the house was steep, Mr. Murdstone wasn't visible at first. But then he appeared, also on a donkey. I informed my aunt. The Murdstones dismounted and came to the door.

"Shall I go away, Aunt?" I asked, trembling.

"Certainly not," she answered. She pushed me into a corner near her and fenced me in with a chair.

The Murdstones entered the room. "Miss Trotwood," Mr. Murdstone said.

"You're the Mr. Murdstone who married the widow of my late nephew David Copperfield?" my aunt asked.

"I am," Mr. Murdstone said.

"I think it would have been better if you had left that poor child alone," my aunt said.

"I agree that our lamented Clara essentially was a child," Miss Murdstone said sourly. "I also agree that my brother probably never should have married her."

My aunt rang the bell for Janet and said, "Janet, ask Mr. Dick to come down." Until he came, my aunt sat perfectly upright and stiff, frowning at the wall. When Mr. Dick came, my aunt introduced him: "Mr. Dick. He's an old and intimate friend. I rely on his judgment." Mr. Dick, who had been biting his forefinger and looking foolish, now took his finger out of his mouth and stood with a grave, attentive expression.

"Miss Trotwood," Mr. Murdstone said, "this boy has run away from his friends and his job. He has caused much trouble and worry, both during the life of my dear departed wife and since. He has a sullen, rebellious spirit; a violent temper; and an unruly disposition. My sister and I have tried to correct his vices but failed."

"I believe he's the worst boy in the world," Miss Murdstone added.

"Strong words," my aunt said shortly.

"Not overly strong," Miss Murdstone replied.

Mr. Murdstone's face had darkened. He and my aunt observed each other. "Acting on my best judgment," he said, "I placed this boy under the eye of a friend, in a respectable business. He ran away, making himself a common vagabond, and came to you in rags. So far, Miss Trotwood, you have apparently aided and abetted him."

"If he had been your own boy, you wouldn't have put him to work as you did," my aunt said.

"If he'd been my brother's boy, his character would be entirely different," Miss Murdstone commented.

"You also wouldn't have put him to work if his poor mother were still alive, would you?" my aunt asked Mr. Murdstone.

"I believe that Clara wouldn't have disputed anything that my sister and I thought was best," Mr. Murdstone replied.

"Hmph!" my aunt responded. "Unfortunate baby." After a pause she asked, "Did she leave nothing to the boy, such as her house?"

"Her first husband left everything to her. When she and I married, I took possession of all of the property, as befits a husband. I am here to take David back. I'll dispose of him as I think proper and deal with him as I think right. If you step in between him and me now, you step in forever, Miss Trotwood. I won't be trifled with. I'm here for the first and last time to take him away. Is he ready to go? If you say that he isn't, my doors will shut against him forever, and yours, I assume, will always be open to him."

My aunt, who was looking grim, turned to Miss Murdstone, "Have you anything to add, madam?"

"My brother has stated the situation exactly as I would," Miss Murdstone replied.

My aunt turned to me. "What do you say, David? Are you ready to go?"

"No, Aunt! Please don't make me go with them! They've never liked me or been kind to me. They made my mother unhappy. Being with them was horrible! Please protect me, for my father's sake!"

"Mr. Dick," my aunt said, "what should I do with this child?"

Mr. Dick considered, brightened, and replied, "Have him measured for a suit of clothes."

"Mr. Dick," my aunt said triumphantly, "your common sense is invaluable." Pulling me toward her, she said to Mr. Murdstone, "You can go when you like. I'll take my chances with the boy. If he's all that you say he is, I can at least do as much for him as *you* have. But I don't believe a word of it."

"Miss Trotwood, if you were a gentleman . . . " Mr. Murdstone began.

"Stuff and nonsense!" my aunt interrupted. "Do you think I don't know how unhappy you must have made poor Clara? Do you think I don't know what a sad day it was for her when you came into her life? Do you think I don't see what you are? I'm sure you kept your wife like a poor caged bird. You were a tyrant, and you broke her heart. You gave her the wounds that she died of. That's what I think."

Pale and breathing heavily, Mr. Murdstone went to the door.

"Good day to both of you," my aunt said. "Don't ever come here again."

Miss Murdstone put her arm through her brother's and walked haughtily out of the house. My aunt remained in the window looking after them. Her face gradually relaxed and became so pleasant that I was emboldened to kiss and thank her, which I did with great heartiness and with both my arms clasped around her neck. I then shook hands with Mr. Dick, who shook hands with me many times and repeatedly laughed.

"Mr. Dick," my aunt said, "you and I will be the child's guardians."

"I'll be delighted to be the guardian of David's son," Mr. Dick said.

"Good," my aunt said. "That's settled, then."

Chapter 16

Mr. Dick and I soon became the best of friends. We often went out together to fly his kite. It was quite touching to see him with the kite when it was high in the air. When he was outside, looking up at the kite in the sky and feeling it tug at his hand, he looked entirely serene. I used to imagine, as I sat near him on a green slope and watched him, that the kite lifted his mind out of its confusion. As he wound the string in and the kite came down out of the beautiful light, lower and lower until it fluttered to the ground and lay there like a dead thing, Mr. Dick seemed to gradually awaken from a dream. Sometimes he would take up the kite and look around him in a lost way.

My aunt took so kindly to me that within a few weeks she was calling me Davy. "Davy," she said one evening when she and Mr. Dick were playing backgammon as usual, "we mustn't neglect your education."

This was my only cause of anxiety, so I was very glad to hear her mention it.

"Would you like to go to school in Canterbury?" she asked.

"Very much," I answered. "I'd still be near you."

"Good," my aunt said. "Would you like to go to Canterbury tomorrow?"

Although I was somewhat taken aback, I promptly answered, "Yes."

"Good. Janet, arrange for a pony and carriage to be here tomorrow morning at ten. Pack Master David's clothes tonight."

I was delighted except when I noticed that the news had made Mr. Dick sad. He started playing very poorly. After giving him a few warning raps on the knuckles with her dice box, my aunt closed the backgammon board and refused to play with him anymore. However, on hearing from my aunt that I could sometimes come home on Saturdays and he could sometimes go to see me on Wednesdays, he cheered up and vowed to make a new, even bigger kite for those occasions.

In the morning Mr. Dick was downhearted again. He wanted to give me all of his gold and silver coins. My aunt limited his gift to five shillings but then, at his pleading, allowed him to give me ten. We affectionately parted at the garden gate. Mr. Dick didn't go into the house until my aunt had driven me out of sight.

My aunt drove the pony through Dover in a masterly manner, sitting high and stiff like a professional coachman. When we came into the country road, she let the pony rest and, looking at me, asked, "Are you happy, Davy?"

"Very happy. Thank you, Aunt."

She seemed pleased.

"Is it a large school, Aunt?" I asked.

"I don't know," she replied. "We're going to Mr. Wickfield's first."

"Does he run the school?"

"No, Davy. He runs a law office. He's my lawyer."

I asked no more questions about Mr. Wickfield. My aunt and I discussed other subjects until we reached Canterbury, where it was market day. Making hairbreadth twists and turns, my aunt maneuvered the pony and carriage around carts, baskets, vegetable stands, and other obstacles. Finally we stopped in front of a very old house with long, low lattice windows. The low, arched door was ornamented with carved garlands of fruits and flowers; its brass knocker sparkled. The two stone steps in front of the door were as white as clean linen. Every windowpane was shiny and clear.

I saw a cadaverous face appear at a small window on the ground floor and quickly disappear. The door opened, and the face came out. It belonged to a boy of about fifteen. His red hair was cropped so short that it was stubble. His eyebrows and eyelashes were so pale that he hardly seemed to have any. His eyes were reddish brown. He was dressed in black, with a white wisp of a neck cloth, and was buttoned up to the throat. High-shouldered and bony, he had a long, lank, skeletal hand, with which he rubbed his chin.

"Is Mr. Wickfield home, Uriah?" my aunt asked.

"Yes, ma'am," he answered. "Please walk in there." With his long hand he pointed to a parlor.

We got out and, leaving Uriah to take care of the pony, went into a long, low parlor that faced the street. Opposite the tall, old chimneypiece were two portraits: one of a middle-aged gentleman, with gray hair and black eyebrows, who was looking over some papers tied together with red tape; the other of a lady with a sweet, placid expression.

The gentleman depicted in the first portrait entered through a door at the far end of the room. His hair was white now, but his eyebrows still were black. "Miss Trotwood, please come in," he said.

"Thank you, Mr. Wickfield," my aunt said.

We went into Mr. Wickfield's office, which had the books, papers, and desk accessories typical of law offices. The room looked out on a garden and had an iron safe built into the wall.

"Well, Miss Trotwood," Mr. Wickfield said, "what brings you here?" Although he was overweight, he had a handsome, very agreeable face. He was very cleanly dressed in a blue jacket, striped vest, and cotton trousers. His fine frilled shirt and linen neck cloth looked unusually soft and white. His complexion had a rosiness that I had learned to associate with heavy drinking.

"This is my nephew," my aunt said.

"I wasn't aware that you had one," he said.

"Actually he's my grand-nephew. I've adopted him. I've brought him here so that he can attend a school where he'll be well taught and well treated. What's the best school here?"

"He couldn't board at our best school," Mr. Wickfield said.

"Well, he could board somewhere else, then," my aunt said.

"Certainly," Mr. Wickfield said. After some discussion he proposed to take my aunt to see the school. The three of us were about to go when Mr. Wickfield said, "I think it might be best if David stayed here."

My aunt seemed disposed to disagree, but I said that I didn't mind staying behind. I sat back down in Mr. Wickfield's office to await their return. My chair was opposite a narrow passage that ended in the room where I had seen Uriah's pale face looking out of the window. Having taken the pony to a neighboring stable, Uriah was at work at a desk in this room. He was holding up a document and writing. Every so often he slyly peeked around the raised document and stared at me. Discomfited, I went to look at a map on the other side of Mr. Wickfield's office and then read a newspaper.

After a fairly long absence, Mr. Wickfield and my aunt returned. My aunt was pleased with the school but hadn't liked any of the boarding houses proposed for me. "I don't know what to do, Davy," she said.

"I'll tell you what, Miss Trotwood," Mr. Wickfield said. "I don't mind if you leave your nephew here for now. He seems like a quiet fellow. He won't disturb me. This is an excellent house for study. It's as quiet as a monastery and almost as roomy. He's welcome to stay here."

My aunt was pleased but hesitated to accept the generous offer.

"Come now, Miss Trotwood," Mr. Wickfield said. "It's only a temporary arrangement. In the meantime you can look for another place."

"I'm very obliged to you," she said, "but I don't see how I can accept . . . "

"Don't worry. You can pay for his room and board if you like—whatever you think is fair."

"In that case I'll be very glad to leave him here. Thank you," my aunt said.

"Then, come see my little housekeeper," Mr. Wickfield said.

We went up a wonderful old staircase, with a banister so wide that we might have gone up that almost as easily, and into a small parlor lit by three quaint windows with oak seats in them. The floor was shining oak. The room was prettily furnished, with lively red and green furniture, a piano, and some flowers. Every little nook and corner had some delightful little table, cupboard, bookcase, or seat. Everything was clean.

Mr. Wickfield tapped at a door in a corner of the paneled wall, and a girl of my own age quickly came out and kissed him. Her face reminded me of the woman depicted in the second portrait downstairs. It had the same sweet, placid expression.

"This is my little housekeeper," Mr. Wickfield said, "my daughter Agnes."

Agnes had a little basket hanging at her side with keys in it. Her father told her about me. She listened with a pleasant face. When he had concluded, he proposed to my aunt that we go upstairs and see my room. We all went together, with Agnes leading the way. The room was charming, with oak beams and diamond-shaped windowpanes.

My aunt and I were very pleased. We went back downstairs. My aunt wouldn't stay for supper because she wanted to return home before dark, but some refreshment was provided for her.

Agnes went back to her governess, and Mr. Wickfield went to his office, so my aunt and I could say goodbye privately. She told me that Mr. Wickfield would arrange everything for me and that I wouldn't lack anything. "Davy, be a credit to yourself, me, and Mr. Dick. Heaven be with you."

I was so overcome with emotion that I just kept saying "Thank you" and asked her to give my love to Mr. Dick.

"Never be mean, false, or cruel," she said. "Avoid those three vices, and I'll always be proud of you."

"I promise to do my best," I said. "I'll always remember your kindness and your advice."

"The pony's at the door. I have to go." She embraced me hastily and went out of the room, shutting the door after her. Looking out, I saw her look dejected as she got into the carriage.

At first I felt very sad at being separated from my aunt and Mr. Dick, but by suppertime I had a hearty appetite. Mr. Wickfield, Agnes, and I had dinner together. Then we went upstairs into the drawing room again. Agnes set out a decanter of wine and some glasses in one snug corner. Her father sat there, drinking heavily, for two hours while Agnes played the piano, worked, and talked to him and me. For the most part, Mr. Wickfield was cheerful, but sometimes his eyes rested on Agnes and he fell into a brooding state and was silent. She always quickly noticed his changed mood and tried to cheer him with a question or caress. Then he cheered up and drank more wine.

Agnes made tea and presided over it. The time passed quickly until Agnes bid her father and me good night. Mr. Wickfield took her in his arms and kissed her, and she went to bed. Then I went to bed, too.

Chapter 17

The next morning after breakfast, I returned to school life. Accompanied by Mr. Wickfield, I went to a grave building that had a learned air. In the courtyard, rooks and jackdaws walked on the grass, having flown down from the towers of the nearby cathedral.

I was introduced to Dr. Strong, the principal, who was in his library. He looked almost as rusty as the tall iron rails and gates outside the school building, and almost as heavy and stiff as the large stone urns that sat, at regular intervals, atop the red-brick wall that surrounded the courtyard. Dr. Strong was thoroughly untidy. His clothes needed brushing, and his hair needed combing. His breeches were unbuckled, his long black leggings were unbuttoned, and his shoes yawned like two caverns on the hearth rug. Looking at me with lackluster eyes, he said, "I'm glad to meet you," and gave me his hand.

Sitting at work not far from Dr. Strong was a cheerful-looking, pretty young lady whom Dr. Strong introduced as his wife Annie. She knelt to put his shoes on him and quickly buttoned his leggings.

When she finished, Dr. Strong, Mr. Wickfield, and I headed out to the schoolroom

Dr. Strong walked with an odd, uneven pace. "By the way, Wickfield, have you found any suitable position for my wife's cousin, Jack Maldon?"

"Not yet," Mr. Wickfield answered.

"I'd like him to have a job as soon as possible. Currently he's needy and idle, and that's a bad combination."

"I think I understand your meaning," Mr. Wickfield said with an expression that suggested some dislike of Mr. Maldon.

"I'd especially like to see him taken care of for Annie's sake," Dr. Strong said. "He's not only her cousin but an old playmate."

"Maybe I can arrange for him to take some position abroad," Mr. Wickfield said.

"Either abroad or here in England," Dr. Strong replied. "Either would be fine."

"But you would prefer abroad, right?" Mr. Wickfield said as if hinting at something unexpressed.

"I don't have any preference," Dr. Strong replied.

"You don't?" Mr. Wickfield responded with apparent surprise.

"No," Dr. Strong answered. "Why would I?"

Looking uncomfortable, Mr. Wickfield made no reply.

The schoolroom was a large, attractive hall on the house's quietest side. It overlooked an old, secluded garden where peaches were ripening on the sunny south wall. About twenty-five boys were studying from books when we entered. They rose to bid Dr. Strong good morning and remained standing when they saw Mr. Wickfield and me.

"A new boy, young gentlemen," Dr. Strong said. "David Copperfield."

The head boy, Adams, stepped out of his place and welcomed me. In his white cravat he looked like a young clergyman, but he was very friendly and good-humored. He showed me my place and presented me to the other boys in a gentlemanly way that put me at ease.

Having had no schooling for such a long time, I did miserably when tested and was placed in the school's lowest grade. The minute that school ended at 3:00, I hurried off because I felt shy.

As soon as I knocked at the door of Mr. Wickfield's house, I felt my uneasiness slipping away. I went up to my airy room and sat there intently reading from my schoolbooks until dinner time, when I went downstairs. Agnes was in the drawing room waiting for her father, who was detained by someone in his office. She met me with her pleasant smile and asked, "Do you like the school?"

"I think I'll like it very much," I said. "But it seems hard and strange right now. You've never been to school?"

"Oh, yes. Every day," she answered.

"At home, you mean?" I asked.

"Papa couldn't spare me to go anywhere else," she answered, smiling. "I'm his housekeeper."

"I can see that he loves you very much," I said.

"Yes. Mama has been dead ever since I was born," Agnes said in her quiet way. "I know only her portrait downstairs. I saw you looking at it yesterday. Did you guess who it was?"

"Yes, because she looked so much like *you*."

"Papa says so, too," Agnes said, pleased. "There he is now." Her bright, calm face lit up with pleasure as she went out onto the landing to meet her father as he came up the stairs. They came in hand in hand.

Mr. Wickfield greeted me cordially. "I'm sure you'll be happy at Dr. Strong's school, David. He's one of the kindest of men. Some people take advantage of his generous and trusting nature."

Dinner was announced. We went down and took the same seats as before. When we had dined, we went upstairs again, where everything proceeded as on the previous day. Agnes set the decanter and glasses in the same corner, and Mr. Wickfield sat down and drank a lot of wine. Agnes played the piano, sat by her father, worked, talked, and played some games of dominoes with me. Then she made tea. Afterwards I brought down my books. Agnes looked through them and told me about their content. She knew quite a lot, although she believed otherwise. She gave me advice regarding the best way to study. Her manner was modest and placid, and she spoke in a beautiful, calm voice.

When Agnes went off to bed, I said good night to Mr. Wickfield. "Would you like to stay with us, David, or go elsewhere?" he asked.

"I'd like to stay," I quickly answered.

"Are you sure?"

"Yes, if it's all right with you."

"I'm afraid we lead a dull life here," he said.

"Not dull for me, sir."

"I'm glad. Stay with us, then, David. You're wholesome company for both Agnes and me."

"I'm glad to be here, sir."

"You're a fine fellow. Stay here as long as you want to."

We shook hands, and he clapped me on the back. "When you have some studying to do at night after Agnes has left us, or if you wish to read for your own pleasure, feel free to come down to my office and sit with me."

"Thank you."

Mr. Wickfield went down soon afterwards. Because I wasn't tired, I soon went down, too, with a book in my hand. I was planning to join him. However, seeing a light in Uriah's little office, and being fascinated by Uriah, I went in there instead. I found him reading a heavy book. His lank forefinger followed every line as he read. "You're working late tonight, Uriah," I said.

"Yes, Master Copperfield." As I was getting onto the stool opposite to talk to Uriah more conveniently, I realized that he never smiled. The closest he came to a smile was to widen his mouth and make two hard creases down his cheeks, one on each side. "I'm not doing office work," he said.

"What work, then?" I asked.

"I'm improving my legal knowledge, Master Copperfield. I'm going through a book on the practice of law."

From my tower-like stool, I watched Uriah resume reading and observed that his nostrils, which were thin and pointed, expanded and contracted. "I suppose you're quite a lawyer."

"Me, Master Copperfield? Oh, no! I'm a very 'umble person." Uriah repeatedly wiped his hands on his pocket handkerchief. "I'm the 'umblest person there is. My mother is very 'umble, too. We live in an 'umble house. My father's former calling was 'umble. He was a sexton."

"What is he now?" I asked.

"He's in heaven now, Master Copperfield," Uriah said. "But my mother and I have much to be thankful for. I'm very thankful to be living with Mr. Wickfield."

"Have you been with Mr. Wickfield long?"

"About four years, Master Copperfield." Uriah closed his book after carefully marking his place. "Since a year after my father's death. It's Mr. Wickfield's kind intention to give me my legal training, which would otherwise not lie within the 'umble means of my mother and me."

"When your training period is over, you'll be a lawyer?" I asked.

"With heaven's blessing, Master Copperfield."

"Perhaps you'll be a partner in Mr. Wickfield's business one of these days, and it will be Wickfield & Heep," I said.

"Oh no, Master Copperfield," Uriah replied, shaking his head. "I'm much too 'umble for that." He eyed me sideways, with his mouth widened and his cheeks creased. "Mr. Wickfield is a most excellent man."

"I'm sure he is," I replied. "My aunt certainly thinks so."

"Your aunt is a sweet lady, Master Copperfield." He writhed with apparent enthusiasm. "She greatly admires Miss Agnes."

"Yes," I said, although I had no idea whether or not my aunt admired Agnes.

"I guess you also admire her, Master Copperfield."

"I think everyone must," I returned.

Uriah began to prepare to go home. "Mother will be expecting me, Master Copperfield. Although we're very 'umble, we're much attached to each other. If you would come and see us some afternoon and take a cup of tea at our lowly dwelling, Mother would be as proud of your company as I would."

"Thank you. I'd be glad to come," I replied.

"Thank you, Master Copperfield," Uriah said, putting his book onto a shelf. "Will you be staying here long?"

"As long as I remain at school, I think."

"Oh, indeed!" he exclaimed. "Then, I would think that *you* would come into the business, Master Copperfield."

"I certainly have no such intention," I protested.

Before leaving, Uriah asked, "May I put out the light?"

"Yes."

He put out the light. Then we shook hands. Uriah's hand was clammy. He opened the door to the street only enough to slide out, exited, and shut the door behind him.

Chapter 18

By the time two weeks had passed, I felt thoroughly at ease both at school and at home. Dr. Strong's school was excellent. I worked very hard and earned praise. The students were expected to be honorable and good, and they were. To my knowledge, every one of us felt attached to the school and proud of it. Canterbury's residents called us "Dr. Strong's boys" and spoke well of us.

I learned that Dr. Strong was sixty-two years old, whereas his wife Annie was only twenty. They had been married only a year. Dr. Strong had been a friend of Annie's father, now deceased, and had known Annie since she was an infant. She had been very poor, and he had married her for love. Dr. Strong had a fatherly, benign way of showing his fondness for his wife. I often saw them walking in the garden or sitting in the parlor. Mrs. Strong appeared to take great care of her husband and to feel much affection for him. I saw a lot of her because she had taken a liking to me on the morning we had met, she always was kind to me, and, being very fond of Agnes, she often visited Mr. Wickfield's house. I sensed some tension between Mr. Wickfield and

Mrs. Strong. I got the feeling that Mr. Wickfield didn't trust her and that she slightly feared him.

One night the Strongs gave a small party to celebrate Dr. Strong's birthday. Mrs. Strong's mother, Mrs. Markleham, was among the guests. A little, sharp-eyed woman, she wore a cap decorated with artificial flowers and two artificial butterflies hovering, on wires, above them. We boys had been given the day off, and we had given Dr. Strong presents in the morning. Adams had made a speech in Dr. Strong's honor, and we all had cheered until we were hoarse. Dr. Strong had shed tears. Now, in the evening, Mr. Wickfield, Agnes, and I went to have tea with him. Two teachers and Adams also went. Mrs. Strong's cousin Jack Maldon was there. As arranged by Mr. Wickfield, Mr. Maldon was about to leave for India as a soldier. Dressed in white with cherry-colored ribbons, Mrs. Strong was playing the piano when we entered. Mr. Maldon, very handsome and with a conceited air, was leaning over her to turn the pages. He was to leave that night to take a ship from Gravesend. Although Mrs. Strong was a beautiful singer, she didn't sing that night. She tried a duet with Mr. Maldon but couldn't even begin. Her head drooped over the keys. Dr. Strong noticed her discomfort and proposed a card game. We had a merry game. Mrs. Strong had declined to play on the ground that she wasn't feeling well. She and Mr. Maldon sat together, talking, on the sofa. Mrs. Strong looked pale. At supper Mr. Maldon tried to be talkative, but he seemed uneasy.

"Jack, it seems only yesterday that you were a little boy making baby-love to Annie behind the gooseberry bushes in the back garden," Mrs. Markleham said.

Blushing with embarrassment, Mrs. Strong said, "Mother, never mind that now."

"Now Annie is a married woman, and you're off to India," Mrs. Markleham continued. "And we have Dr. Strong to thank for both. He has been wonderfully generous to our family. I'll never forget how surprised I was when he first told me that he wanted to marry Annie. Not that there was anything out of the way in his proposal. Not at all. It's just that I hadn't thought of him in that way. I went to Annie and told her, 'My dear, Dr. Strong has made you the subject of a handsome offer.' Annie cried and said that she was very young. I told her that we had to give Dr. Strong an answer. She continued to cry and asked if Dr. Strong would be unhappy without her. She said, 'If he would, I'll marry him because I honor and respect him so much.' So it was settled. I told Annie that Dr. Strong would be both a husband and a father to her."

Mrs. Strong had listened to her mother in silence, looking down at the floor. Mr. Maldon stood near her, also looking down. In a trembling voice, Mrs. Strong now said, "Mother, I hope you're finished."

The conversation now turned to Mr. Maldon— his imminent journey to India and his prospects and plans. He expected to stay in India for some years. "Annie, my dear," Dr. Strong said, looking at his watch and filling his glass, "it's past Jack's time. We mustn't detain him. Jack, you have a long journey and a new country ahead of you." Dr. Strong stood, and all the rest of us did the same. "We wish you a good voyage, a thriving career abroad, and a happy return home." We all drank a toast and shook hands with Mr. Maldon. Then he hurriedly left.

Conversation resumed. After a time Mrs. Markleham asked, "Where's Annie?" She called out, "Annie?" There was no reply. We all started looking for Mrs. Strong and found her lying on the hall floor. She had fainted. Dr. Strong lifted her head onto his knee, put her brown curls aside with his hand, and said, "Poor Annie! She's so faithful and tenderhearted. I'm sure she's upset at parting from her old playfellow and friend, her favorite cousin."

When Mrs. Strong opened her eyes and saw where she was and that we were all standing around her, she rose with her husband's assistance, putting her head against his shoulder. We guests started back to the drawing room, to leave her with her husband and mother, but she said, "I'm feeling much better now. I'd rather stay with all of you." Dr. Strong helped her into the drawing room and sat her on a sofa. She continued to look white and weak. When the gathering broke up, Mr. Wickfield, Agnes, and I walked home.

Chapter 19

I had, of course, written to Peggotty after my safe
arrival at my aunt's and had continued to write to
her since. With considerable pride I had sent her a
half-guinea to repay my debt to her. Peggotty always
replied right away. She expressed surprise that my
aunt was being so good to me and indicated that
she must have misjudged my aunt. She informed
me that the Murdstones had sold my mother's
furniture, left the house, and put it up for sale.
Peggotty said that weeds grew tall in the garden,
and fallen leaves lay thick and wet on the paths. It
pained me to think of my childhood home empty
and neglected. Peggotty said that Mr. Barkis was an
excellent husband, although somewhat stingy, and
that he sent his regards. My little bedroom, she said,
always was ready and waiting for me should I ever
want it. Mr. Peggotty and Ham were well, Emily
sent her love, and Mrs. Gummidge was the same as
always.

I also wrote regularly to my aunt. Every third
Saturday I went home, and Mr. Dick visited me every
other Wednesday. He would arrive on the noon
stagecoach and stay until the next morning. Mr. Dick

was very partial to gingerbread. To make his visits more agreeable, my aunt had instructed me to open an account for him at a bakery but to tell the baker that he mustn't be served more than one shilling's worth of gingerbread on any one day. His bills at the inn where he slept also were referred to my aunt.

On one visit, Mr. Dick said to me, "David, who's the man who hides near our house and frightens Miss Betsey?"

"Frightens my aunt?"

Mr. Dick nodded. "I thought nothing ever frightened her. I was walking with her after tea, right after twilight, and there he was, close to our house."

"What was he doing?" I asked.

"He came up behind her and whispered. She turned around and looked terrified. I stood still and looked at him, and he walked away. Last night it happened again. We were walking, and he came up behind her."

"And she was frightened again?"

"Oh, yes. She cried," Mr. Dick answered. "Why did she give him money?"

"Maybe he was a beggar."

Mr. Dick emphatically shook his head, "No. Since then, late at night, I've looked out of my window and seen Miss Betsey give him money outside the garden rails in the moonlight. Then he slinks away, and Miss Betsey hurriedly and secretly comes back into the house. Lately she's been quite different than usual."

I was skeptical about Mr. Dick's story. On the

Wednesdays that followed, he said that he hadn't seen the man again.

Soon, every boy in the school knew Mr. Dick. Although he never actively participated in any game except kite flying, he was deeply interested in all our games. He would watch a game of marbles or Spin the Top with such absorption that he hardly would breathe at the critical moments. As we boys played ball or went down the slide in the playground, Mr. Dick would clap his hands in delight. He was a universal favorite, wonderfully adept at doing small things. He could cut an orange into all sorts of amazing shapes; turn metal scraps into chess pieces; make a miniature boat from a block of wood or just about anything else; and create Roman chariots out of cards, with empty spools of thread as the wheels.

The Strongs, too, became Mr. Dick's friends. Mr. Dick thought Dr. Strong the wisest, most learned man in the world. Dr. Strong was compiling a dictionary. He would talk about his work to Mr. Dick as they walked along. Mr. Dick would listen with a face shining with pleasure and pride.

One day Uriah invited me to come to his house for tea that evening. I said I'd mention the invitation to Mr. Wickfield and gladly come if he approved. Mr. Wickfield approved, so at 6:00 that evening Uriah and I walked to his house.

"Mother will be proud, indeed,'" he said as we walked along.

"Have you been studying much law lately?" I asked.

"Oh, Master Copperfield, my reading can hardly be called study. I sometimes pass an hour or two in the evening with a book on the practice of law."

"Do you find it difficult?"

"Sometimes. There are Latin words and such that are difficult for a person of my 'umble education." When we reached Uriah's house, he said, "Here's my 'umble dwelling, Master Copperfield."

From the street we directly entered a low, old-fashioned room. There we found Uriah's mother, Mrs. Heep. She looked like an older, female version of Uriah, only shorter. She received me with the utmost humility. She gave her son a kiss and said, "You'll have to excuse me, Master Copperfield. Lowly as we are, we have our affections." The room was respectable but not at all cozy. It was half-parlor and half-kitchen. The tea things were on the table, and the kettle was boiling on the stove. The room contained the usual furniture, a corner cupboard, and a chest of drawers with a desktop at which Uriah could read or write in the evenings. Papers and books also indicated that Uriah did some studying at home. Still, overall the place looked bare. Although her husband had died some time ago, Mrs. Heep still wore mourning.

"It's a day to be remembered, my Uriah, when Master Copperfield pays us a visit," she said, making the tea. "My Uriah has looked forward to this for a long time, sir. We both feared that our 'umbleness might prevent you from coming."

The Heeps respectfully plied me with the choicest food on the table. Little by little they wormed information out of me: about my aunt, my parents, even my stepfather (my aunt had advised me not to discuss him with other people). When there was nothing more to be pulled out of me, they began to talk about the Wickfields: Mr. Wickfield's excellence, my admiration for Agnes, the extent of Mr. Wickfield's business and resources, Mr. Wickfield's habit of drinking too much wine. I felt uncomfortable and wanted to leave. Because the weather was warm, the door to the street had been left open to let in air.

Suddenly a man walked by who stopped, put his head in, and loudly exclaimed, "Copperfield! Is it possible?"

It was Mr. Micawber! He looked the same as ever—with his monocle, cane, high shirt collar, genteel air, and dramatic manner. "My dear Copperfield," he said, extending his hand, "this is a most extraordinary meeting. My dear fellow, how are you?"

Although I would have preferred to encounter Mr. Micawber in some other place, I heartily shook his hand and asked, "How is Mrs. Micawber?"

"Thank you, she's well," Mr. Micawber answered. "The twins have been weaned. Mrs. Micawber is traveling with me. She'll be overjoyed to renew her acquaintance with such a worthy friend." He smiled and looked around. "I'd be honored to be introduced to the people with whom you're taking tea."

I had no choice but to introduce everyone. The Heeps abased themselves before Mr. Micawber, who took a seat. "Any friend of my friend Copperfield has a personal claim on me," Mr. Micawber declared.

"My son and me are too 'umble, sir, to be Master Copperfield's friends," Mrs. Heep said. "He's been good enough to have tea with us."

Mr. Micawber bowed. "Ma'am, you're very obliging. What are you doing, Copperfield? Still in the wine trade?"

Reddening, I answered, "I'm a pupil at Dr. Strong's school."

"A pupil?" Mr. Micawber said, raising his eyebrows. "I'm extremely happy to hear it. Your mind is rich soil."

Uriah intertwined his long hands and writhed.

Anxious to leave, I said to Mr. Micawber, "Shall we go see Mrs. Micawber, sir?"

"If you'll do her that favor, Copperfield," Mr. Micawber replied, rising. "Good evening, Mrs. Heep. Mr. Heep. At your service."

I thanked the Heeps, and Mr. Micawber and I left. As we walked along, he hummed a tune.

The Micawbers occupied a small room in an inn, over the kitchen. When we entered, Mrs. Micawber was lying on a small sofa with her head close to the fire. "My dear," Mr. Micawber said, "allow me to introduce a pupil of Dr. Strong." Mrs. Micawber was delighted to see me. After we exchanged an affectionate greeting, I sat down near her on the sofa. "My dear," Mr. Micawber said, "while you fill Copperfield in regarding our present situation, I'll go read the newspaper to see if there are any suitable jobs."

As he went out, I said to Mrs. Micawber, "I thought you were at Plymouth, ma'am."

"My dear Master Copperfield, we went to Plymouth, but Mr. Micawber wasn't given a job at the customhouse. No one seems to appreciate his abilities. So we borrowed money from my relatives with which to return to London. The children currently are in a lodging there. Mr. Micawber and I came to Canterbury to look into the possibility of his finding work here. So far, however, nothing has turned up. Now we're waiting for some money to arrive that will enable us to pay our bill at this inn and return to London."

When I left the Micawbers, they both insisted that I come dine with them as soon as they received the money. Two days later Mr. Micawber came to Dr. Strong's to invite me to dinner. When I asked him if the money had arrived, he didn't answer. He just pressed my hand and left.

As I was looking out of the window that evening, I was startled to see Mr. Micawber and Uriah walk past arm in arm. When I went to the inn the next day at 4:00, the time set for dinner, I learned that Mr. Micawber had gone home with Uriah and had drunk brandy there. "My dear Copperfield," Mr. Micawber said, "your friend Heep is a young fellow who will go far." I was very uneasy at the thought of what Mr. Micawber might have told Uriah about my past.

The Micawbers and I had an extravagant dinner, with fish, veal, pudding, and ale. They were very merry. So I was surprised when, at 7:00 the next morning, I received the following note, dated only fifteen minutes after I had left the Micawbers:

> My dear young friend,
>
> This evening I hid our troubles behind a mask of merriment. We didn't receive the money to pay our inn bill, and we won't be receiving it. I had to sign a promissory note agreeing to pay within fourteen days. I know, however, that I won't be able to pay. I'm doomed! This is the last communication, my dear Copperfield, that you'll ever receive from me.
>
> The beggared outcast,
> Wilkins Micawber

I was so shocked by the note that I hurried to the inn. However, halfway there I saw the Micawbers sitting on a coach bound for London. They were smiling, conversing, and eating walnuts out of a paper bag. A bottle was sticking out of Mr. Micawber's pocket. They didn't see me, so I decided not to speak to them. Relieved that they soon would be gone, I turned toward school.

Chapter 20

I worked so hard that Dr. Strong soon was publicly referring to me as a promising scholar. By the time I was seventeen and my school days ended, I was the head boy. When graduation came, I was sad to leave the school. I had been very happy there, I was greatly respected there, and I was very attached to Dr. Strong.

My aunt and I had many discussions regarding what profession I should enter. I had no particular liking for anything except reading. "Davy, I'll tell you what, my dear," my aunt said one morning. "A little change, a glimpse of life away from here, might help you decide on a profession. Would you like to see that woman you're so fond of—Peggotty?"

"More than anything else, Aunt!"

"It's a pity your poor, dear mother isn't alive. She'd be so proud of you," she said, looking at me approvingly. "You remind me of her very much. You look like her. You resemble your father as well. It's time you developed self-reliance, Davy. You have to learn independence now. I want you to have strength of character and a will of your own. You'll go on your trip alone."

For my trip my aunt gave me a large suitcase and a purse filled with a generous amount of money. At parting, she gave me many kisses. She suggested that I spend a few days in London if I wanted to. I was free to do as I wished for three or four weeks. Nothing was required of me except to be sensible, think about what I'd like to do for a career, and write to her three times a week.

Before leaving, I went to Canterbury to say goodbye to Agnes, Mr. Wickfield, and Dr. Strong. Agnes was very glad to see me. "The house hasn't been the same since you left, Davy," she said.

"I've missed you, too," I said. "I think I'm at my best when I'm with you. You aren't like anyone else. You're good, sweet, and always right."

"How you talk!" Agnes laughed as she sat at work.

"I'd like to always confide in you. When I fall in love, I'll tell you. How is it that you aren't in love yet? Of course, I don't know anyone who deserves your love. The right man for you will have to be nobler than anyone I've ever met."

Agnes looked me in the eyes and said, "David, I want to ask you something. Have you observed a gradual change, for the worse, in my father?" I had, but I was reluctant to say so. My answer must have shown in my face because tears came into Agnes's eyes, and she looked down. "Tell me what it is," she said quietly. "Please be candid."

"He often seems nervous," I said. "I think he harms himself by drinking so much. Sometimes his hands tremble, his speech is unclear, and his eyes look wild. I've noticed that he's often asked to attend to some business matter when he's in an unfit state."

"Asked by Uriah," Agnes said.

"Yes. And afterwards your father seems upset. He looks haggard. Don't be alarmed by this, Agnes, but just the other evening I saw him lay his head down on his desk and weep like a child."

Having heard her father approaching, Agnes silenced me by gently putting her hand to my lips. In a moment she met her father at the door to the room and had her arm in his. Her beautiful face showed deep love for him.

We were to have tea at Dr. Strong's. We went there at the usual hour and found Dr. Strong, Mrs. Strong, and Mrs. Markleham around the fireside in the study. Dr. Strong received me as an honored guest. He called for a log to be thrown onto the fire so that he could see the face of his former pupil lit up by the blaze. "I won't see many more new faces in place of David's, Wickfield," Dr. Strong said, warming his hands. "I feel the need to rest. I'm going to retire in six months. The head teacher will take over as principal. I'll devote myself to the dictionary that I'm compiling and to Annie," he said, smiling.

Mr. Wickfield glanced at Mrs. Strong, who was sitting next to Agnes at the tea table. Mrs. Strong seemed to avoid meeting his gaze. After a short silence Mr. Wickfield asked Dr. Strong, "What have you heard from Jack Maldon? I feel somewhat responsible for him because he went to India at my recommendation."

"Here's a letter from him to Dr. Strong," Mrs. Markleham said, taking a letter from the mantel. "Poor Jack. India's climate is very taxing, and he's never been strong. The dear fellow says, 'I'm sorry to inform you that my health is suffering severely. I fear that I may have to return home if I hope to recover.' A letter that he wrote to Annie is even plainer. Annie, show me that letter again."

"Not now, Mama," Mrs. Strong softly pleaded.

"My dear, you're unnatural to deny your mother. Dr. Strong wouldn't even have known about the letter if I hadn't asked for it. Do you call that confidence toward your husband? I'm surprised. You should know better."

With a trembling hand, Mrs. Strong reluctantly handed over the letter.

"Now let's see," Mrs. Markleham said, putting on her reading glasses. "Where's that passage? 'The remembrance of old times, my dearest Annie...' No. That's not it. 'The amiable old doctor . . . ' No. Here it is. 'You may not be surprised to hear, Annie, that I have suffered so much in this distant place that I have decided to leave it at all hazards— on sick leave if possible, otherwise by resigning. What I have endured here, and continue to endure, is insupportable.'" Mrs. Markleham refolded the letter and looked at Mr. Wickfield for his opinion.

Mr. Wickfield sat silent with his eyes fixed on the floor. Long after the subject was dismissed and other topics occupied us, he remained that way, seldom raising his eyes except to rest them for a moment, with a thoughtful frown, on Dr. Strong, Mrs. Strong, or both of them.

Dr. Strong was very fond of music. Agnes and Mrs. Strong both sang with great sweetness and expression. They sang together and played duets. Mr. Wickfield seemed to dislike the intimacy between Agnes and Mrs. Strong and watch it with uneasiness. I started to wonder if there was any sort of love relationship between Mrs. Strong and Mr. Maldon. Still, the evening went pleasantly.

When Agnes and Mrs. Strong were taking leave of each other, Agnes went to embrace and kiss Mrs. Strong. Mr. Wickfield stepped between them and quickly drew Agnes away. I left feeling worried for Dr. Strong.

In the morning, I packed up the books and clothes that still needed to be sent to Dover from my room in Mr. Wickfield's house. It pained me to pack up my things and leave the room that had been mine for years. Uriah seemed glad to see me go.

Somehow, I parted from Agnes and her father without crying and took my seat on the London stagecoach. It was strange to sit in a coach—well educated, well dressed, and with plenty of money in my pocket—and pass the places where I had suffered from lack of food, shelter, and money when I ran away to my aunt. In London the coach stopped at a small inn in a crowded neighborhood. A chambermaid showed me to my room, a small, stuffy room that smelled like a horse-drawn cab. Then I went back down to the dining room. I had a meal of veal, potatoes, and wine and then went to

Covent Garden Theater, where I saw *Julius Caesar*. When the play ended at midnight, I was forced to emerge from a magical world onto a rainy street. I walked back to the inn, where I had some wine and oysters and sat thinking about the play past 1:00 in front of the dining-room fire.

At last I rose to go to bed. Going toward the door, I passed a handsome, elegantly dressed young man with dark, curly hair. I instantly recognized him: James Steerforth. I went up to him and, with a fast-beating heart, exclaimed, "James!" He looked at me but didn't recognize me. "You don't remember me, I'm afraid," I said.

"My God!" he suddenly exclaimed. "It's little David!"

I grasped him by both hands. "I never was so glad. My dear James, I'm overjoyed to see you."

"I'm overjoyed to see you, too." He shook my hands heartily. I was so moved that I brushed away tears and laughed. We sat down side by side. "How do you come to be in London?" he asked, clapping me on the shoulder.

"I arrived today from Canterbury. I've been adopted by an aunt who lives in Dover, and I've just finished my education in Canterbury. How do *you* come to be here?"

"I'm on my way to my mother's. She lives just beyond London. You haven't changed at all, my dear David. Same friendly expression." James turned to a waiter, "Waiter, where have you put my friend, Mr. Copperfield—in which room?"

"He's in room forty-six, sir," the waiter

answered with an embarrassed air.

"What the devil do you mean by putting Mr. Copperfield in a smelly little loft over the stable?" James demanded.

"We wasn't aware that Mr. Copperfield was particular, sir," the waiter said apologetically. "We can give him number seventy-two, next to you, if it would be preferred."

"Of course it would be preferred," James said. "See to it at once." The waiter immediately left to arrange the room change. James ran his hand through his curls, laughed, and clapped me on the shoulder again. "Why don't we have breakfast together tomorrow? How about half past eight?"

I eagerly accepted the invitation. We took our candles and went upstairs, where we parted with friendly heartiness at his door and where I found my new room a great improvement. It wasn't at all musty, and it had an immense four-post bed. Among enough pillows for six people, I soon fell asleep in a state of bliss.

Chapter 21

The next morning when I went down to the dining room, James was waiting for me in a snug private room with red curtains and a Turkish carpet. The fire burned bright, and a fine hot breakfast was set forth on a table covered with a clean cloth. James was so elegant and self-possessed that I felt bashful. "Now, David," he said, "tell me what you've been doing, where you're going, and all about yourself."

I told him that my aunt had proposed my trip in the hope that I would choose a profession.

"Since you're in no hurry, come home with me to Highgate, and stay a day or two. You'll be pleased with my mother, and she'll be pleased with you. She likes anyone who's fond of me."

"Thank you. I'd be delighted," I said.

"Good."

After breakfast I wrote to my aunt and told her of my fortunate meeting with my admired former schoolfellow and my acceptance of his invitation. James and I went out in a cab, saw some sights, and took a walk through the British Museum, where I observed how much he knew on a wide variety of subjects. He was a student at Oxford University. "I'm sure you'll graduate with honors," I said confidently.

"My dear David, I don't know that I plan to graduate at all. It's all quite boring."

Taken aback, I said nothing more on the subject.

James and I had lunch and then did some more sightseeing. The short winter day went by so quickly that it was dusk when the coach brought us to an old brick house in Highgate on a hill's summit. A middle-aged lady with a proud manner and a handsome face was in the doorway as we alighted. "My dearest James," she said, folding him in her arms. James introduced me to his mother, and she gave me a stately welcome.

The house was genteel and old-fashioned, very quiet and orderly. I was shown to my room, where I dressed for dinner. From the windows I saw London in the distance.

When I entered the dining room, there was another lady. About thirty years old, she was thin, short, and handsome. She had black hair, intense black eyes, and a thin vertical scar that started above her mouth and went down through her upper lip, altering the lip's shape. She was introduced as Miss Dartle. James and his mother called her Rosa. I found that she lived there and had been Mrs. Steerforth's companion for a long time.

At one point during dinner I mentioned my intention of going down to Yarmouth. "I'd be delighted if James would go with me." I said. "I'm going to see my old nurse and her family. James, do you remember the boatman you met at Salem House—Mr. Peggotty? He and his family live in Yarmouth."

"Oh! That good-natured fellow," James said. "Wasn't his son with him?"

"His adopted son, actually his nephew," I replied. "He also has a very pretty niece whom he adopted as a daughter. His house is a barge on dry land. It's full of people indebted to his kindness and generosity. You'd be delighted to meet the household, I think."

"Would I?" James responded. "Well, I'll think about it. It would be interesting to see what such people are like in their own home."

"I would think that they're clods," Miss Dartle commented.

"There's certainly a wide separation between them and us," James said. "We can't expect them to be as sensitive or delicate in their feelings. Some of them might be virtuous, but they don't have fine natures. They're like their coarse, rough skin—not easily wounded."

"Yes. I doubt that they really can suffer at all," Miss Dartle said.

At first I thought that James and Miss Dartle were joking, but no one laughed or even smiled.

Later, when James and I were alone, I asked him how Miss Dartle had gotten her scar. James's face fell, and he paused a moment. "Actually, *I* did that."

"By an unfortunate accident."

"No," James said. "I was a young boy, and she exasperated me, so I threw a hammer at her. As you see, she was permanently scarred. Rosa was the motherless child of a cousin of my father. When her father died, my mother, who was already a widow, brought her here to be company for her. Rosa has her own income: a couple of thousand pounds a year. That's her history."

"I guess she loves you as a brother," I said.

"Hmph!" James responded, looking at the fire. "But, come. Let's have a drink." And he was his merry self again.

Mrs. Steerforth doted on her son. She loved to talk about him. She showed me his picture as an infant, in a locket with some of his baby hair. She showed me his picture as he had been when I first knew him. She wore at her breast a locket that contained his picture as he was now. In a cabinet near her chair by the fire, she kept every letter that he'd ever written to her. "My son tells me that you first met at Mr. Creakle's," she said as she and I were talking at one table while James and Miss Dartle were playing backgammon at another.

"He was very kind and generous to me when I needed a friend, ma'am. I would have been crushed without him."

"He always is kind and generous," Mrs. Steerforth said proudly. "The school was far from suitable for my son, but there were particular circumstances to be considered at the time. My son's high spirits made it desirable to place him with a man who would recognize his superiority and bow before it. Mr. Creakle was such a man. If James had been at all constrained, he would have rebelled. Instead, he was treated like a lord and acted accordingly. My son informs me, Mr. Copperfield, that you were quite devoted to him and that when you met yesterday you made yourself known to him with tears of joy. I'm not surprised that my son inspires such devotion. I'm glad that you appreciate his merit, and I'm very glad to have you here."

When the evening was pretty far spent and a tray of wine decanters and glasses came in, James promised that he would seriously consider going down to Yarmouth with me. There was no hurry, he said; a week hence would do. His mother hospitably said the same.

After Mrs. Steerforth and Miss Dartle went to bed, James and I lingered for half an hour over the fire, talking about Tommy Traddles and all the others at Salem House. Then we went upstairs. James's room was next to mine. I went in to look at it. It was a picture of comfort, full of armchairs, cushions, and footstools. A portrait of his mother hung on the wall.

I found the fire burning clearly in my room, which looked snug. The window curtains had been drawn. I sat down in an armchair by the hearth to meditate on my happiness. Finally I undressed, extinguished my light, and went to bed.

Chapter 22

Before I was out of bed, James's personal servant, Mr. Littimer, was in my room to set out my clothes. About forty years old, he epitomized respectability. He was soft-spoken, deferential, always at hand when wanted, and otherwise inconspicuous. Mr. Littimer had an inexpressive face, a stiff neck, and close-cropped hair. He seemed utterly self-contained. When I opened the bed curtains, I saw him setting my boots upright and blowing specks of dust off my jacket as he laid it down. "Good morning," I said. "Can you tell me what time it is?"

Mr. Littimer took a watch out of his pocket, opened the lid, looked at the time, closed the lid, and said, "It's eight-thirty, sir. Did you rest well?"

"Yes, thank you."

"Is there anything else I can do for you, sir?"

"No. Thank you," I answered.

"A bell will ring at nine," Mr. Littimer said. "The family eats breakfast at nine-thirty. Thank you, sir." With a slight bow he went out, delicately shutting the door.

The week passed delightfully. James gave me riding, fencing, and boxing lessons. He treated me as if I were a plaything, but I didn't mind because he did so in an affectionate way. I rejoiced at the thought that he might come to consider me his closest friend.

James decided to accompany me to Mr. Peggotty's, and the day arrived for our departure. I thanked Mrs. Steerforth and bid Miss Dartle goodbye, and James and I set off for the stagecoach to Yarmouth. Upon our arrival in Yarmouth, we went to bed at an inn. The next morning we ate a late breakfast. James was in high spirits. He had been strolling on the beach before I was up and said that he had made the acquaintance of a number of boatmen. We decided to surprise Mr. Peggotty's household by going there in the evening.

"We'll see the natives in their true condition," James commented. "What are you going to do until then?"

"I want to see Peggotty," I answered.

James looked at his watch. "Suppose I leave you to go and be cried over for a couple of hours. Will that be long enough?"

"I think that should be enough time," I answered, laughing. "Why don't you come meet Peggotty after that?"

James agreed. I gave him directions to the Barkis residence and set out. It was a sunny but crisply cold day. All the streets looked the same as before. When I came to Mr. Omer's shop, the sign now read "Omer and Joram" instead of just "Omer's." The description "Funeral Clothing and Supplies" was the same. Minnie was sitting at the back of the shop, bouncing a little girl in her arms. A little boy clung to her apron. Entering, I asked, "Is Mr. Omer in?"

"Yes, sir," Minnie answered. "Joe, call your grandfather."

The little boy gave a lusty shout, and Mr. Omer soon stood in front of me, panting and wheezing. He didn't remember me until I reminded him of his preparations for the funeral of my mother and her baby. Once he remembered, he was very warm and friendly. "How have you been since?" he asked.

"Very well. Thank you," I answered. "How are you and your family?"

Minnie had married Bob Joram and had the two children I saw before me. "Bob's working on a coffin at the moment," Mr. Omer said.

I heard the hammering out in the yard. "I've come to visit Mrs. Barkis, and Mr. Peggotty and his family," I said.

"Emily Peggotty works for us," Mr. Omer said very quietly. "She makes elegant dresses. She's such a beautiful young woman that half the women in Yarmouth are jealous of her. She hasn't taken much to anyone here in the shop. To my knowledge, she doesn't have any friends or sweethearts. Lots of people think she's a bit spoiled and uppity. She wants to be a lady. But I have no complaints. She's worked here for two years now, and she's done excellent work."

"Is she here now?" I asked.

"Yes." Mr. Omer nodded toward the workroom door. "Go speak to her if you like, sir. Make yourself at home." I walked over to the parlor and looked in. Emily was as beautiful as ever. Feeling too shy to make my presence known to her, I took leave of Mr. Omer and Minnie and headed to Peggotty.

I knocked at the door, and Peggotty opened it. "Peggotty!" I cried.

It had been seven years since Peggotty and I had seen each other, so she hesitated. Then, recognizing me, she cried, "My darling boy!" We both burst into tears and embraced. "Mr. Barkis will be so glad to see you," Peggotty said. "It will do him a world of good. He's in bed with rheumatism. Will you come up and see him, my dear?"

I went upstairs with her. She went in alone to prepare Mr. Barkis and then came out to bring me in. Mr. Barkis received me with enthusiasm. I sat down by the side of his bed. "It does me a world of good to see you," he said. "I feel as if I'm driving you to Blunderstone again." He lay in bed completely covered except for his face. "What name did I write on the cart, sir?" he asked with a smile.

"Ah," I said. "We had some serious talks about that matter, didn't we?"

"I was willing a long time," he said, "and I don't regret it. Do you remember your telling me that Clara made all the apple pastries and did all the cooking?"

"I remember very well," I replied.

"Clara Peggotty Barkis is the best and most useful woman in the world. She deserves all the praise that anyone can give her and more." He said to Peggotty, "My dear, you'll prepare a special dinner today, something special to eat and drink, won't you?"

I was about to protest that they shouldn't go to any trouble on my account when I saw that Peggotty, on the opposite side of the bed, didn't want me to object.

"Clara," Mr. Barkis said, "take a guinea from the box." Peggotty kneeled down to take a box from under the bed and removed a guinea. "I'm feeling tired," Mr. Barkis said. "If you and Mr. David will leave me for a short nap, I'll rest a bit."

Peggotty and I left the room. I prepared her for James's arrival. He soon came. His high spirits, friendly manner, and handsome looks completely won Peggotty over. James visited Mr. Barkis in his bedroom, and Peggotty, James, and I had dinner together. Then we made merry in the little parlor. When Peggotty spoke of what she called "Davy's room," of its being ready for me at night, and of her hope that I'd occupy it, James said to me, "You must sleep here while I sleep at the inn."

"But to bring you so far and then separate seems like bad companionship, James," I said.

"This is where you belong," he insisted.

At 8:00 James and I set out for Mr. Peggotty's house. We walked over the dark, wintry sands toward the old barge. The wind sighed around us. "This is a wild kind of place, isn't it, James?" I said.

"Dismal enough in the dark," he answered. "And the sea roars as if it were hungry for us. Is that the barge over there, where I see a light?"

"Yes."

We said no more as we approached the light. A murmur of voices was audible from the outside.

I knocked on the door. Ham opened it and cried, "Master Davy! It's Master Davy!"

In a moment we all were shaking hands with one another and asking, "How are you?" Laughing with joy, Mr. Peggotty kept shaking hands with me, then with James, and then with me again. "That you two gentlemen have come here tonight of all nights!" he said. "Emily, my darling, come here. Here's Master Davy's friend. He's the gentleman you've heard about." Turning back to me, Mr. Peggotty said, "This is the happiest night of my life. This very night Emily has agreed to marry Ham, who first proposed two years ago. I can't imagine any man could love her more or with a truer, braver heart."

Embarrassed but pleased, Ham said, "I've loved her ever since we were children, Master Davy. I'd cheerfully lay down my life for her. She's more to me, gentlemen, than I ever could say. I love her as much as any man ever loved any woman."

I was very moved, and happy for Ham and Emily. James said, "Ham and Emily, congratulations."

Emily blushed and seemed very shy. James and Mr. Peggotty talked about boats, ships, tides, and fishes, and we soon were all at ease. Emily said very little all evening, but she looked and listened. Much of the time her eyes were fastened on James. He was charming. He told humorous stories that made everyone laugh. He even sang a sailor's song, beautifully. When Emily grew more courageous, she talked across the fire to me of our old wanderings on the beach. I asked her if she remembered how devoted to her I had been, and we both laughed and reddened. When Emily and I talked, James watched both of us closely. Although Emily sat next to Ham, she leaned away from him.

We had dried fish and biscuits for supper. James and I didn't leave until about midnight. All members of the Peggotty household stood crowded around the door as we walked away. Emily's blue eyes peeped after us from behind Ham, and she called to us to be careful.

"A most engaging little beauty," James said. "It's a quaint place, and they're quaint company. It's quite a new sensation to mix with such people."

"And how fortunate we are to have come just when Ham and Emily announced their engagement!" I said.

"He seems like something of a knucklehead, don't you think?" James responded. "He doesn't seem up to such a girl."

At first I was shocked. Then I said, "Come now, James, you may talk that way, but I know that you delight in their happiness. It was clear tonight that you have empathy for even the poorest people."

James laughed and then started to sing. We walked briskly.

Chapter 23

James and I stayed in Yarmouth two weeks. He was a much better sailor than I, so he sometimes went boating with Mr. Peggotty while I remained ashore. I continued to sleep at Peggotty's while James continued to sleep at the inn. On some days we went our separate ways after breakfast and didn't meet again until supper.

I sometimes went to Blunderstone to visit my parents' graves or visit someone, such as Dr. Chillip, who had been kind to me. There were changes in my old home. The windows were shuttered, and the garden had run wild. The house was occupied by an elderly lunatic and the people who took care of him. The last part of my return to Yarmouth was by ferry. The ferry landed me on the flats between the town and the sea. I then walked straight across the flats. Along the way I always looked in at Mr. Peggotty's house. James was all but certain to be there, expecting me. Then we went on together through the frosty air and gathering fog toward the town's twinkling lights. One dark evening when I was later than usual, I found James alone in the barge, sitting thoughtfully in front of the fire.

"You're so late!" he said when I entered. "Where have you been?"

"Saying goodbye to Blunderstone."

"David, I wish to God I'd had a wise father to guide me these past twenty years."

"My dear James, what's the matter?" I asked.

"I wish with all my soul that I'd been better guided!" he exclaimed. "I wish I could guide *myself* better." There was a passionate dejection in his manner that amazed me. I'd never seen him in such a state. Getting up and leaning against the mantel with his face toward the fire, he said, "I'd rather be this poor Daniel Peggotty or his lout of a nephew than be myself, twenty times richer and twenty times wiser."

"What on earth has happened?" I pressed.

He gave a laugh. "It's nothing."

"Where is everyone?"

"Who knows?" James replied. "After going to the ferry to look for you, I strolled in here and found the place deserted."

We left, and James soon was his usual self. "So, we abandon this buccaneer life tomorrow," he said merrily. "I enjoyed the boating so much that I've bought a boat here."

"What? When you may never even be here again?"

"I've taken a fancy to the place. I bought a clipper. Mr. Peggotty will take care of it in my absence."

"Now I understand you, James," I said with joy. "You pretend to have bought the boat for yourself, but you've really bought it as a present for

Mr. Peggotty. My dear James, thank you so much for your generosity."

"Tush," he answered. "The less said, the better. The boat's name was *Stormy Petrel*. I had it repainted to be *Emily*. But here comes the real Emily," he said. "And there's her true knight, who never leaves her."

Ham had matured into a skilled boat builder. He was in his work clothes and looked very rugged. His face glowed with pride in and love for the woman at his side. As James and I stopped to speak to them, Emily removed her hand from Ham's arm and blushed as she gave it to James and me. When she and Ham passed on, she didn't take his arm again. Instead they walked without touching.

James and I had supper at the inn and then sat talking. We parted for the night, and I headed to Peggotty's. When I arrived, I was surprised to find Ham pacing in front of the house.

"Ham! What are you doing here?"

"Emily's inside, Master Davy," he said. "She's talking to a young woman named Martha Endell who used to work at Mr. Omer's. Martha's a few years older than Emily and was at school with her. Martha came to the house. She wanted to talk to Emily, but she hurried away when Mr. Peggotty was coming home. He wouldn't have wanted her there because . . . " Ham hesitated. "She got into trouble with a man."

"I see," I said.

"Most of the people in Yarmouth won't have anything to do with Martha now. Before Martha hurried away, Emily told her to meet her here. Later Emily told me what had happened and asked me to come here with her. So here I am. I'm not comfortable about Emily being with such a woman, but how could I refuse Emily's request?"

I now paced with Ham for a few minutes. Then the door opened, and Peggotty appeared, beckoning us to come in. Martha was near the fire. She was sitting on the ground, with her head and one arm lying on a chair. Emily appeared to have just risen from the chair. Martha's hair fell loose and scattered. She had a fair complexion. I could see that Peggotty and Emily had been crying. Not a word was spoken when we first entered. The table clock by the dresser seemed, in the silence, to tick twice as loudly as usual.

Emily spoke first. "Martha wants to go to London," she said to Ham.

"Why to London?" Ham asked.

"Better there than here," Martha answered. "No one knows me there. Everyone knows me here."

"What will she do there?" Ham asked, again addressing Emily.

"If you'll help me to leave, I'll try to do better," Martha said.

Emily took out a small purse and gave it to Martha. "Will that be enough?" she asked softly.

Martha opened the purse, looked inside, and said, "More than enough." She took Emily's hand and kissed it. Then she rose and gathered her shawl around her, covering her face. Weeping aloud, she slowly went to the door. She stopped a moment before going out, as if she were going to say something or turn back, but then she left.

As the door closed, Emily started to sob. "Don't, Emily," Ham said, gently touching her shoulder. "Don't, my dear."

"Oh, Ham!" she cried. She then did what I never had seen her do before. She kissed Ham on the cheek and pressed against him, as if for support. When they left, she held his arm with both hands and stayed close to him.

Chapter 24

The next morning at breakfast I was handed a letter from my aunt. She said that she would be waiting for me in London at a particular hotel. James and I parted from the Barkises and Peggottys. We had a pleasant coach trip, at the end of which he went home and I drove to the hotel indicated by my aunt. I found her there, with Janet, awaiting supper. My aunt wept with joy as she embraced me.

"Mr. Dick stayed behind, Aunt?" I asked.

"Yes," she answered.

"How are you, Janet?" I asked.

Janet curtsied. "Fine, sir. I hope you're well."

Later in the evening I made my aunt a glass of hot wine and water and a slice of toast cut into thin strips. She sat opposite me drinking her wine and water, soaking her strips of toast in it before eating them, and looking at me affectionately. "Well, Davy," she said, "what profession do you think is right for you?"

"I don't know," I answered.

My aunt proposed that I become a proctor, a lawyer specializing in marriages and wills. She suggested that she and I go to Doctors' Commons, the ecclesiastical court where such matters were attended to and proctors were trained. Having nothing against being a proctor, I agreed to consider that profession. My aunt then told me that my training would cost £1,000.

"You've been so generous to me, Aunt. I really don't want you investing so much in my training," I protested. "Surely I can try my hand at something less expensive."

"Now, now, Davy. You've been nothing but a credit and a pleasure to me. I want you to be a fine, self-reliant, happy man. Nothing could give me more satisfaction. Please let me do this. Besides, proctors make good money. It's a sound investment."

Seeing that my aunt clearly wanted me to accept her generous offer, I agreed.

About noon the next day, we set out for the law offices of Spenlow & Jorkins, in Doctors' Commons. We were almost there when my aunt looked frightened and greatly increased her speed. An ill-dressed man who had stopped and stared at us was hurriedly coming up to us. "Davy!" my aunt whispered in terror as she pressed my arm. "I don't know what to do."

"Don't be alarmed," I said. "Step into a shop, and I'll get rid of this man."

"No! No, child. Don't speak to him. I order you!"

"Good heavens, Aunt! He's nothing but a beggar," I said.

"You don't know what he is!" my aunt replied. We stopped in an empty doorway, and the man stopped, too. "Don't look at him," my aunt said. "Get me a cab, and wait for me outside Spenlow & Jorkins."

"Wait for you?"

"Yes. I have to go with him," she said.

"With that man?" I cried, aghast.

"I know what I'm doing," she said. "I tell you, I have to. Get me a cab."

Astonished, I hurried away a few paces and hailed an empty cab that was about to pass. Almost before I could let the steps down, my aunt sprang in, and the man followed. She waved her hand to me to go away. I heard her say to the driver, "Drive anywhere." And the cab set off. I now remembered what Mr. Dick had told me about a man who lurked by the house and frightened my aunt.

After I had waited outside Spenlow & Jorkins for half an hour, the cab returned. My aunt was sitting alone in it. Still agitated, she asked me to get in and told the driver to drive slowly up and down awhile. "My dear child," she said, "never ask me who that man was, and don't refer to this incident." After a while she said, "I'm myself now. We can get out."

We entered the central room of Spenlow & Jorkins. It had a high ceiling and a skylight. Several clerks sat copying legal documents. One of these, a dry little man who sat by himself and wore a stiff brown wig, rose to receive us and show us into Mr. Spenlow's office. "Mr. Spenlow has just returned from court," he said. "He'll be right with you. Please make yourselves comfortable." He left.

The room's furniture was old-fashioned and dusty. The green felt desk pad was withered and pale. There were many bundles of papers on the desk. Mr. Spenlow, wearing a black gown trimmed with white fur, hurried in, taking off his hat as he entered. He was a small, light-haired gentleman with a stiff white cravat and stiff shirt collar. His whiskers were carefully curled. His gold watch chain was massive. After mutually courteous introductions, he said, "So, Mr. Copperfield, you are thinking of entering our profession. When I spoke to Miss Trotwood the other day, I mentioned that we have a vacancy here."

"I'm very agreeable to that, sir," I said, "although I'd like to see if the profession suits me before I commit to it."

"Surely," he responded. "We always have a trial month. During that time if you decide that the profession doesn't suit you, you'll be under no financial obligation."

It was settled that I would begin as soon as I pleased. Mr. Spenlow offered to take me to the courtroom then and there and show me what sort of place it was. So the three of us went out. Mr. Spenlow led us through a paved courtyard surrounded by grave brick houses and into a large, drab room. The room's upper part was fenced off from the rest. On each side of a horseshoe-shaped platform, gentlemen in red gowns and gray wigs sat on chairs of the type used at dining-room tables. The presiding judge, an elderly gentleman who looked like an owl, sat blinking over a little pulpit-like desk in the horseshoe's curve. Below, gentlemen of Mr. Spenlow's rank, in black gowns with white fur, sat at a long green table. They looked haughty and stiff but always answered the judge in a quiet, timid way. A shabby, genteel man furtively eating crumbs out of his coat pockets and a young boy were warming themselves at a stove in the center of the courtroom. The place's languid stillness was broken only by the crackling of this fire and the voice of one of the attorneys, who was slowly wandering through a library of evidence. Satisfied with the situation, I soon informed Mr. Spenlow that I had seen enough for now.

My aunt and I returned to our hotel, where we had a long talk about my plans. She said, "There's a small furnished apartment for rent in the Adelphi, Davy. I think it would suit you perfectly." She took an advertisement, cut out of a newspaper, from her pocket and showed it to me. The flat was on Buckingham Street, with a view of the river. We went off again to look at the apartment. We rang the bell several times before the housekeeper, Mrs. Crupp, appeared. She was a stout lady in a cotton dress. "We'd like to see the apartment, please," my aunt said.

"For this gentleman?" Mrs. Crupp asked, feeling in her pocket for her keys.

"Yes," my aunt answered.

The apartment was at the top of the house. It consisted of a little entryway, small pantry, sitting room, and bedroom. The furniture was rather faded. Sure enough, the river was outside the windows. I was delighted with the place, so my aunt and Mrs. Crupp withdrew to the pantry to discuss the terms while I remained on the living room sofa.

They returned. My aunt rented the apartment for a month, with the option of then renting for another eleven months. Mrs. Crupp was to keep me provided with clean bed and bath linen and to cook my meals. I was to take possession in two days.

On our way back to the hotel, my aunt said, "I trust that your new life will make you firm and self-reliant, Davy." The next day I saw her safely seated in the Dover coach with Janet at her side. When the coach was gone, I turned my face toward my new home.

Chapter 25

During the day it was a fine thing to walk around London with the key to my apartment in my pocket and to know that I could invite anyone to my apartment. It was a fine thing to let myself in and out and to come and go without a word to anyone. At night, however, I felt lonely. I missed Agnes.

On the third day, I left Spenlow & Jorkins early and walked to Highgate to visit James. Mrs. Steerforth was very glad to see me. She said that James had gone away with one of his Oxford friends to visit someone who lived near St. Albans, but that she expected him to return the next day. She pressed me to stay for dinner, so I did. We talked about James the whole day. I told Mrs. Steerforth how much the people at Yarmouth had liked him and what a delightful companion he'd been.

The next morning I was having my breakfast, before going to Spenlow & Jorkins, when James walked in. Delighted, I said, "My dear James, I began to think I'd never see you again."

Looking around, he said, "I see you have your own bachelor pad now."

With no small pride I showed him the whole apartment. "Have some breakfast," I said.

"No. I can't. I'm meeting two fellows for breakfast."

"Will you come back for dinner?"

"I can't. I have to stay with them. The three of us are off again tomorrow morning."

"Then, bring them here to dinner," I said.

"That would inconvenience you."

"Not at all." I made James promise to bring his two friends to my apartment for dinner at 6:00.

When he was gone, I rang for Mrs. Crupp. She recommended a man who could serve the meal and a woman who could wash the dishes. She also recommended that I purchase all of the following, already prepared: stewed beef, two roasted chickens, vegetables, tarts, and a jelly mold. She would prepare potatoes, cheese, and celery. I took her advice. I also asked a wine store to deliver a dozen bottles of wine. When I came home in the afternoon, I saw the bottles standing together on the pantry floor.

Around 6:00 James arrived with his friends Grainger and Markham, who were lively fellows about twenty years old. Referring to my apartment, Markham said, "A man might get on very well here, Copperfield."

Dinner was excellent, and we didn't spare the wine. The more I drank, the merrier and more talkative I became. Then we all smoked, and I started to feel sick. Someone said, "Let's go to the theater, Copperfield!" James, Grainger, and Markham all seemed to be in a mist and far away.

"Absolutely," I said. I started to feel my way to the door but ended up in the window curtains. Laughing, James took me by the arm and led me out. We went down the stairs. Near the bottom, someone fell and rolled down the rest of the way. Someone else said it was Copperfield. I was angry at the slander until I realized that I was lying on my back in the passage.

The night seemed very foggy. There were great mists around the street lamps. There was indistinct talk of its being wet. I considered it frosty. James dusted me off under a lamp post and put my hat, which someone produced from somewhere, onto my head. He said, "Are you all right, David"?

I answered, "Never berrer."

At the theater a man in a booth looked out of the fog and took money from someone, inquiring if I was one of the gentlemen paid for. Soon afterwards my companions and I were very high up in a very hot theater looking down into a large pit, which seemed smoky because the people crammed into it were so indistinct. There was a large stage, and there were people on it talking about something. There were bright lights, music, and I don't know what else. The whole building looked as if it were learning to swim. I tried to steady it. Someone suggested that we go downstairs to the boxes occupied by formally attired ladies and gentlemen. One such gentleman, lounging on a sofa with an opera glass in his hand, passed before my view. I also saw myself in a full-length mirror. Ushered into one of the boxes, I found myself saying something as I sat down. People around me cried, "Silence!" Ladies glanced at me indignantly. And—

what?—Agnes was sitting in the seat in front of me, in the same box, with a lady and gentleman beside her whom I didn't know. She looked at me with wonder and regret.

"Agnes!" I said thickly. "Lor' bless me! Agnes!"

"Hush! Please," she answered. I couldn't imagine why. "You're disturbing people." She shrank into her corner and put her gloved hand to her forehead.

"Agnes!" I said. "I'm afraid you're nor well."

"I'm fine, David," she said. "I think you should leave."

"You thin' I sood leeb?" I asked.

"Yes."

I told her I was going to wait to escort her downstairs. She looked at me and quietly said, "I know you'll do as I ask you if I tell you I'm very earnest about it. Go away now, David, for my sake. Ask your friends to take you home."

Saying "Goo ni" (which I intended to be "Good night"), I got up and went away. My companions followed. I stepped out of the box door directly into my bedroom. Only James was with me, helping me to undress. I alternately talked about Agnes and told him to open another bottle of wine.

That night someone lay in my bed in a feverish dream. The bed continually rocked. The someone slowly materialized into myself. I started to feel as if my skin were a board, my tongue were burning, and the palms of my hands were hot plates.

But the agony, the remorse, the shame that I felt when I awoke! Remembering the look on Agnes's face, I felt horror. And—oh—my painful head! The smell of smoke permeated the room. There were wine bottles and glasses all around. It seemed impossible for me to go out or even get up. In the evening I sat down by my fire to a bowl of mutton broth, dimpled all over with fat, and thought that I was dying.

The next morning, I was just going out when I a courier came upstairs with a letter in his hand. "Mr. David Copperfield?" he asked.

"Yes," I said.

He gave me the letter, which he said required an answer. Shutting him out on the landing, I went back into my apartment. I opened the envelope to find a note from Agnes:

> My dear David,
>
> I'm staying at the house of Papa's agent Mr. Waterbrook, at 42 Ely Place, Holborn. Will you come and see me today at any time you'd like to appoint?
>
> Ever yours affectionately,
> Agnes

Feeling enormously grateful that she hadn't berated me for my drunken behavior at the theater, I responded:

> My dear Agnes,
>
> Your letter is just like you, and what could I say of it that would be higher praise than that? I'll come at 4:00.
>
> Affectionately and sorrowfully,
> D.C.

I gave my reply to the courier, and he left.

I worked at Spenlow & Jorkins until 3:30 and then went to Mr. Waterbrook's house. I was shown into a pretty but rather small parlor. There sat Agnes, knitting a purse. She looked so quiet and good, and I was so overcome by shame and self-reproach, that I made a fool of myself: I wept. "If it had been anyone but you, Agnes," I said, turning my head away, "I wouldn't have minded half as much. But it was *you* who saw me. I almost wish I'd died first." She put her hand on my arm for a moment. I felt so befriended and comforted that I gratefully kissed her hand.

"Sit down," Agnes said cheerfully. "Don't be unhappy, David. If you can't trust me, whom *can* you trust?"

"Oh, Agnes! You're my good angel."

She smiled—rather sadly, I thought—and shook her head.

"Yes. You're my good angel."

"Then, let me warn you against your *bad* angel," she said, looking at me steadily.

"My dear Agnes, if you mean James Steerforth . . ."

"I do, David."

"Then you wrong him. He never could be anyone's bad angel. He never could be anything but a guide, support, and friend. It isn't like you to judge him based on what you saw the other night."

"I don't judge him based on only that," she replied quietly.

"On what, then?"

"On many things. I judge him partly based on your account of him, David, and your character, and the influence he has over you."

I sat looking at her as she cast her eyes down on her work.

Looking up again, she said, "I know very little of the world, so it's bold of me to give you advice so confidently or even to have this strong opinion. But I speak as I do because I care so much about you and because I'm quite certain that I'm right. I warn you: your friend is dangerous. I'm not so unreasonable as to expect that you can immediately change your feelings toward him. And I know that your disposition is a naturally trusting one. I only ask that you always keep my warning in mind."

Still loyal to James, I changed the subject. "Will you forgive me for the other night?"

"When I recall it," she said.

She would have dismissed the subject, but I insisted on telling her how it happened that I had disgraced myself. It relieved me to do this.

Then it was Agnes who changed the subject. "Have you seen Uriah?"

"Uriah Heep? No. Is he in London?"

"Yes—on disagreeable business, I'm afraid."

"On some business that makes you uneasy, I see. What is it, Agnes?"

She laid her work aside, put one hand on top of the other, and looked at me pensively with her beautiful, soft eyes. "I think he's going to become Papa's partner."

"What? That mean, fawning fellow?" I cried indignantly. "Haven't you spoken out against the partnership, Agnes? Consider what a connection it's likely to be. You must speak out. You mustn't allow your father to take such an unwise step. You must prevent it while there's still time."

Agnes shook her head while I was speaking, with a faint smile at my warmth. "Do you remember our last conversation about Papa? A few days later he indicated that he might let Uriah become his partner. Uriah forced him into it, David. He has cultivated Papa's weaknesses and exploited them. Papa fears him. Uriah professes humility and gratitude, but his position really is one of power. He told Papa that he was going to leave, because he could do better elsewhere, unless Papa made him a partner. Papa was afraid that he couldn't manage without Uriah, and so was I. I actually supported Papa in his decision. Oh, David! I almost feel as if I were Papa's enemy instead of his loving child. I wish I could set this right!" She started to cry.

I never had seen Agnes cry before. "Please, Agnes, don't! Don't, my dear sister."

She quickly regained her usual calm manner. "Please be friendly to Uriah, David. I don't know any certain ill of him."

"He's a scoundrel."

The door opened, and Mrs. Waterbrook came sailing in. I had a dim recollection of having seen her at the theater. Clearly, she remembered me. At first she looked at me somewhat harshly, but she gradually softened and ended up inviting me to dinner the next day. I accepted and took my leave.

The next day I arrived at the Waterbrooks' for dinner. Mr. Waterbrook was a middle-aged gentleman with a short neck and large shirt collar. He looked like a pug. He told me, "I'm happy and honored to make your acquaintance." When I had paid my respects to Mrs. Waterbrook, Mr. Waterbrook presented me with much ceremony to Mrs. Spiker, a lady in a black velvet dress and a large black velvet hat. Her husband was there, too. Mr. Spiker was a cold man, a prominent lawyer.

Uriah Heep was there, in a black suit. When I shook hands with him, he said, "I'm proud to be noticed by you, Master Copperfield." He hovered about me the rest of the evening. Whenever I said a word to Agnes, Uriah was sure to be watching us.

When I heard that a "Mr. Traddles" was present, I became excited, wondering if the man was my old schoolmate Tommy. I looked for him and found a steady-looking young man, with comically unruly hair and wide-open eyes, standing shyly in a corner. It was, indeed, Tommy. I asked Mr. Waterbrook about him. He said that Tommy was studying to become a lawyer. "He's quite a good fellow. A professional friend recommended him to me. Traddles has a talent for writing legal briefs. He can state a case in plain language."

Dinner was announced. Mr. Waterbrook took Mrs. Spiker's arm and escorted her into the dining room. Mr. Spiker escorted Mrs. Waterbrook. I would have liked to escort Agnes, but a simpering fellow with weak legs took her arm. Being the youngest men, Uriah, Tommy, and I were the last to enter the dining room. I made myself known to Tommy, and he greeted me with great delight. Tommy and I sat far apart at the dinner table. The dinner was very long, and the conversation was largely about the aristocracy and breeding. Mrs. Waterbrook repeatedly emphasized the importance of good breeding, a quality that she regarded as exclusive to the most privileged members of society and that she considered far more important than intelligence or service to others.

I was greatly relieved when the boring dinner ended and I was able to talk with Agnes. I introduced Tommy to her. He was as good-natured as ever. He had to leave early because he was going away the next morning for a month, so we didn't talk nearly as much as I would have liked. But we exchanged addresses and promised to get together when he returned to London. It was a great delight to talk with Agnes and hear her sing. Knowing that she would be leaving in a few days, I stayed until nearly all of the other guests had gone. I took my leave only when it would have been rude to stay longer.

Uriah was close behind me when I prepared to leave and close beside me when I walked away from the house. I didn't want his company, but I remembered Agnes's request that I be nice to him, so I invited him to my apartment for coffee.

"Oh, really, Master Copperfield," he said, "I don't want you to trouble yourself for someone as 'umble as me."

"It's no trouble. Will you come?"

"I'd like to very much," he said with a writhe.

We took the shortest route and didn't speak much along the way. I led Uriah up the dark stairs to my fireside. When I lit candles, he fell into meek transports about the room. I served him coffee, and he said, "Oh, Master—I mean, Mister—Copperfield, I never could have expected to see you waiting on me! But so much has happened to me that was unexpected. Have you heard about the change in my prospects?" He sat on my sofa with his long knees drawn up under his coffee cup, his hat and gloves on the floor, and his spoon going round and round inside his cup. His red, seemingly lashless eyes turned toward me without looking at me.

"Yes," I answered, hating him.

"Ah. I thought that Miss Agnes would know about it," he said. "Do you remember saying to me once that perhaps someday I'd be a partner in Mr. Wickfield's business?"

"Yes, I remember."

"It just goes to show, Mr. Copperfield, that even the 'umblest people can be instruments of good. I'm glad to think that I've been an instrument of good to Mr. Wickfield and that I may be more so. He's such a worthy man. But he's been imprudent."

"Has he?"

"Yes. Very imprudent indeed. I wouldn't say this to anyone but you. If anyone else had been in my place during the last few years, he would have had Mr. Wickfield completely under his thumb by now. Mr. Wickfield would have faced loss and disgrace. I'm his 'umble servant. You won't think the worse of my 'umbleness if I share a secret with you, will you, Mr. Copperfield?"

"No."

"Thank you." He took out his pocket handkerchief and began wiping the palms of his hands. "Didn't you think that Miss Agnes looked beautiful tonight, Mr. Copperfield?"

"I thought that she looked as she always does: superior in every way to everyone around her," I replied.

"Oh, thank you!"

Irritated, I said, "I don't see why you should thank me."

"Well, that's what I wanted to tell you," Uriah replied. "The image of Miss Agnes has been in my 'umble breast for years. I love the ground my Agnes walks on."

I was so horrified and shocked that I felt dizzy for a moment. Somehow I managed to calm myself enough to ask, "Have you made your feelings known to Miss Agnes?"

"Oh no, Mr. Copperfield! Oh dear, no. Not to anyone but you. You see, I'm only just emerging from my lowly station. I rest a good deal of hope on her observing how useful I am to her father. She's so attached to her father that I think she may come, on his account, to be kind to me. If you would be good enough to keep my secret and not do anything to stand in the way, I'd take it as a special favor. You wouldn't want to create any unpleasantness. Having known me only at my 'umblest, you might decide to go against me with my Agnes. I call her mine, you see. There's a song that goes, 'I'd crowns resign to call her mine.' I hope to do it one of these days. My Agnes still is very young, and Mother and me will have to work our way upwards and make many new arrangements before it would be quite convenient. So I'll have time to gradually make her aware of my hopes. Oh, I'm much obliged to you for this confidence! It's such a relief to know that you understand our situation and are certain not to go against me."

He offered his damp hand, and I felt I had to shake it. Then he left.

I had trouble sleeping that night. I kept thinking about Agnes and Uriah. I considered what I should do and reached the conclusion that revealing Uriah's intentions would only upset Agnes, so I decided to say nothing.

Chapter 26

The day of Agnes's departure from London, I went to the stagecoach office to see her off. Uriah was there, returning to Canterbury by the same coach. It was some small consolation to me to see his purple coat and umbrella on the back seat on the coach's roof, indicating that he would ride on the outside. Agnes already was seated inside the coach, so I spoke to her through the coach window. As at the dinner party, Uriah hovered about Agnes and me, listening to every word that we exchanged. When the coach departed, Agnes waved her hand and smiled farewell from the window while Uriah sat on the roof.

When I wasn't at Spenlow & Jorkins, I was alone. I corresponded with Agnes and James. At the end of my trial month at Spenlow & Jorkins, I stayed on at the law firm and rented my apartment for another eleven months. To celebrate my commitment to becoming a proctor, I had sandwiches and sherry delivered to the office for the clerks. Mr. Spenlow said that he would have invited me to his house to celebrate except that he was busy preparing for the return of his daughter, who had completed her education in Paris. He said that he hoped I'd come over after her return. I thanked him. I knew that he was a widower with one child.

A week later, Mr. Spenlow invited me to his house in Norwood for the weekend. He would drive me there in his carriage and bring me back. I happily accepted the invitation. When the day arrived, the clerks regarded me with awe and envy because I was going to Mr. Spenlow's house. One of them said he'd heard that Mr. Spenlow always ate off china plates. Another hinted that champagne was constantly available. Mr. Tiffey, an elderly clerk who wore a wig, had been to Mr. Spenlow's house several times in the course of his career, on business. Each time, he had seen the dining room. He described it as a sumptuous room in which he had drunk the highest-quality sherry. Mr. Spenlow and I drove off in a handsome carriage. The horses arched their necks and lifted their legs high. Mr. Spenlow and I had a very pleasant conversation along the way. He gave me some advice on my profession, which he considered to be the most genteel in the world. Then we talked about the court until we arrived at his house.

The house had a beautifully kept garden, a charming lawn, clusters of trees, and walks overarched with trellis work on which shrubs and flowers grew in season. Upon entering the house, which was cheerfully lit, we came into a hall with all sorts of coats, hats, gloves, whips, and walking sticks. "Where is Miss Dora?" Mr. Spenlow asked the servant. We turned into a nearby room, and Mr. Spenlow said, "Mr. Copperfield, my daughter

Dora." I found Dora Spenlow so beautiful that I instantly fell passionately in love with her. I bowed and murmured something. Mr. Spenlow continued, "And her companion Miss Murdstone."

Miss Murdstone! As I was absorbing this extremely unwelcome surprise, Miss Murdstone said, "I have seen Mr. Copperfield before."

"How do you do, Miss Murdstone?" I managed to say. "I hope you're well."

"Very well," she answered.

"How is Mr. Murdstone?"

"My brother is very well, thank you."

Mr. Spenlow said, "I'm glad to find, Copperfield, that you and Miss Murdstone are already acquainted."

"Mr. Copperfield and I were acquainted in his childhood days," Miss Murdstone said with severe composure. "Circumstances have separated us since then. I wouldn't have recognized him."

"I would have known *you* anywhere," I said.

"Miss Murdstone has had the goodness to accept the position of my daughter's companion," Mr. Spenlow said to me. "My daughter has no mother, so Miss Murdstone has agreed to provide a woman's companionship and guidance."

A bell rang. "That's the first dinner bell," Mr. Spenlow informed me. "I'll show you to your room."

When Mr. Spenlow left me there, I sat thinking about captivating, girlish, bright-eyed, lovely Dora. Her face, her figure, and her graceful manner all enchanted me. The bell rang again so soon that

I scrambled into my dinner clothes and hurried downstairs. There was some company. Dora was talking to a gray-haired gentleman. I felt madly jealous. But then I was seated next to Dora. I talked to her. She had the most delightful little voice, the gayest little laugh, and the most pleasant and fascinating little ways. When she left the room with Miss Murdstone, I worried that Miss Murdstone might disparage me to her.

When we went into the drawing room, Miss Murdstone said to me, "David Copperfield, a word." We stood apart, and she said, "I need not enlarge upon family circumstances. They aren't an appealing subject."

"Far from it, ma'am," I returned.

"Yes," she agreed. "I don't wish to revive the memory of past differences. I won't deny that I formed an unfavorable opinion of you in your childhood. It may have been a mistaken one, or you may have ceased to justify it. That is not an issue now. I may have my opinion of you. You may have your opinion of me."

I nodded.

"It isn't necessary that these opinions cause any unpleasantness here," she said. "Under the current circumstances it would be better if they didn't. It would be best if we didn't speak about each other. Do you agree?"

"Miss Murdstone," I said, "I think that you and Mr. Murdstone used me very cruelly and treated my mother with great unkindness. I'll always think so. But I quite agree with your proposal."

Miss Murdstone shut her eyes and bent her head. Then she walked away, arranging the little fetters on her wrists and around her neck. They seemed to be the same set, in exactly the same state, as when I'd last seen her.

For the rest of the evening I listened to Dora sing French ballads, accompanying herself on a small guitar. I was in bliss. When Miss Murdstone led Dora away, Dora smiled at me and gave me her hand.

The next morning on my way through the hall, I encountered Dora's snub-nosed, little black dog, Jip. I approached him tenderly, but he bared his teeth and growled. I walked out to the garden, which was cool and solitary. I walked around, imagining how happy I'd be if I ever became engaged to Dora. I hadn't been walking long when I turned a corner and encountered her. "You're out early, Miss Spenlow," I said.

"It's so stupid at home," she replied, "and Miss Murdstone is so absurd! She talks such nonsense about its being necessary for the day to be aired before I come out. Aired!" She laughed. "I told Papa last night that I must come out early in the morning. It's the brightest time of the whole day, don't you think?"

I stammered, "Yes. It's very bright at this time and much brighter since you appeared."

"Do you intend that as a compliment, or do you mean that the weather has changed since I came out?" Dora asked.

"I meant that it seems brighter to *me*." I thought that her curls were the most beautiful I'd ever seen and that her straw hat with blue ribbons was the loveliest hat I'd ever seen. "You've just come home from Paris?"

"Yes. Have you ever been there?"

"No."

"Oh. I hope you'll go soon. You'd like it so much," she said.

The thought that she wanted me to go somewhere far away from her filled me with anguish. I said, "I wouldn't leave England now for anything!"

Jip came running up to us, barking at me. Dora took him up in her arms and caressed him, but he continued to bark. Jip wouldn't let me touch him when I tried. Dora patted his blunt nose as a scolding, but he continued to growl. Finally he was quiet, and we walked away to look at a greenhouse.

"You aren't at all close to Miss Murdstone, are you?" Dora asked.

"No," I replied. "Not at all."

"She's a tiresome creature," Dora said, pouting. "I don't know what Papa was thinking when he chose such an annoying thing to be my companion. Who wants a protector? I certainly don't. Jip can protect me much better than Miss Murdstone, can't you, Jip dear?" She kissed the top of his head. "Papa calls her my confidential friend. She's no such thing, is she, Jip? Jip and I aren't going to confide in such a cross person. We'll bestow our confidence where we like and find our own friends, won't we, Jip? It's very hard that we should have a sulky, gloomy old thing like Miss Murdstone always following us around, isn't it, Jip?"

The greenhouse contained beautiful geraniums. We loitered in front of them. Dora often stopped to admire one, and I stopped to admire the same one. Laughing, Dora childishly held Jip up in her slender arms to smell the flowers. Miss Murdstone had been looking for us. She found us in the greenhouse and presented her uncongenial cheek, the little wrinkles in it filled with powder, to Dora to be kissed. Then she took Dora's arm in hers and marched us into breakfast. After breakfast we went to church, where Miss Murdstone sat between Dora and me.

We had a quiet day: no company, a walk, a family dinner of four, and an evening of looking over books and pictures. Miss Murdstone kept her eye on Dora and me. When Mr. Spenlow sat opposite me after dinner, he had no idea how fervently I was, in my imagination, embracing him as his son-in-law.

Mr. Spenlow and I left early the next morning. In the carriage I had the melancholy pleasure of taking my hat off to Dora as she stood on the doorstep with Jip in her arms.

Day after day, week after week I thought of Dora. The first week of my passion, I bought four fancy vests, new boots, and straw-colored kid gloves in anticipation of the next time that Dora would see me. I took to walking to Norwood Road in the hope of encountering her. In the same hope, I walked on the streets with the best ladies' shops. Every so often I saw her. I saw her glove waved in a carriage window. Or I met her, walked with Miss Murdstone and her a little way, and spoke to her. I kept hoping for another invitation to Mr. Spenlow's house.

Chapter 27

I decided to visit Tommy Traddles. He lived on a little street in Camden Town. The street was littered. The houses all looked alike. I arrived at the door as a servant girl opened it to a milkman.

"Now," the milkman said to her, "will you pay me what I'm owed?"

"Master says he'll attend to it," the servant answered.

Glaring down the passage and speaking as if to someone lurking there, the milkman said fiercely, "Payment is long overdue. You won't have any milk tomorrow unless I'm paid!"

The servant looked relieved that she'd be given milk at least one more day. The milkman opened his can and poured milk into the family jug. Then he went away, muttering.

"Does Mr. Traddles live here?" I asked the servant.

"Yes."

"Is he at home?"

"Yes. He's upstairs."

I walked in and went upstairs. When I got to the top of the stairs, Tommy, dressed in old clothes, was on the landing to meet me. Delighted to see me, he welcomed me to his room with great heartiness. It was in the front of the house and extremely neat but sparsely furnished. There was a sofa bed in it. Shoe polish and other paraphernalia appeared amid the books on the book shelves. A table at which Tommy apparently had been studying was covered with papers. He had made various ingenious arrangements to disguise his chest of drawers and accommodate his boots, shaving mirror, and other items.

"Tommy, I'm delighted to see you," I said, shaking hands with him again after I had sat down."

"I'm delighted to see *you*, David."

"Mr. Waterbrook said you're studying to be a lawyer," I said.

"Yes," Tommy answered. "I've also been working as a copy clerk and doing other jobs such as helping to compile a new encyclopedia. I have to do such work because I need the money. My uncle died soon after I left Salem House, and I didn't inherit anything. I'm on my own. But I'm engaged now! Her name is Sophy Crewler. She's the daughter of a Devonshire clergyman. "She's a little older than me but a dear girl. I told you I was going out of town. I've been down there. I walked there and back. I had the most delightful time. Our engagement is likely to be a long one, but our motto is 'Wait and hope.' Meanwhile I get on as well as I can. I don't make much, but I don't spend much either. I board with the people downstairs, who are very nice. Both Mr. and Mrs. Micawber have seen much of life and are excellent company."

"Mr. and Mrs. Micawber! I'm intimately acquainted with them!" I exclaimed.

There was a double knock at the door. Tommy opened it, and there was Mr. Micawber. He hadn't changed a bit. His tights, shirt collar, and monocle were the same as in earlier years.

Not recognizing me, Mr. Micawber said, "I beg your pardon, Mr. Traddles. I didn't realize that you had a quest." He slightly bowed to me.

"How are you, Mr. Micawber?" I asked.

"I'm very well, thank you, sir," he answered.

"And how are Mrs. Micawber and the children?" I said, smiling.

"Very well, sir." He now examined my features, fell back, and cried, "Is it possible? Have I the pleasure of again beholding Copperfield?" With great fervor he shook me by both hands. "Good heavens, Mr. Traddles! To think that I should find you acquainted with the friend of my youth!" He called down the stairs to Mrs. Micawber, "My dear, there's a gentleman here who wishes to be presented to you." Turning back to me, he said, "And how is Dr. Strong and everyone else at Canterbury?"

"I have nothing but good accounts of them," I answered.

Mrs. Micawber entered, looking more untidy than previously. "My dear," Mr. Micawber said, leading her toward me, "Mr. Copperfield wishes to renew his acquaintance with you." She was delighted to see me. We all talked for half an hour.

When the Micawbers left Tommy's room, I said, "Tommy, Mr. Micawber doesn't mean any harm. However, if I were you, I wouldn't lend him any money."

"My dear David," Tommy said, smiling, "I don't have any money to lend."

"You have your good name, though," I said. "Don't let Mr. Micawber buy anything on credit in your name."

"Oh," Tommy responded. "I've already done that."

"I urge you not to do it again," I said earnestly.

Tommy thanked me, and I left.

The next day I was delighted to receive a visit from James. After we exchanged warm greetings and inquired about each other's families, I said, "Yesterday I visited an old schoolmate of ours."

"Who?"

"Tommy Traddles."

"I don't remember him," James said.

"Tommy Traddles," I repeated. "Don't you remember? He was in our room at Salem House."

"Oh. That fellow," James said as he stirred the fire. "He was odd. Is he as soft as ever?"

"Tommy's a fine fellow," I replied. "He's working hard to become a lawyer, and he's engaged to a clergyman's daughter."

James smiled. "Well, I'd be glad to see him again." He sat beating a lump of coal with a poker. "I've just come from Yarmouth. I've been seafaring."

"You've been at Yarmouth! For how long?"

"A week or so," he answered.

"How is everyone? Have Emily and Ham

married yet?"

"Not yet. I haven't seen much of them. By the way, I have a letter for you, from your old nurse." He took a letter out of his pocket. "I think it's about her husband. He's in a bad way, I think."

I anxiously read Peggotty's letter. "She says that Mr. Barkis is in a hopeless state."

"Well, people die every minute," James said with indifference.

"I'll go to Peggotty, to give her what support and comfort I can. You've just come back, but do you want to go with me?"

"I feel I should go to Highgate," James answered. "I haven't seen my mother for quite a while. I actually came to invite you to join *me*. Can you delay going to Yarmouth by one day?"

After hesitating, I said, "All right."

When James had left and I was getting ready for bed, a boy delivered a letter from Mr. Micawber:

Sir (I dare not say "My dear Copperfield"),

I am crushed. I cannot pay the rent. Lodgings were granted on Mr. Traddle's credit to a sum of £23 and 4 shillings, and payment now is overdue.

Wilkins Micawber

I thought, *Poor Tommy*. By this time I knew enough of Mr. Micawber to foresee that he'd recover, but my night's rest was sorely disturbed by concern for Tommy.

Chapter 28

I asked Mr. Spenlow for a few days' leave. Because I was paying, rather than being paid, to learn law, he granted my request. With my voice sticking in my throat, I took the opportunity to say, "I trust that Miss Spenlow is well."

"Very well. Thank you," he replied.

Mrs. Steerforth and Miss Dartle were pleased to see me. When they joined James and me for an afternoon walk, Miss Dartle grasped my arm with her thin hand to keep me back while James and his mother went on ahead, out of hearing. "What has James been doing?" she asked me.

"What do you mean?" I asked.

"Has he been with you these past weeks? He's been away from home more than usual."

"He hasn't been with *me*. Until the other day, I hadn't seen him for weeks."

Miss Dartle looked at me intently. Her face paled, and the old wound lengthened until it cut through her disfigured lip and deep into her underlip. Her black eyes glittering, she asked, "What has he been doing?"

"Miss Dartle, I really don't understand what you're asking," I said.

She gave me another long look and then dropped the subject.

Mrs. Steerforth was especially happy in her son's company, and James was very attentive and respectful toward her. There was a strong physical resemblance between them. They also were very similar in personality and manner. Both were proud, although the son was haughtier and brasher than the mother.

James was unusually attentive to Miss Dartle. At one point when Mrs. Steerforth wasn't present, James laughingly put his arm around Miss Dartle and said, "Rosa and I always will love each other." Miss Dartle slapped him in the face and stormed out of the room.

"What's wrong with Rosa?" Mrs. Steerforth said, entering.

"She was an angel for a while and then turned into a devil to compensate for that," James answered.

"You should try not to irritate her, James," Mrs. Steerforth said. "You know that she's unhappy."

Miss Dartle didn't return, and no other mention was made of her until I accompanied James to his room to say goodnight. Then he laughed about her and asked, "Did you ever see such a fierce little piece?"

"I certainly was astonished when she slapped you. Do you know why she got so angry?"

"Heaven only knows," he answered. "She's always tense, always ready to snap. She's always dangerous. Good night."

"Good night," I responded. "I'll be gone before you wake up."

He placed a hand on each of my shoulders and said, "If anything ever should separate us, you must think of me at my best, old boy. Let's make that bargain."

"To me, you have no best or worst, James. You always are loved and cherished."

"God bless you, Davy, and good night!"

We shook hands and parted.

I was up at dawn. After dressing as quietly as I could, I looked into James's room. He was fast asleep, lying with his head on his arm, as I often had seen him at school.

Chapter 29

I got down to Yarmouth so late in the evening that I went to an inn rather than disturb Peggotty at that hour. At 10:00 I went out. Many of the shops were closed. When I came to Omer and Joram's, I found the shutters closed but the door open. I saw Mr. Omer smoking his pipe by the door, so I entered and asked him how he was.

"Why, bless my soul!" he said. "How are you? Have a seat. Would you like a smoke?"

"No, thank you," I answered.

He placed a chair for me and sat back down, panting from the slight exertion.

"I'm sorry to have heard bad news about Mr. Barkis," I said. "Do you know how he is tonight?"

"No, sir," he answered. "A man in my profession can't go around asking how sick people are doing. I'm sure you understand."

"Oh, yes," I said, realizing the problem.

"We feel we can ask Emily, though, because she knows we mean well. In fact, Minnie and Bob have just stepped out to the Barkises' house. Emily goes there after work to help her aunt a bit. If you'd like to wait for their return, they'll be able to tell you how Mr. Barkis is doing."

"Thank you. I'll do that. How's Emily?"

Mr. Omer removed his pipe and rubbed his chin. "Well, sir, she seems unsettled lately. She works as hard as ever, but she seems distracted and somewhat depressed. I think she'll be better after she's married. I have a high opinion of Ham, who has steady work and has done very well for himself. He's bought a comfortable little house and furnished it. He and Emily have postponed the wedding, I suppose because Mr. Barkis is so ill."

"I see. Have you heard anything about Martha?"

Shaking his head, he said, "Oh. That's a sad story." Hearing Minnie and Bob coming, Mr. Omer fell silent.

Minnie reported that Mr. Barkis was "as bad as bad could be." He was unconscious, and Dr. Chillip had declared that the case was hopeless. I decided to go to Peggotty at once. I bade everyone good night and left feeling very downcast.

Mr. Peggotty answered my soft knock at the door. I shook hands with him, and we went into the kitchen. Emily was sitting by the fire with her hands in front of her face. Ham was standing near her. We spoke in whispers, listening for any sound in the room above. "It was very kind of you to come, Master Davy," Mr. Peggotty said.

"Yes. Very kind," Ham said.

Emily silently gave me her hand. Then she hugged Mr. Peggotty and buried her face against him. "She's all upset, Master Davy, because she has such a kind heart," Mr. Peggotty said. "It's getting late, my dear," he said to Emily. "Ham will take you home now."

"Please let me stay here with you, Uncle," Emily said softly, as if afraid.

"Whatever you wish, my dear," Mr. Peggotty answered.

Ham kissed Emily, but she continued to cling to her uncle. Then Ham went home alone. When I closed the door behind Ham, Mr. Peggotty said to Emily, "I'm going upstairs to tell Aunt Clara that Master Davy's here. That'll cheer her up a bit. Sit by the fire, my dear, and warm your cold hands."

"I'll go up with you," Emily said. So they both went upstairs. As I sat waiting by the fire, I wondered why Emily was clinging to her uncle and why she seemed so afraid. I concluded that she must be alarmed by the prospect of Mr. Barkis's imminent death.

When Peggotty came down, she took me in her arms. "Bless you, my dear," she said. "Thank you for being such a comfort to me. Please come upstairs." She sobbed, "John always has liked and admired you. He's often spoken of you. If he regains consciousness, the sight of you will do him good."

When I saw Mr. Barkis, I doubted that he'd ever regain consciousness. While Mr. Peggotty, Emily, and I stood at the foot of the bed, Peggotty bent over Mr. Barkis and said, "John, my dear, here's my dear boy. Here's Master Davy, who brought us together. You sent messages by him. Remember? Won't you speak to Master Davy?"

There was no response. We remained there, watching Mr. Barkis, for hours. Finally he began to mutter something about driving me to school.

"He's coming to," Peggotty said. "John, my dear!"

"Clara Peggotty Barkis. No better woman anywhere," Mr. Barkis said faintly. He opened his eyes.

"Look. Here's Master Davy," Peggotty said to him.

I was about to speak to Mr. Barkis when he tried to stretch out his arm and said to me with a smile, "Barkis is willing." With those words he died.

Chapter 30

I stayed with Peggotty, comforting her as much as I could. I was pleased to take charge of Mr. Barkis's will. We found it in his money box, along with an old gold watch and chain, a silver tobacco stopper, 87½ guineas, £210 in crisp bills, and receipts for Bank of England stock. The worth of Mr. Barkis's property and other belongings was nearly £3,000. He left everything to Peggotty except for £500 for Emily and £500 for me. I attended to all the necessary legal matters so that everything would be taken care of for Peggotty. I didn't see Emily the whole week that I spent with Peggotty before the funeral. Emily and Ham planned to be married in two weeks.

The funeral was a small, quiet one. Peggotty was to go to London with me the next day, to take care of business related to the will. That night Peggotty and I went to Mr. Peggotty's house. It was raining heavily. Inside the fire was bright. Mrs. Gummidge was sitting next to it.

"Take off your wet things," Mr. Peggotty said to Peggotty and me.

"Thank you, Mr. Peggotty," I said, giving him my coat to hang up.

"Sit down, sir," he said.

"Thank you," I said.

Mr. Peggotty said to Peggotty, "Clara, there isn't a woman in the world who could feel more at ease in her mind than *you* should. You did your duty by John, and he knew it. He did right by you." Mr. Peggotty put a candle in the window as a guide for Emily and a sign that he was home.

Ham entered, wearing a large fisherman's rain hat. "Where's Emily?" Mr. Peggotty asked him. Ham made a motion with his head as if she were outside. Mr. Peggotty took the candle from the window and put it on the table. He stirred the fire.

Not having moved, Ham said, "Master Davy, will you come outside for a minute and see what Emily and I have to show you?" Ham and I went out, and he closed the door behind us. Emily wasn't there, and Ham was pale.

"Ham, what's wrong?" I asked, alarmed.

He started to weep.

"Ham! Tell me what's wrong."

"My love, Master Davy, the pride and hope of my heart, the one I'd die for, has gone!"

"Gone?"

"Emily's run away!" He trembled. "Oh, Master Davy, what should I tell everyone? What should I tell Uncle Daniel?"

Mr. Peggotty opened the door. He instantly realized that something was terribly wrong. His expression changed from one of joy to one of intense fear. The next thing I remember was a great wailing. We all stood in the room, and the women tried to comfort Mr. Peggotty. I had a letter in my hand that Ham had given to me. In a trembling voice, Mr. Peggotty said to me, "Read it, sir—slowly, please."

I said, "Emily's letter is addressed to Ham and dated last night." Then I read aloud, "'When you who love me so much better than I ever have deserved read this, I'll be far away. Tomorrow morning I'm leaving my dear home. I won't ever return unless he brings me back a lady. My heart is torn. I wish that you whom I have wronged so much and who never can forgive me could know what I suffer. I know that I'm wicked. For mercy's sake, please tell Uncle Daniel that I love him more than ever. Please don't remember that you and I were to be married. Try to think instead that I died. Be Uncle Daniel's comfort. Love some good woman who will be true to you and worthy of you. Please don't remember how affectionate and kind you all have been to me. God bless all of you! I'll often pray for all of you. My parting love to Uncle Daniel. My last tears and my last thanks for him.'"

Mr. Peggotty stood looking at me. I took his hand and begged him to be comforted. Without moving, he answered, "Thank you, sir." After some time he said in a low voice, "Who's the man? I want to know his name."

Ham glanced at me and then looked back at his uncle. "James Steerforth, and he's a damned villain." Overcome with shock, I sank into a chair. "Emily was seen with his servant last night," Ham continued. "At dawn they were seen going to a fancy carriage, with horses, on the edge of town. Steerforth was inside."

At first Mr. Peggotty stood perfectly still. Then he pulled his rough coat from its peg, put it on, and put on his hat.

"Where are you going?" Ham asked him.

"I'm going to find Emily," Mr. Peggotty answered.

"Where?" Ham cried, putting himself in front of the door.

"Wherever she is!" Mr. Peggotty cried. "I'm going to find my poor niece in her shame and bring her back. No one stop me! I tell you I'm going to find Emily!"

"No!" Mrs. Gummidge cried, coming between Ham and Mr. Peggotty in a fit of crying. "No, Daniel. Don't go in the state you're in. Wait."

Mr. Peggotty started to cry, and so did I.

Chapter 31

As I passed along the streets the next morning, I overheard people, standing in front of their doors, talking about Emily's flight. Many spoke harshly of Emily. Only a few spoke harshly of James. Everyone spoke of Mr. Peggotty and Ham with sympathy and respect. I found Mr. Peggotty and Ham walking on the beach. It was obvious that they hadn't slept all night. They both were as grave and steady as the sea, which lay beneath a dark sky, without breaking waves but with a heavy roll in it.

The three of us walked as Mr. Peggotty said to me, "Ham and I have talked. I'm still determined to find Emily. Are you going to London tomorrow?"

"Not if I can be of service to you here," I answered.

"I'd like to go to London with you, sir," Mr. Peggotty said. "I'd like to go tomorrow if you're agreeable."

"Certainly," I said.

The three of us walked for a while in silence. Then Mr. Peggotty resumed, "Ham will stay here. He'll live with his aunt and continue at his work. Mrs. Gummidge will continue to live in my house.

Every night she'll put a lit candle in the window as a welcome and encouragement to Emily, in case she . . . in case she comes back." Ham didn't look at either Mr. Peggotty or me. His eyes seemed fixed on the horizon.

We approached the old barge and entered. Mrs. Gummidge was preparing breakfast. She took Mr. Peggotty's hat and placed a chair for him. "Daniel, my good man," she said, "you must eat and drink and keep up your strength. You won't be able to do anything without it. Try. That's a dear soul. If I disturb you with my chattering, just let me know, and I'll stop." When she had served all of us, she withdrew to the window, where she set to mending some of Mr. Peggotty's shirts and other clothes and neatly folding and packing them in an old bag of oiled, waterproof cloth such as sailors carry. "I'll always be here, Daniel," she said. "While you're away, I'll write to you care of Master Davy. Please write to me sometimes, Daniel, and let me know how you're doing."

"I'm afraid you'll be lonely here," Mr. Peggotty said to her.

"No, Daniel. I'll be busy keeping up the house. When the weather's nice, I'll sit outside."

That evening Mr. Peggotty, Mrs. Gummidge, and I sat together until Mr. Peggotty fell asleep from exhaustion. Then Mrs. Gummidge broke into a half-suppressed fit of crying. Taking me to the door, she said, "Bless you, Master Davy. Be a friend to him, poor dear." Then she ran out of the house to wash her face and came back to sit beside Mr. Peggotty.

I left. It was around 9:30 when, strolling in a melancholy manner through the town, I stopped at Omer and Joram's. Minnie told me that her father had taken Emily's running away so hard that he was feeling sick and had gone to bed early. "She's deceitful and bad-hearted," Minnie angrily said of Emily. "She always was."

"Don't say that," I objected. "You know it isn't true."

Minnie started to cry. "What will she do? Where will she go? What will become of her? How could she be so cruel, to Ham and to herself?" Bob Joram entered the room and started to comfort his wife. Leaving them together, I went to Peggotty's.

Early the next morning Peggotty, Mr. Peggotty, Mrs. Gummidge, Ham, and I went to the stagecoach office. "Master Davy," Ham whispered, drawing me aside while Mr. Peggotty was placing his bag among the luggage, "my uncle's broken in two. Be a friend to him."

"I will indeed," I said earnestly, shaking hands with Ham.

"Thank you, sir."

"I hope that . . . that you'll be happy again some day, Ham," I said.

He shook his head. "No one could ever fill the place that's empty now."

When the coach started off, Mrs. Gummidge ran alongside it, looking at Mr. Peggotty, who was sitting on the roof, through her tears and bumping into pedestrians.

In London we set out to find lodgings for Peggotty and Mr. Peggotty. We found clean, inexpensive rooms just two blocks from my apartment. Mr. Peggotty arranged to rent them. I bought some cold cuts, and Peggotty and Mr. Peggotty came to my apartment for some refreshment.

On the way to London, Mr. Peggotty had told me that he wanted to meet with Mrs. Steerforth. I wrote to her that night. As mildly as I could, I told her what had happened. I said that Mr. Peggotty was a fisherman of a gentle, upright character. I said I hoped that she wouldn't refuse to see him in his heavy trouble. I mentioned 2:00 in the afternoon as the hour of our coming, and I sent the letter.

At 2:00 Mr. Peggotty and I stood at the door of Mrs. Steerforth's house. A maid answered and showed us to the parlor. Mrs. Steerforth was sitting there. As we entered, Rosa Dartle glided from another part of the room and stood behind Mrs. Steerforth's chair. Mrs. Steerforth's face was very pale. She sat upright in her armchair, looking imperturbable. She looked at Mr. Peggotty very steadfastly when he stood before her, and he looked as steadfastly at her. For some moments not a word was spoken. Mrs. Steerforth motioned to Mr. Peggotty to be seated. He responded in a low voice, "I wouldn't feel comfortable sitting in this house, ma'am. I'd rather stand."

Another silence followed. Then Mrs. Steerforth said to Mr. Peggotty, "I know, with deep regret, what has brought you here. What do you want of me? What are you asking me to do?"

Mr. Peggotty put his hat under his arm and took Emily's letter from his jacket. He unfolded it and gave it to Mrs. Steerforth. "Please read that, ma'am. My niece wrote it." Mrs. Steerforth read the letter with no show of emotion and returned it to Mr. Peggotty. "I've come to know if they are going to marry," he said.

"Certainly not!" Mrs. Steerforth answered.

"Why not?" Mr. Peggotty asked.

"It's impossible. My son would disgrace himself. You can't fail to know that she's far below him."

"Raise her up, then," Mr. Peggotty responded.

"She's uneducated." Mrs. Steerforth said.

"Then, teach her."

"You oblige me to speak more plainly. Her humble connections would render such a thing impossible even if nothing else did."

Slowly and quietly Mr. Peggotty said, "Ma'am, you know what it is to love your child. So do I. You *don't* know what it is to lose your child. I do. I'd give all the riches in the world to have her back. If you disapprove of her family, we're all willing to never see her beautiful face again. We'll be content to let her be, to think of her, to trust her to her husband. We'll bide our time until we're all before God, equal in rank."

Mrs. Steerforth preserved her proud manner, but there was a new touch of softness in her voice as she answered, "I'm sorry to repeat that it's impossible. Such a marriage would blight my son's career and ruin his prospects. If there is any other compensation . . . "

With a steady but newly fiery eye, Mr. Peggotty interrupted, "I'm looking at the likeness of the face that has looked at me in my home, at my fireside, and in my boat smiling and friendly while it was treacherous. Offering me money for my child's ruin is as bad as what your son has done."

Mrs. Steerforth flushed with anger. Gripping the arms of her chair, she said, "What compensation can you make to *me* for opening such a pit between my son and me? What is *your* love compared to mine? What is *your* separation compared to ours? My entire life has been devoted to my son. Since his childhood I've gratified his every wish. I've had no separate existence from him since his birth. Now he's taken up with a miserable girl and avoids me! He has repaid my confidence with systematic deception, for her sake, and abandoned me for her. He has set this wretched attraction against my claims on his duty, love, respect, and gratitude. If he drops her now and begs my forgiveness, I'll welcome him back. Otherwise I'll have nothing further to do with him." I now realized how alike mother and son were. Both were overly defiant, proud, and unyielding. Turning to me, Mrs. Steerforth said, "Mr. Copperfield, it's useless for me to hear or say anything more. This interview is at an end." With a dignified air she rose to leave the room.

"I have no more to say, ma'am," Mr. Peggotty said. "I came to you because I thought that I should, not because I hoped that you would be kind or just. Your house has brought my family too much evil for me to have believed that my coming here would do any good."

With this, Mr. Peggotty and I left the room. Before we opened the house's front door, Miss Dartle was upon us. She flashed at me, "How dare you bring this man here!"

"He is a deeply injured man, Miss Dartle," I replied.

"I know that James Steerforth has a false, corrupt heart and is a traitor. But I don't care about this man or his common niece. She deserves to be whipped!"

Without a word Mr. Peggotty left the house. "Shame, Miss Dartle!" I said indignantly. "You have caused an innocent, afflicted man even more pain."

"I'd like to see her branded on the face, dressed in rags, and cast out into the streets to starve!" Miss Dartle raged. "I detest her. I'd like to hunt her down. I'd like to . . . "

I left her raving. When I joined Mr. Peggotty, he was walking down the hill. He said, "Now that I've done what I had to do in London, I'm going to set out in search of Emily. I'm going to leave tonight."

We went back to Mr. Peggotty's lodgings and had dinner with Peggotty. After dinner we sat for an hour or so near the window without talking much. Then Mr. Peggotty rose, got his cloth bag and stout stick, and laid them on the table. He accepted a small sum from Peggotty's stock of ready money. He promised to communicate with me when he had any news. He slung his bag over his shoulder, took his hat and stick, and bade us goodbye. "All good attend you, dear sister," he said, embracing

Peggotty. "You, too, Master Davy," he said, shaking hands with me. "I'm going to look for Emily. If any harm should come to me, remember that my last words for her were 'My unchanged love is with my darling child, and I forgive her.'" Putting on his hat, he went down the stairs and away.

Peggotty and I followed to the door. It was a warm, dusty evening. At the corner of our shady street, Mr. Peggotty turned into a glow of light from the setting sun and was gone.

Chapter 32

All this time I had remained in love with Dora Spenlow. The night after Mr. Peggotty's departure, I walked to Norwood and went around and around her house and garden for two hours, looking up at the lights in the windows. I told Peggotty about my love for Dora. Thinking so highly of me, Peggotty couldn't understand why I hesitated to make my feelings known to Dora and her father. "The young lady should consider herself lucky to have such a beau," she said. "And her father couldn't expect more in a gentleman."

One day Mr. Murdstone came to Spenlow & Jorkins. He looked much as before. His hair was as black and thick as ever. When he saw me in the outer office, he was disconcerted. Then he said, "I hope that you're doing well."

"Yes, but that hardly can interest you," I responded.

"You always rebelled against my just authority, exerted for your benefit and reform, so I wouldn't expect you to show me any goodwill now." He passed into Mr. Spenlow's office and paid for a marriage license. Mr. Spenlow handed him the license, shook his hand, and wished him and his future wife happiness. Mr. Murdstone left.

When I was alone with Mr. Spenlow, I asked him about Mr. Murdstone's upcoming marriage. Mr. Spenlow said, "Judging from what the gentleman said and what Miss Murdstone has mentioned, he's going to marry a wealthy beauty, so young that she's just come of age." I, of course, pitied the bride-to-be.

In the course of further conversation, Mr. Spenlow mentioned that Dora's birthday was in a week. He invited me to her birthday picnic. I eagerly accepted. The next day I received a little lace-edged note from Dora repeating the invitation. I was wild with joy. I bought a new cravat and new boots for the occasion. I sent Dora a hamper filled with crackers with tender sayings stamped into them. At 6:00 a.m. of the day of the picnic, I was in Covent Garden Market buying a bouquet for her. At 10:00 I was on a gallant gray horse I had rented for the occasion, trotting down to Norwood.

When I dismounted at the garden gate, I saw Dora sitting on a garden seat under a lilac tree. She was wearing a sky-blue dress and white bonnet. Dora introduced me to a woman of about twenty who was with her: Julia Mills. Jip was there, and, as usual, he barked at me. When I presented my bouquet to Dora, he growled with jealousy. "Oh, thank you, Mr. Copperfield. What dear flowers!" Dora said, laying the flowers against her little, dimpled chin. Then she held the flowers to Jip to smell. He growled. Dora laughed and held them a little closer to Jip. He bit a geranium and tore at it. Dora pouted and said, "My poor, beautiful flowers. You'll be glad to hear, Mr. Copperfield, that that cross Miss Murdstone isn't here. She's gone to her brother's wedding. She'll be away at least three weeks. Isn't that delightful?" She turned to Miss Mills. "You can't believe how ill-tempered and tiresome she is, Julia."

Mr. Spenlow came out of the house, and Dora went to him. "Look, Papa, what beautiful flowers!" she said. We all walked from the lawn toward the open carriage that was being readied. I rode behind the carriage, in which Mr. Spenlow and Miss Mills sat facing forward and Dora sat facing me, with her back to the horses. Dora kept the bouquet close to her on the cushion and wouldn't allow Jip to sit on that side of her, for fear he'd crush it. She often took it in her hand and smelled it. At those times our eyes often met. I was so oblivious to everything but Dora that I rode in a constant whirl of dust kicked up by the carriage's wheels.

We arrived at a green spot, on a hill, carpeted with soft turf. There were shady trees, heather, and, as far as the eye could see, a rich landscape. Because I didn't like sharing Dora's company with anyone else, I was annoyed to find people waiting for us. I was especially jealous of any young man who might compete for Dora's affections.

We all unpacked our baskets. A young man with red whiskers ate lobster while sitting at Dora's feet. In retaliation for Dora's ignoring me, I flirted with a young woman named Miss Kitt. Her mother soon separated us. When the leftovers were being put away, I strolled off by myself among the trees, despondent at not having talked with Dora.

Dora and Miss Mills soon appeared. "Mr. Copperfield, you seem subdued," Miss Mills said.

"Not at all," I claimed.

"And Dora, *you* seem subdued," Miss Mills said.

"Not at all," Dora claimed.

"Dora, Mr. Copperfield, enough of this. Be glad in each other's company," Miss Mills said.

Without thinking, I took Dora's small hand and kissed it. She and I briefly strolled among the trees, with her arm drawn through mine. Then, much too soon, we heard the others laughing, talking, and calling, "Where's Dora?" So we went back. They wanted Dora to sing. I got her guitar from the carriage, gave it to her, and sat by her. I held her handkerchief and gloves and drank in every note of her voice. When evening approached, we had tea.

I was happier than ever when the party broke up, and Dora, Miss Mills, Mr. Spenlow, and I headed back through the twilight. Having drunk too much champagne, Mr. Spenlow fell asleep in a corner of the carriage. I rode alongside the carriage and talked to Dora. She admired my horse and patted him. Her shawl wouldn't stay in place, so now and then I drew it around her.

"Mr. Copperfield," Miss Mills said, "please come to my side of the carriage for a moment. I want to speak to you." I rode around and bent at her side. She said, "Dora will be coming to visit me the day after tomorrow. If you'd like to call, you'll be most welcome."

"Thank you," I said with the utmost feeling.

Then she dismissed me. "Go back to Dora."

I went. Dora and I talked all the rest of the way. I rode my horse so close to the wheel of the carriage that it grazed one of his legs. When I later returned him, the owner made me pay £3 and seven shillings for the injury.

Shortly before we reached Norwood, Mr. Spenlow awoke and said, "You must come in, Copperfield, and rest." We had sandwiches and wine. Finally I tore myself away. I went to sleep that night in a state of bliss.

When I awoke the next morning, I was determined to propose to Dora. I spent three days in an agony of trepidation. Then, having bought and dressed myself in very expensive clothes, I went to Miss Mills' house, where I was shown into an upstairs room. Miss Mills, Dora, and Jip were there. Miss Mills was copying music, and Dora was painting flowers. I was overjoyed to see that they were the flowers I had given her. Miss Mills said that she was very glad to see me. She spoke to me for a while and then, laying down her pen, left the room.

"I hope your poor horse wasn't tired when he got home last night," Dora said, lifting her beautiful eyes. "It was a long way for him."

"It was a long way for *him* because *he* had nothing to sustain him on the journey," I said.

"Wasn't he fed, poor thing?" she asked.

"Yes. I mean that he didn't have my unutterable happiness in being near you."

Dora bent her head over her painting. After a pause, during which I sat very tense, she said, "You didn't care for that happiness in the least when you were sitting with Miss Kitt, although you're certainly free to do as you wish."

In a moment I had Dora in my arms and was telling her how much I loved her. "I worship you," I said. "I'd die without you. I've loved you every minute, day and night, since I first saw you. No one could love anyone more than *I* love *you*." Jip barked the whole time. Then, somehow, Dora and I were sitting on the sofa, with Jip lying peacefully in her lap. Dora agreed to marry me. She fetched Miss Mills, who gave us her blessing and the assurance of her lasting friendship. I measured Dora's finger for a ring.

I wrote Agnes a long letter in which I went on and on about how happy I was and how darling Dora was. I bought a ring of blue stones and sent it to Dora. We secretly met in her garden and sat in the summer house. A week after we had become engaged, we had our first quarrel. Dora sent me back the ring, enclosed in a note that said, "Our love began in folly and ended in madness." I sent a message to Miss Mills, asking her to intercede. She did. Dora and I then met again, cried, and made up.

Chapter 33

Tommy Traddles came to visit me, and I told him about Dora. He then talked more about his own fiancée, Sophy. I asked how Mr. Micawber was.

"He's quite well, but I'm not living with him anymore. Because of his debts, he has changed his name to Mr. Mortimer. He doesn't leave his residence except after dark, and then he wears eyeglasses. The Micawbers couldn't pay the rent, so I gave my name as credit. I've been living in a furnished apartment since then. The creditors took what little furniture I had."

"What a hard thing for you!" I exclaimed indignantly. "Promise me that you won't lend your name ever again in behalf of the Micawbers."

"I promise," Tommy said.

Soon after and entirely to my surprise, Aunt Betsey and Mr. Dick came to my apartment. My aunt had a quantity of luggage, her two canaries, and her cat. Mr. Dick had his kite and more luggage. "Aunt Betsey, what an unexpected pleasure!" I cried. She and I embraced, and Mr. Dick and I shook hands.

"How are you?" my aunt asked Peggotty.

"Well. Thank you, ma'am." Peggotty curtseyed and took my aunt's hand. Then she made tea.

"Davy, my dear," my aunt said, "I'm ruined." If the house and every one of us had tumbled into the river, I hardly could have been more shocked. "All that I have left in the world is in this room, except for the house, which I've left Janet to rent out." She fell onto my neck. "I'm grieved mainly for you, my dear boy."

"What happened?" I asked.

"I lost my money in bad investments," my aunt answered.

I proposed that she take my bed, that I sleep in the sitting room, and that Mr. Dick stay in the room that Mr. Peggotty was renting. Peggotty brought Mr. Dick there.

I told my aunt about Dora. "I hope she isn't silly," she said.

It never had entered my head to consider whether or not Dora was silly, so I was taken aback. "I know that we're young and inexperienced, Aunt, but we love each other."

"I don't doubt your earnestness, Davy. I only hope that she's equally earnest."

When my aunt went to bed and I lay down to sleep in the sitting room, it suddenly hit me that I now was poor. What would Dora think? What would her father think? Would he think that I had proposed to Dora under false pretenses? And how would I live now? When I finally fell asleep, I had nightmares about poverty.

When I awoke, I decided to see if my arrangement with Spenlow & Jorkins could be cancelled and the

£1,000 refunded. I arrived at the office so early that I had to wait outside half an hour before Mr. Tiffey, who always was the first to arrive, appeared with his key. Then I sat down in my corner thinking about Dora until Mr. Spenlow came in.

"How are you, Copperfield?" he said. "Fine morning."

"Beautiful morning, sir. Could I have a word with you before you go into court?"

"By all means," he said. "Come into my office." I followed Mr. Spenlow into his office, and he began putting on his gown and touching himself up in front of a little mirror that hung inside a closet door.

"I'm sorry to say that I've had some bad news, sir. My aunt has met with large financial losses. In fact, she has nothing left."

"You astound me, Copperfield!" Mr. Spenlow cried.

"Indeed, her circumstances have changed so drastically that I need to ask if I can cancel our arrangement and have all, or at least some, of my thousand pounds refunded."

"Cancel our arrangement, Copperfield? Cancel?"

"I have to earn a living now," I said.

"I'm extremely sorry to hear this, Copperfield, but Mr. Jorkins wouldn't hear of your getting some sort of refund."

"Do I have your permission to speak to him, sir?"

Taken aback, Mr. Spenlow said, "Yes."

I went up to Mr. Jorkins' office. "Come in, Mr. Copperfield," he said. Mr. Jorkins was a large, mild-looking, smooth-faced man of sixty. "Have a seat." I sat and then explained my situation. "You've mentioned this to Mr. Spenlow, I suppose?" Mr. Jorkins asked when I was done.

"Yes."

"He said that I'd object?"

"He thought so," I answered.

"I'm sorry to say, Mr. Copperfield, that I can't help you," he said nervously. The fact is . . . But I have an appointment at the bank. Please excuse me." He rose in a great hurry and started to leave the room.

"There's no way to arrange any refund, then?" I asked.

"No," he said, stopping at the door to shake his head. "If Mr. Spenlow objects, then I must, too."

"He didn't object," I responded. "He said he thought that *you* would."

"In that case I do object, Mr. Copperfield. I have to object. What you wish can't be done." He hurried away.

Realizing that I couldn't recover any portion of my aunt's £1,000, I headed home despondent. As I was walking, a cab came up to me and stopped. I looked up and saw Agnes sitting inside, reaching out her hand to me. "Agnes!" I cried joyfully. "I'm so glad to see you. I want to talk to you so much. There's no one I could have wished for more than you."

"What?" Agnes returned.

"Well, perhaps Dora," I admitted with a blush.

"Certainly Dora, I hope," Agnes said, laughing.

"But you next. Where are you going?"

"To see your aunt. She wrote to me."

I dismissed the cab driver. Agnes took my arm, and we walked on together. My aunt had written Agnes a note saying that she had fallen into adversity and was leaving Dover for good. Agnes said, "Papa and Uriah Heep are partners now. They were coming to London on business, so I took the opportunity to come. I wanted to see your aunt and also didn't want Papa to be alone with Uriah."

"Does he exercise the same influence over your father, Agnes?"

"More," Agnes said, shaking her head sadly. "Home is so different now that you scarcely would recognize it. Uriah and his mother live with us now. He sleeps in your old room." She looked into my face. "I often have to bear Mrs. Heep's company when I'd rather be alone. She has nothing but praise for her son." After a pause she said, "Do you know how the reversal in your aunt's circumstances came about?"

"She said that she made bad investments," I answered.

We found my aunt alone. She was greatly pleased to see Agnes. Agnes laid her bonnet on the table and sat down beside my aunt. We began to talk about my aunt's losses, and I told Agnes and my aunt what I had tried to do that morning. "You meant well, Davy, but that was unwise," my aunt said. "We've invested time and money in your becoming a proctor, and I still hope that you'll become one. You're a generous boy—I guess I should say 'young man' now—and I'm proud of you, my dear. Now, Agnes, you have a wise head. You do, too, Davy, about some things. What's to be done? Renting the house will bring in about seventy pounds a year. Mr. Dick will be all right because he has an income of a hundred a year. So what should Davy and I do, Agnes?"

"I must earn a living," I interposed.

"Would you mind being a personal secretary, David?" Agnes asked me. "Dr. Strong has retired. He lives in Highgate now. He asked Papa if he could recommend someone to be his secretary. I'm sure he'd love to have his favorite old pupil. Could you continue studying to be a proctor while working for Dr. Strong part-time?"

"Dear Agnes, what would I do without you?" I said. "You're always my good angel." I was delighted with the prospect of earning a living and doing so in the employ of my old mentor and friend. "I have time every morning before my day starts at Spenlow & Jorkins, and I have time every day after work. My day at Spenlow & Jorkins always finishes by five o'clock." I immediately sat down and wrote to Dr. Strong. I stated my object and said that I'd call on him the next day at 10:00 a.m. Then I posted the letter.

When I came back, I found my aunt's birdcage hanging just as it had hung in the parlor window of her Dover house and my armchair at the open window. Agnes was arranging my neglected books in the old order of my school days. There was a knock at the door. "It's Papa," Agnes said. "He said he'd come." I opened the door and admitted Mr. Wickfield and Uriah Heep. Mr. Wickfield's appearance shocked me. He looked many years older.

He face was overly red, his eyes were bloodshot, and his hands trembled. "Papa," Agnes said, "here are Miss Trotwood and David, whom you haven't seen for so long." Mr. Wickfield gave my aunt his hand and shook hands with me.

"Well, Wickfield," my aunt said, "Agnes has been giving me her good advice." She added coldly to Uriah, "How are you, sir?"

"Well, thank you. I hope you are, too. And you, Mr. Copperfield. I'm very glad to see you well. Your present circumstances aren't what your friends would wish for you, but it isn't money that makes the man. If there's anything that Wickfield & Heep can do, just let us know."

"I quite agree, David," Mr. Wickfield said.

"I have a business engagement," Uriah said, "so I'll be off. Miss Agnes, ever yours. I wish you good day, Mr. Copperfield, and leave my 'umble respects for Miss Betsey Trotwood." With those words he left, kissing his hand and leering at us.

We sat talking about our pleasant old Canterbury days for an hour or two. Then I walked with Mr. Wickfield and Agnes to the place where they were staying. My aunt stayed with Peggotty.

Agnes, her father, and I dined together. After dinner Agnes sat beside Mr. Wickfield and poured out his wine. He took what she gave him and no more. The three of us sat at a window as evening came. When it was almost dark, Mr. Wickfield lay down on a sofa, Agnes pillowing his head and bending over him a little while. When she came back to the window, she listened to me praise Dora.

The next day I went to Highgate. Dr. Strong's cottage was a pretty old place that appeared to have just been renovated. I saw him walking, gaiters and all, in the garden at the side of the house, as he had during my student years. I opened the gate and walked after him. When he turned around and saw me, his face showed delight. He took me by both hands. "My dear Copperfield, you're a man. How are you? I'm delighted to see you."

"I hope you're well, and Mrs. Strong," I said.

"Oh dear, yes. Annie will be delighted to see you. You always were her favorite among the students. She said so last night, when I showed her your letter." Dr. Strong walked with his hand on my shoulder and his kind face turned encouragingly to mine. "Now, my dear Copperfield, in reference to this proposal of yours—it's very gratifying and agreeable to me, but don't you think you could do better? You achieved distinction when you were with us. You're qualified for many good things. It seems a shame for you to accept the lowly position that I can offer."

"I'll continue to prepare to be a proctor," I said. "In the meantime I need an income."

"Well, your studying to be a proctor does make a difference. But, my good young friend, what's seventy pounds a year?"

"It doubles our income, Dr. Strong."

"Dear me!"

"If you'll accept my services in the mornings and evenings for seventy pounds a year, you'll do me a great service," I said.

"If you promise to take a better position if one comes along," Dr. Strong insisted.

"I promise," I said, smiling.

"Then, it's settled," Dr. Strong said, clapping me on the shoulder and keeping his hand there as we walked. "You'll be working on the dictionary that I'm compiling."

We agreed to start the next morning at 7:00. We would work two hours every morning and two or three hours every night, except on Saturdays and Sundays. Dr. Strong took me into the house to see Mrs. Strong, whom we found in his new study, dusting his books. They had postponed their breakfast on my account, and we sat down at the table together. We hadn't been seated long when I saw an approaching arrival in Mrs. Strong's face before I heard any sound of it. A gentleman on horseback came to the gate. As if he were quite at home, with the bridle over his arm, he led his horse into the little courtyard and tied him to a ring in one wall of the empty coach house. Then he entered the breakfast parlor, whip in hand. It was Jack Maldon.

"Jack," Dr. Strong said, "do you remember David Copperfield? As you can see, David, Jack has returned from India."

Mr. Maldon shook hands with me but not warmly, with an air of languid patronage.

"Have you breakfasted, Jack?" Dr. Strong asked.

"I rarely eat breakfast, sir," he replied with his head thrown back in an armchair. I came to ask if Annie would like to go to the opera tonight." He turned to her. "It's the last good night there will be this season, and there's a singer there you really should hear. She's exquisite."

Dr. Strong turned to his wife. "You must go, Annie."

"I'd rather not," she said. She was so visibly disturbed that I wondered how Dr. Strong, buttering his toast, could be blind to her emotion.

"You're young and need some entertainment, my dear," Dr. Strong said to his wife. "You mustn't be made dull by a dull old fellow." He persisted in making the engagement for her.

Mr. Maldon was to come back to dinner. He rode off. However, the next morning I learned that Mrs. Strong had not accompanied Mr. Maldon to the opera. She had sent him a note saying that she wouldn't go.

The whole time that Dr. Strong and I worked, Mrs. Strong sat in the window. She looked unhappy. When I got up to leave at 9:00, she knelt at Dr. Strong's feet and put his shoes and gaiters on him.

Every day I was up at 5:00 a.m. and not home until 9:00 or 10:00 at night. I felt energetic and proud to be so busy. I felt that the harder I worked, the more I deserved Dora. I hadn't told her about my changed circumstances yet. She was coming to see Miss Mills in a few days, and I planned to tell her then. She and I had continually corresponded, with Miss Mills as our go-between.

I went to see Tommy, who now lodged in Holborn, and brought Mr. Dick with me. Mr. Dick and I found Tommy hard at work with his inkstand

and papers in his small apartment. Tommy received us cordially and instantly made friends with Mr. Dick.

I said to Tommy, "I've heard that many men distinguished in various pursuits began by reporting on the debates in Parliament. What do I need to do to get such a position?"

"You need to learn shorthand," Tommy answered.

"I'll do that, then," I said. "Is there anything that Mr. Dick can do to earn money? His penmanship is excellent."

"Then he can be paid to copy documents," Tommy said.

From then on, Tommy procured legal documents that needed to be copied, and Mr. Dick was given the work of copying them, which he did very well. When Mr. Dick received his first pay, there were tears of pride and joy in his eyes. "We'll be all right now, David," he said. "I'll provide for your aunt."

Having been invited to dinner at the Micawbers' new residence, Tommy and I went there one evening. The apartment was so small that we found the twins, now nine years old, reposing on a bed in the living room. Young Wilkins was thirteen, his sister Emma twelve. "My dear Copperfield," Mr. Micawber said, "you and Traddles find us about to undertake another move and will excuse any little discomforts incidental to that."

Glancing around, I observed that the family's scant possessions were already packed. "Where are you going?" I asked.

"To Canterbury," Mr. Micawber answered. "I'm going to be the confidential clerk of our mutual friend Uriah Heep." Amazed, I stared at Mr. Micawber, who greatly enjoyed my surprise. "I placed an advertisement, and my friend Heep responded," Mr. Micawber said. "He hasn't offered a high starting salary, but he has indicated that the salary will increase if I prove invaluable. I intend to devote myself to his service." I managed to congratulate the Micawbers, and we all started to drink homemade punch.

"My dear Copperfield, the companion of my youth, and my esteemed friend Traddles," Mr. Micawber said, rising with one thumb in each of his vest pockets, "I thank you for your good wishes. Mr. Thomas Traddles has, on two occasions, taken debts of mine upon himself. I couldn't leave London without acquitting myself of my financial obligation to him, so I hereby present him with an IOU for the full amount that I owe him: forty-one pounds, ten shillings, and eleven and a half pence." Mr. Micawber placed his IOU in Tommy's hands.

We parted with great heartiness on both sides. When I had seen Tommy to his own door and was going home alone, I wondered why Mr. Micawber never had asked *me* for money. I could only assume that he still thought of me as a boy.

Chapter 34

Being uncommonly neat and practical, my aunt made so many small improvements in my apartment that I felt richer rather than poorer. Among other things, she converted the pantry into a dressing room for me. I was the object of her constant solicitude. My poor mother herself couldn't have loved me more.

Peggotty and my aunt had quickly become close friends. But the time now had come for Peggotty to return to Yarmouth and look after Ham. I took her to the stagecoach office and saw her off. She cried at parting and asked me to be a friend to her brother. We had heard nothing from Mr. Peggotty since he had gone away. "My dear Davy, if you should need any money, please let me be the one to lend it to you," Peggotty said.

"I will, Peggotty. Thank you."

"And tell the pretty little angel Dora that I would so have liked to meet her. Tell her that I'll come and make your house beautiful for you before she marries my boy, if you'll let me."

"I will, Peggotty."

At the appointed time in the evening, I went

to Miss Mills's house. Her father (her only living parent) had gone out. I was shown into the drawing room. Dora came in, with Jip following. As soon as we had seated ourselves on the sofa, I said, "My dear Dora, can you love a beggar?"

Startled, she stared at me. Then, pouting, she said, "How can you ask me anything so foolish? Love a beggar!"

"Dora, my dearest, I'm a beggar."

Slapping my hand, she said, "How can you be such a silly thing as to sit there telling such stories? I'll make Jip bite you."

"Dora, I'm ruined," I said solemnly.

She laid a trembling hand on my shoulder, looked scared, and began to cry.

"Don't break my heart!" I cried.

"Oh dear!" she exclaimed. "Oh dear!" She looked at me with a horrified expression.

I soothed her until her soft, pretty cheek was pressed against mine. Embracing her, I told her how much I loved her. "Because I'm poor now, I'll release you from our engagement if you want me to. But I couldn't bear to be without you. Is your heart still mine, dear Dora?" I asked.

"Yes. But no more talk of being poor," she said. "Will Jip still be able to have a mutton chop every day? He must have a mutton chop every day at noon."

"I promise that Jip will continue to have his daily mutton chop."

"Will we have to live with your aunt?" Dora asked. "If so, I hope she'll keep to her own room much of the time. And I hope she isn't a scolding old thing."

"Not at all," I assured her. "My love, perseverance and strength of character will enable us to bear much worse things."

Shaking her curls, she said, "But I haven't got any strength, have I, Jip?" Holding Jip up, she said to me, "Kiss Jip, and be agreeable now."

I did as commanded. Then I said, "Dora, because we'll have to be careful about money, it would be good if you learned how to keep house without undue expense."

Dora reacted with a sound that was half a sob and half a scream.

"It would be wonderful if you could learn to cook."

She looked terrified. While I was begging Dora's forgiveness, Miss Mills came in. Embracing her, Dora exclaimed, "Oh, Julia, he's a poor laborer!" She sobbed.

I quickly explained to Miss Mills what had happened. She comforted Dora and gradually convinced her that I was not a laborer. When we all were composed and Dora had gone upstairs to put some rosewater to her eyes, Miss Mills rang for tea. "Miss Mills," I said, "you always are my friend. I'll never forget your assistance and sympathy."

"A cottage of contentment is better than a palace of unhappiness," she said, "Where there's love, there's everything."

"Exactly, Miss Mills," I responded.

Dora returned. After tea, she played her guitar and sang French songs. When I got up to leave, I said that I had to get up at 5:00. "Don't do that, you naughty boy," Dora said. "It's nonsensical."

"'My love, I have to work," I replied.

"Don't do it. Why should you?"

"I have to earn money."

"Oh, how ridiculous!" Dora cried.

Chapter 35

I bought a book on stenography and started to teach myself shorthand. I always was punctual at the office and at Dr. Strong's. I worked very hard.

One day when I went to Spenlow & Jorkins as usual, I found Mr. Spenlow in the doorway looking grave and talking to himself. Instead of returning my "Good morning" with his usual affability, he looked at me in a distant, ceremonious way and coldly asked me to accompany him to a nearby coffeehouse. Apprehensive, I complied. When I allowed Mr. Spenlow to walk in front of me because of the passageway's narrowness, I observed that he held his head with a lofty air that was unpromising. I feared that he had found out about my engagement to Dora.

I followed Mr. Spenlow into an upstairs room. Miss Murdstone was there. She gave me her chilly fingernails and sat severely rigid. Mr. Spenlow shut the door, motioned me to a chair, and stood on the rug in front of the fireplace. "Miss Murdstone, have the goodness to show Mr. Copperfield what you have in your purse," he said. Compressing her lips, Miss Murdstone opened her purse's steel clasp and produced my last letter to Dora, teeming with expressions of devoted affection. "I believe that is your writing, Mr. Copperfield?" Mr. Spenlow said.

I felt very hot, and the voice that I heard was very unlike mine. "It is, sir."

Miss Murdstone now took an entire bundle of letters, tied with blue ribbon, from her purse. "I believe," Mr. Spenlow said, "those are also from your pen, Mr. Copperfield?" I took the letters from Miss Murdstone. They began with phrases such as "My ever dearest and own Dora," "My best beloved angel," and "My blessed one forever." I blushed deeply and offered the letters back to Mr. Spenlow. "No, thank you," he said coldly. "Miss Murdstone, be so good as to proceed."

"I confess to having entertained suspicions regarding Miss Spenlow and David Copperfield for some time," she said. "I observed Miss Spenlow and David Copperfield when they first met. When I returned to Norwood, after the absence occasioned by my brother's wedding, and Miss Spenlow returned from her visit to her friend Miss Mills, Miss Spenlow's manner gave me greater occasion for suspicion. Therefore I watched her closely. I found no proof until last night. It appeared to me that Miss Spenlow received too many letters from Miss Mills. Last evening after tea, I observed the little dog growling around the drawing room, tearing at something. I said to Miss Spenlow, 'Dora, what does the dog have in his mouth? It's paper.' Miss Spenlow put her hand to her chest, gave a cry, and ran to the dog. I interposed and said, 'Dora, my love, you must permit me.' The little dog retreated under the sofa on my approaching him and was with great difficulty dislodged with fire irons. Even when dislodged, he kept the letter in his mouth. When I tried to take it from him, at the risk of being bitten, he continued to grip it so firmly in his teeth that I held him suspended in the air by means of the letter. Finally I obtained it. After reading it, I told Miss Spenlow that I suspected she had many such letters in her possession. Finally I obtained from her the packet that is now in David Copperfield's hand. Miss Spenlow implored me to say nothing of the matter. She even tried to bribe me with kisses and pieces of jewelry." Miss Murdstone shut her mouth at the same time that she snapped her purse shut.

Turning to me, Mr. Spenlow said, "You've heard Miss Murdstone, Mr. Copperfield. Do you have anything to say in reply?"

"There's nothing I can say, sir, except that all the blame is mine. Dora . . . "

"'Miss Spenlow' if you please," Mr. Spenlow said majestically.

"I persuaded . . . Miss Spenlow to consent to this concealment, and I bitterly regret it."

"You're very much to blame, sir," Mr. Spenlow said, pacing on the hearth rug. "Your behavior has been deceptive and unbecoming, Mr. Copperfield. When I take a gentleman to my house, whether he is nineteen, twenty-nine, or ninety, I take him there in a spirit of confidence. If he abuses my confidence, he commits a dishonorable act."

"I feel it, sir. I assure you," I responded. "But I never thought it dishonorable before. I love Miss Spenlow so much that . . . "

"Rubbish!" Mr. Spenlow said, reddening. "Please don't tell me to my face that you love my daughter, Mr. Copperfield."

"Could I defend my conduct if I didn't, sir?"

"Can you defend your conduct if you *do*, sir?" Mr. Spenlow returned. "Have you considered your age and my daughter's age, Mr. Copperfield? Have you considered what it is to undermine the confidence that should exist between my daughter and me? Have you considered my daughter's station in life and the plans that I might contemplate for her happiness and advancement? Have you considered *anything*, Mr. Copperfield?"

"Very little, sir, I'm afraid," I answered, speaking to him as respectfully and sorrowfully as I felt. "But please believe me. Dora and I were engaged before the change in my financial circumstances."

Mr. Spenlow energetically struck one hand against the other. "You please will *not* speak to me of engagements, Mr. Copperfield!"

Miss Murdstone gave a short laugh.

I resumed, "When I explained my altered position to you, sir, I had already . . . made my feelings known to Miss Spenlow. I have been working very hard to improve my circumstances. I'm sure that they'll improve in time. Will you grant me some time, sir? We're both very young."

Nodding and frowning, Mr. Spenlow said, "You're right that you're both very young. It's all nonsense. Let there be an end to it. Take your letters, and throw them into the fire. Give me Miss Spenlow's letters to throw into the fire. Our future dealings will be restricted to business. We won't mention this again."

"Sir, Miss Spenlow and I love each other," I said.

"Very well, Mr. Copperfield," Mr. Spenlow said. "I'll have to deal with my daughter. Do you decline to take your letters?"

I had laid them on the table. "Yes. They belong to Miss Spenlow."

After a silence Mr. Spenlow said, "Mr. Copperfield, my daughter is the heir of all my worldly possessions. If this youthful folly isn't completely relinquished, I might have to change the provisions that I've made, to protect her from marrying unwisely. I hope you won't force me to do that. Take a week to consider what I've said."

"Yes, sir," I answered, although I had no intention of giving up Dora.

"Confer with Miss Trotwood or any other person with any knowledge of life. Take a week, Mr. Copperfield."

"Yes, sir," I repeated, and I left the room. Miss Murdstone's eyes followed me to the door.

When I got to the office, I sat at my desk in my nook thinking about this earthquake. I was especially distressed by the thought of Dora's being frightened and disconsolate. I wrote a letter to Mr. Spenlow begging him not to punish Dora for my own folly. I begged him to spare her gentle nature. I sealed the letter and placed it on his desk. When he returned, I saw him, through the half-open door of his office, pick up the letter and read it. He said nothing about it all morning, but before he left in the afternoon, he called me in and said, "You needn't make yourself at all uneasy about my daughter's happiness. I've told her that this is all nonsense. I have nothing more to say to her about this. I'm an indulgent father. You can spare yourself any anxiety on my daughter's account. If you're foolish and obstinate, Mr. Copperfield, you may make it necessary for me to send my daughter abroad for another term. But I have a better opinion of you than that. I hope you'll see reason within a few days. All I desire is that this incident be forgotten. All you have to do, Mr. Copperfield, is forget it."

As if I ever could forget Dora! I wrote to Miss Mills, begging her to see me that evening, and sent the message by a courier. At night I went to Miss Mills's house and walked up and down until Miss Mills's maid stealthily fetched me in and took me to the back kitchen. There I raved to Miss Mills, who had received a hasty note from Dora telling her that everything had been discovered. Miss Mills wept with me and said, "Love will win in the end." We resolved that she should go to Dora first thing in the morning and find some way of assuring her, either by looks or words, of my devotion and misery. When I got home, I told my aunt everything. She tried to comfort me, but I went to bed in despair.

The next morning was Saturday, so I didn't go to Dr. Strong. Instead I went straight to Spenlow

& Jorkins. When I entered, the clerks were there, but no one was doing any work. Mr. Tiffey—for the first time in his life, I think—was sitting on someone else's stool and hadn't hung up his hat. "This is a calamity, Mr. Copperfield," he said.

"What is?" I asked.

"Mr. Spenlow is dead."

I reeled. One of the clerks caught hold of me. He and another clerk sat me down in a chair, untied my cravat, and brought me some water. "Dead?" I repeated.

Mr. Tiffey said, "He dined in town yesterday and started to drive home in his carriage by himself. The carriage arrived home without him. The horses stopped at the stable gate. The stable man went out with a lantern. Nobody was in the carriage. The household was roused, and three servants went out along the road. They found Mr. Spenlow more than a mile away, not far from the church. He was lying facedown, partly on the road and partly on the roadside. No one knows whether he fell out or got out because he was feeling ill. He already was dead when they found him."

Horrified, I longed to go to Dora to comfort her. I went to Norwood that night. When I inquired at the door, one of the servants said that Miss Mills was there. I went back home and wrote a letter to Miss Mills. I sincerely deplored Mr. Spenlow's untimely death. In fact, I wept while writing the letter. I begged Miss Mills to tell Dora that I grieved with her and for her and that I would come as soon as Dora wanted me. The next day I received a few lines in reply. Dora was overcome by grief. When Miss Mills had asked her if she should send her love to me, Dora only had cried, "Oh, dear Papa! Oh, poor Papa!"

It turned out that Mr. Spenlow had left no will—none, at least, that anyone at Spenlow & Jorkins could find. I was amazed, especially given that Mr. Spenlow had indicated to me that he had made a will. Little by little it came out that he had been in debt. The furniture from his house was sold, and the house was leased. Mr. Tiffey told me that less than £1,000 in assets probably would remain after everything was settled.

For six weeks I waited in torment to see Dora. Whenever Miss Mills mentioned me to Dora, Dora would say only, "Oh, dear Papa! Oh, poor Papa!" Mr. Spenlow's two sisters, Miss Clarissa and Miss Lavinia, invited Dora to come live with them in Putney. Clinging to them and weeping, Dora exclaimed, "Oh yes, Aunts! Please take Miss Mills, Jip, and me to Putney!" So they went soon after the funeral. I continued to correspond with Miss Mills.

Chapter 36

Worried by my prolonged dejection, my aunt suggested that I go to Dover to see that everything was working well at the house, which was rented, and to arrange a longer lease with the same tenant. Janet had been employed by the Strongs. I agreed to go because I wanted to see Agnes. Dr. Strong readily agreed to my taking a few days' vacation. With Mr. Spenlow dead, business at Spenlow & Jorkins fell off. Easygoing and inept, Mr. Jorkins was a poor manager. Marriage licenses and wills brought Spenlow & Jorkins the most money, and the competition for those was keen.

I found everything in a satisfactory state at the Dover house. Having settled what little business I had to transact there and slept in Dover one night, I walked on to Canterbury early in the morning. It was a cold, windy, but clear winter's day. The crisp weather and sweeping downs cheered me a bit. When I arrived at Mr. Wickfield's house, I found Mr. Micawber sitting in the little ground-floor office previously occupied by Uriah Heep. Dressed in a black suit, Mr. Micawber was writing with great diligence. He seemed glad, but somewhat embarrassed, to see me. He would have led me immediately to Uriah, but I declined.

"I know this house well," I said. "I'll find my way upstairs. How do you like the law, Mr. Micawber?"

"My dear Copperfield," he replied, "to someone with imaginative powers, the law involves a tedious amount of detail." Glancing at some letters he was writing, he said, "Even in correspondence, the mind isn't free to soar to any exalted expression. Still, the law is a noble pursuit." His face brightened when he said, "Mrs. Micawber and I are renting the Heeps' former residence. We'd be delighted to have you visit."

"Thank you. Has Mr. Heep been treating you well?"

"My dear Copperfield," Mr. Micawber said, "Mr. Heep has been kind enough to advance me money to cover my debts."

"I wouldn't have expected him to be so generous," I said.

With a slight air of offense, Mr. Micawber said, "I speak of my friend Heep, because I have experience."

"I'm glad your experience has been so positive," I said. "Do you see much of Mr. Wickfield?"

"Not much," Mr. Micawber said slightingly. "Mr. Wickfield is a man of good intentions, but he's become superfluous."

"I'm afraid his partner seeks to make him so."

"My dear Copperfield," Mr. Micawber said, "allow me to offer a remark. I'm here in a capacity of confidence. I'm here in a position of trust. I'm not at liberty to discuss the affairs of Wickfield & Heep."

"I understand," I said.

Clearly happy to change the subject, Mr. Micawber said, "I'm charmed, Copperfield, with Miss Wickfield. She's a superior young lady of remarkable attractiveness, grace, and virtue."

"She is, indeed," I agreed. Mr. Micawber and I shook hands, and I took my leave, saying, "Please give my regards to Mrs. Micawber and the children."

No one was in the quaint, old drawing room, although there were items that indicated Mrs. Heep's whereabouts. I looked into the room still belonging to Agnes and saw her sitting by the fire and writing at a pretty, old-fashioned desk. My darkening the light made her look up. What a pleasure to be the cause of that bright change in her attentive face and the object of that sweet regard and welcome! "Agnes!" We sat side by side. "I've missed you so much lately. I'm always at my best in your presence. You make me feel calm and peaceful. Whenever you aren't there to advise me, I seem to do all sorts of stupid things." I started to cry. When I had regained my composure, Agnes asked me what had happened since our last meeting. I told her everything, concluding, "Now my reliance is on *you*, Agnes."

"But it shouldn't be on *me*, David," she said. "It should be on Dora."

Somewhat embarrassed, I said, "Dora is rather difficult to rely on. She's a timid little thing, easily disturbed and frightened. What should I do, Agnes? What would it be right to do?"

"I think that the honorable course would be to write to Dora's aunts. Don't you think that any secret course is an unworthy one?"

"Yes, if *you* think so."

"I would relate, as plainly and openly as possible, all that has taken place and ask their permission to visit. I'd ask them not to dismiss your request without speaking to Dora. I wouldn't be vehement. I'd trust to my fidelity and perseverance, and to Dora."

"Yes. Of course you're right. Thank you," I said.

I went downstairs to see Mr. Wickfield and Uriah Heep. Uriah had a new office, which smelled of plaster and had been built out in the garden. Amid numerous books and papers, he received me in his usual fawning way. I felt sure that Mr. Micawber had told him about my arrival, but Uriah acted as if he were surprised to see me. He accompanied me to Mr. Wickfield's room, which was the shadow of its former self. A number of conveniences had been removed to accommodate Uriah. While Mr. Wickfield and I exchanged greetings, Uriah stood in front of the fire, warming his back and scraping his chin with his bony hand.

"Will you stay with us while you're in Canterbury, David?" Mr. Wickfield asked, glancing at Uriah for his approval.

"Is there room for me?" I asked.

"Yes, there's a spare room," Mr. Wickfield answered.

"I will, then. Thank you."

Taking leave of Mr. Wickfield and Uriah until dinner, I went back upstairs and drafted a letter to Dora's aunts, as Agnes had advised. I had hoped to have no companion but Agnes. However, Mrs. Heep had asked permission to knit near the fire in that room, under the pretext that it was the least drafty room in the house and therefore most suited to her rheumatism. I forced myself to give her a friendly greeting. "I hope you're well, Mrs. Heep."

"I 'umbly thank you, sir," she said. "If I could see my Uriah well settled in life, I couldn't expect much more, I think. How do you think my Ury is looking, sir?"

I thought that he looked as villainous as ever. "I see no change in him."

"Oh. Don't you think he's thinner than before?" she said.

"I didn't notice," I replied.

"Didn't you? Well, you don't take notice of him as a mother does." Her glance shifted to Agnes. "Don't *you* see a wasting and a wearing in him, Miss Wickfield?"

"No," Agnes said, pursuing her work. "You worry about him too much. He's perfectly well."

With a loud sniff Mrs. Heep resumed her knitting. She sat on one side of the fire, I sat at the desk in front of it, and Agnes sat a little beyond me on the other side. Whenever I lifted my eyes from the letter I was writing and met Agnes's eyes, I saw that Mrs. Heep was watching us. At dinner Mrs. Heep maintained her watch. After dinner, when Mr. Wickfield, Uriah, and I were left alone together, Uriah leered at me. In the drawing room Mrs. Heep sat knitting and watching again. The whole time that Agnes played the piano and sang, Mrs. Heep sat at the piano. Once she asked for a particular ballad, which she said her Ury (who was yawning in an armchair) doted on. Every so often Mrs. Heep would look at Uriah and report to Agnes that he was in raptures over the music. She hardly ever spoke without some reference to her son.

When I went to bed, I hardly slept because I was so disturbed by the Heeps' presence in the house. The next day was a repeat of the first. Agnes and I were constantly watched by Mrs. Heep or Uriah. I didn't have even a few minutes alone with Agnes. I barely could show her my letter to Dora's aunts. I asked her to take a walk with me, but Mrs. Heep then complained so much about her rheumatism that Agnes charitably remained to keep her company. Toward twilight I went out by myself and considered whether I should tell Agnes that Uriah wanted to marry her. I hadn't walked far when someone behind me hailed me. The shambling figure and purple coat couldn't be mistaken. I stopped, and Uriah came up.

"Well?" I said.

"How fast you walk!" he said. "My legs are pretty long, but you've given them quite a workout."

"Where are you going?"

"With *you*, Mr. Copperfield, if you'll allow me the pleasure of a walk with an old acquaintance."

"To tell you the truth, I came out to walk alone because I've had so much company," I said.

Uriah looked at me sideways and said with his hardest grin, "You mean my mother."

"Yes, I do," I responded.

"Well, all stratagems are fair in love, sir." He rubbed his chin and softly chuckled. "You're a dangerous rival, Mr. Copperfield. You always were, you know."

"You dare to keep watch on Miss Wickfield?" I said with indignation.

"Oh! Mr. Copperfield! Those are harsh words."

"Do you suppose that I regard Miss Wickfield as other than a dear sister?"

"I can't say, sir," Uriah answered.

"I'm engaged to another young lady. I hope that satisfies you."

"Really?" He caught my hand and gave it a squeeze. "Oh, Mr. Copperfield, if you'd only condescended to return my confidence, I never would have doubted you. Now I'll ask Mother to leave you alone. I know you'll excuse the precautions of affection. What a pity that you didn't condescend to return my confidence. But then, you've never condescended to me as much as I would like. You've never liked me as much as I've liked *you.*"

"Before we leave the subject," I said, "you should understand that I consider Agnes Wickfield as far above you as the moon."

"All along you've thought me too 'umble," he replied.

"It's not humbleness that I object to," I said. "It's a *pretense* of humbleness."

"I can't help being 'umble, sir. Both father and me was brought up at a charitable school for boys. Mother also was brought up at a charitable establishment. We were taught 'umbleness, and little else, from morning to night. We had to take our caps off to this person and bow to that person and always know our place and abase ourselves before our betters. Father was made a sexton because he was so 'umble. The gentlefolks thought him such a well-behaved man. 'Be 'umble, Uriah,' Father said to me, 'and you'll get on. People like to think that they're above you.' He was right."

We walked back, side by side, saying little more. Uriah was merry at dinner and talked more than usual. He asked his mother if he was getting too old to be a bachelor. When Mr. Wickfield, Uriah, and I were left alone after dinner, Uriah intentionally got Mr. Wickfield drunk. "We seldom see Mr. Copperfield, sir," Uriah said to Mr. Wickfield. "Let's drink a toast to him. Mr. Copperfield, to your health and happiness!" Then he asked Mr. Wickfield to toast someone else. Then he himself made another toast. Then he asked Mr. Wickfield to toast yet another person. And the toasts went back and forth. It made me sick at heart to see Mr. Wickfield become intoxicated. Finally Uriah called for a toast to Agnes, "the divinest of her sex." Mr. Wickfield set down his empty glass, looked at the portrait of his dead wife, put his hand to his forehead, and shrank back in his chair. "I'm an 'umble individual to give you her health," Uriah continued, "but I adore her. Agnes Wickfield is the divinest of her sex.

To be her father is a proud distinction, but to be her husband . . . "

With a cry Mr. Wickfield rose from the table.

"What's wrong?" Uriah said, reddening. "I have as good a right as any other man to make your Agnes *my* Agnes. I have a *better* right."

"Look at him," Mr. Wickfield said to me, pointing to Uriah. "Look at my tormentor. Step by step I've abandoned my reputation and home to him."

"I've *kept* your reputation and home for you," Uriah retorted.

"See what he is," Mr. Wickfield said to me.

"You'd better stop him from saying something he'll regret, Copperfield," Uriah said to me.

"I'll say anything I choose!" Mr. Wickfield cried. "David, how far have I sunk since you first came to this house? Weakness has ruined me." He dropped back into his chair. "Uriah Heep is a millstone around my neck. He runs my business, and he runs my house."

The door opened, and Agnes glided in, looking pale. She put her arm around her father's neck and said, "Papa, you aren't well. Come with me." Mr. Wickfield laid his head on her shoulder and went out with her. Her eyes met mine for only an instant, but I saw how much she knew of what had passed.

Without speaking to Uriah, I went upstairs into the quiet room where Agnes had so often sat beside me at my books. I took up a book and tried to read. I heard the clocks strike midnight and was still reading, without knowing what I read, when Agnes touched me.

"You'll be leaving early in the morning, David," she said. "Let's say goodbye now." She had been weeping. "Heaven bless you." She gave me her hand.

"Dearest Agnes, I see that you don't want to speak about what happened tonight, but is there nothing to be done? Is there anything that I can do? Agnes, I'm too poor in everything in which you're rich—goodness, resolution, and other noble qualities—to doubt or direct you, but you know how much I love you and owe you. Tell me that you won't ever sacrifice yourself to a mistaken sense of duty and marry someone unworthy of you. Say you have no such thought, dear Agnes, much more than sister! Think of the priceless gift of a heart such as yours, of love such as yours."

"You needn't fear for me, my brother," she said, and she was gone.

The next day at dawn, I got onto the stagecoach. I sat thinking about Agnes. When the coach was about to start, Uriah appeared. "Copperfield," he said, "I thought you'd be glad to hear before you left that everything is fine between Mr. Wickfield and me. I've already been into his room, and we've sorted it all out. Although I'm 'umble, I'm useful to him. When he isn't intoxicated, he understands his interest. He's an agreeable man. Last night I plucked a pear before it was ripe, but it'll ripen yet. I can wait." He left as the coachman took his seat.

Chapter 37

When I got home, I talked to my aunt about the Wickfields' situation. I also showed her my letter to Dora's aunts. She approved of it, so I mailed it the next morning.

Nearly a week later I was walking home from Dr. Strong's on a bitterly cold day through a heavy snowfall. The noise of wheels and tread of people were as hushed as if the streets had been strewn with feathers. On my way a woman passed me who looked familiar. Then I saw a man stooping on the steps of a church. He had put down some burden on the smooth snow to adjust it. He and I looked into each other's faces. It was Mr. Peggotty. Then I realized that the woman I had seen was Martha Endell.

"Master Davy!" Mr. Peggotty exclaimed. We shook hands. Gripping me, he said, "It does my heart good to see you, sir."

"My dear old friend!"

"I was going to come see you tomorrow morning before going away again."

"Where are you going and where have you been?" I asked. But then I said, "Come, we must get you in out of this weather."

I took Mr. Peggotty into the nearest inn, into a room with a good fire burning. When I saw him in the light, I observed that his hair was long, ragged, and grayer. The lines in his face and forehead were deeper. He looked as if he had toiled and wandered through all sorts of weather. But he looked strong. He shook snow from his hat and clothes and brushed it from his face. He sat down opposite me at a table, with his back to the door. He put out his rough hand and grasped mine warmly. "I've been far, Master Davy, but I've learned very little."

I rang the bell for some hot ale. While it was being warmed at the fire, Mr. Peggotty sat thinking. Soon after we were left alone, he lifted his head and said, "When Emily was a child, she used to talk to me a lot about faraway coasts where the sea was bright blue and sparkled in the sunlight. When she ran off, I thought that Steerforth might have taken her to a warm country. He might have told her wonders about countries like Italy and Greece, so I crossed the Channel to France. In France I traveled mostly by foot, sometimes in carts along with people going to market, and sometimes in empty stagecoaches. When I came to any town, I described Emily and asked if anyone had seen her. Sometimes I was directed to a particular woman. When I saw that she wasn't Emily, I moved on. Many people treated me kindly, giving me food and drink and a place to sleep."

Suddenly I saw Martha listening at the door. I concealed this fact from Mr. Peggotty because I thought it would only upset him. Martha's face was haggard.

"Next I went to Italy, where I wandered as I had in France," Mr. Peggotty continued. "The people were just as good to me. Finally I got news that Emily had been seen in a particular place in Switzerland. Someone who knew Steerforth's servant Littimer had seen the three of them there. I headed for the place right away, traveling day and night."

Martha continued to listen at the door.

"But when I got there, I was too late," Mr. Peggotty said. "They'd gone. So I went home to Yarmouth. I just came from there four days ago. Mrs. Gummidge was overjoyed to see me. She handed me this bundle of letters." He took the bundle from a breast pocket and placed it on the table. "The first letter came before I'd been gone a week. Well, it wasn't actually a letter. It was a fifty-pound note in a sheet of paper addressed to me and slid under the door during the night. It's Emily's handwriting. The second letter came to Mrs. Gummidge three months ago. Please read it, sir."

I read, "Please have pity on a wicked woman and send me word whether my uncle is well and what he said about me when he learned that I'd gone away. Please also tell Ham that I bless him and pray for him to have a happy home. Emily." A five-pound note was enclosed in this letter, which instructed Mrs. Gummidge to send her reply to a particular post office in Switzerland.

"What answer did Mrs. Gummidge send?" I asked.

"She and Ham wrote that I'd gone to find Emily. They told her what my parting words were."

"Is that another letter in your hand?" I asked.

"It's money, sir: ten pounds with the message 'From a true friend.' It came in the mail the day before yesterday. I'm going to seek Emily at the place of the postmark." Mr. Peggotty showed me the postmark. It indicated a town on the upper Rhine River. He had obtained a map of the area. He laid it between us on the table and traced his course with one hand. "Because the money comes from Steerforth, there's no way on earth that I'd accept it. I hope to give it back to him."

I nodded. "How's Ham?"

Mr. Peggotty shook his head. "He works hard and is well respected. He never complains, but he's deeply wounded. He holds his life cheap now. Whenever a man is wanted for dangerous service in rough weather, he goes." Mr. Peggotty gathered up the letters, put them into their little bundle, and put it back into his breast pocket. Martha no longer was at the door. "Well," Mr. Peggotty said, arranging his bag, "it's done me good to see you, Master Davy." He rose, and I rose too. We grasped each other by the hand again before going out. "I'll search for Emily until I die or find her," Mr. Peggotty said quietly. We went out into the snowy night. I saw Martha nearby, but Mr. Peggotty didn't notice her. He spoke of an inn on the Dover Road where he knew he could find clean, simple lodging for the night. I accompanied him over Westminster Bridge and parted from him on the Surrey shore.

Chapter 38

At last an answer came from Dora's aunts. They presented their compliments to me and invited me to call on a certain day—if I liked, with a companion. I replied that I would have the honor of visiting the Misses Spenlow at the appointed time, accompanied by my friend Thomas Traddles. I lost Julia Mills as a go-between and supporter because she and her father moved to India, where he had a business.

On the appointed day of my visit to Dora's aunts, I spent much time deciding how to dress. I decided to look neither poor nor wealthy. When Tommy arrived, I was dismayed to see that his hair was standing straight up so that it looked like the end of a broom. As we were walking to Putney, I took the liberty of asking, "Tommy, could you smooth your hair down a bit?"

"My dear David," he said, removing his hat and rubbing his hair all kinds of ways, "I wish I could, but nothing I've tried will smooth it down. If I were to place a hundred-pound weight on it all the way to Putney, it still would stick straight up again the moment the weight was removed. You have no idea how obstinate my hair is. I'm quite a porcupine."

Although disappointed, I laughed with delight at Tommy's humor and good nature. "Your hair must have all the obstinacy that is lacking from your good nature. By the way, when you became engaged to Sophy, did you make a regular proposal to her family? Was there anything like what we're going through today?"

"Actually, it was a rather painful transaction. Sophy is so useful to her family that they were very unhappy at the thought of her marrying. Mrs. Crewler, especially, was unhappy at the prospect of Sophy's leaving home. However, Reverend Crewler is an exemplary man. He pointed out to his wife that she should, as a Christian, reconcile herself to the sacrifice and bear no uncharitable feeling toward me."

"And *has* she reconciled herself?" I asked.

"Not really," Tommy admitted.

By the time we reached the Spenlows' house, I was terribly nervous. When the maid opened the door, I had a vague feeling of being on view and of somehow moving my body across a hall into a small first-floor drawing room that looked out on a neat garden. Tommy and I sat on a sofa. I heard the clock ticking on the mantel. I looked around for Dora, but there was no sign of her. I thought I heard Jip bark once in the distance and then be muffled.

When Clarissa and Lavinia Spenlow entered, Tommy and I rose and bowed. The sisters wore black. Their bearing was formal and composed. They were small but upright in posture and had round, twinkling eyes like a bird's.

"Please be seated," Miss Lavinia, the younger of them, said quietly. Tommy and I sat back down. Miss Lavinia had my letter in her hand. Turning to Tommy, she said, "Mr. Copperfield?"

"*I'm* Mr. Copperfield, ma'am," I said. "This is my friend Thomas Traddles." We all heard Jip give two more barks and be muffled again.

Miss Clarissa said, "Being familiar with matters of this nature, my sister Lavinia will state what we consider most likely to promote the happiness of both parties." Like her sister, Miss Clarissa leaned a little forward when she spoke, shook her head after speaking, and became upright again when silent.

"We won't enter on the past history of this matter," Miss Lavinia said. "The death of our poor brother Francis has cancelled that and substantially changed our niece's situation. We have no reason to doubt, Mr. Copperfield, that you are a young gentleman possessed of good qualities and honorable character and that you have an affection for our niece."

"No one ever loved anyone more than I love Dora," I replied. Tommy gave an affirming murmur.

Miss Lavinia said, "You ask permission, Mr. Copperfield, to visit here as the accepted suitor of our niece. We have considered your letter carefully, shown it to our niece, and discussed it with her. We've been in doubt as to what course we should take with regard to the affections of people as young as you and our niece. We've decided that we need to observe your feelings for each other. Therefore, we agree to your visiting here."

Greatly relieved, I exclaimed, "Dear ladies, I'll never forget your kindness!"

"However," Miss Lavinia continued, "we'd prefer to regard those visits as, at present, visits to us rather than to our niece. We won't recognize any engagement between you and our niece, Mr. Copperfield, until we've had the opportunity of further observation. If you agree to this, you must give us your word of honor that no communication of any kind will take place between you and our niece without our knowledge."

I eagerly agreed to the aunts' terms.

"In that case, Mr. Copperfield," Miss Clarissa said, "we would be happy to have you come to dinner every Sunday at three o'clock."

"Thank you." I bowed my head.

"Your aunt, mentioned in your letter, will perhaps call on us," Miss Clarissa continued.

"She would be proud and delighted to make your acquaintance," I said, although I wasn't at all sure of that.

The interview being at an end, I expressed my gratitude, rose, and kissed Miss Clarissa's hand and then Miss Lavinia's. Miss Lavinia then rose and, asking Tommy to excuse us for a minute, asked me to follow her. I obeyed, trembling. Miss Lavinia led me into another room. There I found Dora with her ear pressed to the wall and Jip with his head tied up in a towel to prevent him from barking. How beautiful Dora was in her black dress! Miss Lavinia left us, Dora sobbed, and I was in bliss. "My dearest Dora! Now, indeed, my own forever!" I exclaimed.

"Doady!" she said, revealing what was, apparently, to be my nickname. She showed me Jip's new trick of standing on his hind legs.

Miss Lavinia soon came to take me away. Tommy and I left feeling very happy. "They're very agreeable ladies," he said. "I wouldn't be at all surprised if you and Dora were married years before Sophy and me."

My aunt was delighted to see me so happy. I sent Agnes a grateful letter telling her the good that had come of my following her advice. She replied right away with a hopeful, cheerful letter. A few days later my aunt visited Dora's aunts. I was greatly relieved that she got along well with them. A few days later they returned her visit. After that, visits were exchanged every few weeks. The only member of our small society who refused to adapt himself to circumstances was Jip. He never saw my aunt without growling.

One thing troubled me: everyone seemed to regard Dora as a pretty toy. My aunt called her "Little Blossom." Dora's aunts waited on her, curled her hair, made ornaments for her, and treated her like a pet child. One day when I was out walking with Dora, I said to her, "I wish that you could get people to treat you like an adult."

"You're being cross," she responded. "They're very kind to me, and I'm happy."

"Well, you could still be happy if you were treated like a rational being."

Dora gave me a reproachful look and began to sob. "If you don't like me, why are you engaged to me? If you can't bear me, why don't you go away?"

I kissed away her tears and told her that I doted on her.

"I'm very affectionate, Doady," she said. "You shouldn't be mean to me."

"Mean, my precious love? As if I ever could be mean to you!"

"Then, don't find fault with me," she said, pouting.

I was charmed by her presently asking me, of her own accord, to give her a cookbook and show her how to keep accounts. I had a cookbook prettily bound, so that it would look more inviting, and brought it on my next visit. I also gave Dora an accounts book that my aunt had used, a new accounts book, and a pretty box of pencils so that she could practice keeping accounts. But the cookbook made her head ache, and writing numbers made her cry. They wouldn't add up, she said. She would cross them out and draw little nosegays and likenesses of Jip and me all over the accounts book.

Then I tried verbal instruction in domestic matters as we walked. When we passed a butcher's shop, I said, "Now suppose, my pet, that we were married and you were going to buy a shoulder of mutton for dinner. Would you know how to buy it?"

Dora's pretty little face fell, and she pouted. She thought a while, and then her face brightened.

"Why, the butcher would know how to sell it, so I wouldn't need to know anything, you silly boy!"

Once I asked Dora what she would do if I said I'd like an Irish stew. She answered, "I'd tell the servant to make it," clapped her little hands together, and laughed in a charming way.

At some point it dawned on me that I, too, treated her like a plaything.

Chapter 39

Agnes and her father came to Dr. Strong's for a two-week visit. Uriah Heep and his mother rented lodgings in the neighborhood and also visited the Strongs. Forcing himself on me when I was walking in Dr. Strong's garden, Uriah said, "You see, Mr. Copperfield, someone who loves is anxious to keep an eye on the beloved."

"Of whom are you jealous now?" I asked.

"No man at present," he answered.

"Do you mean that you're jealous of a woman?"

Uriah gave me a sidelong glance out of his reddish eyes and laughed. "Not jealous, just wary. When I was an 'umble clerk, Mrs. Strong looked down on me. She always was having Agnes over to her house, and she was a friend to you, but I was too far beneath her to be noticed. She's just the sort of person to make my Agnes look down on me. I won't allow people to stand in my way. I could pull her down off her high horse!"

"I don't understand you," I said.

"Don't you? I'm astonished, Mr. Copperfield. You're usually so quick. Let me just say that in

286

pulling her down off her high horse, I could pull someone else down with her: Mr. Jack Maldon."

A feeling of dread came over me.

"I think that's him ringing at the gate now," Uriah said with satisfaction.

"It looks like him," I replied as nonchalantly as I could.

Uriah put his hands between his knobby knees and doubled up with silent laughter. Repelled, I walked away without saying goodbye.

That Sunday I took Agnes to meet Dora. I had arranged the visit beforehand. Agnes was expected to tea. I was in a flutter of pride and anxiety: pride in Dora and anxiety as to whether Agnes would like her. Dora had been fearful about meeting Agnes. She had told me that she considered Agnes "too clever" for her. But when she saw Agnes looking so cheerful, thoughtful, and kind, Dora gave a small cry of pleased surprise and put her arms around Agnes's neck and her cheek against her face. I was overjoyed.

Agnes and Dora sat side by side. We all had a wonderfully pleasant tea. Miss Clarissa presided, and Miss Lavinia looked on with benign patronage. I cut a cake and handed out the pieces. Agnes's cheerfulness and grace made a favorable impression on everyone. Even Jip accepted her. Agnes showed interest in everything that interested Dora.

After tea Dora said to Agnes, "I'm so glad that you like me. I didn't think that you would, and I want to be liked more than ever now that my friend Julia has gone to India."

"I'm afraid that David must have given an unpromising description of me," Agnes said.

"Oh, no!" Dora said, shaking her curls. "It was all praise. He values your opinion so much that I was afraid of it."

"His attachment to you needs no strengthening from my good opinion," Agnes said with a smile.

I made merry about Dora's wanting to be liked.

"You're a goose," Dora said to me. "I don't like *you*, at any rate."

The evening flew. When I was standing alone in front of the fire, Dora gave me a kiss. Her eyes shone, and she played with a button of my coat. "Don't you think, Doady, that if I'd had Agnes for a friend a long time ago, I would have been more clever?"

"My love, what nonsense!" I said.

"Do you think it's nonsense?" she said without looking at me. "Are you sure it is?"

"Of course I am," I said.

"I've forgotten what relation Agnes is to you, you dear bad boy."

"No blood relation," I replied. "We were brought up together like brother and sister."

"I wonder why you ever fell in love with *me*," Dora said.

"Because I couldn't see you and *not* love you," I replied. She kissed me three times and left the room.

The coach arrived, and there was a hurried but affectionate parting between Agnes and Dora. They promised to write to each other. "Don't mind my letters being foolish," Dora said.

As Agnes and I traveled back to Dr. Strong's house, she praised Dora's gentle, trusting nature, and I thanked her for making Dora feel so comfortable. "Are things better at home?" I asked.

"They're the same," Agnes answered.

"Uriah Heep hasn't said anything about . . . ?" I hesitated.

"Don't worry about me, David," she said. "I'll never take the step you dread my taking."

"No. Of course not." But I felt relieved. "When will you come to London again?"

"Probably not for a long time," she replied. "I think it would be better for Papa to stay at home. I'll write to Dora regularly, and we'll frequently hear about each other that way." When we reached Dr. Strong's, I accompanied Agnes inside. She gave me her hand and said, "I'm so happy that you're happy. God bless you always." And she went upstairs.

I turned to leave. However, seeing a light on in Dr. Strong's study, I decided to bid him good night before leaving. I looked in and saw Uriah, Dr. Strong, and Mr. Wickfield. Dr. Strong sat in his study chair with his hands covering his face. Mr. Wickfield, who looked distressed, was leaning forward touching Dr. Strong's arm. At first, I thought that Dr. Strong was ill. I entered.

"I felt it incumbent upon me, Mr. Copperfield," Uriah said, "to call Dr. Strong's attention to Mrs. Strong's goings-on. It's much against the grain with me to be concerned in anything so unpleasant, but

I felt duty-bound to tell Dr. Strong that anyone can see that Mr. Maldon and Mrs. Strong are too sweet on each other. You've long suspected as much, haven't you, Mr. Wickfield?" Mr. Wickfield didn't say anything. "Come now, partner," Uriah said. "Speak up."

"My friend," Mr. Wickfield said to Dr. Strong, "don't attach too much weight to any suspicions I may have had."

"There!" Uriah cried.

"You've doubted her, Wickfield?" Dr. Strong asked.

"Yes," Mr. Wickfield answered. "I thought that *you* did, too."

"No," Dr. Strong said in a tone of grief. "Never."

"I thought that you wanted to send Maldon abroad to separate them," Mr. Wickfield said.

"No," Dr. Strong said. "I wanted to give Annie pleasure by helping her childhood companion in his career. Nothing else."

"I thought that such a young, beautiful woman, however real her respect for you, might have married you partly because she was influenced by worldly considerations. After all, there's a great disparity in your ages," Mr. Wickfield continued. "So I doubted her. But I never mentioned my doubts to anyone."

"Mr. Copperfield also had doubts," Uriah said.

"How dare you refer to me!" I exclaimed.

"When I alluded to this the other night, you immediately knew what I meant," Uriah responded. "I saw it in your face. Can you deny it, Copperfield?" I didn't say anything.

Dr. Strong looked at me and saw the answer in my face. He rose and paced, occasionally putting his handkerchief to his eyes. "I'm much to blame. I've exposed my dear Annie to trials and aspersions. I utterly believe in her truth and honor. I admit, though, that I may have unwittingly ensnared her in an unhappy marriage. I married her when she was very young. I never meant to take advantage of her, but perhaps I unknowingly did. If she views Jack Maldon, her long-time companion, with some regret regarding what might have been, that is only natural. However, that doesn't mean that she's in any way at fault. It is she who should reproach, not I. Wickfield, give me an old friend's arm upstairs. I ask that none of you refer to this discussion ever again." Mr. Wickfield hastened to Dr. Strong. Without a word they slowly left the room together.

After watching them go, Uriah said, "Well, Mr. Copperfield, the results haven't been as I expected. Dr. Strong is as blind as a stone."

Enraged, I cried, "Villain!" and slapped him in the face with my open hand, so forcefully that my fingers tingled.

We stood looking at each other. Then he said, "Copperfield, have you taken leave of your senses?"

"I'll have nothing more to do with you!"

"Won't you? Maybe you won't be able to help it," he responded.

"I despise you. You cause harm to everyone around you."

"Copperfield, you've always gone against me. You were against me even when you were a schoolboy."

"Think whatever you like," I responded. I took up my hat and left.

For the remainder of Agnes's visit, Dr. Strong kept to himself a considerable part of each day. Agnes and her father had been gone a week before we resumed our usual work. Dr. Strong was as kind to Mrs. Strong as ever, but he seemed to have aged. She seemed to sense that something was wrong, and she had become increasingly unhappy.

About this time I received a letter from Mrs. Micawber. She said that she sought my advice because Mr. Micawber had recently stopped confiding in her. "He has entirely changed," she wrote. "He's secretive. His life is a mystery to me. He spends it, from morning to night, at the office. Also, he's become morose and severe. He is estranged from our older children and takes no pride in the twins. If you'll advise me, you'll add yet another reason for me to feel grateful to you. With love from the children, Emma Micawber." I sent a reply offering the only advice that I could—that Mrs. Micawber be patient and kind toward her husband, as I knew she would be in any case.

Chapter 40

Seasons passed, and I turned twenty-one. Using shorthand, which I had mastered, I covered events in Parliament for a newspaper. Then I started writing stories for magazines. I had a good income. My aunt sold her house in Dover and planned to move into a cottage. I bought a pleasant cottage for Dora and me. We were about to be married.

Dora's aunts were all abustle with wedding preparations. Miss Clarissa and my aunt roamed all over London, finding pieces of furniture for Dora and me. Peggotty cleaned the cottage over and over, scrubbing everything until it shone. Agnes and Sophy were to be bridesmaids. Sophy arrived at the house of Dora's aunts. She had a pleasant face and was frank, genial, and engaging. Tommy presented her to Dora and me with great pride, and I heartily congratulated him on his choice. I picked up Agnes at the Canterbury coach.

The next day we all went to see the cottage in which Dora and I would live. It was a beautiful little place, with everything bright and new. The flowers on the carpets looked freshly gathered. The leaves on the wallpaper looked as if they'd just come out.

The curtains were spotless muslin. The furniture was rose-colored. Dora's blue-ribboned garden hat already hung on a peg. Her guitar case was in a corner.

The day of the wedding my aunt dressed in lavender silk and wore a white bonnet. She and Peggotty were both very excited. Mr. Dick, who was to give the bride away, had his hair curled. Tommy wore a light-blue jacket and cream-colored trousers. We all rode in an open carriage. My aunt sat with her hand in mine the whole way.

At the church Miss Lavinia and my aunt cried. Dora whispered her responses. When we knelt side by side, she trembled less but kept hold of Agnes's hand. I proudly walked down the aisle with my sweet wife on my arm. As we passed, people whispered how beautiful Dora was and how young we both were. Like the wedding ceremony, the reception passed in a joyful haze.

It was strange and wonderful to find myself sitting in my own house with Dora. Sometimes in the evenings, when I would look up from my writing and see her seated opposite me, I'd lean back in my chair and think how strange it was that we finally were alone together. When there was a Parliamentary debate and I was kept out late, it seemed strange, as I walked home, to think that Dora was there waiting for me. It was wonderful to have her softly come downstairs to talk to me as I ate my supper. We had a servant, Mary Anne Paragon, who kept house for us. A severe woman in the prime of life, she was the cause of our first quarrel.

"My love," I said to Dora one day, "do you think that Mary Anne has any idea of time?"

"Why, Doady?" Dora asked, looking up from her drawing.

"Because it's five o'clock, and we were supposed to eat at four."

Dora glanced at the clock and said, "I think the clock is fast."

Looking at my watch, I said, "On the contrary, my love; it's a few minutes slow."

Dora came and sat on my knee to coax me to be quiet. With her pencil she drew a line down the middle of my nose.

"Don't you think, my dear, it would be better for you to remonstrate with Mary Anne?" I asked.

"Oh, no! Please. I couldn't, Doady."

"Why not?" I gently asked.

"Because I'm such a little goose, and she knows that I am."

I frowned.

"Oh, what ugly wrinkles in my bad boy's forehead," Dora said. Still on my knee, she traced them with her pencil.

"Come, Dora. Let's talk sensibly. It isn't comfortable to have to go to work without having eaten dinner, is it?"

"No," Dora replied faintly.

"My love, you're trembling."

"Because I know you're going to scold me," she said.

"My sweet, I'm only going to reason."

"Reasoning is worse than scolding!" she exclaimed. "I didn't marry you to be reasoned with. If you meant to reason with such a poor little thing as I am, you should have told me so, you cruel boy."

I tried to pacify Dora, but she turned her face away and shook her curls from side to side. "Dora, my darling."

"I'm not your darling. You must be sorry that you married me, or else you wouldn't reason with me."

"You're being childish, Dora, and talking nonsense. Yesterday I had to leave after eating only half of my dinner. The day before that I felt sick after eating undercooked veal. Today I haven't eaten at all. I don't mean to reproach you, but this won't do."

"Oh, you're a cruel, cruel boy to say that I'm a disagreeable wife!"

"I never said that!" I protested. "I'm not blaming you, Dora. We both have a lot to learn. I'm only trying to show you that you really must get after Mary Anne."

"You're ungrateful," Dora said, starting to cry. "The other day when you said you'd like some fish, I went out myself and ordered it."

"And that was very kind of you, my darling."

I got home late that night and found my aunt sitting up waiting for me. Alarmed, I asked, "What's wrong, Aunt?"

"Nothing, Davy," she replied. "Sit down. Little Blossom has been out of spirits, and I've been keeping her company. That's all."

I sat down with a sigh. "I meant no harm, Aunt. I only asked Dora if she could look to our domestic affairs."

"You must have patience, Davy," she said.

"Of course. I don't mean to be unreasonable."

"No, no. But Little Blossom is a very tender little blossom, and the wind must be gentle with her."

"I know," I said. "Do you think that you could advise her a little?"

"No, Davy," my aunt answered with some emotion. "Don't ask me to do that." Her tone was so earnest that I raised my eyes in surprise. "I'm not going to meddle," she said. "I want our pet to like me and be as carefree as a butterfly. Remember your own home during your mother's second marriage, and never ask Dora to be something that she isn't." I immediately realized that my aunt was right. "You chose your wife, Davy. She's very pretty and very affectionate. It's your duty to judge her as you chose her—by the qualities that she has, not by the qualities that she lacks. Your future is between the two of you. No one can assist you. You must work it out for yourselves." My aunt kissed me. "Now light my lantern, and see me to my cottage."

When I returned, Dora came down in her little slippers. She cried on my shoulder and said, "You were hardhearted and naughty."

"So were you. But we won't quarrel ever again, will we?" And we made up.

I fired Mary Anne, but not before she stole some of our silverware. After that we had a succession of servants who cheated us. One washerwoman even pawned our clothes. Without servants we were in an even worse state. Our house always was in disorder. Jip walked on the tablecloth during dinner, often putting his foot into the salt or butter. The food always was undercooked or overcooked.

Dora asked me to think of her as my "child wife." She said, "Whenever you're going to be angry with me, say to yourself, 'It's only my child wife.' Whenever I'm disappointing, think, 'I knew a long time ago that she would make only a child wife.' When you miss what I'd like to be but never can be, think, 'Still, my foolish child wife loves me,' because I certainly do." Shortly afterwards Dora told me that she was going to become a wonderful housekeeper. She bought an immense accounts book, carefully stitched up all the pages of the cookbook that Jip had torn out, and desperately tried to "be good," as she phrased it. But the figures still wouldn't add up. Looking dejected, Dora would say, "They won't come out right. They make my head ache."

Then I'd say, "Let's try together. Let me show you, Dora." I'd begin a demonstration, and Dora would pay attention for maybe five minutes, after which she'd begin to feel dreadfully tired. Then she'd curl my hair or turn my shirt collar down, and I'd remember her injunction to think of her as a child. I often wished that I could go to Dora for advice and support. I took all the toils upon myself and had no partner in them. Still, Dora was happy and loved me, so I was largely content.

However late I got home from a Parliamentary debate, Dora always came downstairs to greet me. When I wrote at home, she sat quietly near me. "Oh, what a weary boy," Dora said one night when I met her blue eyes as I was closing my desk.

"What a weary girl is more to the point," I responded. "You shouldn't stay up so late just because *I* do, my love."

"I like to watch you write," Dora said. "Will you let me hold the pens? I want to have something to do while you're writing. May I hold the pens?" To her joy, I said yes. The next time I sat down to write, and regularly afterwards, she sat with a spare bundle of pens at her side. I often pretended to need a new pen because it greatly pleased her to give me one. Sometimes I also pretended to need a page or two of manuscript copied. Then Dora was in her glory. In preparation for this great work, she would put on a bibbed apron to protect her clothes from ink. When she finished, she would bring me the pages with great pride. I would praise them, and she'd hug me around the neck.

In this way we continued. Dora was hardly less affectionate to my aunt than to me. My aunt was more pliant with Dora than with anyone else. She courted Jip, although he never responded; listened day after day to Dora playing the guitar, although she didn't care for music; walked distances to purchase, as surprises, any trifles that Dora wanted; and never entered and found Dora absent without calling out, at the foot of the stairs, "Where's Little Blossom?"

Chapter 41

It was some time now since I had stopped working for Dr. Strong. Living in his neighborhood, I saw him frequently, and Dora, my aunt, Mr. Dick, and I occasionally went to his house for tea or dinner. Also, Dora and my aunt sometimes went to the theater, the opera, or a concert with Mrs. Strong and her mother. Ever since the night that Uriah Heep had suggested that Mrs. Strong was unfaithful to her husband, I had believed her faithful.

One evening when my aunt, Mr. Dick, and I were visiting the Strongs, Mr. Dick suddenly said to them, "What is it that's wrong between the two of you?"

Everyone else was taken aback. But then Mrs. Strong said, "My husband, Mr. Dick is right. Let us both know what has come between us."

"Annie," Dr. Strong said, "there has been no change in my affection, admiration, and respect for you. My only wish is to make you happy."

"David, Miss Trotwood, do either of you know what this is about?" Mrs. Strong asked.

After a few moments of painful hesitation, I said, "Mrs. Strong, I know something that Dr. Strong asked me to conceal. I believe it would be wrong to conceal it any longer."

"Please do tell me, David," Mrs. Strong pleaded.

"Do I have your permission, Dr. Strong?" I asked.

He winced but answered, "You do."

I then related how Uriah had suggested that Mrs. Strong was unfaithful to her husband. When I finished, Mrs. Strong remained silent for some moments, with her head bent down. Then she took her husband's hand and kissed it. "I'll tell you everything," she said to him in a soft, tender voice.

"There's no need, my love," Dr. Strong said. "I've never doubted you."

"I know that," she said, "but there *is* a need, a great need." She then said to her husband, "I have loved and venerated you ever since I was a child. I was proud and honored to marry you. My only unhappiness after we married was to see how my mother and others took advantage of your generosity. I saw that Mr. Wickfield, who had your welfare very much at heart, rightly resented this. I started to see that some people doubted my motives in having married you. They doubted my love for you. My mother asked you to help my cousin Jack Maldon. We had been childhood sweethearts. If circumstances had been otherwise, I might have come to persuade myself that I loved him. I might have married him. If I had, I'm sure I would have been miserable. I have long known that Jack and I have nothing in common. There can be no disparity in marriage greater than disparity of mind and purpose."

Those words struck me powerfully and echoed in my mind: "There can be no disparity in marriage greater than disparity of mind and purpose."

Mrs. Strong continued, "If I were thankful to you for nothing else, instead of for so much, I would be thankful to you for having saved me from mistaking my childhood affection for Jack for something deeper and more solid. He was the object of your generosity, so freely bestowed for my sake. I thought he should have made his own way. But I didn't have a low opinion of him until the night of his departure for India. That night I learned that he had a false and thankless heart. He spoke words of love to me that I found shocking and repellant. I saw, too, how Mr. Wickfield looked at me. I saw that he doubted my faithfulness to you. I thought of telling you what Jack had said to me, but the words died on my lips because I found them so repugnant and so likely to distress you. Since that night I've never spoken to him except in your presence and then only enough to avoid questions. Years have passed since I made clear to him that I don't welcome him here. I consider myself unworthy of you. You're so wise, good, and generous. But I never have wronged you, and I never will." She embraced her husband, and he leaned his head down over her, mingling his gray hair with her dark brown tresses.

My aunt, Mr. Dick, and I went home very happy for the Strongs. But I kept thinking of some of Mrs. Strong's words, especially "There can be no disparity in marriage greater than disparity of mind and purpose."

Chapter 42

About a year after my wedding I was returning from a solitary walk thinking about the book I was then writing—my first work of fiction—when I passed Mrs. Steerforth's house. I was startled by a woman's voice at my side. It belonged to the little maid who had formerly worn blue ribbons in her cap. Now her cap was decorated only with one brown bow. "If you please, sir, would you have the goodness to walk in and speak to Miss Dartle?" she asked.

"Has Miss Dartle requested that?" I responded.

"Yes. Miss Dartle saw you pass a night or two ago. She instructed me to sit at work on the staircase and ask you to step in when I saw you pass again."

We turned back toward the house. "How is Mrs. Steerforth?" I asked.

"Poorly," the maid answered. "She rarely comes out of her room."

When we arrived at the house, I was directed to Miss Dartle in the garden. She was sitting on a seat at one end of a kind of terrace, overlooking London. It was a somber evening with a lurid light in the sky. Miss Dartle saw me as I approached and rose to receive me. She was even thinner and paler than the last time I had seen her. Her dark eyes were brighter and her scar more noticeable. Our meeting wasn't cordial. She showed disdain.

"I'm told you wish to speak to me, Miss Dartle," I said, standing near her and declining her gesture of invitation to sit down.

"Has the girl been found?" she asked.

"No."

"She left him," she said. I assumed that "him" referred to James. "If she hasn't been found, maybe she's dead," Miss Dartle said with undisguised satisfaction.

"I see that time hasn't softened you, Miss Dartle."

She gave a scornful laugh. "Do you want to know what is known of her?"

"Of course."

She rose and took a few steps toward a wall of holly that divided the lawn from a kitchen garden. "Come here," she ordered someone. Mr. Littimer appeared through an arch in the holly and bowed. "Now," Miss Dartle said without glancing at him, "tell Mr. Copperfield about her flight."

Mr. Littimer began, "Ma'am, Mr. James and I . . . "

"Don't address yourself to *me*," Miss Dartle interrupted.

Mr. Littimer turned toward me. "Sir, Mr. James and I have been abroad with Miss Peggotty ever since she left Yarmouth under Mr. James's protection. We've been in France, Switzerland, and Italy. Mr. James took uncommonly to her. He was less restless with her than I've ever seen him before. Miss Peggotty picked up the foreign languages and was much admired wherever we went." Mr. Littimer stole a glance at Miss Dartle and slightly smiled to himself. "Miss Peggotty went on in this way for some time, being occasionally low-spirited, until I think she began to weary Mr. James by giving way to depression and bad temper. Then things became uncomfortable. Mr. James began to be restless again. The more restless he became, the worse Miss Peggotty got. Still, they would patch things up over and over again. At last, when there had been many words and reproaches, Mr. James set off one morning from the neighborhood of Naples, where we had a villa. (Miss Peggotty was very partial to the sea.) Under the pretense of returning in a day or so, Mr. James left me to tell Miss Peggotty that their relationship was over. But Mr. James behaved very honorably. He proposed that Miss Peggotty marry a very respectable man who was prepared to overlook her past and who was at least as good as anyone she could have aspired to under ordinary circumstances, her connections being very common."

I was convinced that the scoundrel spoke of himself, and I saw my conviction reflected in Miss Dartle's face. Mr. Littimer continued, "Mr. James also asked me to restore harmony between Mrs. Steerforth and him. She has undergone so much on his account. When I told Miss Peggotty that Mr. James was done with her, her violence was beyond all expectation. She raved and had to be held by force. I thought that otherwise she might kill herself."

Miss Dartle smiled with satisfaction.

"When I came to the part about her marrying the respectable man," Mr. Littimer said, "she was completely ungrateful. If I hadn't been on my guard, I'm convinced she would have had my blood."

"I think the better of her for it," I said indignantly.

Mr. Littimer bent his head as if to say, "Indeed, sir? You're young." He resumed, "For a time, it was necessary to keep her away from anything with which she might injure herself or someone else and to lock her up. She escaped during the night by forcing open a window lattice that I had nailed shut and climbing down a vine. I have no further knowledge of her."

"Maybe she's dead," Miss Dartle said with a smile.

"She may have drowned herself, Miss," Mr. Littimer said. "Or she may have had assistance from the boatmen and their families. She was in the habit of talking to them on the beach and sitting by their boats. Once, Mr. James was far from pleased to find out that she had told the children that she was a boatman's daughter and that in her own country, long ago, she had roamed the beach like them. When it was clear that she was not to be found, I went to Mr. James, at the place where I was to write to him, and told him what had happened. Words passed between us, and I felt obliged to leave him.

I've borne many insults from Mr. James. This time he went too far. I came home to England and related . . . "

"He didn't relate anything until I paid him," Miss Dartle said to me.

"I related what I knew," Mr. Littimer continued. "At present I'm unemployed. I'd welcome a respectable situation."

Miss Dartle glanced at me as if to ask if there was anything that I wished to ask.

I asked Mr. Littimer, "Did Miss Peggotty receive a letter from home, or did you intercept it and keep it from her?"

He answered, "I'll say only this: Mr. James didn't encourage her receiving letters likely to increase her low spirits and make things unpleasant."

"Is that all?" Miss Dartle asked me.

"I have nothing more to say," I answered.

Mr. Littimer bowed to me and then to Miss Dartle. Then he left through the arch in the wall of holly. After a pause Miss Dartle said to me, "Littimer also told us that James currently is sailing off the coast of Spain. But I suppose that's of no interest to you. The rift between his mother and him is wider than ever. I wanted you to know all of this because I want you to find this low girl and convince her to stay away from James."

I saw by the change in Miss Dartle's face that someone was approaching behind me. It was Mrs. Steerforth. She gave me her hand coldly. She was greatly changed. Her fine figure was far less upright, her handsome face was deeply marked, and her hair was almost white. But when she sat down on the seat, I saw that she still was handsome. "Has Mr. Copperfield been informed of everything, Rosa?" she asked.

"Yes."

"He's heard Littimer?" Mrs. Steerforth asked.

"Yes."

Mrs. Steerforth turned to me. "My sole interest, Mr. Copperfield, is to save my son from falling into the snares of this designing woman again."

"Madam, the woman you speak of is far from designing. She's the victim here. And after the way your son has treated her, I doubt that she would so much as take a cup of water from his hands."

Miss Dartle was about to interpose, but Mrs. Steerforth said, "Let it be, Rosa. You're married now, sir?"

"Yes."

"And are doing well? I hear that you're beginning to be famous."

"I've been very fortunate," I answered.

"You have no mother?" Mrs. Steerforth asked.

"No."

"It's a pity. She would have been proud of you. Good night." I took her hand, which she held out with a dignified, unbending air.

The next day I went to London to see Mr. Peggotty, who was renting a room over a candle shop. I found him in. "Master Davy, thank you for this visit," he said. "You're kindly welcome, sir."

"Mr. Peggotty," I said, taking the chair he handed me, "don't expect much. I've had some news of Emily."

He nervously put his hand to his mouth and turned pale. He fixed his eyes on mine.

"I don't know where she is now, but she's no longer with James Steerforth."

Mr. Peggotty sat down, looking at me intently, and listened in profound silence to all that I had to tell. When I finished, we both were silent for some time. "What do you think, Master Davy?" he asked.

"I think she's alive," I replied.

"If the shock was too great, she might have thrown herself into the sea. Still, I believe she's alive."

"She's likely to come to London because it's so easy to remain hidden here," I said.

"Yes," Mr. Peggotty said. "She won't go home. She might have if she had left Steerforth, but *he* left *her*." He shook his head sadly.

"If she comes to London, I believe there's one person she might go to. Do you remember Martha?"

"Martha Rendell?"

"Yes," I answered.

"I've seen her in the streets," Mr. Peggotty said.

"Emily was charitable to her. That snowy night that we talked at the inn, Martha listened at the door."

"Master Davy!"

"I haven't seen her since. I was unwilling to add to your troubles by mentioning her to you then, but she's the person with whom I think we should communicate. Do you understand?"

"Too well, sir," he replied.

"Do you think that you can find her?"

"I think I know where to look."

"Shall we go out now and try to find her?" I asked.

"Yes." Mr. Peggotty prepared to accompany me. He adjusted some furnishings in the little room, apparently to make it ready for Emily's arrival. He put a candle and match at hand; arranged the bed; took one of Emily's dresses out of a drawer, where it was neatly folded with some other garments; and placed the dress and a bonnet on a chair. When we descended the stairs, Mr. Peggotty said, "There was a time, Master Davy, when I thought of Martha as almost like dirt under Emily's feet. God forgive me."

As we walked along, I asked about Ham. Mr. Peggotty said that Ham was the same, taking no care for his own safety, never complaining, and liked and respected by all. "Do you think that Ham would become violent if he ever encountered Steerforth?" I asked.

"I don't know, sir," Mr. Peggotty replied. "I've often thought about it. I don't believe that Ham would do anything violent, but I'd certainly prefer that he never see Steerforth again."

We weren't far from Blackfriars Bridge when Mr. Peggotty turned his head and pointed to a solitary woman flitting along the opposite side of the street. I immediately recognized Martha. We crossed the road and were pressing on toward her when it occurred to me that she might be more disposed to talk in a private place or even might lead us to Emily. I therefore advised Mr. Peggotty that we shouldn't address her yet but should follow her. He agreed, and we followed at a distance. Martha continued a long way. Finally she turned down a dark, deserted street. I said, "We can speak to her now." We quickened our pace. We were now in Westminster. Martha proceeded so quickly that we were in the narrow waterside street by Millbank before we came up behind her. At that moment she crossed the road and, without looking back, walked even more rapidly. As quietly as we could, Mr. Peggotty and I kept pace on the opposite side of the road, keeping in the shadow of the houses.

There was a small, dilapidated wooden building, probably an obsolete ferry house, at the end of that low-lying street. As soon as Martha reached that building and saw the water, she stopped as if she had reached her destination. She slowly approached the river. The neighborhood was dreary. The melancholy waste of road had neither wharves nor houses. A sluggish ditch deposited mud at a prison's walls. Coarse grass and rank weeds straggled over all the marshy land in the vicinity. In one section, skeletal houses, inauspiciously begun and never finished, rotted away. In another section the ground was littered with rusty steam boilers, wheels, cranks, pipes, furnaces, paddles, anchors, diving bells, windmill sails, and other strange objects half sunk into the mud. Heavy smoke poured from the chimneys of factories whose fiery glare shone along the polluted river. Slimy gaps and causeways, winding among old wooden piles to which a sickly substance clung like green hair, led down through the ooze and slush to the ebb tide. The remnants of last year's handbills, offering rewards for drowned people, fluttered above the high-water mark. Martha went down to the river's edge and stood looking at the water. I realized that she was contemplating drowning herself. Some boats and barges were lodged in the mud. These enabled Mr. Peggotty and me to come within a few yards of Martha without being seen. I motioned to Mr. Peggotty to stay where he was and emerged from the shadows to speak to her. Grabbing her by the arm, I said, "Martha."

She screamed in terror and struggled so fiercely that I doubt I could have held her alone. Mr. Peggotty's stronger hands took hold of her. When she looked into his face, she dropped down between us. We carried her away from the water to some dry stones and laid her down. She cried. In a little while she sat up, holding her head with both hands. "I belong in the river," she said. "Like me, it came from a country place. Like me, there once was no harm in it, but then it crept through the dismal streets and became defiled. I belong in the river." Then she cried again. Mr. Peggotty and I waited for her to stop crying and regain some calm.

"Martha," I said, leaning down and helping her to rise, "I'm David Copperfield, and this is Mr. Peggotty, Emily's uncle. Do you recognize us?"

"Yes," she said faintly. She was haggard. Her sunken eyes indicated a long period of deprivation, perhaps illness.

"Martha," Mr. Peggotty said, "I'm searching for Emily. I've been searching for her a long time." Martha trembled. Mr. Peggotty picked her shawl up from the ground and gently put it around her. "She's ashamed to see me, but she shouldn't be. I love her as much as ever. I just want her back safe. Please help us find her."

"Will you trust me?" Martha asked.

"Fully," Mr. Peggotty said.

"I'll look for her," Martha said, "If I find her, I'll shelter her. Without her knowledge I'll come to you and bring you to her."

"Thank you, Martha!" Mr. Peggotty and I said in unison. We now told Martha everything that we knew about Emily. She listened with great attention. Her eyes occasionally filled with tears. When we finished, Martha asked where she could reach us. Under a dull streetlamp, I wrote our two addresses on my pocket notepad, tore out the piece of paper, and gave it to her. She tucked it into her dress.

"Where are you living, Martha?" I asked.

"I don't stay at any one place for very long," she answered.

Mr. Peggotty whispered to me what I had already thought of. I took out my purse, but I couldn't persuade Martha to accept any money.

"Mr. Peggotty and I have money to spare, Martha. We don't want you undertaking a search without resources."

She thanked us but still refused to take any money. "I couldn't accept money to help Emily," she said. "This gives me something to work for, to live for."

"Martha," I said, "you mustn't ever again think of taking your own life. We all can do some good in this world."

She nodded. Promising again to do her best to find Emily, she went her way along the desolate road. Mr. Peggotty and I headed back. We parted with a prayer for the success of this fresh effort.

It was midnight when I arrived home. I was surprised to see that the door of my aunt's cottage was open and that a faint light in the entryway was shining out across the road. I went to speak to her. Shocked to see a man standing in her little garden, I stopped short amid the thick foliage outside the garden. The man was eating hungrily and drinking from a bottle. I recognized him as the man who had previously frightened my aunt. He seemed curious about the cottage, as if it were the first time he'd seen it. After stooping to place the bottle on the ground, he looked up at the windows and looked around with an impatient, secretive air. My aunt came out. She was agitated and put some money into his hand. "What's the use of this?" he demanded.

"I can't spare any more," my aunt said. "You stripped me of most of what I had. You closed my heart against the whole world. You treated me falsely, ungratefully, and cruelly. Go, and repent of it." The man slouched out of the garden, and my aunt went back inside.

I entered my aunt's house and said, "Aunt, this man has alarmed you again. Let me speak to him. Who is he?"

We sat down in her little parlor. She said, "Davy, he's my husband."

"Your husband! I thought he was dead."

"There was a time that I completely believed in that man. I loved him. He used up my fortune and broke my heart."

"Aunt!"

"When I left him, I provided for him generously. He soon wasted what I had given him. He sank lower and lower. He became an adventurer, a gambler, and a cheat. You see what he is now. He was a fine-looking man when I married him. I thought he was the soul of honor." She gave my hand a squeeze and shook her head. "He's nothing to me now, Davy. But when he periodically reappears, I give him money to go away. I was a fool when I married him, and I'm still enough of a fool that I continue to help him." My aunt sighed. "There, my dear. Now you know the whole story. It's just between us. Let's not mention it again."

Chapter 43

I worked hard on my novel while continuing my
newspaper work. When my novel came out, it was
successful. I now was financially secure enough to
stop covering Parliamentary debates. Because I
wanted Dora to share my love of literature, I talked
to her about my favorite works of literature and read
Shakespeare to her. The only result was that she was
bored and depressed. Feeling contrite, I bought a
pair of earrings for Dora and a fancy collar for Jip
and abandoned my attempt to make Dora educated
and thoughtful. I sat down with her on the sofa, put
the earrings into her ears, and said, "I've been poor
company lately, my dear."

"You've been trying to make me clever, haven't
you, Doady?" she asked with her eyebrows raised. I
nodded assent and kissed her lips. "It's no use," Dora
said, shaking her head. "You've forgotten what I said
about being your child wife. If you can't accept me as
I am, you'll always be annoyed with me."

"Dora," I said with remorse, "I love you dearly
as you are."

"It's better for me to be stupid than for me to
be unhappy, isn't it?"

"It's better for you to be what you naturally are," I responded. I loved Dora dearly and was fairly content, but I wished that she could be more of a partner and helpmate. I bore the full weight of our cares. I couldn't really share my projects or deeper thoughts with Dora. I often remembered Mrs. Strong's words "There can be no greater disparity in marriage than disparity of mind and purpose."

When Dora and I had been married two years, she had a miscarriage that left her in a weakened state. She said to my aunt, "When I can run around again as I used to, Aunt, I'll give Jip a good run. He's getting slow and lazy."

"He's getting old, my dear," my aunt said gently.

Astonished, Dora said, "You think that Jip is old? How strange to think of him as old! Poor little fellow." Dora helped Jip up onto the sofa, where he barked at my aunt. Dora finally got him to lie down beside her. She drew one of his long ears through her hand again and again, repeating, "Poor little fellow. You're not so old, Jip, that you'll leave me yet, are you?"

Dora became so weak that I carried her downstairs every morning and upstairs every night. She would clasp me around the neck and laugh as if I carried her for fun. Jip would bark, caper around us, go ahead of us, and—short of breath—look back from the landing to see that we were coming. I felt that Dora was becoming lighter in my arms.

By this time some months had passed since Mr. Peggotty and I had spoken to Martha. I hadn't seen her since, but she had communicated with Mr. Peggotty several times. She hadn't learned anything about Emily's whereabouts. I began to think that Emily was dead, but Mr. Peggotty remained convinced that he would find Emily alive, and he continued to search for her.

One evening I was walking alone in my garden at twilight. It had rained all day, but now the rain had ceased. There was a damp feeling in the air, and the tree leaves were heavy with moisture. Suddenly Martha appeared, dressed in a plain cloak. "Martha!" I exclaimed.

"Can you come with me?" she asked in an agitated whisper. "Emily is in my lodging!"

"Emily!" I was overcome with joy.

"I went to Mr. Peggotty, but he wasn't in," Martha said. "I wrote down where he should come and left the note on his table. Can you come now?"

"Immediately. Your lodging is in London?"

"Yes," she answered.

I took her arm, and we hurried to the street. I stopped an empty cab that was coming by, and we got in. "Where should I tell the driver to go?" I asked her.

"Anywhere near Golden Square. Quickly!"

"How is Emily? Is she well?" I asked.

"Yes."

We proceeded without another word being spoken. Sometimes Martha glanced out of the window as if she thought we were going too slowly, although we were going fast. We alighted at an entrance to Golden Square. Martha laid her hand on my arm and hurried me to a street of rundown tenements. Releasing my arm, she entered through the open door of one such tenement and beckoned me to follow her up the dirty, rotting stairs. Several of the rear windows on the staircase had been boarded up. There was scarcely any glass in the other windows. Bad air seemed to enter, but never exit, through the crumbling window frames. Through the windows I saw that the rear courtyard was used as a garbage dump. Martha and I proceeded to the top floor. As we turned to ascend the last flight of stairs, we heard someone coming up the stairs behind us. We paused, looked down, and saw Mr. Peggotty ascending. When he reached us, we all continued upward to Martha's room.

Martha knocked on the door and said, "It's me, Emily. Open up."

Emily opened the door, saw the three of us, and cried, "Uncle!" Mr. Peggotty and Emily embraced and wept. Martha and I also wept.

When Emily was sufficiently calm, she asked about Ham, Peggotty, and Mrs. Gummidge. She also asked about me. After Mr. Peggotty and I told her all the news, she told us how she had escaped from Mr. Littimer. "I fled at night," Emily said. "I ran to the home of a woman who had become my friend—a young woman whose husband was a fisherman. They took me in and kept my presence a secret. When I thought it was safe to leave, I wanted to pay them for having fed and sheltered me, but they wouldn't take a penny. I took a ship north to Leghorn, Italy and another ship to France. Then I crossed the Channel to Dover. All the way to England I intended to go home to Yarmouth, but when I arrived in England . . . Uncle, I felt too unworthy to go home. I didn't feel I should burden you and Ham with my shame. I wanted with all my heart to be with all of you again, but I . . . " Mr. Peggotty embraced her again, and we all started to cry again.

After a while Emily resumed her narrative. "I came to London. I was frightened and almost out of money, but I thought that I'd be able to earn a living as a seamstress. While I looked for a job, I slept in horrible places, the only places that I could afford. Then I saw Martha. I was overjoyed to see a friend. She told me that she'd seen you, Uncle. She said she knew you still loved me and that you completely forgave me."

"Thank you, Martha!" Mr. Peggotty said. Martha wiped tears from her eyes.

"Martha brought me here," Emily said.

"I didn't tell her when I went to fetch you, Mr. Peggotty," Martha said, "in case she'd run off. When I didn't find you in, I went to Mr. Copperfield."

Mr. Peggotty then took Emily to his lodging. The next day he came to see me and told me that he and Emily were going to emigrate to Australia. "No one can reproach my darling in Australia," he said. "We'll begin a new life there."

"When do you plan to leave?" I asked.

"A ship will be sailing in two months."

"Will you and Emily go alone?" I asked.

"Yes, Master Davy. My sister wouldn't want to leave you, Ham, or England."

"Poor Ham," I said.

"Clara keeps house for him. He sits and talks to her with a calm spirit when he won't open his lips to anyone else. Poor fellow." Mr. Peggotty shook his head.

"And Mrs. Gummidge?" I asked.

"I intend to leave her an allowance so that she'll be comfortable. At her time of life I don't think she's up to a long voyage or life in a wild, faraway country. Emily will stay with me, in my London lodging, until we go to Australia. She'll make the clothes that we'll need. I hope that will occupy her so that her thoughts will be on the future, not the past." Mr. Peggotty now took £50 and 10 shillings from his breast pocket. "That's the money Emily sent me after running away with James Steerforth. It came from him." He took some more money from another pocket. "And that's the money Emily had when she fled from Littimer. I want all of it to go back to Steerforth. Will you send it to him, care of his mother, after Emily and I have gone to Australia? I'd like you to tell Mrs. Steerforth that we don't want anything that was her son's."

"I'll certainly do that, Mr. Peggotty," I said.

"I've written to Ham and told him everything that has happened. I told him I'm coming to Yarmouth one last time, to see to things and say goodbye."

"Would you like me to go with you?" I asked, sensing that he would.

"If you'd do me that favor, Master Davy. I know that seeing you would cheer Ham up a bit."

The next morning Mr. Peggotty and I were on a coach to Yarmouth. When we arrived, I went to visit Mr. Omer so that Mr. Peggotty would have some time alone with Peggotty and Ham. I entered Omer and Joram's and said, "How are you, Mr. Omer?"

He fanned away the smoke from his pipe so that he could see me better and soon recognized me with delight. "I'd get up, sir, to acknowledge such an honor as this visit, but my limbs are out of sorts and I wheel myself around now," he said. "Otherwise I'm hardy." I saw that his armchair had wheels. Following the direction of my glance, he said, "It's an ingenious thing, don't you think? It runs as light as a feather and tracks as true as a coach. My little granddaughter likes to push me around in it."

"Is everything fine with Minnie and Bob?" I asked.

"Oh, yes. They're as happy together as ever, and the business is doing well."

"I'm glad to hear that."

"And you've become a well-known author," Mr. Omer said. "I read your novel and enjoyed it very much. It didn't make me the least bit sleepy."

"That's one of the best compliments I've received," I said, laughing. I then gave him a general account of Emily.

He listened with the utmost attention. When I had finished, he said enthusiasitically, "I rejoice at it, sir! It's the best news I've heard in a long time. And what will be done for poor Martha?"

"I'm sure that Mr. Peggotty has something in mind, but I don't know what it is yet."

"If some sort of fund is collected for her, I'd like to contribute," he said. "Put me down for whatever amount you think is right, and drop me a line as to where I should send the money. What about Ham? He's as fine a fellow as there is in all of Yarmouth. Sometimes he comes and talks or reads to me for an hour or so. He's all kindness."

"I'm going to see him now," I said.

"Are you? Please give him my respects. Minnie and Bob are at a dance. They'll be sorry they missed you."

I shook hands with Mr. Omer and wished him good night. After a stroll around the town, I went to Ham's house. Peggotty now lived there and rented out the house she had shared with Mr. Barkis. I found Peggotty, Mrs. Gummidge, and Mr. Peggotty in the neat kitchen. Mr. Peggotty had told Peggotty, Mrs. Gummidge, and Ham everything about Emily. Both Peggotty and Mrs. Gummidge had their aprons to their eyes. Ham had just stepped out to take a walk along the beach. When he returned, he was very glad to see me. We all spoke, with some approach to cheerfulness, of Mr. Peggotty's growing rich in Australia and of the wonders that he'd describe in his letters. Ham seemed serene.

But when Peggotty lit my way to a little room where the crocodile book lay ready for me on the night table, she said of Ham, "He's brokenhearted. He's as brave as he is sweet. He works harder and better than any other boat builder. But he's brokenhearted. Sometimes he speaks of Emily as a child, but he never mentions her as a woman."

Mr. Peggotty spent the next day packing what he thought would be useful to him and disposing of everything else. Because I had sensed the previous night that Ham wanted to speak to me alone, I walked where I'd encounter him on his way home from work. I met him on the sands, and we started to walk together. "Master Davy," he said, "will you be seeing Emily again?"

"I hadn't planned to, Ham, but if you'd like me to convey some message to her, I certainly will."

"Thank you, sir," he said. "I *would* like to send her a message. It isn't that I forgive her. It's that I want her to forgive *me*. I want to beg her forgiveness for having pressed my affections on her. Sometimes I think that if I hadn't pressed her to promise to marry me, she would have told me what she was thinking of doing and sought my advice, and I might have protected her." I squeezed his hand. "I loved her," Ham continued, "and I still love her too much to have her believe that I'm happy without her. At the same time, I want her to be comforted. I'd like her to know that although I mourn her going away, I'll be all right. I'd also like her to know that I think of her as blameless. I don't want her to think that I ever could marry anyone but her, but I'd like her to think that I haven't given up on life. Could you somehow convey that, Master Davy?"

"I will, Ham."

"Thank you, sir. It was kind of you to come down with Uncle Daniel. After he leaves Yarmouth,

I don't expect to ever see him again. When you see him for the last time, will you give him my love and thanks for being the best of fathers to me?"

"I'll tell him, Ham."

"Thank you again, sir." We heartily shook hands. With a slight wave of his hand, as if to explain to me that he couldn't enter the old barge, Ham turned away. I watched him cross the flats in the moonlight. He turned his face toward a strip of silvery light on the sea and passed on, looking at it, until he was a distant shadow.

The door of the barge stood open when I approached. On entering, I found it emptied of all furniture except for one of the old footlockers. Mrs. Gummidge sat on this footlocker, with a basket on her knee, looking at Mr. Peggotty. He leaned his elbow on the mantel and gazed at a few expiring embers in the grate. "Come to bid the place farewell, eh, Master Davy?"

"Yes," I said.

"That's the very locker you used to sit on with Emily," he said. "I'm going to take it with me." The wind around the house made a low sound that sounded like a mournful moan. "It's likely to be a long time before the house has new tenants. The people around here consider it unlucky now."

"Does it belong to anyone in the neighborhood?" I asked.

"It belongs to a mast maker in town. I'm going to give him the key tonight." Mr. Peggotty asked Mrs. Gummidge to rise so that he could take the footlocker.

"Daniel," she said, clinging to his arm, "don't leave me behind!" Taken aback, Mr. Peggotty looked from Mrs. Gummidge to me and back to Mrs. Gummidge. "Don't, dearest Daniel," she pleaded. "Take me with you and Emily. I'll be happy to be your servant."

Shaking his head, Mr. Peggotty said, "My good soul, you don't know what a long voyage is ahead and how hard life will be in Australia."

"Yes, I do, Daniel. I can guess. I don't want the allowance. I want to be with you and Emily. I want to help you both. I want to share your labors and ease your burdens. Let me go with you!" Mrs. Gummidge took Mr. Peggotty's hand and kissed it.

We brought the footlocker out, extinguished the candle, and left the old barge locked up, a dark speck in the cloudy night.

The next day when Mr. Peggotty and I were returning to London on the outside of the coach, Mrs. Gummidge was seated on the inside. She was happy.

Chapter 44

I arrived home to find a mysterious invitation from Mr. Micawber. He asked that Tommy Traddles and I come to the offices of Wickfield & Heep at 9:30 a.m. on a particular date. At that place and time, he said, he would "expose villainy." I contacted Tommy, who said that we must go. Dora was too unwell to travel, but my aunt and Mr. Dick decided to accompany me because they were eager to see Agnes and Mr. Wickfield. We didn't inform Agnes and her father of our coming because Mr. Micawber's note had urged secrecy.

Several days later my aunt, Mr. Dick, Tommy, and I took a coach to Canterbury, where we checked into a hotel for the night. The next morning we went to Mr. Wickfield's house at 9:30. When we knocked at the door, Mr. Micawber answered. He ushered us all into his office. "Mr. Traddles and I have been in touch regarding the matter at hand," he said.

I looked at Tommy in surprise. "Mr. Micawber has consulted me regarding this matter," Tommy said to me, "and I've advised him to the best of my ability."

"Is Miss Wickfield at home?" I asked Mr. Micawber.

"Mr. Wickfield is in bed with rheumatic fever, but I'm sure that Miss Wickfield will be happy to see old friends. Please follow me," he answered. Mr. Micawber preceded us to the dining room. Flinging open the door of Mr. Wickfield's former office, he announced, "Miss Betsey Trotwood, Mr. David Copperfield, Mr. Thomas Traddles, and Mr. Dick."

I hadn't seen Uriah Heep since I had slapped him in the face. Our visit took him completely by surprise. He frowned. A moment later, however, he was his usual fawning, 'umble self. "This is indeed an unexpected pleasure," he said. "Mr. Copperfield, I hope you're well. How is Mrs. Copperfield, sir? I've been sorry to hear that she isn't well." I felt ashamed to let him take my hand, but I didn't know what else to do. "Miss Trotwood, things have changed in this office since I was an 'umble clerk who took your pony to the stable, haven't they?" Uriah said to my aunt, with his sickliest smile. "But *I* haven't changed, Miss Trotwood."

"No, sir," my aunt returned. "You're the same as ever."

"Thank you for your good opinion, Miss Trotwood," Uriah said. "Micawber, tell the servants to inform Miss Agnes and my mother. Mother will be delighted when she sees the present company," he said, placing chairs.

"You aren't busy, Mr. Heep?" Tommy said.

"No, Mr. Traddles, not as busy as I could

wish," Uriah replied, resuming his official seat and squeezing his bony hands, laid palm to palm, between his bony knees. "But Micawber and I have our hands pretty full in general because Mr. Wickfield is hardly fit for any work. Still, it's both a pleasure and a duty to work for him. Mr. Traddles, I think you haven't been intimate with Mr. Wickfield. I believe I've had the honor of seeing you only once before."

"No, I haven't been intimate with Mr. Wickfield," Tommy said, "or I might have met with you long ago, Mr. Heep."

The tone of Tommy's reply made Uriah look at Tommy with a sinister, suspicious expression. But he replied, "I'm sorry for that, Mr. Traddles. You would have admired Mr. Wickfield as much as we all do. But if you'd like to hear someone speak eloquently about my partner, I should refer you to Mr. Copperfield."

Agnes now entered, ushered in by Mr. Micawber. She wasn't as self-possessed as usual. She looked anxious and fatigued. Uriah watched her while she greeted us. Meanwhile, some signal passed between Tommy and Mr. Micawber. Unobserved except by me, Tommy went out.

"You can go, Micawber," Uriah said. Mr. Micawber stood erect in front of the door, looking at Uriah. "Micawber, didn't you hear me tell you to go?" Uriah said.

"Yes," Mr. Micawber replied, immovable.

"Then, why haven't you gone?" Uriah demanded.

"Because I don't choose to," Mr. Micawber answered.

Uriah paled and breathed more rapidly. "The whole world knows that you're a dissipated fellow," he said with an effort at a smile. "I'm afraid you'll force me to fire you. Go along now. I'll talk to you presently."

"If there is a scoundrel on this earth with whom I've already talked too much, that scoundrel's name is Heep!" Mr. Micawber declared passionately.

Uriah fell back as if he'd been struck. He looked around and said, "So, this is a conspiracy. You've all met here by appointment. You've bought my clerk, Copperfield? Take care. You and I understand each other. There's no love between us. You always were a proud puppy. You envy my rise, don't you? Micawber, be off."

"Mr. Micawber," I said, "there's a sudden change in this fellow in that he speaks the truth in at least one respect. That tells me that he's been brought to bay. Deal with him as he deserves."

Uriah wiped sweat from his forehead. "Micawber, you're the scum of the earth. So were you, Copperfield, before anyone showed you charity. Miss Trotwood, you'd better call a stop to this, or I'll reveal a thing or two about your husband. I know your story, old lady. Miss Wickfield, if you love your father, you'd better not join this gang. If you do, I'll ruin him. Think twice, Micawber, if you don't want to be crushed. I recommend that you take yourself off while there's still time to retreat. Where's Mother?" He pulled the bell rope.

"Mrs. Heep is here, sir," Tommy said, returning with her. "I've taken the liberty of making myself known to her."

"Who are you to make yourself known? And what do you want here?" Uriah asked.

"I'm Mr. Wickfield's legal agent and friend," Tommy said in a composed, businesslike way. "I have a power of attorney from him, authorizing me to act for him in all matters."

"The old ass has drunk himself into a state of senility. You've gotten the power of attorney from him by fraud," Uriah said.

"*Something* has been gotten from him by fraud, Mr. Heep, and you know it," Tommy answered. "We'll refer that question to Mr. Micawber."

"Ury!" Mrs. Heep cried.

"Hold your tongue, Mother," Uriah said. He rubbed his chin with his bony hand and said, "You think it justifiable, Copperfield—you who pride yourself so much on your honor—to sneak around my place eavesdropping with my clerk? You make yourself out to be a gentleman, but Micawber told me you once were in the streets." Seeing that his words had no effect on me or anyone else, he sat on the edge of his desk with his hands in his pockets, stubbornly awaiting what might follow.

Mr. Micawber said, "Ladies and gentlemen, when I first came to Wickfield & Heep, I had to ask Heep for advances in order to support my family. In return for those advances, I signed IOUs. Heep then started asking me to do fraudulent things. Whenever Mr. Wickfield was least fit to undertake business, Heep always was at hand to force him to undertake it. At those times he obtained Mr. Wickfield's signature on important documents that he represented as unimportant. He induced Mr. Wickfield to empower him to withdraw a sum of trust money, which he pretended to use for business expenses. Heep made this withdrawal appear to be Mr. Wickfield's own dishonest act and then used the threat of legal punishment to torment and constrain Mr. Wickfield. Also, on at least several occasions Heep forged Mr. Wickfield's signature. I've given one forged document to Mr. Traddles. Finally, I can show from Heep's account books that Heep has, for years, deceived and stolen from Mr. Wickfield. This culminated a few months ago when Heep induced Mr. Wickfield to relinquish his share in the partnership in return for an annuity to be paid quarterly by Heep. In sum, Heep has falsified accounts, fraudulently obtained and withheld money from Mr. Wickfield, and forced him out of the business. Now I just have to substantiate these accusations."

With a glance at Mr. Micawber, Uriah hastily went to an iron safe that was in the room and threw the doors open. It was empty. "Where are the books?" he cried with a face of fright.

"I gave them to Mr. Traddles," Mr. Micawber answered.

"You receive stolen goods, do you?" Uriah demanded of Tommy.

"Under such circumstances, yes," Tommy answered.

To my astonishment, my aunt rushed at Uriah and grabbed him by his collar with both hands. "I want my property!" she demanded. "Agnes, my dear, as long as I believed that your father had made away with it, I didn't tell anyone, even Davy, that I had placed it with him for investment. But now that I know Uriah Heep is answerable for it, I'll have it back!"

I hurriedly came between my aunt and Uriah. "Aunt, everything possible will be done to force him to make restitution." My words calmed her, and she resumed her seat.

Uriah gave me a ferocious look and asked, "What do you want done?"

"I'll tell you what *must* be done," Tommy said. "First, the document by which Mr. Wickfield gave up his share in the partnership must be given to me now."

"What if I don't have it?" Uriah said.

"You have it," Tommy said. "Second, you must make full restitution. Everything here—all account books, documents, money, and securities—must remain in our possession."

"And if I refuse?" Uriah said.

"We'll fetch the police and have you taken to Maidstone Jail," Tommy answered.

Mrs. Heep cried, "Miss Wickfield, please help us! Don't let them take Uriah! He's very 'umble and never meant no harm."

"Mother, hold your tongue," Uriah growled. "Let them have the document. Go get it."

"Mr. Dick, please accompany her," Tommy

said. Mr. Dick went with Mrs. Heep, and they soon returned with the document. "Good," Tommy said. "Now, Mr. Heep, we'll give you some time to consider whether or not you're going to fully cooperate."

Uriah shuffled across the room. Pausing at the door, he said, "Copperfield, I've always hated you. You've always been an upstart, and you've always been against me. As for you, Micawber, I'll get back at you."

When Uriah left the room, we all thanked Mr. Micawber, who invited everyone to his house. Tommy remained to keep an eye on the Heeps, and Agnes remained to look after her father. I parted from Agnes hopeful that the Heeps would cause her father and her no more harm.

Mr. Dick, my aunt, and I went to the Micawbers' house. Mr. Micawber bolted in and rushed into his wife's arms, exclaiming, "Emma, the worst is over! I won't have anything to hide from you anymore. Now, welcome poverty!" The whole family wept with joy and embraced one another. Then my aunt raised the issue as to what the Micawbers actually would do now. She suggested that the family emigrate to Australia. "We don't have enough money to do even that," Mr. Micawber said.

"You've helped us so much," my aunt said. "We'll be more than happy to provide you with enough money to get there."

"Only on the condition that it's a loan, not a gift," Mr. Micawber said.

"On whatever terms you wish," my aunt

responded. "David knows some people who are going to Australia soon. If you decide to go, you can take the same ship. You could help one another."

"Is the climate healthy, ma'am?" Mrs. Micawber asked.

"The best in the world," my aunt answered.

"Are the circumstances of the country such that a man of Mr. Micawber's abilities would have a fair chance of rising in society? Would there be ample opportunity for his talents?" Mrs. Micawber asked.

"There's no better opportunity anywhere for a man who conducts himself well and is industrious," my aunt said.

"It seems, then, that Australia is the proper place for Mr. Micawber," Mrs. Micawber said.

"My dear madam," Mr. Micawber said, "under the circumstances I believe that Australia is the right place for my family and me and that something extraordinary will turn up there."

Chapter 45

Dora continued to be unwell. Jip seemed to suddenly grow very old. He moped, his eyesight was weak, and his limbs were feeble. He no longer barked at my aunt. When my aunt would sit at Dora's bedside and Jip would lie on the bed, he would crawl over to my aunt and lick her hand. Dora would lie there smiling at us and never complain. "You're very good to me," she said to me. "My dear, careful boy is tiring himself out. Aunt, you've had no sleep." Sometimes Dora's aunts came to see her. Then, remembering happier times, we all would talk about the day that Dora and I married.

I would sit in Dora's quiet, shaded room for many hours. I'd sit by her bed, and she'd look at me with her blue eyes and wrap her small fingers around my hand. One morning after my aunt had made Dora comfortable, Dora said, "Look at my hair on the pillow, Doady. It's still long, bright, and curly." I smiled. "Not that I'm vain about it, you mocking boy. You used to say that you thought my hair was so beautiful. When I first began to think about you, I used to look in the mirror and wonder if you'd like to have a lock of it. When I gave you one, you were so foolish."

"That was on the day that you were painting the flowers I'd given you," I said. "That day I told you that I was in love with you."

"After you left, I cried over the flowers because I believed you really liked me. When I can get out and about as I used to, let's go see the places where we were such a silly couple and take some of the old walks. Shall we, Doady?"

"Yes. We'll do that," I said. "So you must hurry and get well, my dear."

"Oh, I'll do that soon. I'm much better, you know."

But Dora no longer went downstairs, even in my arms. She was completely bedridden. One night as I sat by her bed, she said, "Doady?"

"Yes, dear."

"I'd like to see Agnes. I'd very much like to see her."

"I'll write to her, my dear."

"What a good, kind boy!" she said.

"I'll write to her right away. I'm certain that she'll come."

"Are you very lonely when you're downstairs?" Dora asked with her arm around my neck.

"How can I be otherwise, my love, when I see your empty chair?"

"My empty chair." She clung to me for a while in silence. "You really miss me, Doady? Giddy, stupid me?"

"My heart, there's no one on earth whom I could miss more," I said.

"Oh, Doady! I'm so glad and yet so sorry." She embraced me.

"Why sorry, Dora?" I asked.

"Because I don't really think that I'm going to get well," she answered.

"Don't say that, Dora. Dearest love, don't think that."

Agnes came. She, my aunt, and I sat with Dora most of the day. We didn't talk much, but Dora seemed content. I now feared that she was dying, but I kept telling myself that somehow she would get well. At times I went off alone to weep.

When Dora and I were alone that night, she said, "I'm going to say something that I've often thought of saying, Doady. I hope you won't mind. I think I was too young when I married, not just in years but also in thought and experience. I was such a silly little creature. I don't think I was fit to be a wife."

I fought to hold back tears. "Oh, Dora, love, you were as fit to be a wife as I was to be a husband."

"I don't know," she said with the old shake of her curls. "Maybe. But you're very clever, and I never was."

"We've been very happy, my sweet Dora."

"I was very happy. However, as the years passed, you would have tired of your child wife. I would have been less and less a companion for you. You would have been more and more aware of what was missing. I wouldn't have improved. It's best as it is."

"Dora, dearest, don't say such things. Every word seems to be a reproach."

"Not a single syllable is meant to be," she said, kissing me. "You haven't done anything that deserves a reproach, and I love you far too much to say a reproachful word. That's my only merit:

how much I love you." I started to cry. "Oh, my poor boy. Hush. Send Agnes up to me. I want to speak to her alone. When I speak to her, I don't want anyone else to come in, not even Aunt." I continued to cry. "Oh, Doady, with the passing of years I would have disappointed you. I would have tried but disappointed you. You might have come to love me less than you do now. It's best as it is. Now, go downstairs and send Agnes up."

I went into the parlor and asked Agnes to go up to Dora, which she did. I sat by the fire and thought, with remorse, about all the secret regrets that I'd had since I married Dora. Jip whined to go upstairs. "Not tonight, Jip," I said. He came slowly up to me, licked my hand, and lifted his dim eyes to my face. "Oh, Jip." He lay down at my feet, stretched himself out as if to sleep, and, with a plaintive cry, died. Then Agnes was standing in front of me. Her face was so full of pity and grief that I knew that Dora had died.

Chapter 46

At Tommy's request my aunt, Agnes, and I went to the Micawbers' house, in Canterbury. After greetings, Tommy asked everyone but the Micawbers to join him in the parlor. Then he closed the door. "My dear David," he said, leaning back in his chair and looking at me with affectionate sympathy, "I won't make any excuse for troubling you with business because I know you're deeply interested in this matter and it might divert your thoughts. Still, you look quite worn out."

"I'm fine," I said. "I'm anxious to attend to these matters for the sake of Agnes, my aunt, and Mr. Wickfield."

"Mr. Micawber has been untiring in going through all sorts of documents and account books," Tommy said. "He's really been wonderful. Mr. Dick, too, has been a great help. He's been enormously useful in copying, fetching, and carrying. He also has looked after Mr. Wickfield. I'm happy to report that Mr. Wickfield's health has considerably improved. Relieved of the Heeps and all the torment and worry that they caused, he's hardly the same person. His mind is so much sharper and clearer than it was before. He has been able to assist me with regard to some business particulars that I would otherwise have found difficult to sort out." Tommy now looked among the papers on the table. "Having counted the funds and sorted out a mass of confusion and falsification, Mr. Micawber and I can confidently say that Mr. Wickfield can conclude his business and meet all of his financial obligations."

"Thank heaven!" Agnes exclaimed.

"However," Tommy said, "the house might have to be sold. Also, the amount that will remain after all financial obligations have been met is unlikely to exceed a few hundred pounds."

"I'm very grateful to you, Mr. Traddles," Agnes said, "and I rejoice that Papa can pay all of his debts and therefore keep his good name. I intend to open a school in the house." We all expressed our admiration and support for this idea.

"Next, Miss Trotwood, that investment of yours. It was originally, I think, eight thousand pounds?" Tommy said.

"That's correct," my aunt replied.

"I can't account for more than five thousand," Tommy said apologetically.

"That's all there was," my aunt said. "I took out three thousand of the original investment. I paid one thousand for Davy's legal training and kept two thousand. When I lost the rest, I thought it was wise not to say anything about the two thousand pounds but to secretly keep it for a time of need. I wanted to see how you would manage on your own, Davy. You did admirably. You proved persevering, self-reliant, and self-denying. So did Mr. Dick."

"Then, I'm delighted to say that we have recovered all of your money!" Tommy exclaimed, beaming.

"How is that possible?" my aunt asked.

"You believed that Mr. Wickfield had misappropriated it?" Tommy asked.

"Yes," my aunt answered. "That's why I didn't say anything. I didn't want Mr. Wickfield to get into trouble."

"Uriah Heep took your money," Tommy said.

"And you've gotten it back from him?" my aunt asked.

"Actually, Mr. Micawber did," Tommy said. "Heep didn't spend the money. In fact, Heep told me that he took it—not to spend it—but to cause David injury."

"What's become of Mr. Heep?" my aunt asked.

"I don't know," Tommy answered. "He and his mother left on a night coach to London,"

"And now we come to Mr. Micawber," my aunt said.

"I must praise him highly again," Tommy said. "We couldn't have set things right without his help. He did right for right's sake. He would have done much better financially by continuing to work with Heep. His IOUs for advances from Heep amount to 103 pounds. That money, of course, rightly belongs to Mr. Wickfield."

"I'm sure that Papa will absolve Mr. Micawber of that debt," Agnes said.

"That leaves the matter of getting the Micawbers to Australia," my aunt said. "How much should we give them, Davy?"

"I think we should pay for their passage, clothes, and travel provisions. Shall we also give them a hundred pounds?" I said. My aunt and Tommy agreed with my suggestion.

"Finally," Tommy said with discomfort, "I must address Heep's threatening allusion to a . . . husband of . . . Miss Trotwood." Retaining her upright posture and apparent composure, my aunt nodded. "Is there . . . Miss Trotwood, any such person?" Tommy asked.

"There was, my good friend," my aunt said. "He recently died." The rest of us expressed sympathy.

"That concludes our business, then," Tommy said. "We can have the Micawbers in now."

When Mr. and Mrs. Micawber entered, my aunt said, "Our apologies for keeping you out of the room for so long. We've been discussing your emigration. Here's what we propose." My aunt then explained what arrangements we wished to make. The Micawbers were delighted. Thus we concluded our business. Tommy would settle all of Mr. Wickfield's financial obligations. The Micawbers would sell all of their possessions.

My aunt and I spent the night at Mr. Wickfield's house. Freed from the presence of the Heeps, it seemed purged of a disease. I slept in my old room like a shipwrecked wanderer who has come home.

The next day, my aunt and I returned to her cottage in Highgate. When she and I sat alone before going to bed, she said, "Davy, my husband died in a London hospital. He'd been ill a long time. He was a shattered man for many years. When he knew he was dying, he sent for me. He was sorry then, very sorry. I spent a lot of time with him at the end. He died the night before you and I went to Canterbury. No one can harm him now. Uriah Heep's threat is an empty threat. I married my husband thirty-six years ago, when he was a fine-looking man."

Chapter 47

The time rapidly approached when Mr. Peggotty, Emily, Mrs. Gummidge, and the Micawbers would sail for Australia. Peggotty came up to London. I spent much time with her, Mr. Peggotty, and the Micawbers, but I never saw Emily. One evening when I was alone with Peggotty and Mr. Peggotty, our conversation turned to Ham. Peggotty told us how tenderly he had taken leave of her and how manfully and quietly he had borne himself. I never had conveyed Ham's message to Emily because he had asked me to do so right before she departed for Australia. However, I now decided to write to her without further delay. I thought she might want to send some reply to Ham. I felt I should give her that chance.

My aunt and I had vacated our Highgate cottages. I intended to go abroad, and she planned to return to her house in Dover. We had temporary lodgings in Covent Garden. Before going to bed, I sat down in my room and wrote to Emily. I told her that I'd seen Ham, and I conveyed what he had said exactly as I remembered it. I left the letter to be sent in the morning.

The next day, Mr. Peggotty came. "Master Davy," he said when we'd shaken hands, "Emily got your letter, and she wrote this reply. She requests that you read it and, if you see no harm in it, send it to Ham."

"Have you read it?" I asked. Mr. Peggotty nodded sorrowfully. I opened the letter and read as follows:

Dear Ham,

I got your message. Oh, what can I write to thank you for your good and blessed kindness to me? I have put your words close to my heart, and they'll stay there until I die. They are such comfort. I rejoice that there are men such as you and Uncle. Now, my dear, my friend, goodbye forever in this world. If I am forgiven, I may see you in another world. All thanks and blessings.

Farewell evermore.

Emily

The letter was blotted with tears.

"May I tell her that you don't see any harm in it and that you'll send it to Ham, Master Davy?"

"I'll see that Ham gets it, Mr. Peggotty," I replied. "I think I'll go down to Yarmouth. There's plenty of time to go and come back before the ship sails for Australia. I keep thinking of Ham in his solitude. It would be a kindness to put this letter into his hand and to tell Emily, before you leave for

Australia, that Ham received it. I won't mind the journey. To the contrary, travel will do me good. I'm restless. I feel better when I'm moving from place to place. I'll go down tonight."

"Thank you, Master Davy. Thank you."

At my request Mr. Peggotty went to the coach office and reserved the box seat for me on the mail coach. In the evening I headed to Yarmouth. On the first part of the trip, I remarked to the coachman, "Don't you think that's a remarkable sky? I don't remember seeing one like it."

"Nor I, sir," he answered. "That's wind. There'll be mischief at sea."

The clouds were the color of smoke and were tossed into heaps. The moon seemed to plunge through them headlong. It had been windy all day. An hour later the wind had greatly increased and was howling. The sky had become even more overcast. As the night advanced, the clouds thickened until they spread across the whole sky. The wind blew harder and harder. It reached such intensity that our horses scarcely could move forward against it. Many times during that September night, the horses turned around or came to a dead stop. We often feared that the coach would be blown over. Periodically, sweeping gusts of rain came that forced us to take some shelter under trees or by walls.

When day broke, the wind blew even harder. I had been in Yarmouth when the seamen said it blew great guns, but I'd never known the likes of this or anything approaching it. We arrived at

Ipswich very late, having had to fight for every inch of ground since we were ten miles out of London. We found a cluster of people in the marketplace. They'd left their beds in the night, fearful of falling chimneys. Some of these, congregating in the inn yard while we changed horses, told us that strong winds had ripped great sheets of lead off a church tower and flung them into the street. Others told us about country people, coming in from neighboring villages, who had seen great trees lying torn out of the earth and bundles of hay and of wood scattered on the roads and fields. Still the storm's intensity increased.

We struggled on, nearer and nearer to the sea, from which this mighty wind was blowing straight at the shore. Its force was more and more terrific. Long before we saw the sea, its spray was on our lips and it showered salt rain on us. Miles and miles of the flat country adjacent to Yarmouth were flooded. When we came within sight of the sea, the waves on the horizon were like towers above a rolling abyss. Finally we reached Yarmouth. People came to their doors. Aslant, and with streaming hair, they were astounded that the coach had come through on such a night.

I took a room at the old inn and went down to look at the sea. I staggered along the street, which was strewn with sand, seaweed, and flying blotches of sea foam. Slates and tiles fell off roofs. In the fierce winds of street corners, strangers took hold of each other to keep their footing. Coming near the beach, I saw not only the boatmen but half the people of

Yarmouth lurking behind buildings. Now and then, someone braved the storm's fury to look out over the sea and was blown off course in trying to zigzag back. Joining these groups, I found wailing women whose husbands were out in herring or oyster boats, which there was great reason to think must have foundered before they could reach a place of safety. Among the people were grizzled old sailors who shook their heads and muttered to one another as they looked from water to sky. I saw ship owners, excited and uneasy; children, huddling together and peering into older faces; stout mariners, disturbed and anxious, leveling their binoculars at the sea from behind places of shelter as if they were surveying an enemy.

The tremendous sea itself confounded me when I could pause to look at it amid the blinding wind, flying stones and sand, and awful noise. High walls of water rolled in and, at their highest, tumbled into surf. They looked as if they'd engulf the town. As receding waves swept back with a hoarse roar, they seemed to scoop out deep caves in the beach. When some white-headed billows thundered toward land but dashed themselves to pieces before reaching it, all of the fragments seemed wrathful, rushing back together to form another monstrous wave. Hills of water suddenly changed to valleys, and valleys to hills. Masses of water shook and boomed. Every shape tumultuously rolled on, changing shape and place. The whole horizon seemed to rise and fall.

Not finding Ham among the people whom the hurricane had brought together, I made my way to his house. It was shut. No one answered my knocking. I went to the shipyard where he worked. I learned there that he'd gone to Lowestoft to meet some urgent need for ship repair in which his skill was required and that he'd be back tomorrow morning.

I returned to the inn at 5:00. I hadn't sat in front of the coffee room fire for five minutes when the waiter came to stir it, as an excuse to talk. He told me that two coal-carrying ships had sunk, with everyone on board, a few miles away. Other ships had been seen trying, in great distress, to keep away from shore rocks. "Mercy on them and on all poor sailors," he said.

I felt lonely and depressed. I also felt a sharp uneasiness at Ham's not being home. I became afraid that he might try to return from Lowestoft by sea. My fear became so strong that, without having eaten anything, I returned to the shipyard. I found the boat builder, with a lantern in his hand, locking the yard gate. When I asked him if Ham might try to return by sea, he laughed. "There's no fear of that," he said. "No man in his right mind would put off in such wind, least of all Ham Peggotty, who was born to seafaring."

Only somewhat reassured, I returned to the inn. The howl and roar, the rattling of the doors and windows, the rumbling in the chimneys, the apparent rocking of the very building that sheltered me, and the sea's prodigious tumult were even more fearful than in the morning. Now there also was a great darkness, which invested the storm with new terrors. I couldn't eat, sit still, or do anything. My thoughts ran wild with the thundering sea. My uneasiness regarding Ham remained in the foreground. My dinner was removed almost untasted. I tried to refresh myself with a glass of wine but couldn't drink. I sat drowsily in front of the fire but couldn't fall asleep. I remained conscious of the uproar outdoors. Suddenly I felt such intense fear that I bolted upright and then paced. Finally the wall clock's relentless ticking tormented me so much that I resolved to go to bed. On such a night it was reassuring to be told that some of the inn's servants had agreed to sit up until morning in case of an emergency. I went to bed, exceedingly weary. But when I lay down, I was wide awake again. If anything, all of my senses were exaggerated. I lay there for hours, listening to the wind and water. At times I imagined that I heard shrieks out at sea. At other times I thought I heard houses fall. Every so often I actually heard the firing of signal guns. I got up several times and tried to look out, but I couldn't see anything except the reflection in the windowpanes of the faint candle that I'd left burning and of my own haggard face looking in at me from the black void.

Finally my restlessness reached such a pitch that I hurriedly dressed and went downstairs. In the large kitchen, where I dimly saw bacon and ropes of onions hanging from the beams, the servants were gathered around a table that had been moved away from the large chimney and brought near the door. They welcomed my company. One man said to me,

"We've been wondering, sir, if the souls of the coal-ship crews who drowned are out in the storm." I remained there for two hours. Once, I opened the yard gate and looked into the empty street. Sand, seaweed, and flakes of foam were driving by. I had to call for assistance before I could shut the gate again and latch it against the wind.

When I returned to my solitary room, it was filled with gloom. I was so exhausted that this time when I got into bed, I fell into as deep a sleep as if I had tumbled from a precipice. My dreams took me to a variety of places, but in all of them a strong wind blew. I was awakened around 8:00 a.m. by someone knocking and calling at my door.

"What's wrong?" I cried.

"A ship! Close by!"

I sprang out of bed. "What ship?"

"A schooner from Spain or Portugal, most likely loaded with fruit and wine. Make haste, sir, if you want to see it! The people on the beach think that it'll go to pieces at any moment!" The man hurried back down the stairs.

I dressed as quickly as I could and ran into the street. Many people were there, all running to the beach. I ran the same way and soon faced the wild sea, which was even more terrifying than when I'd last seen it. Breakers rose to a great height and bore down on one another. Amid the noise of the wind, waves, and crowd, I looked out to sea for the ship and saw nothing but great waves with foaming heads. A half-dressed boatman who was standing next to me pointed to the left with his bare arm, tattooed with an arrow that pointed in the same direction.

Then I saw the ship close to shore. One mast was broken short, about six feet from the deck, and lay over the side, entangled in a maze of sail and rigging. Broadside on, the ship rolled so violently that I thought its sides would collapse. I saw crew members working with axes. One man with long, dark curly hair was especially active. Then a great cry, audible even above the wind and water, rose from the shore. Sweeping over the rolling ship, the sea made a clean breach and carried men, spars, casks, planks, and bulwarks into the boiling surge. The ship's second mast still was standing, with the rags of a rent sail and a confusion of broken, flapping cordage. Another great cry of pity and horror rose from the beach as the ship went down. Then it re-emerged. Four men were clinging to the rigging of the remaining mast. The curly-haired man was uppermost. The ship rolled and dashed, showing us its entire deck. As the ship rolled first toward the shore and then back toward the sea, its bell rang. The wind carried the death knell to us. Again we lost sight of the ship. Again it rose. Two men were gone. The agony on the shore increased. Men groaned and clasped their hands. Women screamed and turned their faces away. Some ran wildly up and down the beach, futilely crying for help. I frantically implored a group of sailors whom I knew not to let the two men perish before our eyes. Greatly agitated, they told me that some men had bravely manned a lifeboat an hour earlier but hadn't been able to do anything. They said that no man could wade in with a rope and not be washed away, so there was nothing left to try.

Then I saw the people on the beach part. Ham came hurrying through them to the front. I ran to him. As he looked out to sea, his face had the same look of determination that I had seen on it the morning after Emily's flight. I became terrified that he was going to attempt a rescue. I held him back with both arms and begged the men with whom I'd been speaking not to let him leave the shore. Another cry arose on shore. Looking toward the wreck, we saw the sail repeatedly strike the lower of the two men and finally knock him into the sea. The curly-headed man now was alone on the mast. "Master Davy," Ham said, grasping me by both hands, "if my time has come, it's come. Lord above bless you and bless all. Mates, get me ready! I'm going in." People pulled me away and held me. They said that Ham was determined to go, with or without help, and that I'd only increase his danger if I interfered with the preparations. I don't know what I answered, but I saw men come running with ropes from a capstan. They penetrated a circle of people who hid Ham from my view. Then I saw him standing alone in a seaman's shirt and trousers. One long rope was around his wrist, another around his waist. At a little distance several strong men held the end of the rope that was tied around Ham's waist.

The ship now split in two. The lone man continued to cling to the mast. As the few planks between him and destruction rolled and bounced, he waved his red cap to us. Ham stood alone, watching the sea, with the silence of suspended breath behind him and the storm in front of him. When there was a great retiring wave, he glanced backward at the men, held the rope fastened around his waist, and dashed in after the wave. In a moment he was buffeted by the water: rising with the hills, falling with the valleys, lost beneath the foam, then drawn again to land. The men hastily hauled him in. He was hurt. I saw blood on his face. From his gestures I thought that he hurriedly instructed the men to leave him freer. Then he went in again. He made for the wreck, again rising with the water's hills and falling with its valleys, again lost beneath the churning foam. Striving hard, he was borne in toward the shore and then toward the ship. He neared the wreck. He was so near that with one more vigorous stroke he would be clinging to it. Then a high, green hillside of water moved shoreward from beyond the ship. Ham seemed to leap up into it with a mighty bound. And the ship was gone!

I ran to the spot where the men were hauling Ham in and saw some eddying fragments in the sea, as if a mere cask had been broken. Every face showed consternation. The men drew Ham to my very feet. He gave no sign of life. Ham was carried to the nearest house. I remained near him while every means of restoration was tried. But he was dead. As I sat beside the bed, a fisherman who had known me since my childhood whispered, "Mr. Copperfield" at the door. Tears started to his weather-beaten face, which was ashy pale. His lips trembled. "Sir," he said, "will you come yonder?"

"Has a body come ashore?" I asked.

"Yes," he answered.

"Do I know the person?" I asked.

Not answering, the fisherman led me to the shore. On that part of it where Emily and I had looked for shells as children, on that part of it where the wind had scattered some lighter fragments of the old barge—blown down during the night—I saw James Steerforth lying dead, with his head on his arm, as I often had seen him lie at school. Men brought a hand bier, laid James's body on it, covered the body with a flag, lifted the bier, and bore it toward the houses. All the men who carried the body had known James, gone sailing with him, and seen him merry and bold. They carried him through the wild roar, a hush amid the tumult, and took him to the cottage where Ham's body lay. When they set the bier down on the threshold, they looked at one another and at me and whispered. I knew why. They felt it would be wrong to lay James's body in the same room as Ham's. We brought James's body to an inn. As soon as I could collect my thoughts, I arranged for a carriage that would bring me, and James's body, to London. I knew that the care of the body, and the hard duty of preparing his mother to receive it, could rest only with me. I decided to depart late at night so that there would be less curiosity when I left Yarmouth.

At nearly midnight the carriage left the inn's courtyard. I sat alongside the driver, and James's body was inside. Although the hour was late, many people were waiting to see the carriage pass. At intervals along the town, and even a little way out on the road, I saw more people. Finally only the bleak night and open country surrounded me.

I arrived at Highgate about noon. The day was mellow, and bright with sunlight. Fallen leaves perfumed the ground. Many more leaves still hung on the trees, in beautiful tints of yellow, red, and brown. A mile from Mrs. Steerforth's house, I asked the driver to stop the carriage and await my order to advance. I then left the carriage and walked the rest of the way to the house.

The house looked the same as before. The blinds all were down. The dull, paved courtyard, with its covered way leading to the disused door, showed no sign of life. There was no wind. Nothing moved. When I summoned the courage to ring at the gate, my errand seemed to be expressed in the bell's mournful sound. The little maid came out with the key in her hand. As she unlocked the gate, she looked at me earnestly and said, "Are you ill, sir?"

"I'm agitated and fatigued," I answered.

"What's wrong, sir? Has Mr. James . . . ?"

"Hush," I said. "Something has happened that I have to tell Mrs. Steerforth. Is she home?"

"Yes," the maid replied. "Come in." She led me to the drawing room. "Mrs. Steerforth rarely goes out, even in her carriage. She keeps to her room. She doesn't see any company, but I'm sure she'll see *you*, sir. She's upstairs with Miss Dartle. What message should I take upstairs?"

"Please just give her my card and say that I'm waiting here."

The drawing room's former pleasant air of occupation was gone. The shutters were half closed. James's picture, as a boy, was there. So was the cabinet in which his mother had kept his letters. I wondered if she ever read them now. The house was so still that I heard the maid's light step upstairs. The maid returned to say, "Mrs. Steerforth is an invalid and can't come down, sir. But if you'll excuse her being in her room, she'll be glad to see you."

In a few moments I stood in front of her. She was in James's room, surrounded by many tokens of his old sports and accomplishments. After receiving me, she said, "I'm not in my own room because this room is better suited to my infirmity." Rosa Dartle had risen from her chair when I entered. She scrutinized me with her dark, piercing eyes. Her scar sprang into view. "I'm sorry to see you in mourning, sir," Mrs. Steerforth said.

"My wife has died," I said.

"You're very young to know such a great loss. I'm grieved to hear it. I hope time will be good to you," Mrs. Steerforth said.

"I hope that time will be good to all of us, Mrs. Steerforth. We must all trust to that in our heaviest misfortunes," I said. My earnestness and my tears alarmed her. The whole course of her thoughts appeared to stop and change. "James . . . " My voice trembled.

Trying to remain calm, Mrs. Steerforth asked, "Is my son ill?"

"When I was last here," I faltered, "Miss Dartle told me that he was sailing here and there. The night before last was a dreadful one at sea. James was at sea that night and near a dangerous coast. His ship went down. He . . . drowned."

Mrs. Steerforth moaned and fell back stiffly in her chair. Miss Dartle's eyes flashed. Turning to Mrs. Steerforth, she fumed, "This is your fault! Is your pride appeased now? He's made atonement to you with his life. Do you hear? His life!" Mrs. Steerforth stared at Miss Dartle. Her mouth was closed and rigid. "He inherited your cruel, proud nature," Miss Dartle continued. "You pampered his pride and passion, and this is what comes of it!"

"Miss Dartle, for heaven's sake," I entreated.

"I *will* speak," she said, turning on me with her lightning eyes. You be silent." She turned back to Mrs. Steerforth. "You reared him to be what he was—just like you, haughty, spoiled, willful, contemptuous."

"Shame, Miss Dartle!" I protested.

"I loved him more than you ever did!" Miss Dartle threw at Mrs. Steerforth. "If I had been his wife, I would have loved him and asked nothing in return. Unlike you, I would have been truly devoted to him. I *should* have been his wife. Your love always was selfish. Often when you were displeased with him, he would open his heart to me. But then he tired of me. We fell away from each other. Maybe you saw it and weren't sorry. Since then I've been a mere disfigured piece of furniture to both of you. You've both treated me as if I had no feelings. So go ahead and moan—not because you loved him but because you made him what he was."

"Miss Dartle, show some compassion and forgiveness," I said. "Mrs. Steerforth needs your help, not your censure."

"A curse on you!" Miss Dartle flung at me. "It was an evil hour when you came here. A curse on you. Get out!"

Throughout Miss Dartle's tirade, Mrs. Steerforth had remained unchanged: rigid, motionless, staring, sometimes moaning. Miss Dartle now kneeled in front of Mrs. Steerforth and took her in her arms. Weeping, Miss Dartle rocked Mrs. Steerforth as if she were a baby.

I left. Later in the day I returned, and we laid James's body in his mother's room. The servants told me that Mrs. Steerforth was in bed, with Miss Dartle at the bedside. Doctors were in attendance. I went through the dreary house, darkened the windows, and left.

I told Tommy Traddles about both Ham and James. He agreed with me that we should keep the deaths secret from Emily and Mr. Peggotty. I went to see Peggotty and Mr. Peggotty. It wasn't easy to answer their inquiries about Ham. I told them that I had given Emily's letter to Ham and that all was well.

When the time came for the ship to sail from Gravesend, Peggotty and I went down there. We found the ship in the river, surrounded by a crowd of boats. A favorable wind was blowing. The signal for sailing showed at the masthead. I rented a rowboat and rowed Peggotty and me to the ship. We went on board. Mr. Peggotty was waiting for us on deck. He took us down between decks. The area was so confined and dark that at first I hardly could see anything. As my eyes adjusted to the gloom, I saw great beams and ringbolts of the ship; cargo; emigrant berths; and chests, bundles, barrels, and heaps of baggage lit, here and there, by dangling lanterns and elsewhere by yellow daylight straying down a hatchway. In crowded groups, people were making new friendships, taking leave of one another, talking, laughing, crying, eating, and drinking. Some already were settled down into the possession of their few feet of space. Their little households were arranged; in many cases, small children were on stools or in small chairs. Other people, lacking a resting place, wandered disconsolately. The passengers ranged from two-week-old infants to people crooked with age, from farmers with soil on their boots to smiths with soot on their skin. People of every age and occupation seemed to be crammed into the narrow world of "between decks."

The time came when all visitors were warned to leave the ship. Peggotty was crying on a chest beside me. Mrs. Gummidge was busily arranging Mr. Peggotty's possessions. A young woman was stooping to help her. When she stood up and turned toward me, I recognized Martha. "Martha!" I cried with delight. "Are you going with Emily and Mr. Peggotty?"

"Yes, sir," she said, weeping with gratitude and happiness.

"Heaven bless you, Mr. Peggotty," I said, shaking his hand.

The ship was quickly clearing of visitors. I told Mr. Peggotty what Ham had asked me to say at parting. Mr. Peggotty was deeply moved. When he asked me to give Ham his love, it was very hard for me not to break down. I embraced Mr. Peggotty; took Peggotty, who was weeping, on my arm; and hurried away. On deck I took leave of the Micawbers.

Peggotty and I went over the side of the ship into our rowboat. I rowed us a little distance from the ship, but we stayed to watch it begin its journey. The sun was setting. The sky was calm and radiant. The ship lay between us and the sun's red light. Every taper line and spar of the ship was visible against the glow. I never had seen anything at once so mournful and so hopeful and beautiful. As the sails rose to the wind and the ship began to move, three resounding cheers broke from the surrounding boats. Those on board the ship responded by repeating the cheers. I watched the waving of hats and handkerchiefs, and then I saw Emily. She was at her uncle's side. He pointed to us with an eager hand. She saw us and waved her last goodbye to Peggotty and me. Surrounded by the rosy light and standing high on the deck, apart together, Emily and Mr. Peggotty held each other and passed from my sight. When I rowed ashore, night had fallen.

Chapter 48

A long, gloomy night gathered on me. I was haunted by the ghosts of many hopes, dear remembrances, errors, and regrets. Not realizing how wounded I was, I left England. The desolate feeling with which I went abroad deepened and widened hourly. At first it was a heavy sense of sorrow. Gradually it became a hopeless consciousness of lost love and friendship. My life seemed to be a wasteland. I mourned Dora, taken from her blooming world at such a young age. I mourned James Steerforth, who might have won the admiration and love of thousands. I mourned Ham, whose broken heart had found rest in the stormy sea. I mourned the remnants of the simple barge where I'd heard the night wind blow when I was a child. I roamed from place to place, feeling the whole weight of my grief. At times my despondency was so great that I wanted to die. Vainly seeking purpose and comfort, I went from city to city. I visited foreign towns, castles, palaces, cathedrals, temples, and tombs, hardly conscious of what I was seeing.

For many months I traveled with this ever-darkening cloud over my mind. I went to Italy and then traveled over an Alpine pass to Switzerland, where I wandered in the mountains with a guide. I found sublimity and wonder in the dread heights and precipices, roaring torrents, and wastes of snow and ice. One evening before sunset, I started to descend to a valley by a winding track along a mountainside. I saw the valley shining far below. It awakened some long-buried sense of beauty and tranquility, some softening influence. I paused, feeling some renewal of hope. When I reached the valley, I saw beauty all around me. The bases of the surrounding mountains were richly green. Above these bases were forests of dark fir. Higher still were range after range of craggy steeps, gray rock, bright ice, and green specks of smooth pasture, all gradually blending with the crowning snow. Here and there a wooden cottage was a dot on the mountainside. The little village that lay in the valley had a wooden bridge across a stream, which tumbled over rocks and roared away among the trees. In the quiet air was a sound of distant singing: shepherds' voices. I lay down on the grass and wept as I hadn't yet wept since Dora's death.

I found a packet of letters awaiting me and strolled out of the village to read them while my supper was being prepared. Other packets had missed me; I hadn't received any for a long time. Since I had left home, I hadn't had the will to write any letter longer than a line or two saying that I was well and had arrived at a particular place. I opened the packet and read a letter from Agnes. She said nothing about herself except that she was happy, useful, and prospering as she had hoped. All of the rest was encouragement to me. She said she knew that I'd be able to turn affliction into good, that trial and grief would only strengthen me and make me even firmer and higher in my purposes. She said that she rejoiced in my fame and looked forward to its continual increase. She said that, just as my childhood hardships and sorrows had taught me and added to my character, so would later afflictions. "I commend you to God, who has taken your innocent, darling Dora to her heavenly rest. I always cherish you as a brother, and I'm always at your side in spirit. I'm so proud of what you've done but prouder still of what you'll become."

I put the letter into my breast pocket and felt that the night was passing from my mind. There was no name for the love that I bore Agnes, who was dearer to me than ever before. I read her letter many times and wrote to her before I went to sleep. I told her, "I was in sore need of your help. Without you I am not, and never have been, what you think me. You inspire me to be that, and I'll try to be that."

I did try. Nine months had passed since Dora's death. I stayed in the valley for three months and made new friends. Before winter set in, I left the valley, going to Geneva. I returned in the spring. I also returned to my writing. I worked hard on a second novel based on my own experience. When it was done, I sent it to Tommy, who arranged for its publication. News of my growing reputation began to reach me from travelers I encountered. Then

I began a third novel. When it was half written, I thought of returning home. For a long time, though working patiently, I had accustomed myself to robust exercise. My health, severely impaired when I left England, was restored. I had seen much. I had been in many countries and had significantly increased my knowledge. I had also started to think of Agnes in a new way. I now felt that I never had fully appreciated her love. I started to realize that I loved her not only as a brother loves his sister but as a husband loves his wife. I wanted to act on this but dreaded losing her sisterly affection and bringing something uncomfortable into our relationship. I also feared that if she ever had loved me in a romantic way, I had disregarded that love, so that it must have died within her. From the time we both were children, I had thought of her as far above me, unattainable. I had bestowed my passionate tenderness on Dora instead of Agnes, although I had known Agnes first. I started to hope that Agnes might overlook my past mistakes and that I might be so blessed as to marry her. I always had confided in her. She knew every detail of my errant heart. If she never had loved me romantically, would she be able to love me that way now? If she *had* loved me romantically, what must her sacrifice have been in remaining my friend and sister! I always had felt that she was stronger and more constant than I. I still felt unworthy of her. *The time was past when I should have acted*, I thought. I had let it go by and had deservedly lost her. I suffered greatly at the thought of my weakness and foolishness. I had thrown away the chance of marrying her. I now realized how much I loved her, always had loved her. I feared that now it was too late; our relationship must remain undisturbed. I remembered Dora's saying that I would have tired of her if she had lived The truth of that now stung me.

Chapter 49

I returned home three years after I had left. I landed in London on a wintry autumn evening. It was dark and raining. I saw more fog and mud in a minute than I had seen in a year. I walked some distance before I found a coach. Although the house fronts, looking on the swollen gutters, were like old friends to me, I saw that they were dingy friends. As I looked out of the coach window, I saw that an old house had been pulled down in my absence and that a neighboring street was being drained and widened.

My aunt had long been reestablished in Dover. Tommy was practicing law. He had an apartment in Gray's Inn now, and he had told me in his last letters that he hoped to marry Sophy soon. My family and friends expected me home before Christmas but had no idea of my returning so soon. I had wanted to surprise them.

The well-known shops, with their cheerful lights, improved my spirits. When I alighted at the door of the Gray's Inn coffeehouse, I felt cheerful. I went up to my room to change out of my wet clothes. Then I came back down and warmed myself by the coffee-room fire and had dinner.

Then I went to see Tommy. At his residence an inscription on the doorpost informed me that Mr. Traddles occupied an apartment on the top floor. I ascended the stairs, which were feebly lit on each landing by a little oil wick enclosed in dirty glass. I stepped into a hole left by a missing plank and fell down. I groped my way more carefully after that and reached a door with "Mr. Traddles" painted on it. I knocked. Tommy answered the door. "Good God!" he cried. "David!" He rushed into my arms, and I held him tightly.

"Well, my dear Tommy?"

"My long-lost and most welcome friend, I'm so glad to see you!" he said, ushering me in. "And you've grown so famous! When did you return to London? Where did you come from? What have you been doing?" Tommy gestured me to an armchair by the fire and stirred the fire. We hugged each other again, laughing and wiping our eyes. We sat down and shook hands across the hearth. Sophy now emerged from a back room. "I'm so sorry that you missed our wedding," Tommy said to me.

"Your wedding!" I cried joyfully.

"We were married six weeks ago," Tommy said. Sophy laughed and blushed. I never saw a bride who looked more cheerful, amiable, honest, or happy. I kissed her as an old acquaintance would and heartily wished them joy. "What a delightful reunion this is!" Tommy said. "Was it you who stumbled on the stairs, David?"

"Yes," I said, laughing.

"These aren't luxury accommodations," Tommy said cheerfully, "but we'll manage. Sophy's an extraordinary manager. The apartment has only three rooms, but we're quite comfortable."

"I'm so glad that you two are happily married at last," I said.

"Thank you, my dear David," Tommy said.

"Will you have tea?" Sophy asked me.

"Our teaspoons are base metal," Tommy said.

"The silver will be that much brighter when it comes," I said.

"That's exactly what *we* say," Tommy said. "I work hard and read law insatiably. I get up at five every morning, but I don't mind."

There was a loving, cheerful fireside quality in Sophy's bright looks that assured me that my friend had chosen well. Sophy made tea and toast, and the three of us sat around the fire. "Miss Wickfield and your aunt came to the wedding," Sophy said. "They're both well. They talked of nothing but you. Tommy often has spoken of you, too."

After a pleasant evening with Tommy and Sophy, I returned to the inn, where I sat by the fire, thinking. The couple's happiness had returned my thoughts to Agnes. *I might have inspired a dearer love in her,* I thought. "But I taught her to be my sister. She'll marry and have new claimants on her affections. She'll never know the love for her that has grown up in my heart. It's right that I should pay the price of my childish passion for Dora. I've reaped what I sewed." Still, I wondered if I really could bear Agnes's marrying someone other than me. Could I remain her close friend as she had remained mine when *I* married?

Looking up from the fire, I saw a familiar face. Dr. Chillip sat reading a newspaper in the opposite corner. He had left Blunderstone seven years before, and I hadn't seen him since. He sat placidly perusing the newspaper, with his little head tilted to one side and a glass of warm sherry with sugar and lemon at his elbow. I walked up to him and said, "Dr. Chillip, how are you?"

Not recognizing me, he said, "Fine. Thank you, sir. How are *you*? You look familiar, but I'm afraid I can't recall your name."

"You knew it before I knew it myself," I responded.

"Did I, sir? Is it possible, then, that I had the honor of attending your birth?" he said.

"You did, sir."

"Well, you've certainly changed a good deal since then," he joked.

"I'm David Copperfield, sir."

Clearly moved, he shook my hand with great warmth. "Dear me, sir!" He surveyed me with his head to one side. "Mr. Copperfield, is it? I should have recognized you. There's a strong resemblance between you and your poor father, sir."

"I never had the happiness of seeing my father," I said.

"Yes, and that's very much to be deplored," Dr. Chillip said in a soothing tone. "I'm well aware of your fame, on which I congratulate you. The people in my area all know of you. I live in Bury St. Edmund's now." I sat down next to him. "Mrs. Chillip inherited some property in that neighborhood, so I bought a practice down there," he said. "I'm doing well. My daughter is growing quite tall now. Her mother let down the hems of her dresses only last week. Time goes by so quickly. It seems only yesterday that I treated you when you had the measles. Do you have a family, sir?" I shook my head. "I know that you sustained a bereavement some time ago," Dr. Chillip said. "I heard it from Miss Jane Murdstone."

"Where did you see her, Dr. Chillip?"

"Mr. Murdstone is a neighbor of mine again. He married a young lady—poor thing— who is from that area and inherited some good property."

"I was aware of his having remarried. Do you attend the family?" I asked.

"Not regularly."

A look of dislike on Dr. Chillip's face emboldened me to ask, "Are the brother and sister the same as before?"

"They have remained very severe, sir," Dr. Chillip answered.

"What have they been up to?" I asked.

Dr. Chillip shook his head, stirred his sherry, and sipped it. "The present Mrs. Murdstone used to be a charming woman," he said with a plaintive tone. "She was very amiable. Mrs. Chillip believes that her spirit has been entirely broken since her marriage to Mr. Murdstone and that she is all but insane with melancholy."

"I suppose Mr. and Miss Murdstone tried to force her into their own detestable mold, and it broke her. Heaven help her," I said.

"At first there were violent quarrels. Now she's little more than a shadow. If I may take the liberty of saying so, since Miss Murdstone came to live with them, she and her brother have reduced Mrs. Murdstone to a state of near-imbecility."

"I believe it."

Taking another sip of sherry, Dr. Chillip said, "Before marriage, Mrs. Murdstone was a lively young woman. Between you and me, sir, the gloom and severity of Mr. and Miss Murdstone have destroyed her. They go around with her more like her jailors than her husband and sister-in-law."

"Does Mr. Murdstone still profess to be religious?" I asked.

"Oh, yes," Dr. Chillip replied. "He's quite ferocious in his doctrine. He sometimes gives public talks on the subject of damnation. Mrs. Chillip has said that what Mr. Murdstone calls his religion actually is a vent for malice and arrogance."

"I entirely agree," I said.

"Mr. and Miss Murdstone are much disliked," Dr. Chillip continued. "Given that they're very free in consigning everyone who dislikes them to perdition, we really have a good deal of perdition going on in our neighborhood. However, as Mrs. Chillip says, Mr. and Miss Murdstone undergo continual punishment because they've turned inward to feed on their own hearts, and their hearts certainly make bad feeding."

"What brings you here?" I asked.

"I've been called as an expert witness in a case of someone who became deranged from alcoholism." Apparently the topic of derangement made Dr. Chillip think of my aunt because after a pause he said, "I remember being quite unnerved, the night of your birth, by your father's aunt. She seemed very angry and stormed out."

"I'm going down to see her early in the morning," I responded. "She's actually a tenderhearted person. You'd agree if you knew her better."

The mere possibility of his ever seeing my aunt again seemed to frighten Dr. Chillip. He paled and said with a small smile, "Is she indeed, sir?" He called for a candle, took leave of me, and hurried off to bed.

I spent the next day on the coach to Dover. I burst into the parlor and was received by my aunt, Mr. Dick, and Peggotty—who was their housekeeper now—with open arms and tears of joy. My aunt was mightily amused when I told her about Dr. Chillip's continuing dread of her. Both she and Peggotty had a great deal to say about Mr. Murdstone and, in my aunt's words, "that murdering woman of a sister."

When we were left alone, my aunt and I talked far into the night. She told me that Mr. Peggotty's letters from Australia always were cheerful and that Mr. Micawber actually seemed to be earning a living. Janet, having initially resumed her position as my aunt's maid when my aunt returned to Dover, had married a thriving innkeeper. Mr. Dick was well and happy. Patting the back of my hand as we sat in our old way in front of the fire, my aunt asked, "And when will you be going to Canterbury, Davy?"

"I'll get a horse and ride over tomorrow morning, unless you'll go with me."

"No, I'll stay here," she said.

"I would have stopped in Canterbury on my way here if I hadn't been so anxious to see you, Peggotty, and Mr. Dick," I said.

My aunt was pleased but said, "Tut, Davy. My old bones would have kept until tomorrow." She softly patted my hand again as I sat looking thoughtfully at the fire. I was thinking of Agnes and, yet again, feeling regret at not having asked her to marry me years ago. My aunt and I were silent for some minutes. When I raised my eyes, she was watching me steadily. She seemed to know that I had been thinking about Agnes because she said, "You'll find her father a white-haired old man but in other respects a better man, a reclaimed man. You'll find *her* as good, beautiful, earnest, and unselfish as she always has been. If I knew higher praise, I'd bestow it on her." I felt reproached. How had I strayed so far from Agnes and for so long? "If she teaches her young pupils to be like herself," my aunt continued, "she'll be doing all of us a great service. She never could be anything but a blessing to everyone around her."

"Does Agnes have . . . ?"

"Have what?" my aunt asked sharply.

"Does she have any suitors?"

"Dozens!" my aunt cried with indignant pride. "She could have married twenty times over since you went away."

"No doubt," I said. "Does she have any suitor who is worthy of her? Agnes couldn't care for anyone unworthy."

My aunt raised her eyes to mine. "I believe she cares for someone."

I felt a shock of pain. "Are her affections returned?"

"I can't say, Davy," my aunt replied gravely. "I've already said more than I have a right to say. Agnes never has told me that she loves anyone, but I suspect it." She looked at me closely.

"If it's true, and I hope it is . . . "

"I don't know that it is," my aunt said curtly.

"If it's true, Agnes will tell me in her own good time. A sister to whom I have confided so much won't be reluctant to confide in me."

My aunt looked away.

I rode away early in the morning. I felt a mixture of excitement and dread at the thought of seeing Agnes again. I wasn't sure that I could control myself and not burst out with a declaration of love. When I arrived at the house, I saw that the room that had been Uriah Heep's and then Mr. Micawber's office now was a little parlor. Otherwise the old house, as clean and orderly as ever, was just as it had been when I first saw it. A new maid admitted me. I said, "Please tell Miss Wickfield that a gentleman wishes to see her." The maid went upstairs and then returned. She showed me up the old staircase into the unchanged drawing room. The books that Agnes and I had read together were on their shelves. The desk where I had worked on my lessons many a night stood at the same corner of the old table. There was no vestige of the Heeps. Everything was as it had been in the happy time. I stood by a window and looked at the houses across the street, recalling how I had watched them on wet afternoons when I had first come to Mr. Wickfield's house. I remembered how I had watched tramps come into town on wet twilights. They would limp past, their bundles drooping over their shoulders at the ends of sticks. Now, as then, I smelled the damp earth and wet leaves. The very breeze seemed the same as before, all those years ago.

The opening of the little door in the paneled wall made me start and turn. Agnes's beautiful eyes met mine as she came toward me. She stopped and laid her hand on her chest. I caught her in my arms. "Agnes, my dear, I've come upon you too suddenly."

"No, no. I'm rejoiced to see you, David."

"Dear Agnes, what happiness it is for me to see you again!" I pressed her to my heart.

For a little while we both were silent. Then we sat side by side. Her face showed me the welcome that I'd dreamed of, waking and sleeping, for years. She was so dear to me that I scarcely could speak. Her sweet tranquility calmed me. She gently recalled the past in a way that soothed rather than pained me. "And you, Agnes. Tell me about yourself. In all this time you've never said much about your own life."

"What should I say?" she answered with a smile. "Papa is well. Our peaceful home has been restored to us, and our anxieties have been set to rest. Knowing that, dear David, you know everything."

"Everything, Agnes?" I asked. She looked at me with some fluttering wonder in her face and paled a bit. "Is there nothing else, Sister?" She blushed and then paled again. Smiling with a quiet sadness, she shook her head. I had wanted her to confide in me if she loved some man, even though such news would have been very painful to me. I saw, however, that she was uneasy, so I didn't pursue the matter. "Are you very busy, my dear?" I asked.

"With my school?" she said, looking up again in her bright composure.

"Yes. Is it hard work?"

"The work is so pleasant that it doesn't feel like work," she replied.

"Nothing good is difficult for you," I said.

Her color came and went again. She bent her head, and I saw the same sad smile. "Papa is out in the garden. He likes to work there on every pleasant day. Will you spend the day with us?" Agnes asked cheerfully. "Will you sleep in your old room? We still always call it 'David's room.'"

"I can't stay overnight because I promised to ride back to my aunt's tonight, but I'll joyfully spend the day here."

"I have to be with my pupils, but I'll join you when I can," Agnes said. "Here are the old books, David, and the old music."

"Even the old flowers are here," I said, looking around. "That is, they're the same kinds of flowers."

"While you've been absent, I've found pleasure in keeping everything as it used to be when we were children. We were very happy then, I think."

"Heaven knows we were!"

"Every little thing that has reminded me of my brother has been a welcome companion. Even this seems to jingle an old tune." She showed me the little basket, full of keys, still hanging at her side. "I'll see you in a little while," she said, smiling. And she left the room.

Mr. Wickfield came in from the garden. He was as my aunt had described him. He seemed a mere shadow of his handsome portrait on the wall.

At lunchtime, Agnes, Mr. Wickfield, and I sat down to table with six little girls, Agnes's pupils. The peace and tranquility that I used to feel in Mr. Wickfield's house returned to me. When lunch ended, neither Mr. Wickfield nor I drank any wine. We all went upstairs. Agnes and her students worked, sang, and played. After tea the children left. Mr. Wickfield, Agnes, and I sat and talked of bygone days.

"My part in the events that took place is cause for much regret and contrition, David," Mr. Wickfield said, shaking his white head. "But all has turned out well—thanks, in great part, to my dear Agnes. She has worked so hard and endured so much." Agnes gently touched his arm as a way of asking him to stop praising her. "I've never told you about Agnes's mother, David. She married me against her father's wishes, and he renounced her. Her mother had died many years before. Agnes's mother sought to be reconciled with her father, but he was a hard man and would have nothing further to do with her. She had an affectionate and gentle heart, and it was broken. She loved me dearly but never was fully happy because of the break with her father. She died when Agnes was two weeks old." He kissed Agnes on the cheek.

Agnes went to the piano and played some of the old songs to which we often had listened. I came and stood by her. "Are you planning to go away again?" she asked.

"What does my sister say to that?"

"I hope not."

"Then, I have no such intention," I said.

"I think you shouldn't, David, since you ask me. Your growing reputation and success have given you great power to do much good here in England. Even if I could spare my brother, I think that England could not."

"I owe you whatever is good in me, Agnes."

"Me, David?"

"Yes, my dear Agnes," I said, bending over her. "You've always led me to be better than I was, always directed me to higher things." She shook her head. "I'm so grateful to you, Agnes, so bound to you. There's no name for the affection I feel for you. I want you to know that I'll look up to you my whole life and be guided by you, as I've been guided through the darkness that is past. Whatever happens, whatever new ties you may form, whatever changes may come between us, I'll always look to you and love you as I do now and always have. You'll always be my solace and resource—until I die, my dearest sister."

She put her hand in mine. "I'm so proud of you, David. You've praised me far beyond my worth. You don't give yourself nearly enough credit." She resumed playing but continued to look at me.

As I rode back in the lonely night, the wind going by me like a restless memory, I thought of Agnes's sad smile and feared that she was unhappy. *I* was unhappy.

Chapter 50

For the next few months I lived in my aunt's house in Dover and worked on my next novel. Sitting in the window from which I had looked out at the moon on the sea when that roof first sheltered me, I quietly pursued my task. Occasionally I went to London to lose myself in the swarm of life there or to consult Tommy about some business matter. During my absence he had managed my finances for me with the soundest judgment. I was prospering.

Although Sophy worked all day in a back room that overlooked a sooty little strip of garden, I always found her the same bright homemaker, often humming the ballads of her home region of Devonshire. Sophy also acted as Tommy's copy clerk. When I was alone with Tommy, I said, "What a thoroughly good and charming wife Sophy is!"

"David, she's the dearest girl. She manages this place with punctuality, economy, order, and cheerfulness."

"Indeed, you have reason to commend her. You're a happy fellow. I believe you make each other two of the happiest people in the world."

"I'm sure we *are* two of the happiest people," Tommy said. "Sophy gets up by candlelight on these dark mornings and busies herself with the day's arrangements. Whatever the weather, she goes to the market before the law clerks go to work. She devises splendid little dinners out of the plainest ingredients. She makes puddings and pies. She keeps everything in its proper place and always is neat and ornamental herself. However late, she sits up with me at night. She always is sweet-tempered and encouraging. Sometimes I simply can't believe my good fortune." Tommy put on slippers that Sophy had placed by the fire to warm and luxuriantly spread his feet on the fender. "Our pleasures are inexpensive but wonderful. In the evenings here, we draw the curtains—which Sophy made—and couldn't be more snug. When the weather is fine, we go out for a walk in the evening. The streets abound with enjoyment for us. We look into the glittering windows of the jewelry shops. I show Sophy which diamond brooch resting on white satin I'd give her if I could afford it, and she shows me which gold watch she'd buy for *me*. We pick out the spoons, forks, and knives we'd prefer if we could afford them, and we go away feeling as if we owned them. When we stroll into the squares and grand avenues and see a house for rent, we sometimes look up at it and say how nicely that house would do if I were made a judge. Sometimes we get half-price tickets to the theater and thoroughly enjoy a play. When we walk home, we sometimes stop to buy some cooked food at a takeout place or a small lobster at the fishmonger's. Then we make a splendid supper, chatting about what we've seen."

"I almost forgot to tell you: I've received a letter from Mr. Creakle," I said.

"No! Creakle the schoolmaster?"

"Yes. I've never forgiven him for battering you. Because of my increasing fame and fortune, he now professes to always have been much attached to me. The scoundrel. He isn't a schoolmaster anymore. He's a prison warden. He wrote that he'd be glad to show me the perfect prison system, the only certain way to turn convicts into sincere, lasting penitents: a system of solitary confinement. If I accepted the offer, would you go with me?"

"I wouldn't mind," Tommy said.

"Then, I'll write to say that we'll come."

On the appointed day, Tommy and I went to the prison where Mr. Creakle was a warden. It was a massive building erected at vast expense. In a ground-floor office we were presented to Mr. Creakle. He received me as if he had formed my mind and always had loved me tenderly. On my introducing Tommy, Mr. Creakle similarly expressed, but with less fervor, that he always had been Tommy's guide and friend. Mr. Creakle's face was as red as ever. His eyes were as small but more deeply set. The scant, wet-looking gray hair by which I remembered him was almost gone. The thick veins in his bald head protruded.

Our tour began. It was lunchtime, so we went first into the large kitchen, where each prisoner's meal was being set out separately. All prisoners received their meals in their own cell. As we were going down rows of cells, Mr. Creakle particularly praised one prisoner, Number 27, for his repentance. "Number 27 is completely reformed," Mr. Creakle told Tommy and me. "He speaks with piety and writes beautiful letters to his ailing mother." At last we came to 27's cell. Looking through a peephole in the door, Mr. Creakle said with admiration, "He's reading a hymn book." So that we could converse with 27 in all his purity, Mr. Creakle directed the door of the cell to be unlocked and 27 to be invited out into the passage. This was done, and Tommy and I beheld the converted 27. To our amazement, it was Uriah Heep.

Uriah immediately recognized us. "'How do you do, Mr. Copperfield? How do you do, Mr. Traddles?"

Mr. Creakle, of course, was surprised that Uriah knew Tommy and me. This increased his admiration for Uriah. "Well, 27," Mr. Creakle said, "how are you today?"

"Very 'umble, sir," Uriah replied.

"You always are, 27," Mr. Creakle said. "Are you quite comfortable?"

"Yes. Thank you, sir. Far more comfortable here than I ever was outside. I see my follies now, sir. I'm comfortable in my new understanding."

"How do you find the beef?" Mr. Creakle asked.

"It was tougher yesterday than I could wish," Uriah said with a meek smile, "but it's my duty to bear it. I've committed follies, so I should bear the consequences without complaining."

Mr. Creakle murmured approval. He now ordered that Prisoner 28 be let out of his cell. Mr. Littimer walked out, reading a book. I saw that he recognized me, but he didn't acknowledge that recognition. Mr. Creakle said, "28, my good fellow, you complained about the cocoa last week. How has it been since?"

"Thank you, sir. It's been better," Mr. Littimer answered. "However, if I may take the liberty of saying so, I think the milk in it has been watered down."

"What's your present state of mind, 28?" Mr. Creakle asked.

"I see my follies now, sir," Mr. Littimer answered. "I'm greatly troubled when I think of the sins of my former companions, but I trust that they may find forgiveness."

"You're quite happy yourself?" Mr. Creakle asked.

"Perfectly so. I'm much obliged to you, sir."

"Is there anything at all on your mind now? If so, mention it, 28," Mr. Creakle said.

Glancing at me, Mr. Littimer said, "Sir, I attribute my past follies to having lived a thoughtless life in the service of young men and to having allowed them to lead me into temptations that I didn't have the strength to resist. I hope that all young gentlemen will heed my warning and not be offended. I speak for their own good. I'm aware of my own past follies. I hope that all young gentlemen will repent of the wickedness and sin to which they've been parties."

With some difficulty, I kept silent.

"That does you credit, 28," Mr. Creakle responded. "I would have expected it of you. Is there anything else?"

Glancing at me again, Mr. Littimer said, "Sir, there was a young woman who fell into dissolute ways and whom I tried to save but couldn't. I forgive that young woman for her bad conduct toward me and hope that she repents."

"Well said, 28," Mr. Creakle said. "We won't detain you."

"Thank you, sir," Mr. Littimer said. "Gentlemen, I wish you good day and hope that you and your families will avoid wickedness." After exchanging a glance with Uriah, Mr. Littimer returned to his cell, and the door was shut.

"A most respectable man," Mr. Creakle said, "and a perfect example of reform. Now, 27, is there anything that I can do for you? If so, mention it."

"I 'umbly ask leave to write to my mother again, sir," Uriah said with a jerk of his head.

"It's granted," Mr. Creakle said.

"Thank you, sir. I'm anxious about Mother. I fear for her soul. I want her to enter into my state of salvation. This place has saved me. I wish Mother had come here so that she could be saved, too. All people would be better off if they were arrested and brought here." Uriah's last remark gave Mr. Creakle boundless satisfaction. Stealing a look at Tommy and me, Uriah said, "Before I came here, I was given to follies. Now I'm aware of them. There's a great deal of sin outside. There's a great deal of sin in Mother. There's nothing but sin everywhere except here."

"You're quite changed?" Mr. Creakle asked.

"Oh yes, sir!" Uriah exclaimed.

"This is very gratifying," Mr. Creakle said. "You've addressed Mr. Copperfield and Mr. Traddles, 27. Do you wish to say anything further to them?"

"You knew me a long time before I came here and was changed, Mr. Copperfield," Uriah said, giving me a villainous look. "You knew me when, in spite of my follies, I was 'umble among those who were proud and meek among those who were violent. You yourself were violent to me, Mr. Copperfield. Once you struck me in the face." Mr. Creakle looked at me with shock and indignation. "But I forgive you, Mr. Copperfield," Uriah continued, "just as the Lord forgives sinners. I forgive everyone. It would ill become me to bear malice. I forgive you and hope you'll curb your passions in the future. I hope that Mr. Wickfield will repent, and Miss Wickfield, and the whole sinful bunch. You've been visited with affliction, and I hope it will do you good. But it would have been better for you if you had come here. Mr. Wickfield should have come here, too, and Miss Wickfield. The best wish I can give you, Mr. Copperfield, is that you will be arrested and brought here. When I think of my past follies and my present state, I'm sure it would be best for you. I pity everyone who isn't brought here." He slid back into his cell. Tommy and I felt great relief when he was locked in.

When Tommy, Mr. Creakle, and I were walking back to Mr. Creakle's office, I asked Mr. Creakle, "What crime caused Uriah Heep, Number 27, to be arrested?"

"Conspiracy to defraud the Bank of England out of a large sum," he answered. "He was the ringleader."

"What's his sentence?" I asked.

"Life imprisonment," Mr. Creakle answered.

"And Mr. Littimer, Number 28? What was his crime?" I asked.

"28 was a valet. He robbed his young master of about 250 pounds' worth of money and valuables the night before they were going to go abroad. 28 was caught right before he was going to board a ship to America. His sentence, too, is life imprisonment."

Tommy and I had seen all there was to see. It would have been useless to tell Mr. Creakle that Uriah and Mr. Littimer were completely insincere in their claims of piety, that they were the same hypocritical scoundrels they'd always been. He wouldn't have believed us.

Chapter 51

During my first months at home I saw Agnes frequently. At least once a week I rode to her house and spent the evening with her. I usually rode back the same night. Whenever I read Agnes the novel that I was writing, saw her listening face, moved her to laughter or tears, and heard her speak so earnestly about my fiction, I thought, *Oh, to be married to her! She's everything that I could wish my wife to be.* Her good opinion meant more to me than anyone else's. Still, I continued to feel that I had no right to propose to her, that to do so would be selfish and only upset her and threaten our friendship. Agnes was the same toward me as she always had been. Whenever I mentioned her to my aunt, we both seemed to imagine her as my wife, but neither of us uttered a word to that effect. I think that my aunt read my thoughts and understood why I didn't act on them.

I started to worry that Agnes might not have accepted any suitor because she knew that I was in love with her and she didn't want to cause me pain. This thought began to oppress me. On a harsh winter day shortly before Christmas, I determined to go see Agnes and speak to her about this. There had been snow some hours before; it lay not deep but frozen on the ground. Out at sea, beyond my window, the wind blew ruggedly from the north.

"Are you riding today, Davy?" my aunt asked, putting her head in at the door.

"Yes. I'm going to Canterbury. It's a good day for a ride."

"I hope your horse agrees with you. Right now he's standing in front of the door with his head and ears drooping as if he'd prefer his stable."

"He'll freshen up," I said.

"At any event the ride will do his master good," my aunt said, glancing at the papers on my table. "Child, you spend a good many hours at your desk. When I used to read books, I never realized what work it is to write them."

"It's work enough to read them sometimes. As to the writing, it has its own charms, Aunt."

"Ambition, love of praise, satisfaction in the work, and much more, I suppose. Well, go along." She patted me on the shoulder.

Standing in front of her, I asked, "Do you know anything more about that attachment of Agnes's?"

She looked up into my face a little while before replying. "I think I do, Davy."

"Are you confirmed in your impression?"

"I think so." She looked at me.

I now felt even more determined to make clear to Agnes that she mustn't hesitate to accept the man she loved. I went downstairs, mounted, and rode away. How well I remember the wintry ride:

the frozen particles of ice that the wind brushed from the grass blades and pelted into my face; the hard clatter of the horse's hooves; the snowdrift lightly eddying in the chalk pit as the breeze ruffled it; the smoking team, with the wagon of old hay, stopping to breathe on the hilltop and shaking their bells musically; the whitened slopes and sweeps of lowland lying against the dark sky as if they were drawn on a huge slate.

I found Agnes alone by the fire, reading. Her pupils had gone to their homes for Christmas vacation. On seeing me come in, Agnes put down her book. She welcomed me as usual, took her work basket, and sat in one of the old-fashioned windows. I sat beside her on the window seat. We talked about my novel, the progress I had made since my last visit, and when it would be finished. Agnes was very cheerful. She laughingly predicted that I'd soon be too famous to be talked to on such subjects. "So I make the most of the present and talk to you while I can," she joked. I looked at her beautiful face, focused on her work. She raised her clear, mild eyes and saw that I was looking at her. "You're thoughtful today, David."

"Agnes, shall I tell you what about? I came to tell you." She put aside her work, as she always did when we discussed something very serious, and gave me her whole attention. "My dear Agnes, do you doubt my being true to you?" I asked.

"No!" she answered with a look of astonishment.

"Do you doubt my being what I've always been to you?"

"No," she answered as before.

"Do you remember that I tried to tell you, when I came home, what a debt of gratitude I owed you and how fervently I felt toward you?"

"I remember it very well," she said gently.

"You have a secret. Let me share it, Agnes." She looked down and trembled. "I feel that you've bestowed the treasure of your love on someone. Indeed, someone has suggested this to me. Don't shut me out of what most concerns your happiness. If you can trust me as you say you can and as I know you can, let me be your friend and brother in this matter."

With an appealing, almost reproachful glance, Agnes rose from the window seat. Hurrying across the room as if she didn't know where she was going, she put her hands in front of her face and burst into tears.

"Agnes! Dearest! What have I done?"

"Let me go away, David. I'm not feeling well. I'm not myself. I'll speak to you another time. I'll write to you. Don't speak to me now."

"Agnes, I can't bear to see you this way and think that I've been the cause. You're dearer to me than anything else in life. If you're unhappy, let me share your unhappiness. If you're in need of help or counsel, let me try to give it to you. If you have a burden on your heart, let me try to lighten it. For whom do I live now, Agnes, if not for you?"

"I'm not myself," she repeated.

"I must say more. I can't let you leave me in this way. For heaven's sake, Agnes, let's not mistake each other after all these years and all that has come and gone with them. I must speak plainly. If you have any lingering thought that I could envy the happiness you will confer on your husband, dismiss it. If you think that I could not resign you to a dearer protector of your own choosing and that I couldn't be a contented witness of your joy, you're mistaken. I haven't suffered entirely in vain. You haven't taught me entirely in vain. There's no selfishness in what I feel for you."

She was quiet now. After a little while she turned her pale face toward me and said in a low voice, broken here and there, but very clear, "I don't doubt your pure friendship for me, David. I owe it to you to tell you that you're mistaken. That's all I can say. If, throughout the years, I've sometimes wanted help and counsel, they have come to me. If I've sometimes been unhappy, the feeling has passed. If I've ever had a burden on my heart, it has been lightened for me. If I have any secret, it isn't a new one and isn't what you suppose. I can't reveal it. It has long been mine and must remain mine." She started to leave.

"Agnes, wait." I clasped my arm around her waist. Her words "it isn't a new one and isn't what you suppose" had given me new hope. I exclaimed, "Agnes, I respect, honor, and love you! When I came here today, I thought that nothing could have wrested this confession from me. I thought I could have kept it to myself until we were old. But, Agnes, if I have any newborn hope that I may ever call you something more than Sister, widely different from Sister . . . "

She wept, but apparently with joy.

"Agnes. Ever my guide and best support. If you'd been more mindful of yourself and less mindful of me when we grew up together, I think my heedless fancy never would have wandered from you. But you were so much better than I was, so necessary to me in every boyish hope and disappointment, that to have you to confide in and rely on in everything became second nature, supplanting for the time the greater feeling of loving you as I do. When I loved Dora, even then my love would have been incomplete without your sympathy. And when I lost her, what would I have been without you?" I pressed Agnes to my heart. She was trembling. Her sweet eyes shone on mine through her tears. "Dear Agnes, I went away loving you. I stayed away loving you. I returned home loving you." Then I told her of the struggle I'd had and the conclusion I'd reached. I opened my mind to her, truly and entirely. I told her that my love for her had ripened to be what it now was. "If you love me enough to take me for your husband, you do so on no deserving of mine except my love for you."

"I'm so blessed, David. My heart is overflowing." Agnes laid her gentle hands on my shoulders and looked into my face. "I've loved you ever since I met you." We wept with joy. Never to be separated again!

That winter evening we walked in the fields together. The frosty air seemed to partake of our blessed calm. The stars began to shine. We lingered, looking up at them. We thanked God for having guided us to this tranquility. That night we stood together in the old-fashioned window while the moon was shining. Agnes raised her eyes to it, and I followed her glance. Long miles of road opened out before my mind. I saw a ragged, travel-weary boy, forsaken and neglected, who would come to call the heart now beating against mine his own.

It was nearly lunchtime the next day when Agnes and I arrived at my aunt's house. "She's up in your study," Peggotty said to me. We found her, wearing her reading glasses, sitting by the fire.

"Goodness me!" my aunt said, peering through the dusk. "Why is Agnes here?" She darted a hopeful glance at me.

"We're engaged!" I announced.

With a clap of her hands, my aunt yelled with joy. Peggotty and Mr. Dick came running upstairs. My aunt cried out, "Agnes and Davy are engaged!" Then everyone hugged everyone else.

Two weeks later Agnes and I were married. Apart from the members of our households, the only guests at our quiet wedding were Tommy, Sophy, Dr. Strong, and Mrs. Strong. Agnes and I left everyone full of joy and drove away together. I held her in my embrace. She was the true companion of my heart. My love for her was founded on a rock.

"Dearest husband, now that I may call you by that name, I have something to tell you," Agnes said. "The night that Dora died, she told me that she was leaving me something. Can you guess what it was?"

"I think I can," I said. I drew closer to my side the wife who had loved me for so long.

"She told me that she had a last request of me and that she left me a last charge."

"And it was . . . "

"That only I would occupy this vacant place." Agnes laid her head on my chest. We both wept.

Chapter 52

I had advanced in fame and fortune. My domestic joy was perfect. Agnes and I had been married ten happy years. One spring night when we were sitting by the fire in our house in London and our three children were playing in the room, our servant told me that an older man who looked like a farmer wished to see me. Asked if he had come on business, he had answered no; he had come for the pleasure of seeing me and had come a long way.

Because the visitor was a stranger, the children felt shy. One of our boys laid his head in his mother's lap to be out of harm's way, and little Agnes (our eldest child) left her doll in a chair and peaked out from between the window curtains to see what would happen next. She looked like little more than a heap of golden curls. "Have him come in here," I told the servant.

A hale, gray-haired man soon entered but paused by the door. Attracted by his looks, little Agnes ran to bring him into the room. I hadn't clearly seen his face yet when my wife, starting up, cried out to me in a pleased and excited voice, "It's Mr. Peggotty!"

Although old now, Mr. Peggotty still looked ruddy and strong. When our first emotion had passed and he sat in front of the fire with the children on his knees and the firelight shining on his face, he looked robust and handsome. "Master Davy." The old name in the old tone fell so naturally on my ear. "It's a joyful hour that I see you once more, with your own true wife," Mr. Peggotty said.

"A joyful hour indeed, old friend," I said.

"And look at these pretty little ones," he said of the children. "Why, Master Davy, you were no taller than the littlest when I first saw you. Emily wasn't any bigger, and poor Ham was just a boy."

"Time has changed you little since then," I said. "But let these dear little rogues go to bed. You mustn't sleep anywhere in England but here tonight. Tell me where to send for your luggage. Is the old black bag that went so far among it? Then we'll swap ten years' worth of news over a glass of Yarmouth grog."

"Are you alone?" Agnes asked Mr. Peggotty.

"Yes, ma'am," he said, kissing her hand.

Agnes and I sat Mr. Peggotty between us, not knowing how to give him enough welcome. "It's a great amount of water to cross to stay only a month," Mr. Peggotty said. "But water, especially saltwater, comes naturally to me, and friends are dear, so here I am."

"Are you going back those thousands of miles so soon?" Agnes asked.

"Yes, ma'am. I promised Emily before I left. I'm not getting any younger. I felt that if I didn't make the journey now, I never would. It's always been on my mind that I must come and see Master Davy and your own sweet, blooming self in your wedded happiness before I got to be too old." He looked at us as if he never could sufficiently feast his eyes on us.

"Tell us everything relating to your fortunes," I said.

"Our fortunes are soon told, Master Davy. We've thrived. We've worked as we should. It was a little hard at first, but we always thrived. What with sheep farming and one thing and another, we're well-to-do. We've prospered."

"And Emily?" Agnes and I asked in unison.

"When we first sailed away, she was pretty downcast. I think that if she'd known about Ham's death—which Master Davy kept from us out of kindness—she might not have survived the voyage. There were some poor folks aboard who were ill. Emily took care of them. She also took care of children. So she was busy doing good, and that helped her."

"When did she first hear about Ham's death?" I asked.

"After I heard about it, I kept it from her for about a year. We were living in a solitary place among beautiful trees, with roses covering our house to its roof. One day while I was out working on the land, a traveler came along from Suffolk. Of course, we took him in, gave him food and drink, and made him welcome. Everyone in the colony does that. He had an old newspaper with him that reported on the storm. That's how Emily found out. When I came home at night, I found out that she knew." He had dropped his voice as he spoke, and the gravity that I remembered so well spread across his face.

"Did the news change her much?" I asked.

"Yes. For a long time, if not right up to the present," he said. "But I think the solitude did her good. She had a lot to keep her busy, such as looking after the poultry, so she came through. If you could see my Emily now, Master Davy, I wonder if you'd know her."

"Is she so altered?" I asked.

"I don't know. I see her every day, so it's hard for me to know. But sometimes I think so." Looking at the fire, Mr. Peggotty said, "She's a slight figure, kind of worn, with soft, sorrowful blue eyes, a delicate face, a pretty head that leans down a little, and a quiet, almost timid voice and manner. That's Emily." Agnes and I silently observed him as he sat, still looking at the fire. "Some people think that she bestowed her affection on an unworthy man. Others think that she's a widow. No one knows her story. She might have married well any number of times. 'But, Uncle,' she said to me, 'that's gone forever.' She's cheerful when she's alone with me and shy when others are around. She'll go any distance to teach a child, tend a sick person, or help out with some young woman's wedding. She's loving toward me. She's patient, liked by young and old, and sought out by anyone in trouble." He drew his hand across his face and, with a half-suppressed sigh, looked up from the fire.

"Is Martha still with you?" I asked.

"Martha got married the second year we were there, Master Davy. A young farm laborer came by on his way to market with a wagon of goods and offered to marry her. Wives are scarce there. He said that he'd set up a farm for the two of them. Martha asked me to tell the man her story, and I did. They were married. They live far from us."

"And Mrs. Gummidge?" I asked.

Mr. Peggotty burst into laughter and rubbed his hands up and down his legs as he'd been accustomed to do when he enjoyed himself in the old barge. "Would you believe it? A ship's cook who was turning settler offered to marry her!"

I never saw Agnes laugh so hard. Mr. Peggotty's amusement was so delightful to her that she couldn't stop laughing. The more she laughed, the more she made *me* laugh and the more Mr. Peggotty's delight increased. "And what did Mrs. Gummidge say?" I asked when I could control my laughter.

"Instead of saying, 'Thank you. I'm much obliged to you, but I'm not going to change my situation at my time of life,' she grabbed a bucket that was nearby and hit that ship's cook over the head." Mr. Peggotty again roared with laughter, joined by Agnes and me. When we were exhausted from laughing so hard, Mr. Peggotty wiped his face and resumed. "But I must say this for the good creature: she's been all that she said she'd be and more. She's the most willing, truest, most helpful woman who ever breathed. I've never known her to complain, not even when we were new there."

"And how is Mr. Micawber?" I asked.

With a smile Mr. Peggotty took an envelope from his breast pocket and carefully removed a folded newspaper from the envelope. "Now that we're well-to-do, we don't live in the countryside anymore, Master Davy. We live in a town at Port Middlebay Harbor."

"Was Mr. Micawber in the countryside near you?" I asked.

"Bless you, yes, and he turned to the work with a wonderful will. I've seen his bald head perspiring in the sun until I thought it would melt away. He's a magistrate now."

"A magistrate!" I said.

Mr. Peggotty handed me an issue of the *Port Middlebay Times* and pointed to an article, which I read aloud:

A public dinner honoring our distinguished townsman Wilkins Micawber, magistrate for the district of Port Middlebay, was held yesterday in the Port Middlebay Hotel's banquet room, which was crowded to overflowing. Forty-seven people were served dinner while numerous others filled the hallway and stairs. Port Middlebay's most fashionable and respected residents flocked to pay tribute to the talented, popular, and highly esteemed guest of honor. Dr. Charles Mell, principal of Port Middlebay's grammar school, presided. Mr. Micawber sat on his right. In a speech full of feeling, Dr. Mell toasted "our distinguished guest, the pride of Port Middlebay" and stated, "May Mr. Micawber never leave us unless it is to better himself, and may his success among us be so great that bettering himself is impossible." Much cheering followed. When the cheering subsided, Mr. Micawber expressed his thanks and gave a flowing, polished speech. It was a masterpiece of eloquence. The parts in which he traced his successful career to its source and warned the audience's younger members not to incur debts that they can't repay were especially powerful. The following guests also were toasted: Dr. Mell, Mrs. Micawber, Mrs. Begs (formerly Miss Micawber), Mrs. Mell, and Wilkins Micawber, Jr. At the conclusion of the proceedings, the tables were removed to make room for dancing. Wilkins Micawber, Jr. and the lovely and accomplished Miss Mell were among those who danced until dawn.

I was delighted to learn of the happy circumstances of Dr. Mell, my Salem House friend and mentor. Mr. Peggotty now opened the newspaper to a different page and pointed to a section, which I also read aloud:

To David Copperfield, the eminent author
My Dear Sir,
    Years have elapsed since I had the pleasure of seeing you, the friend and

companion of my youth. Circumstances beyond my control have separated us, but I haven't been unmindful of your famous accomplishments. Nor have I been barred from the intellectual feasts that you've spread before us. I cannot, therefore, allow the departure of Port Middlebay's esteemed Mr. Daniel Peggotty without taking this opportunity to publicly thank you, on behalf of all Port Middlebay residents, for the gratification that your writings provide. You are known and appreciated here. Continue your eagle flight! Port Middlebay's residents watch it with delight, entertainment, and instruction. As long as my eyes have light and life, they will be among those looking up to you from Australia.

Wilkins Micawber, Magistrate

Mr. Peggotty stayed with Agnes and me the whole month that he was in England. Peggotty and my aunt came to London to see him. Agnes and I parted from him aboard ship. But before he left, he went with me to Yarmouth to see Ham's churchyard grave, for which I had provided the tombstone. At Mr. Peggotty's request I copied the tombstone's plain inscription for him. As I did so, he stooped to gather a handful of earth from the grave. "For Emily," he said as he wrapped it in a handkerchief, which he then put into his bag. "I promised."

Chapter 53

And now my written story ends. I look back for the last time. I see myself, with Agnes at my side, journeying along the road of life. I see our children and our friends around us, and I hear many voices, not indifferent to me as I travel on.

What faces are the most distinct to me in the fleeting crowd? Here is my aunt, more than eighty years old, in strong eyeglasses. She still is upright and a steady walker of six miles at a stretch in winter weather. As usual, Peggotty is with her. Also in eyeglasses, Peggotty is accustomed to doing needlework at night very close to the lamp. Her cheeks and arms, so hard and red in my childhood, are shriveled now. Her eyes are fainter, but they still glitter. Her rough forefinger is just as it always was. When I see my youngest child catching at it as she totters from my aunt to Peggotty, I think of the little parlor at Blunderstone when I scarcely could walk. My aunt is godmother to my daughter Betsey Trotwood Copperfield, and my daughter Dora says that my aunt spoils her. There is something bulky in Peggotty's pocket. It is the old crocodile book, with some of the pages torn and stitched. Peggotty exhibits it to the children as a precious relic. I find it strange to see my own infant face—actually that of my son Davy—looking up at me from the crocodile stories. During this summer holiday, I see Mr. Dick among my boys. Now an old man, he is making giant kites and gazing at them in the air with great delight.

Mrs. Steerforth now is bent with age and feebleness. She supports herself by a cane. Her face has some traces of its former beauty and pride. She is fretful and confused. Her mind wanders. She is in a garden. Standing near her is Miss Dartle, dark, withered, with a white scar on her lip. "Rosa, I have forgotten this gentleman's name," Mrs. Steerforth says.

Miss Dartle bends over Mrs. Steerforth and says loudly, "Mr. Copperfield."

"I'm glad to see you, sir," Mrs. Steerforth says. "I'm sorry to see you are in mourning. I hope time will be good to you."

Miss Dartle impatiently scolds her, "He isn't in mourning. Look again."

"You've seen my son, sir," Mrs. Steerforth says. "Are you reconciled?" Looking fixedly at me, she puts her hand to her forehead and moans. Suddenly she cries in a terrible voice, "Rosa, come to me. He's dead!"

Miss Dartle caresses Mrs. Steerforth. Then she fiercely tells her, "I loved him better than you ever did!" Then she soothes Mrs. Steerforth to sleep on her breast, as if Mrs. Steerforth were a sick child.

Julia McPherson, formerly Miss Mills, has come home from India. She is married to a rich, much older Scotsman with large ears. Peevish and spoiled, she has a male servant who brings her people's cards and letters on a golden plate and a female servant who wears a bright headscarf and serves her snacks in her dressing room. Mrs. McPherson continually quarrels with her sour husband. She is steeped in money and talks and thinks of nothing else. She has a stately house, sumptuous dinners every day, and powerful acquaintances. But she has no happiness and does no good.

Jack Maldon works for the patent office. He still sneers at Dr. Strong, whom he describes as "charmingly antique." Dr. Strong, always our good friend, still labors at his dictionary. He has reached the letter D. He's happy in his home and wife. Mrs. Markleham isn't nearly as influential as in the old days.

Tommy is hard at work in his law office. His lawyer's wig has made his hair (where he is not bald) even more unruly than before. His desk is covered with piles of papers. As I look around, I say, "If Sophy were your clerk now, she'd certainly have enough to do."

"You may say that, my dear David," Tommy replies. "Those were wonderful days in Holborn Court, weren't they?"

"Sophy told you that you'd be a judge some day. That's the talk of the town now."

Tommy and I walk arm in arm to his house, for a family dinner. It's Sophy's birthday. On our way Tommy tells me about the good fortune that he's enjoyed. "I've really been able to do all that I hoped for," he says. "Our two boys are receiving the very best education and distinguishing themselves as steady scholars and good fellows."

Tommy's house is one of the very houses that he and Sophy used to look at and daydream about on their evening walks. It's a large house. Tommy, the same simple, unaffected fellow as always, sits at one end of the table, and Sophy beams at him from the other end, across glittering silverware.

Now as I end my task, subduing my desire to linger, all faces but one fade. That face shines on me like a heavenly light by which I see everything else. I turn my head and see it, in its beautiful serenity, beside me. My lamp burns low. I've written far into the night. But the dear presence without which I would be nothing bears me company. Oh, Agnes, my soul, so may your face be by me when my life ends. So may I still find you near me when reality melts from me like the shadows that I now dismiss.

Afterword

About the Author

D*avid Copperfield* is the most autobiographical of Charles Dickens' many novels. The author was born in Portsmouth, England in 1812. He was the second child of Elizabeth and John Dickens, who would have six more children after Charles. The son of servants, John was a clerk in the navy's payroll office. Like the character Clara Copperfield, Elizabeth was pretty, self-centered, and insufficiently protective of her son—an inadequate mother. John, too, was an inadequate parent. Caricatured as Wilkins Micawber, he was genial but pretentious in speech and manner and somewhat unscrupulous. He habitually ate, drank, entertained, and otherwise made merry beyond his financial means.

By the time Charles was 11, the Dickenses had moved to London, then Chatham (a seaport in southeast England), then back to London. John Dickens continually defaulted on loans. When Charles was 12, his parents put him to work in a rundown London warehouse alongside the Thames River, just as David Copperfield is put to work at age 10. Like David, Charles labored from morning to night, earning six shillings a week. Whereas David labels wine bottles, Charles labeled jars of shoe polish. David's coworkers call him "the little gent"; Charles' coworkers called him "the young gentleman."

Like Wilkins Micawber, John Dickens was imprisoned for failure to pay debts. The Micawber family pawns or sells many of its possessions, including books. The Dickens family did the same. Elizabeth and all of the children except for Charles and his older sister moved into the prison with John. Charles lived nearby and regularly visited his family, as David Copperfield visits the Micawbers. Three months after his imprisonment, John was released. Upon his mother's death he had inherited enough money to reach an agreement with his creditors. Charles left the shoe-polish warehouse. John retired with a pension, and the family settled in a lower-class section of London. Like the Micawbers, the Dickenses moved from residence to residence, repeatedly evicted for nonpayment of rent.

For three years Charles attended Wellington House Academy, a London school reportedly run by a severe principal who frequently caned students. Charles's experiences at Wellington House influenced his depiction of David Copperfield's Salem House, headed by the tyrannical Mr. Creakle. Charles's schooling ended when he was fifteen.

Like David, Charles became a clerk at a London law firm. At the same firm, his friend and former schoolmate Thomas Mitton was training to become a lawyer. Overweight, good-natured, and loyal, Mitton likely inspired the character Tommy Traddles. Just as David stays at Spenlow & Jorkins only briefly, Charles remained at the law firm only a year and a half.

At age 18, Charles met and fell passionately in love with Maria Beadnell, probably the primary model for Dora Spenlow. The daughter of a well-to-do bank manager, Maria belonged to a higher social class than Charles. Just returned from finishing school in France, she was pretty, petite, vain, frivolous, and flirtatious—both curly-headed and largely empty-headed. Eager to impress her, Charles, dressing like a dandy, paid her visits and compliments. Maria's parents soon discouraged further communication between the two. Charles then sent secret messages to Maria by way of her friend Mary Anne Leigh. In *David Copperfield,* Julia Mills plays the same role of go-between. Obsessed with Maria and wanting to marry her, Charles pursued her for several years. She doesn't seem to have returned his passion.

Having mastered shorthand, at age 19, Charles became a Parliamentary reporter known for his rapid, accurate recording of House of Commons speeches and debates. This career, recalled in *David Copperfield,* proved brief. When Charles was 21, his first published fiction appeared in a magazine. He quickly became a regular contributor of short stories to various periodicals, including a newspaper edited by George Hogarth.

Invited to Hogarth's home, Charles met

Hogarth's daughters. He soon was engaged to the eldest, 19-year-old Catherine. They married in 1836. Like David and Dora's relationship, Charles and Catherine's was not one of equality. Charles was somewhat bossy and critical, Catherine meek and adoring. Although the marriage never would be truly happy, the couple would have ten children.

Shortly after the wedding, Catherine's younger sister Mary, an excellent housekeeper, came to live with the couple. Charles adored Mary and cherished her companionship. Partly memorialized as the angelically selfless Agnes Wickfield, Mary died in 1837. Grief-stricken, Charles described her as having had no faults. Mary and he had been "happy together," he wrote to a friend; she had sympathized with his "thoughts and feelings" more than anyone else ever had or ever would. Charles wrote this inscription for Mary's gravestone: "Young, beautiful, and good. God in his mercy numbered her with his angels at the early age of seventeen."

In 1842, another of Catherine's sisters, 15-year-old Georgina, joined the Dickens household. She, too, had Agnes-like traits. Graceful, slender, amiable, and capable, Georgina increasingly managed the household.

Having always loved the theater, at the age of 45, Charles began a love affair with actress Ellen Ternan, who was 18. Soon after, Charles and Catherine permanently separated. Only their oldest child stayed with his mother. All of the other children stayed with Charles, as did Georgina, who continued to manage the household. Charles's relationship with Ternan would last for the rest of his life.

When Charles died of a stroke at age 58, he was one of the world's most famous, successful, and beloved writers. His first novel, *The Pickwick Papers* (1837), had been immensely popular, and throughout the years, his reputation had only grown. None of his novels ever has gone out of print. Along with *David Copperfield* (1850), his favorite among his novels, his best-known works include *Oliver Twist* (1838), *A Christmas Carol* (1843), *A Tale of Two Cities* (1859), and *Great Expectations* (1861). He was honored with burial in Westminster Abbey.

About the Book

In *David Copperfield,* malevolent individuals continually threaten benevolent ones. Evil prevails when good people fail to oppose it. The novel presents three kinds of characters: those who are basically good but largely passive, those who are actively evil, and those who are good as well as quick to take action against evil.

David Copperfield's gentle mother, Clara, does not stand up against her cruel second husband, Edward Murdstone. More eager to avoid offending Mr. Murdstone than to protect her son, she allows Mr. Murdstone to abuse David. When Mr. Murdstone starts to beat David severely with a cane, David tries to defend himself by biting Mr. Murdstone. Hearing the commotion, Clara cries out and comes running into the room. However, she then leaves David—cut, bruised, and swollen—locked in his room. Instead of condemning her husband's brutality, she rebukes David for having bitten his stepfather: "Oh, Davy. That you could hurt anyone I love! Try to be better. Pray to be better. I forgive you, but I'm so grieved, Davy, that you should have such bad passions in your heart." Mr. Murdstone, of course, is the one who unjustly hurts others and has "bad passions." Throughout the novel, those passions continue unchecked. In addition to bullying David, Mr. Murdstone bullies Clara herself. After Clara's death, he bullies a second young wife.

At Salem House, David encounters more domination and submission. No one intervenes or even protests when the school's principal, Mr. Creakle, canes and otherwise assaults students. Mr. Creakle's son previously "objected to his father's cruel treatment of the students and of Mrs. Creakle," we read. As a result Mr. Creakle turned him out of the house. This punishment has saddened Mr. Creakle's wife and daughter, but they submit to Mr. Creakle's tyranny, just as Clara Murdstone submits to Mr. Murdstone's.

As much as she loves her father, Agnes Wickfield fails to protect him from Uriah Heep's scheming. Mr. Wickfield falls prey to Heep largely because he's an alcoholic. Instead of helping her father to avoid alcohol, Agnes provides him with a decanter of wine every evening and watches him drink heavily. David, too, simply watches as alcoholism increasingly places Mr. Wickfield under Heep's power. Only when Agnes asks David if he has observed a change in her father does David say, "I think he harms himself by drinking so much." Only then does David reveal that he often has seen Heep ask Mr. Wickfield to attend to some business matter while Mr. Wickfield is intoxicated. When Agnes tells David that Heep probably will become her father's business partner, David asks, "Haven't you spoken out against the partnership?" She hasn't. Afraid that her father wouldn't be able to manage without Heep, she has expressed support for the partnership. One evening after dinner, David is the only other person present while Heep, proposing toast after toast, gets

Mr. Wickfield drunk. It makes David "sick at heart to see Mr. Wickfield become intoxicated." Yet, he in no way intervenes.

Annie Strong is another good individual who is strikingly passive with regard to ill-intentioned people. Faithful to her husband, she is appalled when Jack Maldon makes sexual advances toward her. Even so, when Maldon returns from India, Annie does not bar him from her house. Instead she suffers his visits in silence and allows her husband to continue to trust Maldon. "Years have passed since I made clear to [Maldon] that I don't welcome him here," she later reveals, when pressed. Until then she doesn't confide in her husband or take any other action to end Maldon's frequent visits.

Among the students at Salem House, wealthy James Steerforth has the most influence over Mr. Creakle. Steerforth makes no attempt to curtail Creakle's abuse of other boys. David says of Steerforth, "He didn't defend me from Mr. Creakle, who was very severe with me." In fact, Steerforth himself is an abuser. He publicly insults and humiliates the teacher Charles Mell, who has done no wrong. Spoiled by his mother and others, Steerforth feels free to inflict harm because no one ever has curbed his selfishness and aggression. As a young boy he threw a hammer at Rosa Dartle, scarring her for life, merely because she annoyed him.

In terms of character, Tommy Traddles is Steerforth's opposite. During his boyhood Tommy has no power or influence, yet he opposes injustice. "Tommy was very honorable," David later recalls.

"He considered it a solemn duty in the boys to stand up for one another." Among the students, only Tommy is good enough and courageous enough to protest Steerforth's treatment of Mell. He "bravely" cries out, "For shame, Steerforth! This is unworthy." The result, however, is negative. Mell himself says, "Hold your tongue, Traddles." After Mell leaves the room, every boy except Tommy cheers Steerforth, who has caused Mell to be fired. Because Tommy weeps over Mell's unjust firing, Mr. Creakle canes him and Steerforth publicly mocks him, calling him a "girl" and "Miss Traddles."

Oblivious to Steerforth's true character, David brings Steerforth to Daniel Peggotty's home, thereby introducing evil into the house. When Emily Peggotty runs off with Steerforth, David leaves it almost entirely to Mr. Peggotty, and then Martha Endell, to search for her, even though he himself is heavily responsible for the situation. As when he was a schoolboy, the adult David is notably passive with regard to wrongdoers.

Mr. Peggotty has the courage to stand up against those who are in the wrong and have more power than he does. The haughty, domineering Mrs. Steerforth doesn't intimidate him. "She looked at Mr. Peggotty very steadfastly when he stood before her," but "he looked as steadfastly at her." Mr. Peggotty boldly asks if James Steerforth will marry Emily. "Certainly not!" Mrs. Steerforth answers. When she insultingly offers Mr. Peggotty money as supposed compensation for her son's behavior toward Emily, Mr. Peggotty dares to speak plainly. "With a steady but newly fiery eye" he says, "I'm looking at the likeness of the face that has looked at me in my home, at my fireside, and in my boat smiling and friendly while it was treacherous. Offering me money for my child's ruin is as bad as what your son has done." Mr. Peggotty leaves with his dignity and determination intact.

Like Tommy and Mr. Peggotty, Betsey Trotwood has strength of character. She is willing to speak out, and take action, against cruelty and injustice and to do so alone. She saves both Mr. Dick and David from abuse. When Mr. Dick, harmless and good-natured, would have been permanently confined to a mental asylum, she took him into her home. Rather than send David back with Mr. Murdstone, she tells Murdstone just what she thinks of him—"Do you think I don't see what you are? . . . You were a tyrant"—and becomes David's guardian.

What, then, are *David Copperfield's* messages about good and evil? To some extent the messages are somber. Through a lack of courage and strength, the novel suggests, people who are basically good, regularly allow evildoers to have their way. The book also suggests that good people who lack status and power tend to suffer when they stand alone against evil. Tommy's childhood acts of bravery and conscience result in little more than his being abused. However, *David Copperfield* also conveys this message of hope and encouragement: good people who are weak on their own can overcome evil by joining forces. Uriah Heep's downfall serves as illustration. Wilkins Micawber doesn't expose Heep's crimes until he has enlisted Tommy's help and arranged for Heep's victims to gather. Micawber confronts Heep, declaring him a "scoundrel," only when surrounded by supporters. Looking around, Heep remarks, "So this is a conspiracy. You've all met here by appointment." He refers to the gathering as a "gang." Micawber then publicly charges Heep with fraud. By working together, Tommy, Micawber, Mr. Dick, and Mr. Wickfield set things right. Acting in concert, good people can defeat evil.